THE SPLENDOR OF PORTUGAL

OTHER WORKS BY ANTÓNIO LOBO ANTUNES IN ENGLISH TRANSLATION

The Land at the End of the World
Knowledge of Hell
An Explanation of the Birds
Fado Alexandrino
Act of the Damned
The Return of the Caravels
The Natural Order of Things
The Inquisitors' Manual
What Can I Do When Everything's on Fire?

ANTÓNIO LOBO ANTUNES
THE SPLENDOR OF PORTUGAL

TRANSLATED BY RHETT MCNEIL

DALKEY ARCHIVE PRESS
CHAMPAIGN / DUBLIN / LONDON

Originally published in Portuguese as *O Esplendor de Portugal* by Publicações Dom Quixote, 1997
Copyright © 1997 by António Lobo Antunes
Translation copyright © 2011 by Rhett McNeil
First Edition, 2011

Library of Congress Cataloging-in-Publication Data

Antunes, António Lobo, 1942-
[Esplendor de Portugal. English]
The splendor of Portugal / António Lobo Antunes ; translated by Rhett McNeil. -- 1st ed.
    p. cm.
"Originally published in Portuguese as O Esplendor de Portugal by Publicações Dom Quixote, 1997."
ISBN 978-1-56478-423-0 (pbk. : alk. paper)
I. McNeil, Rhett. II. Title.
PQ9263.N77E7613 2011
869.3'42--dc22
                        2011019090

Partially funded by a grant from the Illinois Arts Council, a state agency, and by the University of Illinois at Urbana-Champaign

The publication of this book was partly supported by the DGLB—Direcção-Geral do Livro e das Bibliotecas / Portugal

www.dalkeyarchive.com

Cover: design and composition by Danielle Dutton, illustration by Nicholas Motte
Printed on permanent/durable acid-free paper and bound in the United States of America

Heroes of the sea, noble people,
Courageous, immortal nation,
Raise today once more
The splendor of Portugal!
From amidst the mists of memory,
Oh Fatherland, hear the voice
Of your illustrious forefathers
Which shall surely guide you to victory.
To arms, to arms,
On land, on sea!
To arms, to arms,
Fight for the Fatherland!
March, march against the cannons.

—PORTUGUESE NATIONAL ANTHEM

1

When I said that I had invited my siblings to spend Christmas Eve with us

(we were eating lunch in the kitchen and you could see the cranes and the boats back behind the last rooftops of Ajuda)

Lena filled my plate with smoke, disappeared in the smoke, and as she disappeared her voice tarnished the glass of the window before it too vanished

"You haven't seen your siblings in fifteen years"

(as her voice enveloped the window frame it took with it the hills of Almada, the bridge, the statue of Christ alone beating its helpless wings above the mist) until the smoke dissipated, Lena reappeared little by little with her fingers outstretched toward the breadbasket

"You haven't seen your siblings in fifteen years"

so that all of a sudden I was aware of the time that had passed since we arrived here from Africa, of the letters from my mother, first from the plantation and later from Marimba, four little huts on a hillside of mango trees

(I remember the regional administrator's house, the store, the ruins of the barracks shipwrecked and sinking in the tall grass)

the envelopes that I kept in a drawer without showing anyone, without opening them, without reading them, dozens and dozens of dirty envelopes, covered with stamps and seals, telling me about things I didn't want to hear, the plantation, Angola, her life, the mailman delivered them to me on the landing of the stairway and an expanse of sunflowers murmuring in the fields outside, sunflowers, cotton, rice, tobacco, I don't care about Angola, a bunch of blacks in the barracks, in the government palace, and in the huts on the island laying out in the sun as if they were us, I closed the door with the letter held between two fingers like someone holding an animal by its tail

letters just like putrid dead animals

Luanda Bay, ignored by its own palm trees, amounted to nothing more than a tiny room in need of a paint job, outfitted with a coatrack and a chest of drawers, Lena filling my plate with smoke and blotting out the world

"You put them out on the street and now, fifteen years later, you want your siblings back"

sitting in front of me waving her hand to waft away the smoke

"If I were you I wouldn't wait up for visitors, Carlos"

she's gotten fat, dyes her hair, complains about some heart condition or another, gets examined at the doctor's office and takes pills, Lena interfering with me and my family, the daughter of a Cuca-beer plant worker living with a bunch of cousins a hundred meters from the Marçal neighborhood, out of shame I never told any of my schoolmates that I was dating her, if it happened that she came up to me, laughing after class

(skinny, hair braided, before she started to go to the doctor or take pills for her heart condition)

I would whisper frantically

"Get lost"

only later, on the bus, after verifying that not even the Jingas were watching us, would I signal to her with my index finger, a house three streetlights down with an awning covered with mosquitoes, mossy vines, her father in boxer shorts reading the paper, mulatto neighbors in clapboard shacks, Lena with her braids undone tugging on my lapel in the café, the city at a standstill, my schoolmates intrigued, beers suspended half-swig, me hoping that they couldn't hear me

"Get lost"

pretending to be as impolite as them, as scandalized as those who mocked your house and your mulatto neighbors, knocked your notebooks to the ground, pulled up your skirt and laughed, yelled at you from afar

"Slum-dweller"

you in tears gathering up your notebooks and your father who didn't have a car like us, he rode an ancient moped, threatening us with a rolled-up newspaper, harmless, tiny, unstable on his little pockmarked legs

"My daughter's better than you bastards"

Lena tugging on my lapel in the café

"I need to talk to you be patient"

tomorrow everyone in Luanda will know about us, the manager throws me out with an irritated gesture

"Get out"

my schoolmates turn their backs on me and plug their noses

"You smell like Sambizanga you stink Carlos"

selfish Lena not caring if they turn their backs on me, at the shore dragging me along the arcade where the birds are perched and waiting for dusk when the trawlers go out to fish, so they can fly around screeching, pecking at splotches of diesel fuel

"Don't telephone me don't call me at all"

lights that shone between the cabanas and palm trees of the island, the city streetlights lit, the sign of the hotel orange and blue missing a few letters, people and cars pay no attention to me due to the darkness, my schoolmates called their friends Guess what the big news is, have you heard, brace yourself, don't faint, guess who Carlos, no, the other one, the jerk from Malanje, is dating, me hating Lena who couldn't even bear me a child getting up from the table in Ajuda to wash off the tablecloth with a sponge, to put on rubber gloves and wash the plates

"You put them out on the street and now you want your siblings back if I were you I wouldn't wait up for visitors Carlos"

she didn't rest until I married her and freed her from Marçal, from her relatives who shivered with malaria in grimy rooms, dressed in black as if they still lived in Minho, tripping over clay pots and little saints with oil lamps at their feet, on Sundays her uncles, sweating beneath their overcoats, cleared five feet of land behind the house in hopes of growing cabbages

you're going out with the slum-dweller Carlos admit that you're going out with the slum-dweller she's not a slum-dweller you're crazy her family's apartment is under construction

fat and with her hair dyed, Lena just finished drying the plates, piled them in the cupboard, took off her gloves and headed for the room where the Christmas tree stood, still with no stand, no silvery star, no decorative balls, no snowflakes

"You haven't seen your siblings in fifteen years"

I was left alone in the kitchen listening to the humming of the refrigerator and looking at the hills of Almada, looking at the plantation from the window of the jeep as we drove away over the potholes of the dirt road that divided the two fields of withered sunflowers until it reached the pavement, the company store where the Bailundos bought cigarettes, dried fish, and warm beer on Sundays appeared around a curve and hid itself among the trees, along with the lime plaster-covered shanties in the field where a setter was barking, withered sunflowers, withered rice, withered cotton, a tractor with no wheels in a ditch, at the spot where the dirt road met the pavement a UNITA patrol car pulled out in front of us and they waved their rifles at us, telling us to pull over, barefoot soldiers with their uniforms in tatters rummaging through our luggage looking for coins or food, anything they could steal, the unbearable damp smell of cassava, filthy fingernails searching between the seats, toothless mouths

"Get out, get out"

my sister to my mother, twisting in fear to escape their reach

"Mother"

"You put them out on the street and now you want your siblings back if I were you I wouldn't wait up for them tonight Carlos"

a sergeant in a Panama hat, oblivious of the other soldiers, grilled a snake at the end of the handle of a cannon brush and didn't bother us, a dust devil made the fallen leaves dance in the convent courtyard in between broken columns, salamanders and geckos crawling on the remains of arches, where my father, walking slowly with his canes, often came to watch the gledes fly about, my father in his bed, a rosary hanging on the headboard, looking at us with the alarmed expression of a blind man

"Give your father a kiss"

his nostrils enormous, his neck ringed with blotches and straining with the enormous task of trying to breathe

(you could tell that his ribs hurt him)

I tripped over one of his canes and it crashed to the ground with the loudest bang I ever heard, to this day, my brother screamed when the thunder struck and submerged himself beneath the furniture on all fours, holding tight to the chair, a glob of chocolate stained his bib

"I won't give him a kiss"

the raspy deterioration of my father's voice, on that day we had lunch in the dining room to the sound of the rain on the roof, the servants made sandwiches, grilled croquettes on wooden skewers, brought them to us on platters held high, cars from the other farms parked in the yard, my sister to my mother, trying to escape from the soldiers in tattered uniforms

"Get out get out"

"Mother"

opening our suitcases, ripping our bags, leaving me speechless, the sergeant with the snake, rotating the brush handle, turned on a battery-operated radio as if this were some kind of holiday and he was at the bar with his buddies, all at once the music blared and crackled from the ditch at the side of the road and deafened us, my mother pushed one of the soldiers with her purse

"Give them your earrings so they'll leave us alone Clarisse give them whatever they want"

it was then that I noticed a body lying near the snake, a soldier missing half his head and covered in blowflies, I pinched Lena's arm, whispered softly to Lena

"Keep quiet"

a soldier hit her in the belly with the butt of his rifle

the belly that never bore a child have you heard the news brace yourself don't faint guess who Carlos is going out with

they tore off her necklace, the beads flew everywhere at the very moment that the sergeant began to cut the snake with his knife, my sister gave up her earrings, her hairpin, her ring, the pavement of the Malanje highway, cracked by all the mortars, vibrated in the heat and in the midst of all this the sound of an airplane, the soldiers hiding in the tall grass, the sergeant cutting the snake into pieces, putting them in a sack, and heading off without any hurry, my mother climbing behind the steering wheel and putting the jeep in gear

"Hurry"

while we shoved clothes into the open suitcases, grabbed shirts, socks, pants, Lena's bag of makeup and perfume and the smashed vials, my mother scanning the tall grass

"Hurry"

Lena couldn't walk because of the blow she'd received, and Rui and I carried her

"You haven't seen your siblings in fifteen years"

"Hurry hurry"

my sister kept gathering up nightgowns, sandals, a round mirror, the beads from the necklace that danced in the sunlight, the sound of the airplane faded away to the north, up past the Pecagranja jungle or Chiquita

I remember the mango trees and the Jinga who was lynched by the head of police, I remember the rest of the Jingas waiting quietly

a bomb, a second bomb, a distant cannon blossomed in the sky, my mother afraid that the UNITA soldiers would return and we'd suffer the same fate as the soldier covered in blowflies

"Clarisse"

the jeep swerved down the highway, Lena clasping her arms around her stomach, skinny, hair in braids, leaving the Malanje church, the organ still blowing its tune, cousins scattering flower petals along the steps, the bishop smiled, the lynching victim thrashed his legs one or two times and twirled in front of the tree trunk, the chief of police pointed at him with his horsewhip

"Buy your dried fish at the company store, not the store in town"

he ordered his men to destroy the crates of fish that belonged to the mulatto merchant, who didn't dare move a muscle, they poured gasoline on it and set it ablaze, burned the bolts of fabric, the packages of tobacco, the racks of buttons, suspenders, elastic, leather belts, and wooden toys, the merchant came with his son on his shoulders to ask my mother for forgiveness, kneeling at her feet straight away

"I swear that I had no idea that they worked for you ma'am I don't sell anything to the farm workers just to the people in Chiquita"

lying through his teeth given that everyone in Chiquita worked for us and he was stealing some of our profits, pretending to be meek, trying to play to our emotions with the child, showing us the shack he lived in

"I'm just a poor man"

kissing my mother's hand, kissing my hand, in the end I asked the native soldiers for a nightstick, the merchant protecting his child, whimpering through his busted lips

"Don't hurt me I'm just a poor man don't hurt me anymore"

to teach him obedience we divided up the suckling pigs and the pork rinds between our foremen, a group of grinning and delighted creatures, as Africans always are when they profit from the misfortune of others, ransacking the mulatto's wares, bumping into the hanging man in a greedy rush to grab ash and garbage, the mulatto's wife watching them silently, an Indian in sandals who worked in the hut that passed for a school teaching children without slide rule or textbooks, writing crooked numbers and letters on butcher paper, the first fruit bats flitted belligerently in the dusk's cautious transition into night, the chief of police addressing my mother, courteously

"Maybe we should hang him"

the terrified merchant, his hair a mess, the muddy mane of an aging horse, his customers already seated on some stones in the cheerful hope that there would be a second execution, free of charge, more fun than the old films they used to show on the side of the gas station on Camões Day, speeches by President Carmona, parades of firemen, the kids from the Portuguese Youth group marching with arms outstretched in the Roman salute, inaugurations of dams and levees, all the festivities feeling dangerous, people shoving, looking for a place to sit, the film likely to burn up at any minute, the projectionist

"Damn"

mending it with glue, the workers hesitating with their green and red flags, not knowing what to do with them, they were given a cup of wine, a package of cookies, and a medallion of our lady of Fátima, the crowd bellowed at them

"Long live the Patria"

they responded unenthusiastically, I never saw them enthusiastic about anything except mischief and shiny metal wristwatches

"Long live the Patria"

and they were left in peace until the next day, waving flags, their stomachs full, dead drunk in the servants' quarters, they beamed at the real possibility of another hanging, especially if they were part of the guy's family and stood to inherit his junk, the broken saucepan, the mug with no handles, the wretched little rug, my mother to the head of police, exacting, but with a sharp eye toward her financial well-being

"If we hang them all then who do I have to put to work, can you tell me that?"

and since the head of police had no intention of harvesting rice from six in the morning on, for fifteen escudos a day, and the added obligation to spend it at the company store and still end up owing money at the end of the month, because the price of fish was so high, triple what the rest of the village paid, the native soldiers abandoned their excellent plan to leave the brute hanging from a tree, legs flailing, for the even better one of giving them all a good bashing with their nightsticks, although the people, oddly enough, weren't too thrilled at this prospect and took off running for the rafts in the river, that ungrateful bunch, their hands holding sore backs or buttocks, corresponding to the whims of the nightsticks, chased by my brother and pellets from the air rifle with which he had terrorized Pecagranja since Easter, my mother worrying

"Call Rui back here, poor thing, I don't want him falling and hurting himself on account of those fools"

Rui

"Why do you think of them now, when you haven't seen them for fifteen years?"

loved to shoot pellets during the sunflower harvest, the medic in taped-up glasses with a crack in one of the lenses took hours to extract them with tweezers and mercurochrome in the cancerous tent they called a clinic, rusty syringes, a rubber enema bag hanging from a nail on the wall, vials of expired quinine in cardboard boxes, all the precautions taken by the people in the Huambo uplands notwithstanding, the foreman gave a sack of seeds to each worker, they just wouldn't stop dying from dysentery, recently arrived on the cattle trucks, they pretended that they were worn-out from the ride so they wouldn't have to work, and they'd soon come down with a fever and start vomiting, the foreman insisted that they were just faking and shoved an ice cube up their chief's anus as an example to everyone else, but by Thursday the chief

"He was as healthy as a horse, ma'am, it's just the spirit of outright defiance these swine have"

was dead and buried, and his subjects, ever loyal, made haste to follow his lead

"Get up stop faking it get up"

they lasted a month at most, even with the help of enemas and quinine, my mother made an agreement with the foreman at Dala Samba and started hiring Bundi-Bângalas, even though they were liars and layabouts they always lasted a little bit longer, some of them lasted through the entire harvest, but couldn't go back home to live it up because they spent so much at the company store that they now owed us twenty harvests' worth of work, that is, twenty if they planted for free and didn't eat anything at all, the native soldiers kept one or two of the workers' children in prison to make sure they stayed on with us, a little weaker, sure, but willing to work, on Saturdays they were able to see their kids, but only from a distance and through the bars of the prison, if my mother were a Bundi-Bângala she would jump for joy for the opportunity to not have her kids bugging her, or her husband if they'd put him in too, the problem is that nobody wanted us, who was looking to take in an invalid with one foot in the grave and three useless kids, just as

I bet

she was glad to send us off to Lisbon eighteen years ago, making up excuses about the civil war, about what they were doing to white people, about the Cubans, about South Africa, and then went straight back to Cassanje to run the plantation without Lena or us slowing her down

"Slum-dweller"

sending letters covered in stamps and seals, as dirty as if they'd come on foot all the way from Malanje to Ajuda, the mailman brought them and I kept piling them up in the drawer without reading them, envelopes from the plantation at first and then from Marimba, a little village that doesn't even show up on maps, mango trees, buildings in ruins, the military barracks crumbling in the rain, my mother living there temporarily, who knows how she managed to eat, in some ramshackle hovel with one or two of the servants who stayed with her, the cook named Maria da Boa Morte

Maria da Boa Morte Maria da Boa Morte Maria da Boa Morte

given that name for having caused the death of her mother when she was born, always smoking a cigarette, with the lit end inside of her mouth, when I was little I loved the smell of her, fried lard, cigarettes, the perfume they made her wear to cover up her body odor, Maria da Boa Morte

Maria da Boa Morte

and maybe Josélia who took care of my grandmother in the room upstairs that looked out on the apple tree that struggled through the dry season, those apple trees that had been dried out by the climate, evaporating branch by branch into a fragrant dust as I got older, as if they had never existed, no trace of them on the earth, no scar, no furrow, no crease, no sign, as if I, correspondingly, didn't exist, after all these years past

Josélia Maria da Boa Morte Josélia Josélia

as if my siblings, correspondingly, didn't exist, despite all the winters spent in this house, where Lena says they'll never return

"If I were you I wouldn't wait up for visitors Carlos"

I sent a telegram to Clarisse in Estoril, I spoke on the telephone with the director of Rui's nursing home, I told them

"Six o'clock"

I told them

"I'll be waiting for you I'll be waiting for him at six o'clock"

and so at any moment they're going to ring the doorbell, I bet that if you start counting they'll ring the doorbell before you can get to one hundred, I can hear a taxi pulling up outside, a car at the corner of the avenue, footsteps on the front steps and I still have to set up the Christmas tree, still need to put the pine tree in the stand and fill it with gravel so it will stand up straight, still need to put the sequined star on top, the cotton snow

cotton sunflower rice the taste of papaya

wreaths, ornaments, to wrap the candies I bought for Clarisse, the necktie I bought for Rui, champagne in the ice bucket, plates of walnuts and pine nuts, embroidered tablecloth on the table, fruit-cake, codfish, if you count down from one hundred to zero, one hundred ninety-nine ninety-eight ninety-seven ninety-six I bet that before you get to ten they'll come through that door, if you get to zero and they haven't it's because my sister went to pick up my brother and got held up in traffic, it's hard to find a trolley, let alone a taxi at this time of night while Lisbon is out shopping in full force, malls, boutiques, supermarkets, my siblings with presents for Lena and me, a book, a record, a trinket, a picture frame, me helping them take off their coats and hang them on the coatrack, putting their umbrellas in the ceramic vase, complimenting her stylishness, his lack of gray hairs

"Don't wait up for visitors Carlos"

Lena envisioning Christmas alone with me

(count to one hundred again, count down from one hundred to zero, count to three hundred)

same as the last fifteen Christmases since

as she insists

I forced them out of Ajuda, getting up out of her chair, surprised, wearing a blouse that's at least better than those rags from Sambila

"She's not a slum-dweller I swear she's not a slum-dweller her parents' apartment is under construction I swear she's exactly like us"

that she usually wears, costume jewelry and tin fripperies, Christmas alone with me, bored, quiet, watching Mass on TV, reading magazines, hearing the clanking of the rain gutters and the wind whistling through the shrubs, Lena offering chairs, offering my spot on the couch that has an indentation the shape of my body

"Sit down, sit down"

the hills of Almada against the sky, the lights of the ships, the spotlights in the shipyard, Lena alone in the living room, me at the doorstep, the bottle of champagne in the ice bucket, the plates of walnuts and pine nuts, the embroidered tablecloth, the fruitcake, rows of lights twinkling on the pine tree, me counting to one hundred, to five hundred, to one thousand certain that they'd come because I sent a telegram to Estoril, spoke on the telephone with the director of the nursing home, certain that they'd come listening to the clanking of the rain gutters and the wind whistling through the shrubs, counting from one to one hundred a thousand times until late at night in front of the untouched platter of codfish.

24 July 1978

There's something terrible in me. Sometimes at night the rustling of the sunflowers wakes me and, in the darkness of the bedroom, I feel my womb growing bigger with something that is neither a child, nor swelling, nor a tumor, nor illness, it's some sort of scream that, instead of coming out of your mouth, comes out of your entire body and fills up the fields like the howling of dogs, and then I stop breathing, grab the headboard hard and a thousand stems of silence slowly float inside the mirrors, awaiting the dreadful clarity of morning. At such times I think I'm dead, surrounded by workers' huts and cotton, my mother already dead, my husband already dead, their places at the table faded away, and now I live in mere rooms, empty rooms whose lights I turn on at dusk to disguise their absence. As a child, before we came back to Angola, I watched the lynching of the town lunatic in Nisa. Kids on the street were afraid of him, dogs ran away from him if he happened to pass by, he stole tangerines, eggs, flour, would install himself in front of the high altar and insult the Virgin, one day he flayed the belly of a calf from its neck to its groin, the animal walked into the town square tripping over its own entrails, the farmers from the nearby farm grabbed the lunatic

me at the end of the appointment while Rui got dressed with the nurse's help

"What's wrong with the little guy Doctor?"

"A hereditary cerebral condition ma'am electrical synapses out of order his behavior could change"

they dragged and shoved him to the threshing floor, began to beat him with hoes and sticks and he didn't defend himself or even scream out, the bum smiled more and more with every blow, I remember a hunchbacked olive tree in the sunlight, men raising and lowering the harrows, the lunatic, always with a smile, pulled his comb out of his pocket to straighten his hair, a second later a stone crushed his chest and the locks of his hair looked like the nest that a group of storks had built on the edge of the water tower

"Become aggressive for example become disobedient give him these pills at lunch and dinner and come in for another appointment in May"

branches and leaves and mud and pieces of cloth, after the farmers took off I remained alone with the man for some time before the police showed up, me and those fearless pigeons returning to the dam, since nobody was looking I took the lunatic's comb, a broken comb with missing teeth, hid it in the dresser drawer behind my pencils and school notebooks, I kept it with me for years and years in a scratched and dented cookie tin with no picture on the lid, any time I touched it I could see the houses in Nisa and the calf walking into the town square tripping over its own entrails, no one else could ever understand what it was, no matter who it was

"Is this a comb Isilda?"

"It's nothing"

"I bet it's a piece of a comb show me"

"I'm not going to show you it's nothing leave me alone"

and I think that it was around this time that I realized there was something terrible in me. I woke up at night to the rustling of the sunflowers

"You wake up because of the sunflowers but not when the little ones cry"

my womb grew bigger in the darkness of the bedroom with something that wasn't a child, it was a sort of scream that, instead of coming out of your mouth, comes out of your entire body filling the fields like the howling of dogs, I smiled the same smile as the man lying facedown on the threshing floor about whom the police chief advised my uncle

"Bury him in the gully where they bury stray dogs it'll serve as compost for the reeds that grow there and this matter is settled"

I agreed to allow Carlos

(no, not Carlos)

to develop inside me in order to smother the scream, in pregnancy my body became a coffin inside which a cadaver was growing

"Are you going to comb the baby's hair with that ghastly comb Isilda?"

"No I'm not leave me alone get out of here"

and after that Clarisse, and after that Rui, me like an eviscerated calf bleeding and tripping over my own entrails each time one was born, sliced open from neck to groin spilling all over myself in exhausted anguish, without any objection, any complaint, any harsh word, facedown on the sheets

"Turn over Mrs. Isilda turn over on your back immediately what are you doing?"

with the comb in my hand, smiling in defiance at whoever was killing me because there is something terrible in me that you all don't know about but that animals and blacks are aware of, the servants are aware of it watching me guardedly any time I step foot in the kitchen to arrange the meals, as if I were wasting away right in front of them, something terrible that was passed on to Rui

"A hereditary condition ma'am a complication that is transmitted from parent to child you can never tell how they're going to behave"

and that Carlos and Clarisse don't have, since neither animals nor Africans are frightened by them, they curl up at their feet, allow themselves to be scratched and petted, smelling them, laugh, another way of being quiet, hanging on them, looking at them, an expression, a smell, the house was different without children, not bigger, different, they say that when children leave home the houses get bigger and become sad, it's not true, upon returning to the plantation from Luanda where the boat had left amid pure chaos, full of baggage and people not to mention refrigerators and ovens and automobiles left on the docks that the Cubans and residents of the slums fought over at gunpoint, willing to die for a hot plate or a broken dishwasher and carrying them out of the city, a trail of ants, upon returning to the plantation from Luanda the house had changed, everyday objects were strange to me, I recognized the chairs and didn't sit in them, the framed pictures showed strangers whose habits and names I happened to know, the cook, the only creature in the world whom Carlos ever liked, he didn't like me, didn't like his siblings, didn't like his wife, he liked her, leaning over the side of the boat to remind me to take good care of her, Maria da Boa Morte who smoked with the lit end of the cigarette inside her mouth, I taught her good manners the way you teach an animal, hired her out of pity to work among the cups and kale, and my son, no one could ever explain this one to me, never letting go of her for a second, drinking out of her hand, eating out of her hand, insisting she tuck him in so he could get to sleep, he never asked for me or his father to do it, Maria da Boa Morte was the one he wanted, just in the door on break from boarding school and he'd be sitting in the dining room talking to her, upon returning to the plantation from Luanda the house had changed, everyday objects were strange to me, I recognized the chairs and didn't sit in them, the past showing in those picture frames no longer belonged to me, who the hell is this, who the hell is that, that lady over there arm-in-arm with my husband is wearing a hat I used to own

"*That hat looks so nice on you Isilda*"

I sent away for it in Portugal, wore it with sapphire earrings to the dinner party at the governor's place, I was radiant at Rui's baptism, took it to Europe with me, visited Paris in it, walked along the seaside wearing it in Barcelona, if I ever felt upset I'd go get it, lock the door to my room, and try it on in front of the mirror even with no lipstick on, even with no eye shadow, and it gave me the urge to sing, back around the time my mother got sick I never went a week without wearing my suede shoes, I'd clamber up into the attic in secret, look for it in the trunk, show it to my mother and my mother

"How beautiful"

not just to please me, but sincerely

"How beautiful"

raising her wrist up off the mattress and gently touching the hat with her fingertips

"How beautiful"

if someday I go to Lisbon to see my children I'll have it mended by the seamstress in Malanje, I'll have its crown fixed, do something with the brim, some small stitches in the holes in the gossamer that will hardly be noticeable, I take the hat that I bought in Rome down off the coatrack and leave it on the landing of the stairs so they can all see it, me at age thirty, happy, no wrinkles on my cheeks, Clarisse and Rui on my lap, Carlos hiding behind the cook

"Let go of me"

with the lit end of the cigarette inside her mouth, eating dried fish with her in the pantry, he doesn't like his siblings, doesn't like his wife, he likes the destitute street urchins and palm oil, chickens wandering in and around the workers' huts, upon returning to the plantation from Luanda the cook had changed too, wearing slippers on the tile floor, unafraid of me for the first time, banging on the broken dinner bell to call everyone to lunch, Maria da Boa Morte Josélia Damião Fernando, they served the food wearing white coats with gold buttons, I lent them to the bishop for the party in honor of the nuncio's visit, outdoor music, yellow canopies, the church choir, the invited guests sweating in their flannel dress shirts, the nuncio surprised by the servants' efficiency

"So much hard work, you shouldn't have"

Fernando with his tight curly hair straightened out with hair spray had one of his incisors pulled out and replaced with a silver one so that when he spoke the words shone, pulling his lips back, tremendously satisfied, showing off the unusual hardware that they'd hammered into his gums, upon returning to the plantation from Luanda where the boat had left amid pure chaos, full of baggage and people, of junk that had been hastily taken from the clutches of the Cubans and soldiers, bursts from machine guns on street corners, groups of ragged soldiers with machetes cutting each other's throats, blond-haired Belgians in camouflage bolting down mortars on the porches of homes, naked corpses or ones wearing nothing but a single boot that were swept down ditches toward the sea by the heavy rain, the prostitutes on the island, without any customers, perched in the palm trees shaking their tits, a bearded mulatto in Muxima who made off with my gas can and spare tire

"Comrade"

whites in the parks, surrounded by beds and tables, sitting on little stools waiting for no one, bandaged elbows, bandaged heads, ashes from the moped they set fire to, the headquarters of National Front for the Liberation of Angola up in flames, the Cuca neighborhood devastated by cannon fire, bodies piled up in front of the morgue, the bearded mulatto unbolted the headlights, pulled off the windshield wipers, cut off the canvas top with scissors, a couple of young hussies were eyeing the ring

"Comrade"

that belonged to my family and that my father gave me before I got married, a ring without precious stones that at first glance looks valuable but isn't worth a cent, one of the hussies grabbed my finger

"Hurry up I don't have all afternoon"

my father with that expression that wasn't a smile but looked like a smile

"See how nice it looks on you Isilda?"

shaved and dressed in a suit and tie for dinner at the plantation underneath the hundreds of lights from the chandeliers reflected in the silverware and plates, my mother looking very elegant, me with a ribbon tied in a bow around my waist and outside, instead of in a city, London for example, the cotton field after harvest, the smell of dirt got in through the open windows the curtains quivering in the wind, Damião brought out the soup with the majesty of one of the three wise men bearing gifts, ladies in low-necked dresses, with scarlet fingernails and scarlet lips, their eyebrows replaced with a curved pencil line that turned their facial features into a perpetual look of surprise, they put a cushion on the chair so I could sit up taller and their eyebrows turned toward me, in soft silky voices

"My God, how you've grown"

gentlemen in tuxedos smoked cigars, the lights turned off for dessert, the rustle of linen and wristwatches, beaded handbags, high heels that tapped on the ground with the sound of jangling crystals, legs crossed on the couches, a bridge table, my father handing out cognac and liqueurs with that expression that wasn't a smile but looked like a smile, kisses that left me dazed in the ladies' aromas, the cars leaving one by one illuminating the sunflowers, the cotton, the trees in the distance, and the workers' huts, the ladies' shoulders as they walked down the stairs, covered with translucent shawls as if it were somehow cold in all that heat, my mother to my father, under her breath

"You couldn't take your eyes off the French woman Eduardo"

a woman with a fake, lozenge-shaped beauty mark who, when she leaned over, embarrassed my godfather, threw the clocks off their rhythm, and disrupted the bridge game, I remember her on horseback behind the church, my father with his hand on the stirrup

"Denise"

my father who was starting to go bald, his hand trembling

"Denise"

the French woman pulling away from him, pointing at me with her crop trying to get him to notice and my father indifferent, raising his fingers from the stirrup to her boot

"Denise"

my mother taking her shoes off and massaging her feet

"These sandals are killing me"

letting her hair down while stretching out in an armchair amid wine glasses, overflowing ashtrays, a six of hearts on the rug,

Damião lined up the bottles in the china cabinet and tidied up the room

"Do you even for a second think that I'm blind to what's going on between you and the French woman Eduardo?"

his thumb creeping up from her boot to her pants, from her pants to her belt, disappearing in between the buttons of her blouse, appearing again, disappearing, the sunflowers standing on end at the threat of rain, the field hands approaching through a shortcut in the grass, the French woman wasn't wearing the lozenge-shaped beauty mark and now during the day, without makeup, she appeared less elegant to me, much older, with gray hairs, hopelessness in her eyes, blowing a kiss, hiding something, riding away at a trot, scraping horseshoes on the flagstones of the chapel where the names of the deceased were written half in Portuguese half in Latin, so worn down that they could hardly be deciphered, the sky completely opaque and in it the first bolt of lightning, the first drop of rain, the horse's head and the woman's head bobbing up and down in the rice paddy, the ceiling lights on, the lamps on the chests of drawers lit, Damião cleaning out coffee sludge from the colander, my father shutting the windows where the wind blasted against the casement and made the curtains flap, avoiding my mother who watched in the mirrors, her attention divided between him and her sore heel

"Why even lie Eduardo don't be a child don't overexert yourself you're a terrible liar"

the French woman after an argument between my father and her husband that made it so that for months no one visited our house and no eyebrows rose in surprise at my entrance

"How you've grown"

sold her property to an Indian from Mozambique and moved to the Congo with her family, I never saw the horse or the lozenge-shaped beauty mark again, never again did the men interrupt their game of bridge, my mother exiled herself to the guest room and only spoke to my father through me

"Ask your father to pass the salt Isilda"

"Ask your father if he's going to have a second helping of fish"

"Inform your father that the chief's daughter died we need to give him a little money for their annoying drum circle I'm going to Luanda because I don't want to deal with any parties"

my father meekly passing the salt, assuring her that he didn't want any more fish, promising to give money to the tribal chief, wandering outside the guest room like a ghost but never daring to call out her name, coughing as loud as he could for my mother to hear but nothing, just a slight illumination below the door, the sound of breathing, an occasional noise, silence like that of a deep well, the bed made very early in the morning, a towel drying on the windowsill, a few bites of toast at breakfast, the butter dish with its lid on backwards, remnants of sugar at the bottom of a teacup, my mother out at a friend's farm the whole day or in Malanje or at the convent, my mother ill, touching my hat with her fingertips

"How beautiful"

and upon returning to the plantation from Luanda where the boat had left amid pure chaos, full of baggage and people, a fat, ungainly boat, only good for cruising calm seas, it gave the impression that it was limping through the water, returning from Luanda, without my ring, without the gas can, without the spare tire, at every step of the way coming upon overturned vans, ruined straw huts, soldiers who were killed crossing the highway, military personnel from Katanga, Zaire, South Africa, upon returning to the plantation before giving orders to the servants and writing letters to my children to let them know I'd arrived just fine, I'm fine, I'll be fine

they put a cushion on the chair so I could sit up taller, just as tall as them and their eyebrows turned toward me, in soft silky voices

"How you've grown"

no problems here, all the workers who run the machines are still here, none of them ran off, on the contrary, those miserable bastards still show up

(the Jingas are so miserable that, fortunately for them, they aren't even aware of their misery)

begging for work, sometimes missing an arm, missing legs, write to my children to tell them that with the high demand for work I can easily reduce their wages right down to nothing they'll stay on for free since they have nowhere to go, tell my children that I'm fine, that I'll be fine, not to worry, we'll start planting on Tuesday, we won't have a late harvest this year, if we don't sell to Portugal we'll sell to Japan, chartering a ship isn't a problem and in terms of transportation all I have to do is make a deal with the Russians or Americans who are drilling on the oil rigs in Cabinda

with the cushion on the chair I was much taller than them, if I need to I'll ask Maria da Boa Morte to get a pillow for me right now and I'll sit down on top of the world with the rest of the universe whirring around insignificantly down below

write to my children to reassure them because in spite of the war going on not a single goat, chicken, or ear of corn has been stolen, everything's the same as usual, absolute peacefulness, reassure them since there's nothing to fear here in Baixa de Cassanje, Carlos opens the letters, reads them to his brother and sister, you can see why he'd be scared to open the envelope, worried that it would be bad news, the hesitation, his thumb trembling at the edge of the flap, anxiety at first then relief, looking out over the chimneys you can see the bridge, the statue of Christ, the shipyard and the hills of Almada, I bought it when my husband was still alive and my husband the poor thing hated the big city

"When I die bury me in Dondo here in Angola"

my husband signing the document

"But why buy it if we rarely leave Africa?"

he complained that it was too cold, that the change in the position of the stars confused him, that he couldn't breathe, that he suffocated in Europe

"I suffocate in Europe"

always getting turned around on the streets, longing for the smell of cassava root, the smell of the earth, his pillow

"I can't get to sleep with this pillow"

so we ended up taking him through the haze brushing spider webs from our faces, the tombs and crosses blurry in the dense mist, Damião in a white coat with gold buttons set chrysanthemums down next to an angel lying in front of an open book and maybe now the chrysanthemums are suffocating him, an unobserved bird on the other side of the wall took pity on us, Clarisse grabbed his canes and without a word disappeared into the field, she didn't have them when she came back at dinnertime and I was thinking that time was as slow as molasses in Dondo yes sir, thinking of how I'd never noticed the slowness of Dondo nor the slowness of the nights in Africa, the rustling of the sunflowers with something that was neither a child, nor swelling, nor a tumor, nor illness, it's some sort of scream throughout your entire body like the howling of dogs, I grabbed the headboard with all my strength until the wind died down

there's something terrible in me

the sunflowers fell quiet and the thousand stems of silence continued to undulate inside the mirrors awaiting the dreadful clarity of morning, the calf walked into the town square, a hoof here a hoof there, talking to myself out loud barely believing I was talking out loud

terrible in me something

"I'm dead"

the eyes of the calf completely white, devoid of iris and pupil, two white spheres without eyebrows, its stomach flayed from neck to groin, Damião very serious wearing an old shirt from back when no one visited us, made from a pajama top that he elevated to the dignity of a cloak, he bent over my husband, placed a coin over each eye, he lit all the tapers in the room, the suddenly gigantic shadows spilled onto the ceiling, swaying separating and fusing, we buried my father in Malanje and months later found out that the French woman killed herself in the Congo, a foreigner with scarlet lips shooing away the servants, taking the revolver out of the drawer, raising it to her ear, her eyebrows must have looked really surprised, a curved pencil line instead of her own eyebrow hairs, drawn with a compass, Carlos impassive, not a single tear, Rui

"A hereditary cerebral condition ma'am electrical synapses out of order epilepsy"
what a word epilepsy epilepsy epilepsy
his behavior could change
without any respect for the visitors or for me, starting to laugh, sitting on his dead father's bed laughing, upon returning to the plantation from Luando, even before writing to my children to re-assure them, I didn't expect a response, didn't expect a phone call especially with UNITA breaking the telephone poles and tearing down phone lines, often the phone rings, I hold the receiver up to my ear and there's no sound or just fragments of words, far-off breathing, hisses and pops that stream out of the phone and fade, or am I the only one who notices, because I'm alone and afraid of the night, that the phone rang and didn't ring, it doesn't ring for entire weeks, I hold it near me as I rest, shake it, unplug it, plug it in in the other room in vain, they finally took Rui outside and I could hear him giggling in the backyard, beaming, shooting his pellet gun at the washerwomen, the farmers took the town lunatic in Nisa, they took Rui, dragged and shoved him to the thresh-ing floor, started beating him with hoes and sticks and my son didn't complain, I recall a hunchbacked olive tree in the sunlight, men raising and lowering the harrows, Rui pulled a comb from his pocket to straighten his hair and a second later a stone crushed his chest, when the farmers left I stayed with him for some time until the police showed up, me and the fearless pigeons who were returning to the empty dam, since no one was watching I took the comb with missing teeth
"I bet it's a piece of a comb show me"

"I'm not going to show you it's nothing leave me be"

that I kept in a scratched and dented cookie tin with no picture on the lid, me with Rui on my lap holding him, hugging him

"Are you going to comb the baby's hair with that ghastly comb Isilda?"

"No I'm not leave me alone get out of here"

Rui wasn't like the others, didn't talk like them, sat motionless in the middle of a meal with his fork up to his mouth as if he were in some far-off place, Carlos and Clarisse glancing at each other, my husband shrugging his shoulders, me worried

"Rui"

"These pills at mealtime and another appointment in May"

Rui with his siblings in Ajuda knowing that Carlos loathes him like he loathes everybody except Maria da Boa Morte with the lit end of the cigarette inside her mouth, Lena's a slum-dweller the daughter of one of those destitute workers at the Cuca-beer plant and Clarisse, with that God-given disposition, doesn't care about him only cares about bars and fancy shops and the cretins who support those tendencies of hers, Rui without me to look after him and take him to the doctor getting himself lost in Ajuda, in Alcântara, sitting among all the retirees in Santo Amaro with his air rifle on his knees waving down at the Tagus River

"You wake up because of the sunflowers but not when the little ones cry"

his hair like the nests made of branches and leaves and mud and scraps of fabric that the storks had built on the edge of the water tower, upon returning to the plantation from Luanda, painfully thirsty, my back hurting from the jarring ride in the jeep, the taste of dust in my mouth, my hands covered in oil, upon returning to the plantation even before writing to my children to let them know that I arrived just fine, that I'm fine, that I'll be fine, there won't be any problems with the harvest this year, if we don't sell to Portugal we'll sell to Thailand, I'll strike a deal with the Russians or Americans who are drilling for oil on the rigs in Cabinda, upon returning from Luanda, not even responding to Damião's obeisance, dusting the china, wearing a gray shirt with the stateliness of a high priest, I went up into the attic, looking in the trunk for the moth-eaten hat, that gauzy skeleton that I took with me when we went to Europe, I visited Paris in it, went sightseeing in it in Barcelona, locked the door to my room, looked at myself in the mirror even with no lipstick and no eye shadow, tomorrow I'll send it to the seamstress in Malanje to mend it, have its crown fixed, find a way to repair the brim, some small stitches in the gossamer that will barely be noticeable, I wait for the bearded mulatto in Muxima to raise his hand and flay me from neck to groin

don't worry we're going to start planting on Tuesday

and I walk into the kitchen, a hoof here a hoof there, tripping over my entrails, toppling over in front of the oven like a dead calf.

24 December 1995

On the desk in the office there was a paperweight, a glass ball with reindeer inside pulling a sleigh and seated in the sleigh a bearded fat man in a woolen suit and red cap. If you turned the ball upside down and right-side up again, snow swirled around the bearded man's sleigh, dusting snow onto the cap, the reindeer, and the microscopic pine tree in the background, my mother put the paperweight on the desk in between a picture of us in Durban and an ostrich made out of *pau-santo* wood with transparent stones for eyes, she explained

"It's Santa Claus"

and I didn't understand how that little plastic figure was able to leave its glass prison, full of water with an air bubble at the top, in order to give us the gifts that appeared in the morning in the dining room, with our names on tags taped to the wrapping paper, and much less understood that Santa Claus bought them at stores in Luanda

(her fingernail wasn't able to scrape off the price tag or the store's label completely)

since it seemed to me unlikely for a couple of reindeer and a sleigh to slide down the coastline under the palm trees in a swirl of snow when it was thirty-eight degrees Celsius in the shade and the houses softened in the heat, people sweating on the boardwalk, and on the beach the sea was boiling, fat bubbling to the top like a soup on the stove. My mother maintained that Santa Claus came down the chimney with a bag full of toy trumpets, colored pencils, and cap guns, a strange story since the chimney led down from the roof and opened right onto the stove top, putting Santa Claus in a dangerous position next to the duck and rice in the oven, and moreover I couldn't understand how such a fat gentleman could fit down a dirty, skinny pipe: as far as I can remember during my childhood, the only thing that ever came down the chimney was an errant canary that emerged from it one morning fluttering around the kitchen in its sooty anguish, chirping desperately and finally escaping out toward the backyard, scattering ash everywhere, leaving dark smudges on the clothes that were drying on the line and turning up dead the next day in the pot of azaleas, spread out on its back, its beak open, skinny because of its sick, deflated lungs. Still my mother reassured us that Santa Claus, very experienced and full of tricks

(it was hard for me to imagine kindness and trickery combined in a single person, from my point of view those characteristics were incompatible) possessed secret wiles that were capable of solving what were, to him, the very simple problems of narrow chimneys and malevolent ovens, always eager to roast anyone who fell into their bellies along with the red potatoes, wiles that my mother, judging by her knowing smile, undoubtedly had access to as well but refused to explain, and since it was November

(thunder boomed in Baixa de Cassanje with the sound of pianos crashing down invisible stairwells, power lines snapped and flailed about, scattering sparks that set fire to the acacia trees)

we spent the rest of the afternoon observing the paperweight, hoping that Santa Claus would decide to take a practice run, with wrapping paper and reindeer and snow, departing from the glass sphere on his sleigh, riding up to the rooftop, first inserting one boot and then the beard and then his entire plump body into the opening where the smoke came out. We turned the paperweight upside down a number of times, trying to stoke his vanity with the whirling white specks, and yet the little creature stubbornly remained motionless, holding the reins with his gloved hands, staring at the tiny pine tree in front of him with absurd concentration. We decided to break the glass with the hammer from the toolbox in an effort to facilitate his endeavors.

(some people are so lazy and self-indulgent that even breaking through a little glass is a chore for them)

Rui, who'd been sent for the hammer, preferred the wrench used for tightening leaky faucets, we had the paperweight on the ground and the wrench in the air when my father opened the door, and in an instant the paperweight was back on the desk, the snow, mocking us, swirled in the water, and we were grounded, sent to our rooms looking out the window at the rainy sky, dark as night at four in the afternoon and the sunflowers bent from the wind, alarmed at the horrible threat of not getting any colored pencils or cap guns for Christmas. I have the globe with me here in Ajuda, on the shelf in the living room for my brother and sister to see, I just put the sequined star on top of the tree, put the gifts down near the stand, a bottle of damn expensive perfume for Clarisse who's no fool and can spot a pinchbeck from across the room, an overstock bargain necktie, very colorful the way he likes it for Rui, who's a fool

and since he won't notice it's all the same to him and I save some money

for the most part, his epilepsy an earthworm gnawing holes in his head, my mother used to take him to the doctor in Malanje, when she returned home with him, even though she'd bought a handkerchief for herself, you could tell she'd been crying, she left Rui in the kitchen went upstairs and took ages to come down to the dinner table, her eyes swollen and her voice worn-out, piercing everything with her stare but not noticing anything at all, refusing to eat the soup, refusing to eat the fish, lying on her bed at night, you could hear her sobbing mixed with the thousands of other noises without origin or cause that inhabit the silence, I shook Clarisse and Clarisse

"It's just a bird"

yet it wasn't a bird or a fox or the tractor drivers mourning a death in the workers' huts or the fever-breath of the cotton, it was the grandfather clock with Roman numerals in the hallway that robbed us of our certainty, the solemn copper pendulum swinging to the right and to the left in the depths of it, it was the straw in the couch cushion crackling, my mother's voice from far away and up close, to my father

"The doctor said that it's a hereditary condition I was the one who gave it to him it's my fault"

and my father, as he had almost every ten minutes ever since Rui got sick, taking a bottle of whiskey out of the bedside table

there wasn't a drawer without a bottle of whiskey in it, the medic from Chiquita warned him that if he kept drinking like this he wouldn't last another year

"He won't even last a year Mr. Amadeu will do himself in with cirrhosis in no time flat"

and in the end he lasted eight, eight years walking with canes because the alcohol had attacked his legs, sitting in the armchair, a blanket over his knees, he never stopped drinking, my father searching for a glass you could hear the bottleneck clink against the rim of it, putting away the bottle, Clarisse

"It's just a bird it's not mother at all it's a bird listen"

the clock, that selfish thing, silent, coughing, then breaking in with its arrogant clanging, disdainful of the world, the bats scolding each other in the poplars, Rui in the other bedroom with Josélia, the small lamp still burning because of his attacks, very calm at first and then all of a sudden his face like a ghost, biting his tongue and frothing at the mouth, the women in the workers' huts as restless as brooding hens

my mother promised she'd look after Maria da Boa Morte that if Maria da Boa Morte fell ill

the bottle clinking as it would continue to clink for months and months and then even more months, instead of calling Rui to his side, talking to him, going to the doctor with him, my father who never left the house opened the cupboard doors knocking over glasses, knocking over cups, drank with his back to us, tumbled down into the closest chair he could find, feeling ashamed in front of us, ashamed of himself, he sat looking down at his hands until we called him

"Come eat dinner with us, father"

Damião held him up at his waist and sat him down at the head of the table and everyone pretended not to notice the potatoes that were spilled everywhere, the waxy tears running down his cheeks that he wiped away with his sleeve and napkin, pretending that they didn't think that my father was drunk, Rui biting his own tongue and foaming at the mouth, Clarisse hoping that I would lie to her

"It's just a bird it's true that it's just a bird right Carlos?"

yet it wasn't a bird or a fox or the women in the workers' huts mourning a death or the fever-breath of the cotton, it was the grandfather clock with the Roman numerals in the hall that always had the wrong time, first it's five o'clock in the morning, then six in the afternoon, and then thirty-six demented clangs, it was my mother's voice in between sobs, from far away and up close

me pushing shoving people aside on the gangway of the boat and my mother promising

"Promise me"

that she would look after her

"It's my fault Amadeu don't try to tell me different it's my fault"

Rui, for whom I bought an overstock bargain necktie, very colorful the way he likes it, strutting around the home with the other residents, proud of his new gift, not thinking about my mother, my father, me, showing off that miserable rainbow tie, the boat leaving Luanda, Rui counting dolphins, pointing at them with his outstretched index finger

"Fifty-one"

it was necessary to go along whenever he went out so that he didn't get lost at the first street corner and didn't get picked up by the police, half naked in the street, pieces of newspaper stuck in his collar, mocked and insulted in Odivelas or Oeiras, trying to strike up conversations with the Cape Verdeans, believing they worked for us

"I can't find the way back to the plantation"

asking the guards at the station, fidgety in his fetid, tattered clothes, eating soup

(it must be soup judging from the noise his tongue is making) out of a tin bowl

"My brother Carlos knows the way back to the plantation"

Rui here with me in the apartment very soon, giving me a picture frame or an ashtray or a book, completely at ease, his shoes shined

"Hi brother"

hair combed, face shaven, fingernails trimmed, wearing a threadbare suit and the secondhand shirt they give to the residents when they leave to visit family, brushing them off in the lobby, handing out sedatives just in case

"Well look at you so well-behaved"

Clarisse and I waiting for five or six years in the darkness of the bedroom and it wasn't a bird, no chance at all it was a bird, it was the clinking of a glass, the ringing of the clock that prevented us from hearing my father, my mother's indignant voice over the voice of the sunflowers

"Put him in a home in Luanda really put him in a home in Luanda do you know what you're asking me to do Amadeu?"

my mother if she could see where I put him would kill me, the way Clarisse and Lena, furious with me, almost killed me, when I told Rui

"Put your things in a suitcase and hurry up that cheat of a cab driver won't shut off his meter"

not quite a clinic, not quite a home, an establishment in Damaia where they take in poor things that are a burden to their families as was our case, people dying of cancer, mentally retarded, blind, there were even beds out on the porch, in the hallway, in the kitchen, they gave them a glass of wine and a bowl of rice pudding on Saturdays, changed the linens every two weeks, they got a hot shower once a month, in Damaia right across the street from the theater, well fed, no need to work, luxuriating looking out the window at the actresses on the movie posters, a grocery store just a few steps away, a moped repair shop, very lively compared to Ajuda, gypsies wearing gold rings selling clothes laid out on canvas tarps on the sidewalk, Clarisse blocking my way on the stairs, hitting me with her fist

"If you go through with this I swear I'll call Mom Carlos I swear I'll call Mom"

caught up in the delusion that the telephone lines actually worked in Africa, that the postal system worked, Rui, whose behavior was always so unpredictable, happened to be in an obedient mood standing behind me with his suitcase and her hitting me convinced that my mother would find out at some point, isolated in Angola by the Cubans with the cotton all lost and spoiling in the field because there was no one to harvest it, at the head of the table in a mansion that had been looted, waited upon by Damião or Fernando

Maria da Boa Morte

their pomaded hair shining, in white coats, white gloves, and gold buttons as if there weren't any bombs or war or corpses on the plantation, eating cassava grits and dry fish on porcelain plates and with silver utensils under the chandelier with its dim light-bulbs and missing crystals, what's become of the grandfather clock that always had the wrong time, the dozens of whiskey bottles in the cupboards, what's become, more to the point, let's be realistic, of the cupboards themselves, Clarisse wearing a blouse more low-cut than usual blocking my way on the stairs, under the mistaken impression that it mattered to me at all and Rui to Clarisse

"Let go of Carlos sister"

a brother who took his word of honor seriously, nicely dressed, loving, submissive, agreeing with me, if the whole world were like Rui was in the times between his attacks we would never get worn-out and would relish being alive, Rui understanding that my only concern was his well-being and it's true, the proof that it's true is that he's not late at all that he arrives here despite the traffic and the Christmas shopping

"Let go of Carlos sister"

the bottleneck against the glass again, that's what always pops into my mind, the bottleneck against the glass, my father drinking with his back to us for eight years, his back bent over at the waist, his neck red, even after the point when he could no longer stand up he turned his back or hid his face under a blanket, then came the bottleneck, doing it in secret, shaking against the glass, the bottleneck against the glass again, the endless, selfish clanging of the clock, my mother's now solitary voice, not a bird, not a fox, not the women mourning a death in the workers' huts, a dead man all teeth, with phalanges like teeth as well, not the fever-breath of the cotton, my mother's now solitary voice distinct from the thousand interwoven voices of which the silence is composed

"Put him in a home in Luanda frankly put him in a home in Luanda do you know what you're asking me to do Amadeu?"

Rui liked Damaia, liked the home, he above all liked the movie poster with an American actress in a bikini

In Mussulo nothing but Rhodesian blondes on the beach ugly old women I slept with a redhead on the island it was rushed and without any pleasure at all I didn't feel what I felt with

Maria da Boa Morte

Angolan women

he was glad not to have to share the sofa bed with Clarisse because the bedroom, come on, was for Lena and me, Rui greeting the cancer patients, the blind, those who were just inconveniences to their families and who would in no time, judging from the commotion, be inconveniences to him

a redhead with red pubic hair and freckles her nipples identical to freckles her eyes freckles that winked when it was over I wanted to die freckles forming constellations like the ones on the atlas with a map of the heavens Orion Cassiopeia Gemini Centaurus the smell of sour milk from the freckles her name was Flannery

Clarisse tried to spit on me but the spit wouldn't come out of her mouth, she threw a ceramic harlequin figurine at me and it shattered against the wall, as a child if my mother ever yelled at her or contradicted her or prohibited her from this or that she would take off

like me

up the stairs with her head obscured by a sea of skirts, pausing on the way to kick the grandfather clock, which quickly responded with a hundred wounded clangs

"I can't stand you all, I can't stand you, I can't stand you"

she slammed the door with such force that the hinges shuddered, Josélia terribly upset downstairs, her hands together in an attitude of prayer

"Child"

we could hear her breaking jewelry boxes and trinkets in her bedroom while my father, shuffling around in silence, headed toward the cupboard to clink the bottleneck against the rim of his glass

bottleneck against the glass bottleneck against the glass

and returned to the table as if his legs were stilts, holding the napkin to his mouth, Clarisse slamming the door to the kitchen in Ajuda with such great force that the pots fell from their hooks, Lena trying to get in

"Open up Clarisse"

Lena in such a state that it was readily apparent that she hated me

"Are you satisfied Carlos you've probably never been so satisfied in your life as you are now"

the hatred of the daughter of the Cuca-beer plant worker, who used to read the newspaper in his front porch garden on the outskirts of town, sitting in a canvas chair, harmless and tiny, the house full of provincials in coats freezing in the African heat, praying to plaster saints that failed to protect them from misery and the rain, the hatred of the slum-dweller humiliated by the rich guy from Malanje who was ashamed of her and pretended not to know her in front of his friends, Lena quick to take revenge calling my mother

"Carlos put Rui in a home in a hovel"

and me shoving her aside and hanging up the phone, on the off chance they'd fixed the phone lines

"Don't even think about it"

Clarisse wrote letters to Angola

"You'll see Carlos you'll see"

she messed up, tore up the paper, threw it on the floor, started over, she waved an envelope right in front of my face with the wrong address on it, and I quieted down, even if the postal service were miraculously working the accusations and complaints wouldn't reach Baixa de Cassanje, getting lost in one city then the next on an endless journey, covered in dust and stamps until one of the employees of a little isolated hut they call a branch office tosses it into the trash can out of exhaustion, or into the river where the wreckage of war floats by chaotically, calves, adolescents, baskets, Maria da Boa Morte cooking the last quail on the gas stove top and my mother cutting the cartilage from its bones with a rusty razor, if my father weren't disintegrating in the Dondo cemetery he would be clinking the bottleneck against his glass, raising his silent eyes to us, my father who would like to be here in Ajuda with my brother and sister and I, I would tuck the blanket over his legs, give him the best cut of the turkey, buy him an art book, talk with him, my mother insisted that I didn't like anyone except Maria da Boa Morte but maybe I've changed and I miss people, it's hard to live here and see the hills of Almada, the Christ statue, the bridge, to nod off in front of the TV with Lena next to me, her ankles swollen, reading magazines, going to bed before me, abandoning me in this neighborhood with no streetlights, the window open onto the disorder of the leaves, the garbage truck comes at eleven, men in gloves and fluorescent vests, they dump me out into the back of the truck and take me with them, along with the scraps of food, duvet covers with no stuffing, detritus, I happen to think of Rui, very pleased with the blond actress

freckles forming constellations like the ones on the atlas at school Orion Cassiopeia Gemini the smell of sour milk from her nipples take a shower wash my body

in a bikini on the façade of the theater, thinking of Rui not out of remorse, but out of envy, and maybe out of envy

(it can only be envy)

for fifteen years I never went to see him at the home, one day after another given the gift of a free afternoon to go to the market or watch the gypsies, like he watched the sowing of the rice seeds with his pellet gun in hand, the tribal chief complained to my mother, my mother complained to the police chief, the police chief complained to the native soldiers, and the native soldiers stomping their cannabis plants, piglets, and chicks called for the women with children on their hips and beat the tribal chief right in front of them to teach them all to have manners, the tribal chief came to beg Rui's forgiveness and give him a dozen eggs, Rui dropped the eggs on the ground

"I don't want this shit no way"

little mottled eggs

freckles

from the African chickens, ones that the gledes, crucified, their wings outstretched and still in the immense still sky, spot from the air, all of a sudden descending with their talons extended, Clarisse

"No"

who in no time

(that's how she is)

will be hugging me around the neck, grateful for the perfume, grateful for me putting Rui in a place where they understand him and care for him, when I stopped paying the monthly bills the owner of the home warned me sir, if you don't pay what you owe I'll have no choice but to give the bed to someone else, artificial and idiotic, exactly like a character out of the theater, didn't say another word, imagine an actor with a mustache and gold chain entering stage right and reciting that at the front of the stage, his fingers spread out between the buttons of his vest, sir, if you don't pay what you owe I'll have no choice but to give the bed to someone else, I almost wanted to applaud, give him flowers, beg for an autograph, visit him in his dressing room bravo, once more bravo, encore, sir, if you don't pay what you owe I'll have no choice but to give the bed to someone else, and then me to the great actor, admiring his dramatic pauses

"Go ahead"

the fake mustache, the gold chain, his restless eyes, frowning lips, the way he conveyed emotion through gestures, haughty with his awesome threat that I would stand in line all night at the ticket booth to hear

"And a suit in civil court in order to recoup my losses"

speaking to the judge in cuff links seated on high, identifying me with a dramatic flourish of his sleeve to an audience of bailiffs who are fascinated

"Behold the villain who threw his brother into the gutter"

such a stirring performance everyone searching for their handkerchiefs, the lawyers overcome, the judge himself, that unfeeling thing, sobbing at each paragraph and preposition, and I, the villain of the piece, cackling like an ogre

ha ha ha

the audience wanted to jump up on stage and beat me

"It's true"

and so did Lena and Clarisse, my mother too if the news ever made it to Africa there's no danger of that, it wouldn't make it there, me trying to play my part with the gentleman, although of course never attaining the dramatic perfection of this genius

"It's true"

I was even worried for a little while that this mustachioed actor would show up on my doorstep some day with Rui and his suitcase, I called the home, disguising my voice, and asked the receptionist who answered the phone to connect me to my brother, saying he was just a friend of a friend, the sounds of screams, arguments, furniture being dragged along the floor, the receptionist

"Just a moment"

the phone was set down, the receptionist in the distance

"Quiet down Mr. Teodoro"

in the midst of this Rui breathing through his mouth, the whishing sound of pieces of gravel rubbing against each other that I've heard ever since he was born

"Yes?"

relieved, I hung up the phone, feeling kindness toward the actor, even capable of hugging him, being his friend, inviting him to lunch at a reasonably priced restaurant, not an expensive one, but reasonable, almost even trying to send him an occasional small payment by wire transfer, but I finally thought better of it and refrained from sending anything, I reminded myself that I wasn't the one who brought Rui into being nor was I under any obligation to financially support shirkers, I make a pittance as a pharmaceutical sales rep enduring the whims of the doctors at the hospitals with a briefcase full of samples, a few months later I put a piece of cloth in my mouth and called on behalf of the Angolan Embassy to get information about Rui, switching the verb tenses just like the blacks who think they're white or

for some patently absurd reason

pretend that we consider them equals, the same sounds of screams, arguments, furniture getting knocked over or dragged across the floor, a different receptionist

"Just a moment"

covering the receiver with the palm of her hand and getting exasperated with Mr. Teodoro

"Quiet down immediately Mr. Teodoro"

Mr. Teodoro who had retained a remarkable vitality for a person dying of cancer, more things being dragged along the floor, more arguments, complaints of someone who'd been stabbed

"So help me God"

me imagining Mr. Teodoro determined to slaughter his fellow residents with nothing more than a bread knife and his enthusiasm and in the midst of all the howling the persevering voice of Rui in my ear

"Yes?"

and then I realized that it was Clarisse who was paying the mustachioed actor, that ravishing stage presence with his fingers tucked in between the buttons of his vest

"Sir, if you don't pay what you owe I'll have no choice but to give the bed to someone else"

since the pittance that Lena got paid immediately turned into payments on the car or the dishwasher, two gadgets that had the common characteristic of generating a hellish noise and an enormous amount of smoke without moving an inch, Clarisse who settled things

settled things what a miracle

with the actor using the money she received from some married executive, three times her age, which he gave her for personal services and incidental expenses, one married executive or a group of them, each of whom were in charge of a piece of my sister, which is what happens as a rule with joint owners of condominium buildings, Clarisse, if my father were alive he would shut himself up in the cupboard full of liquor bottles right away, the bottleneck clinking against the rim of his glass twenty-four hours a day seven days a week and the grandfather clock, out of pity, covering up everyone else's murmuring with its merciful clangs just as my mother shielded him from the curiosity of their friends, locking him away in the bedroom upstairs with a liter of whiskey and a couple of sleeping pills, she came down the stairs with a hesitant smile that ruined her makeup while the visitors winked at each other behind her back

"Amadeu says that he's very sorry but he's come down with a terrible migraine the poor thing" in the middle of dinner while people were discussing one thing or another a clatter on the stairs, a bottle falling down them landing on the floor coming to a halt at the foot of the table, a second bottle sliding underneath the full-length mirror, a metal rod from the stair runner bouncing to a stop against a curtain, where the wind that blew the sunflowers issued in its serene secrecy, Damião running around with a tray in his hand, Fernando gathering up the bottles, my father in his pajamas, framed by the doorway, held up his hand to greet the guests with an uncertain gesture, lost his balance trying to pull his napkin out of its ring, asking Damião to serve him wine

"Good evening everyone"

the sound of the generator out behind the house grating against the silence, slowing down every so often, dimming the lights, the wife of the governor's secretary looking at my father, appalled, the guests with their spoons suspended halfway between their plates and their mouths, my mother quick to hold back her tears, their friends uncomfortable in their chairs, fidgeting with their neckties, my father slamming his hand down on the table as hard as he could

"I said good evening everyone damn it"

the same way that I'm sitting at the table in Ajuda, the linen tablecloth on it, the fruitcake, the dishes of almonds and the corn cakes and raisins and pine nuts, the sparkling wine going flat in the metal bucket where the ice cubes are slowly melting, the tie and the bottle of perfume adorned with ribbons, which, thank God, make them look more expensive, the ridiculous pine tree stuck in the stand decorated with a silvery star on top, like a sad fifty-year-old woman wearing a tiara, the silver of candy wrappers and pathetic little decorative bells, the same way I'm here waiting, alert to every taxi, every truck, every vehicle on the avenue in hopes of hearing the doorbell ring and the voices of my brother and sister in the street, in hopes that Lena will soon finish watching that movie on TV, close her magazine, put out her cigarette

(even after so many years of marriage she still couldn't put out a cigarette properly, there was always a lingering line of smoke that took centuries to disappear)

and bring out the *caldo verde* soup and codfish from the kitchen, Lena in her blouse and pearl necklace, which I like better than those mulatto-style slum-dweller rags she used to wear, Lena, Clarisse, Rui, and I fifteen years later as if we were still in Africa, as if we were listening to the breathing of the cotton in the darkness, as if we were inhaling the smell of the earth, as if Josélia and Maria da Boa Morte

Maria da Boa Morte

were by our side, working right next to us, me dejected about the mute, empty chairs

"Good evening everyone"

raising his arm to greet the guests with an unsure gesture, trying to pull the napkin out of its ring, slamming his hand down on the table as hard as he could

"I said good evening everyone damn it"

but I couldn't get them to hear me since I was covered in snowflakes on the reindeer-pulled sleigh inside the glass ball, protected by my wool suit and red cap, disappearing in a whirl of white specks that hide me from the world.

5 June 1980

When I sit down at my dressing table at night to take off my makeup, I ask myself if it's me or the mirror in the bedroom that has grown old. It must be the mirror: these eyes don't belong to me anymore, this face isn't mine, are these wrinkles and blemishes on my skin the traces of old age or just spots where the acid from the tin has corroded the mirror? In the past, back in my father's day, I never paid attention to the mango trees, the stand of trees in the distance, between the house and the workers' huts where the hill starts to slope down to the river, where there's a grave of an unnamed colonist whose cross was pushed out of the ground by the roots of the mango trees, which stuck out of the ground like arms, waving around in terror at nothing at all, not even any birds because birds, my father assured me, are afraid of the dead and only owls dare to drink their blood

　　blood

and the oil from the oil lamps. Or maybe not a dead person but the ghost of a dead person since on the day the priests from the mission decided to transfer the body to the cemetery at the monastery and brought with them shovels and Latin hymns they didn't find anything except a pile of chalk-white bones held together by the uniform of an ancient explorer and a rifle, dark with rust, that looked like the gramophone's bell-shaped speaker, from which *opéras mélancoliques* used to emerge mournfully in the evenings during the rainy season. I'm positive it's the mirror that's grown old: if I lean toward it I can't even see my hands in the frame, the paintings on the wall and the furniture in the room disappear into some kind of fog, the lace on my nightgown floats into the air with the wild abandon of tapestries in deserted rooms, the priests carry me from the hill to the interior of the monastery, loosening their sandals by the dried leaves in the doorway, what you notice in the mirror is a tremor of absence, an echo of nothingness, a well where the face of a drowning victim, which isn't mine, is withdrawing from the scene with a cotton ball and an eyeliner pencil that aren't mine looking for each other amid the traces of old age and the acid from the tin that's corroded the mirror. It's the mirror that has grown old: it was just now that we returned from dinner at the Belgians' house, my husband and I, the lights were lit from our gate to the front door, illuminating the hydrangeas, the statue in the little pond with its elbows upraised in a joyful balletic movement, the little ones asleep upstairs with Maria da Boa

Morte without us even telling her to do it, lying in the hallway to watch over them

(it's true these people really get attached to the kids)

ready to come to them and calm their fears if they called, my husband loosened his tie, took off his suit coat, looked around for the ashtray among the silver-handled hairbrushes and looked for the bottle of whiskey in the drawer and after he shut the drawer he had regained some enthusiasm and there was color in his face, his irises shone as brightly as his cuff links, I swear it's the mirror that has grown old, not me, because we've just now returned from the Belgians' and I was smiling, I didn't notice a single trace of old age on my skin, not my back either, not my gallbladder, my kidney stones weren't bothering me, while I took off my necklace I saw my husband lie down, wiping his mouth on the sleeve of his pajama top, hiding a second bottle among the countless bottles of aspirin and cough syrups in the nightstand, no potbelly, no gray hairs, no canes, no shaking hands that made him spill alcohol on his clothes shaking his head back and forth

"Get the spiders off my chest Isilda don't let them bite me"

I'd go get a broom or a towel and pretend that I was shooing away the spiders, I'd look for them under the mattress, on the floor, my husband terrified, curling up against the wall as if he wanted to knock it down and disappear into the fields

"That one there on my foot Isilda the huge one on my foot"

his stomach swollen and his feet so emaciated my God, two gnarled pieces of cassava root, my parents promised me the world and then some if I would refuse to marry him, they sent me to live in Lobito for a year, they tried to enroll me in a school in Cabo

"You'll go straight to Cabo and in a few months you won't even remember this guy"

they offered me a trip to France, they told me that all the agronomists who worked for Cotonang, without exception, had mulatto lovers and mulatto children with whom they secretly lived in the neighborhood near the company headquarters, I took a bus to Malanje, puttering along gravel roads, Amadeu shared a prefabricated house with a Dutch chemist, a couple of rooms so messy and dusty that you could tell that it had been centuries since the last time a woman, even a mulatto woman, had been in there, the flower vase was just an empty Coca-Cola can, the dinner table was a piece of plywood on top of a barrel the bathroom was a pigsty, the bristles on the shaving brush and the toothbrush pointing up at the lizards on the ceiling, no sign of any children, no sign of any lovers, pictures of dancing ladies on the wall, like the ones in the cabarets in Luanda, my husband standing in front of them to block my view

"I promise these are the Dutchman's don't worry about them"

the Dutchman went along with this story, checking out my legs, lying to me but making sure that I knew he was lying, since he liked my legs

"Not a day goes by that Amadeu doesn't plead with me to take those down"

a worthless little miscreant sitting on a beer crate where he could get a good look at my backside, me pulling my skirt close against my legs and telling my husband that we should head out to the street, uncomfortable around this foreigner

"It's stuffy in here Amadeu"

they weren't streets but filthy dirt roads covered with trash that no one bothered to pick up, mules dozing in the sunlight on the embankment, a setter with its paws outstretched, reckless in its rage, barking at a guy who was frying up thin slices of liver in a little garden the size of a handkerchief that had nothing more than a single begonia growing in it, the return bus broke down out of that idiotic stubbornness that things have when they just refuse to work, a profound and unshakable obstinacy, the next bus didn't leave until the following morning, I had dinner in the Cotonang cafeteria, embarrassed, with dozens of engineers staring at me through the haze of wine, the cafeteria looked for the most part like my husband's prefabricated house, the same mess, the same dust everywhere, the same Coca-Cola cans used as vases for the flowers, the same tables made out of barrels and plywood, the same dancing ladies from the cabarets bashfully covering up their nakedness with a ribbon tied in a bow around their necks, engineers who seemed to be waiting, like the café owners in Uíge who wore ten rings on each finger, for me to strip off my clothes right there and shake my ankles in a frenzied can-can, the Dutchman tried to get my husband drunk so that he could toss him aside like a rag doll and have his way with me, while a filthy cafeteria worker wearing a soiled uniform and with manners almost as bad as the men dumped disgusting potatoes onto their plates with a mason's trowel, after one or two flashes of lightning we suddenly became aware of the roof and the thousand drops of rain pounding against the zinc rooftop, the lights dimmed, accentuating the filth and squalor, I don't know why I then thought of home and had to fight back tears, my father and mother worried, the dancing ladies were watching me from inside their pictures

(each photograph was surrounded by a border of little sketches and words that I preferred not to read)

out of a feeling of solidarity for a fellow woman, the type of detached benevolence usually reserved for escorts on their first day on the job, and we ran from one boggy field to the next, tripping over each other, up to our shins in mud, the lightning periodically illuminating the fence posts and piglets, appearing briefly, their images as clear as ghosts before evaporating in the darkness, the guesthouse in Malanje was nothing more than an oil lamp at the top of some stairs, an old woman with a toothpick in her mouth behind the counter and no rooms available, they were all taken by farm-equipment salesmen and diamond smugglers who passed the time arguing at the top of their lungs about whether they shouldn't give a damn about Portugal and just keep getting rich here among the Bailundos or should give a damn about Portugal because my wife's from Chaves and my in-laws send us kilos of *alheira* sausage at Christmas, the Dutchman

(I swear it was his hand that was groping me as if by accident)

pulled Amadeu, who could barely stay on his feet, out into the murkiness of the rain

"Why doesn't the little lady come sleep at our place tonight?"

if my parents had heard him my father would have shot him and my mother would have fainted, my husband closer to fainting than to shooting anyone vomited violently, holding himself up in the doorway, throwing up out of fear of the Dutchman rather than devotion to his girlfriend, I helped Amadeu, my little hands on his rib cage, holding him up, my hair wet and matted against my forehead and my dress in tatters like the clothes of a shipwreck survivor

"Breathe slowly don't choke don't die on me now"

my husband practically holding himself up on my back alone, tripping over himself from one dirt road to the next, blowing his vinegary breath down my neck in between apologies and grumbles, the foreigner kicked open the gate to the house, lit a kerosene lantern that turned us into mummies with its white light, our movements like the jerky gestures of marionettes, butterflies did themselves in on the hot wire mesh around the lantern making a sound like the crackling of cellophane, lizards stuck the suckers at the end of their fingers to the cork panels on the ceiling, the palm trees near the chapel snapped in the north wind, a couple of voices started to shout in German, one of the voices fired a pistol and then they both fell silent, when one of his friends showed up dead in the back of a jeep with a deep wound in his chest, my father after returning from the funeral asked no one in particular what is life worth here, can someone tell me what life is worth here, and I think he died without knowing it, among the sunflowers, with the blade from one of our hoes stuck in his kidney, the sergeant feigned outrage and interrogated some of the foremen without finding the culprits, threw a few of them into prison in Luanda so that we'd stop complaining, all of them piled into a bus and wailing out of fear, I was able to get my husband to lie down under the mosquito net after taking off his shoes and his clothes, putting up with his stammering and whining, his tears

"I'm worthless Isilda just leave"

the Dutchman turned out the kerosene lantern that continued to hiss in the darkness, the prefab house faded into the night, a group of sleepless topographers argued in the rain, the bell at the administrative building split the silence with its warning clangs, the chemist was snoring, my husband was snoring, a field mouse chirped in despair in a baobab tree, I felt a desire to flee but I couldn't, I felt a desire for my home, for my parents, for my varnished furniture

"What is life worth here can someone tell me what life is worth here?"

I cuddled my wet body up close to my husband, put my arm around his waist, and submerged myself in that vinegary breath I'll never forget, trembling at every flash of lightning, every sound, every buzzing insect until the morning light brightened the window with a murky lilac color, I didn't sleep at all, didn't even rest, afraid that the sleepless topographers would abduct me and I guess that was my honeymoon, with a Coca-Cola can for a flower vase on a plywood table balanced on top of a barrel where a branch from an orange tree was slowly drying out and rotting. It's the mirror that has grown old: it was just yesterday that I took the bus from Malanje back to the plantation, the bus losing metal parts over every pothole on the highway, screws, staples, mud flaps, little pieces of the engine, passengers stumbling off the running board, thatched huts, trees, soil the color of red bricks, a cow lying in the road, drowsy and peaceful, the driver whooping at it trying to scare it off, my husband in his wrinkled linen suit hurriedly combing his hair with his fingertips

"What are your parents going to think of me Isilda?"

my mother horrified at the sight of us, dropping the sugar dish she was holding onto the teapot, breaking it, my father with a cigar in his mouth, the ashes falling down the front of his vest, jerking Amadeu around by the lapels, making him jitter and dance with every shove

"Where did you dig up this clown Isilda?"

in the armchair my mother fanned herself with a napkin, Damião on all fours picking up shards of the teapot without losing one bit of his priestly dignity, my husband with his feet in the air warning my father

"Where did you dig up this clown Isilda?"

"Let go of me sir I'm going to vomit"

turning to run out of the room, knocking over end tables, the crystal bear figurine, the lamp imported from China, which my mother adored, with the dragons that blew smoke from their mouths, running into Damião, who was taking the pieces of the broken teapot to the kitchen, and falling into his lap, the two of them forming some sort of Pietá, Our Black Lady of the Golden Buttons, Damião, who could only write his name if you gave him a year to do it, and the dying Christ who had lost a shoe along the way, looking at me from across the room, hoping that I would come to his aid, while Damião was taking him to the trash can along with the shards of china, determined to dump all of it, Amadeu included, into the trash can and be rid of him, rid of the shabby suit and breath that reeked of wine, rid of this pest who was once again warning

(a white man, can you believe it, a white man)

"Let go of me sir I'm going to vomit"

Damião let go of him, the petunias outside were whispering, making the curtains swell, the peacocks that my mother imported from Egypt so that she could keep up with the French woman who loved the chirping of birds, the peacocks fanned out their ruby-colored tails, my husband stretched out on the rug protected himself from my father who poked at him with the tip of his shoe, bemused, making sure that this lump of dirty linen was still alive and breathing

"Where the hell did you dig up this clown Isilda?"

the lump pulling on the drapes in an attempt to stand up, tearing them off their loops, pulling them off the curtain rod, getting hit in the head by the rod and disappearing behind the damask fabric, over in the armchair my mother's mouth was a tunnel of shock, the draped figure zigzagged his way over to her, the curtain loops jingling, and held out his damp hand, a corolla of well-trimmed fingernails that my mother refused to shake

"Pleased to meet you"

and after the introductions, after the draped figure talked with my father, after my father warned me, pointing with disgust at that motley mess of damp drapes and curtain loops

"Over my dead body young lady"

we married in the church in Malanje, the bishop, the music, the lavender, the hundreds of guests buried in a sea of feathers, English wool, and fur coats, my mother overjoyed in her new outfit, ordering the photographers around, my father showing me the very tip of his thumb

"You're as good as dead to me you're not going to get a thing not even this much young lady"

his coworkers from Cotonang, a pack of savages with carnations in their lapels, rounded up all the brandy in the pantry in
one second flat and tried to catch the peacocks so they could roast
them for dinner, the Dutchman growled pick-up lines at me in a
language made up of consonants and thorns, my mother's only
real complaint was that the peacocks had disappeared from the
garden, she had no idea how it could have happened, there wasn't
even a single feather left behind on the grass, and since it was
as if I were already dead and didn't even realize it, my husband,
finally untangled from all the drapes and the curtain loops that
dropped to the ground all around him, much to the disapproval
of the Bailundos, who thought he was more handsome that way,
my husband began to run the plantation, not from the field but
from the second-story balcony, with a glass of whiskey in his hand
and other liters of it stashed in every drawer and cupboard, never
looking after the rice, the corn, the sunflowers, the cotton, never
looking after me and the children, wiggling and dancing around
the room in his pajamas the buttons in the wrong buttonholes,
trying to escape the spiders

"That one on my stomach Isilda the huge one on my stomach"

especially after Rui became ill and starting having the seizures
and the doctor confirmed that it was hereditary, Rui, who maybe
can get treatment now that he's in Europe at least near all those
hospitals and has Carlos to help him, I sent a check with the last
letter in case it becomes necessary to take him to Germany or
London so he can undergo brain surgery and be cured, the most
intelligent of all my children, the most sensitive, the most fun, always playing fun little games with everyone with his pellet gun, a

tiny pellet in the buttocks, a tiny pellet in the thigh that you could pick out in a split second with a pair of tweezers, my husband instead of laughing and seeing the humor in it grabbed a bottle from the cupboard without saying a word he never said a word to the ungrateful workers who fled the plantation and the African overseers or the regional administrator who brought them back to him in shackles for punishment

"Here they are sir"

Amadeu wouldn't touch the horsewhip he'd just lower his eyes, worried about the spiders

"Let them go"

indifferent to the planting season, the harvest, the broken-down threshers that were rusting in the fields, the loans, the bills, the deferred payments, the threats from lenders, closing drawers and cupboards, opening the bottle, taking a glass out from under his robe, wiping his lips on his shirttails without a word, ambling over to another room to find more whiskey

"Where the hell did you dig up this rank clown Isilda?"

and it was me, a woman who'd been raised to be a housewife and to have a husband who would look after her business affairs and look after me, it was me who had to talk with the middle-men, haggle with the suppliers, convince the government to help us out, argue with banks to put off paying our debts, it was me, a woman who deserved a life like the neighbors' wives had, playing cards, going horseback riding, having drinks at the club, me who took Rui to the doctor and brought him back home, God knows how, who forbade Clarisse from dating the entire high school and coming home after midnight, who scolded Carlos for never talking to my husband or to me and despising the both of us as if we hadn't done our best for him, Carlos who on the rare weekend that he actually came home locked himself up with the cook or went fishing by himself without even a short chat with anybody, so much so that I now wonder if it was a good idea to put the apartment in Ajuda in his name just because he was the oldest of the three, I wonder now whether it will occur to him to do some sort of harm to his siblings taking advantage of Rui's kindness, Rui who is innocence incarnate, and Clarisse's foolishness and her obsession with clothes and parties, not treating his siblings with respect, making them feel like guests in their own home, because I can't believe he would throw them out, that's just a step too far, me without any news because they cut off my phone line and my children won't respond to my letters if the letters actually even get to them, so it's only natural, given the life that I lead, that when I sit down at my dressing table I ask myself if it's me that has grown old or the mirror in the bedroom, if these wrinkles and blemishes on my skin are the traces of old age or the acid from the tin that's corroding the mirror, I prefer to think that it's the mirror, it's certainly the mirror because just now, just a few minutes ago, if that, we returned from dinner at the Belgians', the lights were lit from the gate to the front door of our house, illuminating the hydrangeas, the statue in the pond with its elbows upraised in a joyful balletic movement, Amadeu loosened his tie, took off his coat, I saw him lean over the bedside table, sorting through bottles of aspirin and cough syrup, smiling at me just now, just a few minutes ago, if that, I went down to the workers' huts to count the field workers that they sent me from Huambo for the rice harvest and the supervisor there, an absolute cheat, guaranteed me that they were all healthy, obedient, and eat very little as if there had ever been an African that fit that description, if I were to go down there right now, after the short time that's passed between then and now

(it's the mirror that has grown old of course it's the mirror that has grown old there's no other possibility it's the mirror)

and find ten or fifteen brute beasts barely able to move around their huts, feebleminded from rheumatism and malaria, then it would be a lucky day, ten or fifteen brute beasts wasting away in tattered rags and what's left of the cotton withering in the fields, the unharvested sunflowers devoured by crows, ten or fifteen brute beasts as old as the mirror

(the same resignation the same wrinkles the same white hairs that aren't mine)

to whom I take a pot of soup not out of kindness but in hopes that they might help me salvage a measly square meter of corn that will allow me to stay here through one more rainy season, neither the MPLA nor the Cubans have the right to kick me off the land that is rightfully mine, this house with its roof that's missing shingles, this sideboard table with missing plates, this corner cupboard with no forks, these closets with no hangers, stolen by the soldiers passing through, a ragtag group that doesn't answer to anybody, they just ransack whatever they can get their hands on, livestock, telephones, clocks, broken pots, killing each other just to pass the time, all of them with the same red handkerchiefs, the same old-fashioned pistols and the same wiry frames, wasting away from hunger and dysentery, a result of drinking brackish water, even the lepers from Marimbanguengo are dragging themselves along by their stumps in ragtag armies, dismembering other lepers with machetes, the priest who was still at the monastery preaching in Latin to the baobab trees was found one morning in the well, his body covered with stab wounds, Fernando and Damião pulled him out with a hook and when they brought him to the surface he had such a sinister grin on his face that I told them to dig a shallow grave in the grass and bury him as quickly as possible, Damião fashioned a cross out of two sticks that started to grow leaves soon thereafter, determined to become a tree, when my husband was still alive the priest ate lunch with us on Thursdays, with his sermons about whites and blacks living together peacefully in heaven, Rui very interested in this project

"And what about the pellet gun?"

in the same way that Clarisse wished that there were shops selling baubles and jewelry so that she could go bankrupt as fast as she could, and the same way that Carlos, without any real reason at all for it, wished that he didn't have to live with any of us, sometimes I ask myself what we did to him that was so bad that he never wanted anything to do with us, never wanted to visit us, despised us, you could see it in the way that he wouldn't respond to us when we called him down to dinner, Amadeu putting the whiskey bottle away in the sideboard table

"Carlos"

and Carlos sitting there in silence fidgeting with his soup spoon, when he was little and we happened to scold him for whatever reason, a broken window, a stain on his bib, the frog he kept in his bedroom, instead of feeling sorry or apologizing or crying like his brother and sister did he would clench his fists, mouthing words at me, becoming visibly distressed, holding back tears, me almost afraid of my own son

"What did you say?"

Carlos mouthing words, becoming visibly distressed, holding back tears

"I didn't say anything ma'am"

I'm still afraid of him, my own son, even though he's far away from here, in Lisbon, he doesn't respond to my letters, doesn't ask about me, all alone here on the plantation, with no money, with ten or fifteen half-dead dimwits, and despite being young and strong I

(these wrinkles are from the acid that's corroding the tin frame and streaking the mirror they're not mine why just a few minutes ago I had black hair and was coming back home from dinner at the Belgians' place)

need a kind word, a comforting word that will make me believe that they're harvesting the cotton and selling it, that our money's multiplying in the bank, tomorrow when I wake up there will be tractors busy at work instead of deserted rows of cotton, and two hundred workers in the fields, all I ask for, God knows I don't ask for much, is a hopeful word from time to time on a little piece of paper even though we both know for certain that our hope dried up as fast as our money and credit, that the next time I walk down to the workers' huts I won't find a single soul, just me, Maria da Boa Morte, and the rain leaking into the bedrooms, me pretending to give orders and her pretending to obey them, there are times when I sit in front of the telephone, positive that they're going to call from Ajuda, that I'll hear them, talk to them, lie to them, say that the Americans or the French bought the whole harvest, I get dressed up, put on perfume, put on my pearl earrings to talk to them, I hold the receiver to my ear and nothing, not even

"Mom"

or

"Hi Mom"

or

"We've been thinking about you how are things going Mom?"

in the earpiece, a silence as expansive as the earth's, the silence of the sunflowers during the rainy season, a gust of wind that yanks the azaleas out of the ground and blows them into the pond, the statue of the young lady with her elbows upraised, the look on her face exactly the same as the one on Carlos's face, mocking me as she dances, all she lacks is his scrunched-up face, all she lacks is the ability to mouth words like he did, me holding the telephone in my hand, opening the door that leads out to the garden almost in fear, questioning the statue

"What did you say Carlos"

the statue becoming visibly distressed, holding back tears

"I didn't say anything ma'am"

me in the long dress that I wore to that dinner, an evening gown that even the bishop swore looked beautiful on me when I kissed his ring

"God forgive me for saying so but you look like a holy saint Dona Isilda"

the evening gown, the pearl earrings that I hid underneath one of the floorboards so the Cubans don't steal them from me whenever they come back to steal whatever they didn't take last week,

the hot plate, the stove, my father's Spanish-language encyclopedia, the last remaining sofa, I styled my hair, powdered my cheeks,
curled my eyelashes to get ready to talk to my children, put the
stool from the kitchen next to the telephone and not even

"Mom"

or

"Hi Mom"

or

"We've been thinking about you how are things going Mom?"

nothing, a silence as expansive as the earth's, the girl carved
out of stone dancing in the pond, mocking me, a hundred-year-
old Bailundo climbing up the hill from the workers' huts, first his
cane and then him, first his cane and then him, first his cane and
then him, dragging his body, hauling it up the hill, looks like he'd
fit right in with this ragged mirror, it's not me because I haven't
grown old, not me, dragging his body toward the house and falling over onto his knees on the grass, a Bailundo

(not me)

who I always see when I'm in the orchard, in the forest, in the
garden, on the porch, he lives down by the river and all the boa
constrictors down there that my father taught me to hunt when I
was still single, the Bailundo on his knees in the grass if you can
call those bloody kneecaps knees, trying to stand up, a tormented
little insect trying to pull himself up with his cane, Maria da Boa
Morte restless in the hallway, drying her hands on her apron and
asking me for the phone so she could hear Carlos's voice, raising it
to her ear with an enormous smile on her face

"Hello there sir"

and me pretending to talk to them, as if I were really talking to them, advising them about this or that, talking excitedly into the deaf-mute receiver, telling them to keep warm, telling them to eat well, sending them my love, pausing for a moment, sending them my love again, hanging up the phone, getting up off the stool, explaining to Maria da Boa Morte

"They hung up"

climbing up the stairs to the second floor in my evening gown which even the bishop swore looked beautiful on me when I kissed his ring

"God forgive me for saying so but you really do look like a holy saint Dona Isilda"

pearl earrings, lipstick, powder, perfume, stretched out on the bed awaiting the Cubans, hoping the Cubans will come and put a bullet in me.

24 DECEMBER 1995

For many years if I happened to wake up before everyone else I thought that the ticktock of the clock on the wall in the living room was the heart of the house, I would lie in the dark with my eyes open for hours and hours listening to its living pulse certain that as long as the pendulum still swayed from one side to the other

systole diastole, systole diastole, systole diastole

none of us would die.

For many years if I happened to wake up before everyone else I thought that the ticktock of the clock on the wall in the living room was my own heart and I would lie in the dark with my eyes open for hours and hours listening to my own living pulse. The bed in my parents' room squeaked when my father leaned over the nightstand groping among the bottles, my grandmother whom the doctor would come to examine with his stethoscope and prescribe medications for coughed in her room at the end of the hallway the sound was like someone shaking a bag of rocks, the threshers started up, Maria da Boa Morte walked up from the workers' huts and came into the kitchen smoking a cigarette with the lit end inside her mouth burning her tongue and I felt responsible for all of them given that it was surely something in me, inside my chest, swinging from left to right and right to left

systole diastole, systole diastole, systole diastole

ensuring our continued existence, the house, my parents, Maria da Boa Morte, me, the others began to get up, the setters barked on the porch, the quails flew down from the top of the wall chirping at the sun, my grandmother, drinking sugar water, kept shaking her bag of rocks, the clock cleared its throat before striking six o'clock and me with my eyes open not even daring to move a finger, aware of the sparrows outside, the brightness of the cotton coming through the window, and the cotton pickers whom the foremen with whistles slung around their necks distributed across the fields, keeping the world from dying, keeping the men in black clothing from bringing the hearse and taking away my grandmother in a coffin, me swinging from left to right and from right to left

systole diastole, systole diastole, systole diastole

worried about Rui's crying that Josélia helped to calm and Clarisse's complaints, refusing to eat, letting my father pour himself a whiskey and then hide the bottle, my mother in her robe, wrinkled from sleep, getting upset in the doorway to my room

"Carlos"

not knowing that it was thanks to me that she was even able to get upset, that the second the clock, or I, stopped beating

systole diastole, systole diastole

the house and my family and all of Angola would disappear, I had to keep quiet, something in my chest going from left to right and from right to left, allowing the continued existence of the Baixa de Cassanje and the day itself and the river, allowing her to roll back the blinds and shake my foot underneath the blanket

"Carlos"

my mother in the morning, older and poorer and shorter and uglier than my mother at night, without her fake eyelashes, earrings, necklaces, high heels, with wrinkles that I'd never noticed that made her mouth look withered, flaps of loose skin between her neck and her shoulders, the clock pausing to gather strength

(everything gave off the impression that it would all dissolve in silence)

rang out with a regal clang and began ticking again and as long as it ticked we all remained alive, my father scrounging for bottles in the study, my mother walking over to me, a stain from grease or a fried egg on her robe, pulling the blanket off my legs

"It's already six-thirty Carlos"

a trail of smoke wafted behind the thresher, it crept along the hillside on its crippled wheels, the dusty driver up on top

Cassiano

(he lived alone, always lived alone in a small brick shack that he stuffed with birdcages full of doves, after they took ill all that was left in the birdcages was a pile of feathers and beaks that were open but no longer sang, he opened the little door to the cage and dumped the dead doves out in the forest without a tear

Cassiano

where are those doves now?)

my mother in the morning covering her tiny yawn with the palm of her hand she put on my shirt and pants, Maria da Boa Morte carried bowls of food out to the setters who jumped excitedly all around her, my father with purple bags under his eyes

(he was the same father in the morning, the same father at night, the same untied shoes, the same general disarray)

he came slowly down the stairs for breakfast, declining milk and toast, pushing away his cup of Postum with a look of disgust, asking Damião, already in his white jacket with the golden buttons, to fix him a cordial

(he called it a cordial)

from the liquors in the sideboard table I straightened my shirt very carefully, slowly, so they wouldn't have to bury my grandmother six feet under and the heart of the house didn't stop beating, as I walked down the hallway, carrying the full glass that was my heart, aware of the back-and-forth nodding of the pendulum, I passed by my sick grandmother's room from which emerged the coughs that sounded like a bag of rocks and the vapors of medicines and agony, since only the copper pendulum with two counterweights, also made of copper, behind the glass case of the clock, kept the men in black clothing from taking her away, one

of the quails flew into the glass window, startling me, startling the
mechanism in my chest that hiccupped and missed a beat

diastole, systole diastole

and flinched, emitting a frail little tick, I was sure that the house
and everyone in it had evaporated, but no, Maria da Boa Morte was
stoking the fire, Clarisse was refusing to eat more oatmeal, and my
mother was cursing under her breath as she locked the cupboard
door of the sideboard table and put the key in her pocket, the smell
of the sunflowers and the glimmer of the sun on the river helped
me to walk without stepping off the rug onto the wooden floor,
the bag of rocks rattled painfully in the distance, too far away now
to distress me, the clock thank God continued to tick, would always continue to tick, ultimately there was no sickness, no death,
Africa, my house, my family, and I were all eternal since nothing
bad would ever happen to us, my father could drink his whiskey
without his liver wasting away because all the warnings from the
medic in Malanje, waving around the pages of results from all the
medical tests, two red Xs here, three red Xs over there, were nothing more than nonsensical drivel, the field workers were the ones
who smelled like corpses and were buried in the cemetery at the
monastery near the old colonist's tomb where the hyenas howled,
we were eternal, we never grew old, we played on the ground beneath the golden rain tree, and in the midst of all this Rui knocked
his dessert to the tile floor, his whole body fell backward, his huge
face with his mouth opening wider and wider exposing more and
more of his teeth, a mass of foam spewing out of his mouth like
rising dough, my mother saying to Damião and Fernando

"Hold him still for the love of God hold him still"

that stupid pendulum swinging from left to right and from right to left determined to keep fooling me with its monotony inside its potbellied case, Rui kept writhing despite the efforts of Damião and Fernando, knocking over Josélia, my father fidgeted with the tablecloth in an effort to console himself, I threw a silver candlestick, who knows what ever happened to it after I left Angola with all the chaos that's been reported in the newspapers, against the glass case of the clock

"I won't let you kill my brother you hear me?"

the chains from which hung the counterweights of the clock got tangled up, the pendulum banged against the back wood panel, swung forward, then back again, tried to recover, gave up

"I won't let you kill my brother"

it started to shake its round little rump once again, incoherently and without any real authority, if it keeps ticking we're all going to die, if it keeps ticking I'll grow up, if it keeps ticking I'll grow a beard and my hair will become white and I'll wear glasses, if it keeps ticking, if it still keeps ticking I'll grow to like soup and pureed spinach and talking about money, Rui's face turned into rows of teeth gnashing and swallowing themselves in a frenzy, Maria da Boa Morte knelt down in the kitchen, my father with no one looking at him kept fidgeting with plates and teacups, if it keeps ticking I'll have dinner at the Belgians' and the governor's palace, when we traveled by car at night the owls submissively let themselves be run over on the backwoods roads, the chrome shine of their eyes, the soft thud on the bumper and that was it, there were rocks and shrubs on the narrow trail, they looked hollow at night in the shadows that you never noticed during the day, and there were rabbits, which looked like rabbits, and a colorless world whose sudden cruelty frightened me, Rui's body writhed and then went slack, like someone who's fainted, his teeth slowly shrank back to their normal size, his face was once more his face, the face of the person who helped me build towers out of mud and chase chickens, the clock on the wall, vengeful, rang out thirteen or fourteen or fifteen clangs driving my mother crazy, my mother in the morning who wiped Rui's forehead with a damp cloth napkin

"Take pity on me and please shut that clock up"

or sixteen or seventeen or eighteen haughty, stupid clangs on the landing where the stairs, with their threadbare carpet runner, turned toward the bedrooms and the bag of rocks rattling up there, the hands of the clock spun around and around from one number to the next, accumulating hours, weeks, months, years, systole diastole systole diastole systole diastole, Lena, who at least today in order to greet my family here with the appearance of prosperity

I guess

traded her lace shirt for a respectable blouse, traded her gaudy costume jewelry for a normal ring, not a gem to swoon over, but a normal one

"What's the matter Carlos?"

the construction cranes above the roofs of the buildings, the hills of Almada and the lights from the shipyard on the opposite side of the Tagus River, the table all set, the champagne, the decorative balls on the Christmas tree, the presents tied with fine ribbons and I'd like to see if my mother could get up the nerve to accuse me, to my face, of not caring about my brother and sister, of not doing all I can, of not getting along with them, I'd like to see her tell me, to my face, who cares about the family and who doesn't, who had the idea of getting us all together, who just up and decided to pay for this dinner, who got dressed to the nines as if going to a cocktail party or an evening reception at the embassy and wasted a fortune at the store on silvery stars and ridiculous wreaths so that his family would feel good, content, comfortable, happy, my mother with her paranoid idea that I don't like other people and yet I'm the one tracking them down, I called, sent telegrams, invited them, I put up with them in Ajuda without a complaint for three years straight tolerating the craziness of the one and the whims of the other, testing the limits of my patience, him flailing around on the carpet and her sleeping with the entire population of Lisbon, she never really went behind my back because I was never there, I had to earn a living, I'd come home exhausted from work and find Clarisse stretched out comfortably on the couch smoking cigarettes with gold-colored filters that stunk like crazy, cheap knockoff of Turkish tobacco, sipping my anisette liqueur with some mustachioed wise guy

"Haven't you met Francisco?"

or Gustavo or João or Feliciano or Manuel, indifferent to Rui writhing like a lizard on the floor in front of her groaning and biting his own lips and tongue, I'd like to see my mother tell me, to my face, that the best option wasn't to put him somewhere where they can take care of him and other nutcases like him twenty-four hours a day, pills, nurses, hot meals, medical examinations of his head with screws or something like that to see what's wrong with his brain, and I helped him out in spite of the protests from Lena, whose practical sense of things excuse me for saying so

is practically nonexistent, what do you expect from the daughter of a poor wretch from the Cuca-beer plant who read the newspaper in shorts in his tiny front-porch garden that had much more dust than chrysanthemums, right next to the misery of the slums, Lena lacking good sense and brains grabbing me by my shirt, certain that I was just trying to get rid of my brother

"I've never known someone so inhumane"

the same way she thought that I wanted to get rid of Clarisse so that I wouldn't have to put up with her shamelessness in my house, I'd like to see my mother swear to me, to my face, if she has the nerve to do it, that she would put up with Clarisse, insulting her over and over, coming home at any hour she pleased, staying out all night long, getting up at one in the afternoon staggering out of her room as if she'd just awoken from a coma, us

"Clarisse"

and her with her eyes closed and traces of lipstick on her face, looking for a chair, slumping down into the seat, waving away our questions to her

"Be quiet my head hurts don't say a single word to me"

drinking a whole mug of coffee, asking for more coffee, spilling some on her chest when she opened her eyelids just a bit and then immediately closed them again because the sun hurt her eyes, Clarisse recovering little by little, with the voice of a little girl

"What time is it?"

a way of speaking that my father could never resist, he gave her money, let her borrow the car, argued with my mother, who disciplined Clarisse, to get her out of her punishments, my father who treated her the way a boyfriend would, following her around in a state of ecstatic worship, an alcoholic with even less sense than her if that's possible, thinking that everything she does is charming, that everything she does is sensible, that everything she does is intelligent, even the basest things, around the time that he was practically on the verge of death, as skinny as a dog, without his dentures, lying on the mattress with his cheeks caved in, with the majestic profile of a corpse, he let out a breath, and I thought

"He's gone"

my mother went over to examine him, he's gone he's not gone, he's breathing he's not breathing, a pause, a hesitation, my father's chest motionless and the stupid clock on the wall that I'll never trust again belying his motionlessness, how could I have ever thought that pendulum was the heart of our house, my mother with her lips up to my father's ear

("If you don't respond we're just going to call the funeral home and make the arrangements we'll save money on the doctor's bill and the medication and spend it on fertilizer since it'll at least help the sunflowers grow")

my mother in doubt with her little hand on the phone ready to call the men dressed in black

"Amadeu"

another breath, another pause, a twitch of his thumb, a movement of his cheeks, the tip of his tongue between his gums

"Clarisse"

Clarisse nowhere near us, far away at some dance in Malanje, laughing, eating hors d'oeuvres, talking with friends, and my father, so naïve, certain that she was there with us and was helping him across a bridge that didn't exist to the bank on the other side that didn't exist either

"Clarisse"

when she got back from Malanje she found him wearing the suit he wore to his wedding, the tie he wore to his wedding, a silk shirt, a white flower on his lapel, clean-shaven, his shoes

(I've never seen such pointy shoes)

shined, ready to accompany her to some bar or nightclub if they would let him leave the coffin, thinking that everything she does is charming, that everything she does is sensible, that everything she does is intelligent, even the basest things, emptying his wallet before my sister even had a chance to open her mouth

"How much do you need honey?"

for the first time in years he wasn't reaching for the bottle, his hands weren't shaking, his nose wasn't running, a version of my father from back when he used to play chess against a German in Biswaden

I think it was Biswaden

and waited every day for a letter to arrive with his next move and we also waited for it because we liked the stamps until one or both of them lost interest and the chessboard sat there for centuries with a variation of the King's Indian Defense on it, back when he could still walk and took us on picnics with egg-salad sandwiches to the Duque de Bragança waterfalls, back when he used to talk to us and let us take a little peek through his telescope, which was just like looking at the sky without any lenses, just more out of focus and dimmer, little bright specks overlapped with gauzy nebulae, a version of my father from back in the old days, perfected by death, watched over by my mother who used her fan to shoo away the blowflies, men smoking in the garden, women blowing their noses in the living room, Damião hung funereal crape drapes in the window and the murmuring of the sunflowers was silenced, the peacocks ran off into the grove of sequoias, Josélia looking after the setters keeping them from barking tightening their muzzles, the setters whimpering, restrained in their muzzles and Josélia hitting them on the napes of their necks

"Be quiet"

Damião opened the glass case of the clock and immobilized the pendulum out of respect for the dead, the heart of the house was dead too, the house was dead, Baixa de Cassanje was dead, Angola was dead, the workers locked in their huts by the foreman, forbidden from picking cotton, Rui and I wearing black felt armbands, one of us on either side of my mother afraid of all the strangers and the smell of the candles, Clarisse

that slut

dressed in red, running in through the door, stopping short at the foot of the bed without paying any attention to my father, looking at my mother, looking at all of us, looking at the women with handkerchiefs who, in turn, looked back at her in indignant outrage and although it might seem impossible I could swear that my father, with a crucifix around his neck, called out

"Clarisse"

turned his body toward her and called out

"Clarisse"

with the same hope, apprehension, and pride of a boyfriend with his girlfriend that was always in his voice when he called her name, not Rui's, not mine, hers

"Clarisse"

the first to get a peek through the telescope, to eat dessert, to trot from the stable to the rice field on our only horse, an emaciated mare with saddle sores

"Clarisse"

it might seem impossible but nevertheless I could swear that my deceased father, dressed like a groom, ignored the house, the plantation, my mother, the men smoking in the garden, even his whiskey, everything but Clarisse who most of the time wouldn't even give him a kiss, she'd come into the room in a whirlwind of perfume and leave in a second whirlwind having emptied his pockets in the meantime, Clarisse at the foot of the bed without a tear, without a look of sorrow on her face, walking down the patio stairs, we could hear her outside and we could hear a car speeding away on the gravel, honking its horn, scaring off the quails, a convertible heading towards Malanje, some military official in uniform who rested his ribbons and medals on her shoulder, their heads leaning against each other, disappearing in the distance, honking when they reach the dogs, Lena, who at least today, in order to greet my family here with the appearance of prosperity, traded her frilly slum-dweller clothes for a respectable blouse, traded her gaudy costume jewelry for a normal ring with a fake diamond on it, Lena who worries about me since, as she says over and over, as if discovering this fact with renewed incredulity every morning, we're no longer twenty years old, stirring the foam with her spoon poking at an open wound

"Did you sleep Carlos?"

me returning from the plantation to watch over Ajuda, the hills of Almada, the shipyard, the bridge, the decorative balls on the Christmas tree, me reduced to two wood-floor rooms with a tiny kitchen and a bathroom with a clogged-up drain and walls stained with soap scum

"I didn't sleep at all I was thinking about Africa"

Lena certain that people our age, meaning people who through no one's fault but their own are no longer twenty years old, usually fall asleep when it's just starting to get dark, no matter where they are, at the table, at church, at the movie theater, and when they're not sleeping they sit on benches in little city parks getting some sun and wearing checkered hats, if I were to take her advice all I'd do is fill my pockets with bread crusts to feed the swans and spend my afternoons playing dominoes with the high-school kids, me who's going to turn forty-three in May, I can still spot a mosquito on the opposite bank of the river and I've never grown a single gray hair, the telephone operator at work who plugs and unplugs the switch jacks at a blinding speed without ever looking up from the comic strips she's always reading told me without any kind of double meaning because first of all she's married and her husband weighs a menacing two hundred pounds and second of all because she has a daughter who has some esophageal medical condition, that I didn't look a day over thirty-five

"Thirty-five or thirty-four Mr. Albuquerque you've still got a lot to learn"

Lena who I saved from the wretchedness of the Cuca neighborhood looking at me as if I were a centenarian with rheumatoid arthritis and bone spurs encircling my spine

"Did you sleep Carlos?"

as if I could ever fall asleep with my brother and sister about to arrive by taxi at any minute, the headlights shining through at the edges of the window frame, the car doors slamming shut, three short knocks at the door from Clarisse, I always remember her three short knocks, the hubbub in the doorway, me quickly turning down the volume on the TV and jumping out of my armchair

"Where the hell have you been?"

three quick knocks, her contented voice, Lena criticizing me without even opening her mouth

of course

not my sister, but me who had spent the evening at home without hurting a fly, boring myself to death with the movie on TV, looking at the clock and tapping the tips of my fingers on the edge of the side table, eleven o'clock, midnight, half past midnight, one o'clock, Lena who thought I was acting like a school principal or a criminal, looking at me out of the corner of her eye, Clarisse, that princess, wouldn't even respond to me, would go into the kitchen and light the stove, take out a frying pan, look for butter in the fridge, opening up the package, cutting off a chunk of it with a knife, my hand wrapped around her wrist in a flash, my nose at her neck sniffing her perfume which smelled like a cabaret on the island in Luanda Bay, about to smack her in the face, to teach her to respect me

"I asked where you've been"

the kitchen with its crooked hooks for the dish towels and the dull metal cans of beans and pasta, the faucet that didn't shut off all the way, the mold growing on the ceiling, the mop and pail, and a pair of sandals that I never knew who they belonged to, Lena

"Let go of her"

my sister trying to break free from my grasp so she could put the butter in the frying pan

"Carlos"

you could see the fence outside through the little window above the washing machine, cups scattered about, the streetlamps along the narrow road by the school that threw the buildings into high relief, the metal bars protecting the front window of the pawn shop, everything built too near to everything else, everything hollow, the blinds on my bedroom window that won't go up, that get stuck, the blinds in the living room that won't go down straight, with a wooden slat that refuses to fit in its slot, not even after hammering on it, breaking it, the carpet that's coming unglued and exposing the cheap cement used by the builder, the fact that my parents, since they didn't like me

(and the proof that they didn't like me was right there in front of us)

forced me to live in a tiny cubicle fit for an old widow getting by on a Montepio pension plan when they could have gotten someplace nice, a respectable apartment, made me grab Clarisse even harder

"I asked you where you've been you slut"

when I was the one who was a wretch, not my sister, counting pennies from the first day of the month to the last, far away from Baixa de Cassanje, from the scent of the cotton, from Maria da Boa Morte, from the servants who did all the things whether cheerfully or begrudgingly that I now do begrudgingly myself, me as my own servant in a hut in Ajuda with the same river, the same solitude, the same bitter eternity ahead of me, all I need to complete the picture is to start smoking with the lit end inside my mouth, a crate of dried fish, and my features eroded by leprosy, all I need to complete the picture are native soldiers pulling me off of my bed of woven straw clubbing me and blowing their whistles, and it was me, not my sister, that I started punishing like the police chief punished the field workers

(systole diastole, systole)

"I asked you where you've been"

(the heart of the house what a lie, the heart of Cassanje what rubbish)

my brother and sister haven't arrived yet because of traffic and last-minute shopping, because of the rain, because of all the Christmas lights and garlands and wreaths along the streets, the turnip greens getting cold, the codfish getting stale, the oil coagulating, the fruitcake with its cheap gemlike fruits sparkling in the lights the crystallized cherries and the fruits that taste like sugary cabbage, if my mother were here, if Maria da Boa Morte were here with me I swear they would be delighted to see us all together here in Ajuda, together in the house on the plantation with Damião and Fernando, their hair styled with pomade, my father making coins appear and disappear they weren't in his jacket or anywhere else they just miraculously appeared

voila

between his index finger and middle finger pulling a stream of coins out of our noses and ears, giving us horsey rides down the hallway, mimicking Charlot, the crippled Belgian who walked with a limp, my mother pretending to get mad while laughing behind her napkin

"Amadeu"

us thinking about our presents the whole time during dinner, discussing them, trading a toy train for a puzzle before we even found out what they'd bought for us, no holes in the roof, the wooden floors waxed, fresh wallpaper, Clarisse free from my grasp in the kitchen, calling me a name that nobody ever called me, a name that everyone knew and avoided using, the teachers, my classmates, my friends from the café in Luanda, the Cuca-beer plant worker, Lena, the name that everyone knew despite the color of my skin, my thin lips, my straight hair, despite me calling her my mom and her calling me her child just like Rui and Clarisse, despite guests treating me the same as if they didn't know my true identity, where I came from, and where they found me, Clarisse, under her breath, without anger, almost out of pity

"You think you can get revenge on white people by beating up a white woman you think you're equal to a white person because you can beat me up?"

Lena standing in front of me like the native soldiers in front of the sickly, parasitic, diarrheic, consumptive field workers, weighing their bags of cotton, refusing to pay them money, to give them the vouchers for the company store, threatening to send them back to Huambo with a stamp branded on their neck, without their wives, without their children, without their battery-powered radios that never worked and took a year to save up for, the sickly workers speaking their jumbled Portuguese, afraid of the foreman from Cela and his yardstick with nails driven through it

"Boss"

"Did you sleep Carlos?"

when I hadn't slept, I couldn't sleep, I could never have slept, I had to keep my eyes wide open for hours and hours and keep quiet in the dark so that nobody would die, because as long as there was something in my chest that was swinging from left to right and right to left we would continue to exist, the house, my parents, my grandmother, Maria da Boa Morte, me, we would all continue to exist, forever.

I realized the house was dead when the dead began to die. My son Carlos, as a child, thought that the clock on the wall was the heart of the whole world, and it made me want to smile when I realized long ago that the heart of the world, the true heart of the world, wasn't in there with us, but out beyond the porch and the grove of sequoias, in the cemetery where they used to bury blacks and whites side by side back in my father's day in the same way that even before my father's day, back in the days of the first owner of the sunflowers and cotton plants, they used to bury the white people who rode on horseback and gave orders the same as the black people who worked on the plantations in this century and the century before it and even the century before that, a rectangular area enclosed by limestone walls, the gate open and waiting for us, with a crucifix on top of it, gravestones scattered everywhere without any order or dates or carved figures in relief or names in the middle of the grass, willow trees that never grew, desiccated cypresses, a plinth along the wall where you could stand to say a final good-bye, on which the feral cats always slept, snarling at us and forbidding us from entering. The real heart of the house was the grass growing on the graves in the late afternoon or early evening, saying words that I couldn't really understand because I was afraid to understand them, not the wind, not the leaves, but voices that told a story which didn't make sense about humans and beasts and murders and war as though incessantly whispering, telling the story of our offenses, accusing us, repeating lies about how my family and the family before mine had come here like a band of marauders and destroyed Africa, my father always advised me

"Don't listen"

given that I live on property that belongs to me, on a farm that we built and that belongs to me, like Maria da Boa Morte and Josélia, I brought them up and they belong to me, yet even so, yesterday, last week, it might have even been last month, the grass went silent, the tops of the willows went silent, the branches of the cypresses stopped talking, my footsteps disappeared from the hallways, I could no longer make out my own shadow, the lights in the faces of the people within the cast metal frames of the photographs all went out, and I understood that the dead were starting to die and the house was starting to die along with them, the skeleton of the house with pieces of cartilage, drapes, and pictures hanging from its bones, the skeleton of the house, completely empty except for me, the servants, and the creeping vines on the porch that enshrouded us in sheets full of insects. This is certainly the reason that Damião left: when he woke me up this morning he wasn't wearing his gloves or his gold buttons: he was barefoot, didn't have any pomade in his hair, wearing one of my husband's old shirts, which I gave him under the condition that he would never wear it in front of me, he looked like the government troops that now live down in the workers' huts awaiting the arrival of the UNITA guerillas or the South Africans or mercenaries, busy chasing after the piglets that the Cubans forgot to take with them when they took off on what they thought was the way to Luanda but was really just a trap at the first or second curve in the dirt road, the government troops had a Cabindan man who wore espadrilles and sunglasses and who called himself lieutenant, who climbed up the steps to our front door, knocking, claiming my bed for himself and claiming the rest of the house for the other soldiers, all of them stoned on marijuana, who held their bazookas backward and planted cassava root in the rice paddies

"Comrade"

me, an elderly woman with two other elderly women in the kitchen eating the same canned foods and the same vegetables that the caterpillars had overlooked and drinking the same brown water from the water tank, or rather the same rainwater, the same rust and the same silt, the three of us picking the cotton and the sunflowers in hopes of one day getting to Caxito, God knows how, in the van with no wheels and no engine that served as a birdhouse for the crows, and selling the harvest to the Americans from the oil company, me at the top of the stairs blocking his way into the foyer

"Get out of here"

the Cabindan taking a broken cigarette and a matchbox with no matches out of his bag, looking around at his buddies, who were laughing at him, my godfather pointing at the jackrabbit

"Don't be a wimp don't be afraid shoot"

the smoke from the kitchen about a quarter mile away, the jackrabbit motionless on the footpath, the barrel of the rifle going up and down disobeying me, pointing variously at tree trunks, fence posts, the witch doctor's hut right in the middle of a field where nobody, not even the police, ever dared to knock, he predicted the future and divined illnesses with shells, stones, and roosters' spurs, turned pale, turned ash-white, cut a rooster's throat and chewed it while his whole body shook, the Cabindan in his lieutenant's ribbons and stripes demanding the keys to my house

"Comrade"

the jackrabbit's ears suddenly alert, its spring-loaded paws ready to jump, my godfather angry with me, staring at me, putting his finger over my finger on the trigger

"You wanna see how to shoot you wanna see how to shoot little girl?"

and I was blinded and deafened by the gun's report, its blast, the blossom of powder from which the bullet emerged and disappeared, such great force against my temples that I didn't see the jackrabbit vanish, I didn't notice, relieved that the animal was still alive, that there was no pile of fur twitching in the dirt, my godfather ripped the rifle from my hands, pulled me up by my elbows until his nose was up against mine, his two eyebrows formed a single eyebrow, his two eyes a single eye ablaze, his chin digging into my chin

"You'll never get anything right little girl"

awaiting another jackrabbit with me, demanding that I hold the rifle, that I carry it, that I take it back into the tall grass into which the jackrabbit had fled, me on my feet and he behind me at the back of my neck, no longer enraged, just disappointed, sad

"You'll never get anything right little girl"

he lived in Dala Samba about a mile from the hills where the remains of the Jinga kings resided

palm trees spurting up from the defoliated tops of the hills, and the ghosts of the Jinga princes in a mysterious silence, surrounded by pans and gourds and pipes and maybe even

so it was said

the cadavers of the cattle that had belonged to them and corpses of their wives and children

in a house with columns out front in the middle of the tobacco plantation with hippopotamus and elephant skulls on the porch, lion heads, leopard heads, and antelope heads among the zebra pelts, arrows, spears, harquebuses, my godfather wearing an old colonial helmet with dozens of mulatto grandchildren fathered by his mulatto bastard children scampering around all the rooms of the house, the old man with a cigar between his teeth who, on the first Sunday of every month, even during the rainy season when the forest trails turned to muddy streams and the sky turned black with clouds, took his mule out of the stable, thrashed it with a whip to train it to be obedient and tame its wild nature, the beast kicking, spooked at every strike of lightning, he saddled it, put on the bridle, kicked it in the ribs three or four more times to jog its memory, wore a slicker made of yellow rubber and trotted through the forest for twenty-six hours until he arrived at Baixa de Cassanje to visit my family with one of his mulatto sons walking behind him with a muzzle-loading rifle slung on his back, as enormous and silent as my godfather was verbose and rail-thin, the son to whom he spoke as if he were some annoying stranger and who in turn treated his father like a boss, following him everywhere even if the old man sat down at the table to have lunch with us, or went for a walk with my father to talk about the crops, look for signs of blight, run their fingers along the length of the stalks, they'd go out to hunt forest buffalo, bouncing in the jeep over the divots and bumps in the ground, the Lwena driver at the wheel, my godfather and my father on the bench seat in the back fixing their eyes on the animal's footprints, the mulatto with the cartridge boxes on his lap and in the middle of all this the jeep stopped at a bend in the river, horns bent over the water, drinking, the old man to his son, not turning around, holding out his open hand

"Sansão"

the mulatto handing him the binoculars and the rifle, my godfather searching through the dense fog for the alpha male, trying to find it based on the arrangement of the females and the calves among all the necks bent down to drink, finding it, spitting out his cigar butt, pulling a new cigar out from under his slicker, shoving it between his lips like some sort of wedge

(I remember the ruddy sideburns, the ruddy mustache, I remember his small head and his crew-cut hair)

measuring up the forest buffalo and felling it, no convulsions on the part of the buffalo, its legs doubled over, completely helpless, the same way my godfather was felled, in turn, two or three Augusts later, during the coldest part of the season, when the tobacco was stiff with hoarfrost in the mornings and we tried to save it covering it with plastic tarps that were attached to a framework made of reeds, constantly harassed by the barking dogs, the old man felled while lying in wait for a single cheetah, an old animal that was missing some of its claws as we could tell from the scratch marks it left devouring one by one the bull calves and she-goats, we tied a goat to a pole, we made a pile of boards and straw to hide ourselves near the anguished cries of the tethered beast, my godfather, my father, me, and the mulatto son, so obedient and silent that you almost forgot he was there holding the guns under his arm, us waiting for the goat to cry out, those shrieks of a murdered child, bleats of pure terror, which attracted the cheetah, a whole night without talking, our bones were chattering, not our teeth, our bones were chattering, listening to the owls, the underbrush, the palm trees on the tombs of the Jinga kings and in the middle of all this the goat stood motionless for the first time since we brought him out there, a long diagonal shadow or the shadow of a shadow

or the shadow of a shadow of a shadow

flowing like water or light over the other shadows, the sound of an acrid, hungry breath that weighed heavy on our blood and thickened it making it vibrate in our veins, rather than course through them, vibrate in our veins

"The cheetah"

my father whispered in the dark shadows of the boards and straw taken from one of the huts, shadows that my insomnia had turned red, shadows that lit candles inside my body, painful

"The cheetah"

my godfather to his son finding a place to rest the barrel of the rifle

"Sansão"

the mulatto taking the binoculars out of their case, cleaning them, loading the carbine, checking the butt of the gun, he paused at the safety as if he foresaw something, who knows what, as if he understood something, who knows what, as if for years and years he had expected something, not tense, calm, not astonished, resigned, something that was going to happen or that my father thought was going to happen now, my godfather who didn't expect anything, didn't mistrust anything, focused on the goat that was standing upright with the air of an offering, the long, straight shadow moving across all the other shadows

"Sansão"

the son who always accompanied him, ambling in his sandals beside the mule's hindquarters, dropping the binoculars, pulling the carbine up to his chest, taking the safety off, unhurriedly raising the barrel to my godfather's shoulder blades, softly calling to him, I didn't even realize that it was the first time that I'd heard his voice, the first and last time that I heard his voice

"Father"

and it was already day now because you could make out the wet branches and the tall grass and the first insects, the cheetah ran off, the goat started bleating again, my godfather stared at the mulatto for an eternity, the eternity of a single life, kept staring at him from the ground where he lay covering the deep purple stain on his shirt as if he were hiding some secret, shameful weakness while his son, in a languid calm, without arrogance or rage, re-loaded the weapon, raised it to his chest, pointing it away from the goat and us, and the old man ordering him in a whisper like me at the top of the stairs to the Cabindan from the government army

"Get out of here"

my godfather trying to get up, trying to kick at him with his boot, trying to hide his entire body behind his fingers, repeating the same words

"Get out of here"

without arrogance or rage as well, as if scolding a child or chid-ing him for some foolish mistake, almost sweetly, affectionately

"Get out of here"

and I only realized that he was trying to catch his breath, re-gain control of his muscles, trying to speak, when the goat got loose from the pole and trotted into the forest, the second bullet silenced him for good and we strapped him onto the mule and brought him, with the mulatto walking behind, past the court-yard and the sequoia grove to the cemetery where they used to bury blacks and whites side by side back before my father's day, back in the days of the first owner of the sunflowers and the cot-ton plants and the men who worked the fields in this century and the one before it and even the one before that, we brought him to the rectangular area enclosed by limestone walls, the gate with a crucifix on top of it, gravestones scattered everywhere without any order or dates or names among the willow trees that never grew and the desiccated cypresses, the police chief told them to dig two graves

(me almost smiling because my son Carlos, my naïve son Carlos believed that the clock was the heart of the world)

in the vacant area near the pomegranate trees, which the mulatto helped the native soldiers dig and decorate without saying a word and without my father or the police chief or the corporal even saying a single word to him, anchoring the wooden crosses in the little piles of rocks at the head of the graves, burying the old man, pouring the quicklime, adorning the damp sand with silk chrysanthemums, he lowered the second coffin into the grave himself with the same care as the first one

(*my son Carlos thinking that I don't like him because*)

he lay down on the pleated satin, rested his neck on the pillow, adjusted the sheet, closed his eyes awaiting the police chief's pistol, and the native soldiers were the ones who poured the quicklime onto the lid of the coffin with its copper figure of Jesus, the native soldiers whom nobody stopped from adorning the damp sand with silk chrysanthemums while my father held the umbrella because it was starting to rain, not a heavy rain but those thick March raindrops, waxen beads trickling down the sides of our shoes, the police chief returned the pistol to its holster, the grass on the graves was telling its ancient story about humans and beasts and murders and war that I didn't understand because I was afraid to understand, incessantly whispering about our offenses, accusing us

such injustice

of having come here like marauders, even the missionaries, the farmers, the medics who cured leprosy, the grass on the graves repeating lies about which my father warned me, covering my ears

"Don't listen"

(*my son Carlos, the oldest, my first child and God knows how hard it was for me to accept him, the one who's looking after his brother and sister in Lisbon and thinks that I don't like him because*)

my father driving with me to the house on the plantation back when the plantation and the house and the mirrors and I were all young, back when the corn hadn't been trampled and there were no broken tiles and no old-age spots on my skin or blotches from the acid in the tin that have corroded the mirror, the setters waiting for their dinner, the native soldiers going down to the workers' huts with pickaxes and shovels, the employee at the company store sold beer and dried fish to the cotton-field workers, kept track of their tabs in a little notebook with a little stub of a pencil, the police chief grabbing my father's wrist so tight that all the color went out of his fingers and my father didn't even get annoyed with him

"There was no other option but to bury him as well before the officials from Luanda showed up to bury him and us too sir you know that we didn't have any other option"

(*I'm not his mother*)

my father walking up the front steps without inviting the police chief in, bumping into a chest full of cloth napkins and towels and bunches of lavender, bumping into another piece of furniture like the goat we used to lure the cheetah, driven insane with fear, staggering around with neither pupil nor iris showing, just the liquefied whites of its eyes, as pale as egg whites in its eye sockets, he sat down with me on the balcony facing the rain that was now as delicate as a spiderweb, transparent, soft, almost happy, intoning a droll little tune that caught the attention of the azaleas, we looked out at the village and the river, the same village and the same river from earlier today with the Cabindan lieutenant claiming my bed for himself and the rest of the house for the rest of this unruly troop that takes orders from the government or that thing that Africans love to call government so that they can pretend they have one, pretend they're not obeying the Russians and the Cubans, pretend they're free from the Portuguese and can boss us around, humiliate us, and ransack our property on the docks as the boats disembark for Lisbon

"Portuguese bitch"

taking our broken vacuum cleaners and our gas stoves with missing parts, the paintings and books they knew nothing about, the photo albums so they could invent relatives for themselves

"I had a white uncle I had a white grandfather look right here buddy"

the unruly government troops planting cassava root in the rice paddies, drunk on palm wine, high on marijuana

"Comrade"

making themselves at home in my living room, in my kitchen, rolling out their sleeping mats in my study, stewing rats out on my terrace, forcing Maria da Boa Morte to cook them swallows for dinner, walking through the hallways wearing grenades around their waists and ammunition belts for suspenders, calling me to my room where the Cabindan man, the lieutenant

(because I'm not his mother, imagine that, as if a person's mother)

was writing at my dressing table, sweeping aside with the back of his hand all the bottles and brushes and tubes and boxes I use for disguising my age, for lying about my age the same way that I lie in the letters to my children and tell them all about the sunflowers and the rice so that neither they nor I get upset, pretending that I still hope to be able to hope, as if a person's mother

(as if a person's mother weren't)

all alone here without a man to protect her, the way my mother had my father and I never had anyone or I had a bottle of whiskey and a pair of pajamas with a few bones rattling around in them, all alone here with two women who are just as worn-out as I am, eating the same canned foods and drinking the same silt from the water tank, with the obligation or humility or fate of having to invent a present that ceased to exist years ago, the Cabindan man writing in Portuguese that was taught at the mission in a little hut with desks, a map, and a plaster bust of the female symbol of the Republic on a pedestal, the priest quizzing them about cities that they would never see, Coimbra Beja Chaves Vila Real Barcelos Évora

"Your name is spelled like this write down the letters of your name so the principal can see"

handing me a piece of paper informing me that the government had just taken possession of that which belonged to me, had decided to make use of that which belonged to me until the end of the war, the Cabindan man seated and me facing him, me, as if I were the black woman, the servant, the Bailunda from Huambo, me facing him reading the paper, reading it again, reading it once more while the lieutenant combed his hair in the mirror with my comb and checked out my nail polish

"Your house belongs to the people now"

my house traded for a sheet of graph paper with grease and soot stains on it, soldiers in my mother's room, in my children's rooms

(*the woman who accepted him ever since he was a baby and grew fond of him and raised him*)

connecting things with screws, putting together mortars, speaking to each other in a dialect that I couldn't understand similar to the murmur of the dahlias during those insomniac nights when something terrible was growing in me watching the mulatto in his coffin breathing so peacefully, which intrigued me but didn't intrigue my father, awaiting or desiring or begging for the policeman's pistol, a jolt, disorder, and peacefulness yet again, the quicklime searing the skin, causing pink boils to form all over the body, my house invaded by a troop that calls itself government so that it can live in the houses on the hill in Luanda with a view of the ocean and the island and the trawlers heading out of the bay at dawn trailing a wake of seagulls and diesel fuel behind them, the houses that were deserted by those who owned the beer, cacao, fruit, and coffee who were now in Brazil and Switzerland, a government composed of ministers who used to work for us back in the time of President Carmona

(and they were grateful to work for us)

as bookkeepers, servants, doormen, errand boys, they got out of bed if we so much as coughed, they smiled out of respect before they spoke to us, they apologized for things they didn't even do like the laborers who fled from the workers' huts in search of some place upland that was much too far given their state of exhaustion and starvation, like me writing this letter that I can't send to my children in Ajuda, who are worried about me, trying to call, get some news about me, mailing packages to me that never arrive, me without a single complaint, facing the seated Cabindan man

"This house belongs to the government comrade"

me, someone who my son Carlos could learn to like, if I were black

(*as if a person's mother weren't*)

and for whom he would feel

God help me I hate this word

pride, like Rui certainly did, like Clarisse maybe did if she ever stopped to think for long enough to realize that her father wasn't a man he was a wretch in pajamas swimming in whiskey like fetuses in specimen jars, drinking up our harvests with all of Angola enclosed in the bottles in our cupboards, my husband who never dared to tell me, receiving a telegram that I held right in front of his face in which a woman who worked in the Cotonang cafeteria asked for money for

(*Carlos never knew who she was and never asked who she was and so I'm certain that he never sought her out in Malanje if in fact she still lives in Malanje if in fact she's still alive*)

her son, the two of us that night in our bedroom, my husband looking at me from the mattress, me disentangling my hair from my earrings, the telegram on top of the bedspread, birds and moths flitting around the light on the other side of the curtains,

I didn't feel disillusioned or enraged nor did I feel like talking, I felt worn-out, I felt the feebleness of someone who hasn't slept for centuries, someone who just hopes that she won't have to talk and that nobody will talk to her, who hopes she can somehow pull myself off of me like a dress and become naked, free from myself, who hopes she could stretch out on the floor and become a mere thing, one of the setters howled out in the orchard at a screech owl or barn owl, spooking the peacocks, I set my earrings on the silver saucer and my mouth spoke yet I did not speak

"I don't want a divorce at all I just want you to leave me alone"

in a voice that I didn't recognize and that mingled with the water in the little pond out front, a voice without words or upon which words floated without any meaning, rotten limp frayed leaves

"I don't want a divorce at all I just want you to leave me alone"

not out of love, not out of that species of resigned selfishness that's called love, not out of fondness for my husband, a need for him, or the fact that I would miss him but rather out of indifference, inertia, out of not being able to endure, at that moment, the upheaval of people leaving, open suitcases, impatient footsteps going this way and that, someone on all fours looking for a lost necktie behind the chest of drawers, pushing aside armchairs and drapes, remarking with cancerous spite

"I can never find anything in this hellhole"

the unkind comments or the offended silences, self-sufficient, rebuffing any help that's offered, the rejection even crueler than the comments, the telegram from the Cotonang cafeteria worker on top of the bedspread, breeding discontent, me putting a nightshirt on over my bra for the first time so that my husband couldn't see my breasts, idly, painfully drawing out the words I spoke, as if each syllable, each letter were an incisor with roots stretching from my chin to my brain that was being wrenched from my mouth

"I just want you to leave me alone leave me alone"

talking to someone who didn't hear me, he was thinking back to months earlier, to the prefab house that lacked any trace of a woman, any sign of a woman, the house he'd shared with the Dutch chemist, the pictures of dancing ladies with lewd comments scribbled in pencil that I preferred not to read, doodles that I preferred not to look at, vases made from Coca-Cola cans, the dinner table made out of slats of wood from a barrel, the filth, the neglect, the ankle sock in the dishwasher, the tube of shoe polish in the bidet, Amadeu who had left the bedroom but was still there on the bed, walking by the light of his lantern along the lanes of Cotonang, heading to a little building in need of a paint job on the other side of the fence, an abandoned infirmary with its little garden of dusty chrysanthemums and mosaics made up of little pieces of colored glass from which the light from the lantern was reflected and off of which arabesques were projected onto the dirt below, a single room that smelled of carbolic acid and moldy cheese, the sky visible through holes in the roof, stars, the sparkling of the slate, and the fog drifting above the roof beams, the metal cot that was once cream-colored, a pail filled with gauze and bandages, medieval medical devices on the shelf, the cafeteria worker

"Don't worry I don't want a divorce lie back down don't make any noise don't bother me I just want you to leave me alone"

just like you'd imagine a cafeteria worker, wearing an apron and rubber boots and a hairnet, a black girl no older than eighteen maybe twenty since we're bad at guessing how old they are, they either look much younger or much older than they actually are, the same way we're bad judges of their temperament, their character, their honesty, their obedience, and their affection for us if it's possible to call whatever it is they feel affection, they don't get attached to us, they aren't loyal, they aren't grateful, they hate us, my father, poor thing, always warned me

"Don't be a fool don't kid yourself they despise you"

for instance after independence was declared my cousin from Lobito was joking around with her servant because she had always bent over backwards for him and they got along so well, as if he was part of the family

"All right don't go and kill me now that you all are in charge of everything"

and the ungrateful wretch in the most serious tone in the world

"Don't worry because I worked it out with the servant of the lady on the sixth floor I'm going to kill his boss and he's going to kill you"

the cafeteria worker squatting on her sleeping mat with her son, a child that looked fully white

(as if a person's mother weren't)

a white person's lips, white person's nose, white person's hair, at most

even if you were to look really closely

something in the shape of his fingernails, though even a doctor would overlook it, a fully white child whose origins and black blood could only be detected without hesitation by the old black ladies who smoke their cigarettes with the lit ends inside their mouths, Josélia, Maria da Boa Morte, who never said anything in order to protect themselves and protect him, my husband at the door of the old infirmary with his hat in his hand, very formal, as if she were a stranger, indecisive, shy, afraid of the woman and above all afraid of me, of what we could say to one another, trying his hardest not to look at anybody, to not seem interested in his son thinking that if he showed interest in his son it would hurt my feelings when it was the fact

(something that he didn't understand the same way men never understand since men don't understand anything about us)

that he wasn't interested that hurt me and me

between two women

to the cafeteria worker, not between a white woman and a black woman, between two women, since even a black woman can understand the things that no man, black or white, ever can, taking out my checkbook resting it on the metal cot

"How much?"

helping her keep her job, making it so they wouldn't have to call her into the office and fire her when they could no longer overlook the presence of this whore among them, the affront of a European baby in the workers' quarters being lugged around by some anonymous African woman, making it so that she wouldn't be disowned by the members of her own race, so that she didn't wind up dead in some alleyway in the neighborhood or disemboweled like a goat on the trail through the tall grass, me holding my pen above the check looking up through the holes in the roof at the clouds that were drifting off to the east, gray clouds followed by darker clouds bringing rain, writing down the amount, not the one that she never got around to asking for but rather the amount that her job and her son or rather my son

(as if a person's mother were someone other than the woman who's accepted him ever since he was a baby and raised him)

my oldest child, was worth, Carlos, in whose name I put the deed to the house in Ajuda to show him that I never resented him, that I never renounced him, that I like him despite the fact that he doesn't believe me, he doesn't write me back, doesn't read my letters, he's forgotten about me like the dead in the cemetery like Damião who woke me up today without wearing his uniform jacket, the gloves, the gold buttons, barefoot, no pomade in his hair, wearing my husband's old shirt that I gave to him centuries ago under the condition that he would never wear it in my presence, Damião who if the bishop saw him wouldn't recognize him

"I'm leaving ma'am"

pointing out at the unplowed fields, the ruined harvest, the silent clock on the wall, the missing armchairs, all the pictures that used to hang on the walls, the silence in the enormous hallways, Damião taking pity on me, confiding to me in a soft voice, revealing the misery and solitude in which I lived

"I can't stay here because this house is dead"

If Lena and I were to separate there would definitely be more dust on the shelves and more dirty clothes in the laundry basket but in recompense I wouldn't have to eat at set times or sleep with the window closed and the apartment would immediately get bigger. There are times when I think that my parents bought such a tiny place on purpose in order to force the people who live in it to hate each other, in order to impel Lena and I to get divorced because it isn't possible for two adults to live their lives constantly bumping into each other, hesitating over who should pass through the door first, back and forth in a comic ballet, me you you me, retreating advancing retreating advancing in unison stepping on each other's toes and muttering insults under our breath

"Idiot"

"You're the idiot you fool"

it isn't possible for two adults to see the other one on the couch every single time we feel like sitting on it, an ogre with an angry fist always huffing at the bathroom door

"Hurry up"

at the exact moment that we turn on the water in the shower, it isn't even possible for a couple to be unhappy because unhappiness is something solitary and so they've even robbed us of the pleasure of sadness here so I end up sitting at the window that looks out on the Tagus which I can't even open because she catches a cold at even the slightest breeze, looking out on the hills of Almada waiting for the smell of hot food and a shrill cry from just a few feet away

"Soup's ready"

our knees touching underneath the tablecloth and then quickly retreating from each other with a shudder of displeasure, our fingers getting entangled indignantly in the breadbasket, our eyes avoiding each other, and the cruel silence, thinking

just like my parents wanted us to think

why won't you die, why won't I die, why don't we both die, my mother still alive in Angola writing me letters first from the plantation then from Marimba that I never read since I already know all her complaints by heart, all her whining, all her suggestions, don't forget about your brother and sister, eat well, don't catch a cold, my father in the Dondo cemetery and my mother in a hut in the village with both her servants in uniform, sowing seeds while wearing that pearl-colored hat

(it was pearl-colored I think)

that she wore to formal dinners, in a measly acre of sprouting crops among the piglets and she-goats, better off than I am here in Ajuda in this apartment where these stupid lights are blinking on the Christmas tree and the codfish is getting colder

and colder and colder and colder

as it sits in the oven in the kitchen. If Lena left the apartment would immediately get bigger: nine-tenths of the clothes in the closet would disappear, the contempt of the African masks on the wall would vanish, I could unlock the window and the living room would stretch from end to end out toward the river, I'd be able to reach out and touch the boats with my hand, if I ever felt like it I could embark with them to Panama or Turkey, I'd be able to smell the boggy banks of the river from a bed that I wouldn't have to share with anyone, there'd be no elbow jabbing me in the ribs no thigh pinning my knee against the mattress, if Lena were to leave I'd take the dirty sheets to the dry cleaner two streets down, I'd have a nice sandwich for dinner, with a book held open between my plate and the pitcher, on Sundays I'd give the table and counters a quick once-over with a washcloth to keep the ants away, I'd leave the Christmas tree up as long as it would last, until the lights went out one by one, I'd let this night continue on for an eternity, forbidding myself to succumb to the moments of weakness that, out of foolishness, come upon me every once in a while, I wonder how Rui's doing, I wonder how Clarisse's doing, remembering that they despise me, my wife despises me, my wife whom I decided to uproot, who knows why, from her home on the edge of the slums, when her father met me for the first time he immediately recognized the true color of my skin and despised me as well and I say that he recognized the true color of my skin because he never stopped staring at me, as if beneath this disguise of my physical appearance, my skin, my hair, there was a different appearance and skin and hair that no white person would ever accept, one that I discovered in myself on the day that Maria da Boa Morte told me in the kitchen, she didn't address me as "child" the way she did my brother and sister, she called me "you" using the informal *tu*, I was sitting at the table drinking a cup of milk watching the April wind across the flower bed, watching the men who were coming up from the workers' quarters carrying heavy sacks, I was seven or eight and my father's footsteps on the floor above rattled the ceiling, Josélia was beating the rugs on the clothesline, Damião was cleaning the silver in the living room, the quails were fluttering about the garden and Maria da Boa Morte didn't call me child she called me *tu* as though she and I were the same, as if she were my equal

"You're black"

the racket steadily pounding dust out of the rug, the foreman dividing up the Bailundos out in the fields with his whistle, me not understanding

"You're black"

Maria da Boa Morte was working at the stove with the lit end of the cigarette inside her lips at the very moment when the peacocks began to repeat in unison

"You're black"

at the moment when the setters and the Bailundos stared at me from the other side of the window frame, standing against a horrendous sky

"You're black"

the six portholes of a ship heading toward the narrow entrance of the port pass in front of the cornice of the Dockworkers' Union building and the lights on the docks, which are blurred by the rain, Lena started taking off her necklace, unlatching the clasp at the nape of her neck

"Are we going to wait up all night for your brother and sister?"

and in the midst of all this, after eighteen years of marriage, I realize in the blink of an eye that she never wanted me to get her pregnant because she didn't want the shame of having a mulatto baby in her womb, contaminating the cradle, contaminating the house, I realized why she always shrank away from me in bed the second that I started to stretch out under the covers

"I've got a headache Carlos"

the rain at the window, each drop lit up and shining like the portholes of the ship, my father used to set up a Nativity scene in Angola, hills made of blotting paper, the cliché ceramic figurine of a Coimbra university student playing guitar, sheep, seraphs, little clay figures, Rui saying to my father without knowing what snow was or even having the slightest idea of what it could be

"What about the snow?"

one of the wise men was black, dressed the same as the white wise men, wearing a crown and everything but black, Clarisse prancing around me and snapping her fingers

"Maria da Boa Morte said that Carlos is black"

my father frozen stiff, my mother frozen stiff, my grandmother frozen stiff, the clock on the wall frozen stiff

(the house should have disappeared as soon as the pendulum stopped moving but it didn't disappear) the black wise man back behind the others, not up front, behind them, black and in last place, Clarisse heading toward the door and looking at them on the verge of tears

"Don't look at me like that don't spank me Maria da Boa Morte was the one who said it not me"

my grandmother

"Clarisse"

my father holding a star made of tissue paper, my mother calling the police chief and an hour later the geese rustling, the setters alarmed, the sound of the jeep's motor in the driveway, shouting, scurrying, clamor in the kitchen, a horsewhip held in air, the native soldiers taking Maria da Boa Morte out to the jeep, the police chief whispering

"Everything's under control Dona Isilda"

the sound of the jeep fading down the road, Lena unlatching the clasp of her necklace

"Are we going to wait up all night for your brother and sister?"

me thinking

"Why the hell don't you just get out of here and leave me alone?"

since if we were to separate there would be more dust on the shelves and more dirty clothes in the laundry basket but in recompense I wouldn't have to eat at set times or sleep with the window closed and the apartment would immediately get bigger, the ship reached the entrance to the port, heading to America, to China, to wherever the hell it wants, there was no taxi outside on the avenue, no bus puttering down the street, nobody calling my name at the doorstep, Rui to his housemates in Damaia

"My brother is black"

Clarisse to the engineer or the lawyer or the colonel who's supporting her now

"Can you believe an African invited me to dinner can you believe the nerve of those people?"

a mulatto baby in her womb, the shame of a mulatto contaminating the house, Maria da Boa Morte back at our house in May, a month during which my father stumbled his way from one bottle to the next removing their stoppers in a sluggish rage, she was skinnier, her head was shaved, with welts on her back, the police chief accepting a cigar, a glass of anisette liquor

"If you keep her here you don't run the risk of her spreading lies about your son all over Baixa de Cassanje Dona Isilda can't you see the trouble she was getting into?"

Maria da Boa Morte limping on her left leg heating up the table scraps in a pan for the setters, me tugging at her apron

"Is it true that I'm black?"

not apprehensive or sad, just curious, tugging at her apron scampering around her

"Is it true that I'm black?"

black like Josélia, Fernando, Damião, the field hands, the foreman was going to come into the kitchen and send me out to work the harvest, they were going to take away my room, my toys, my spot at the dinner table, I was going to have to eat dried fish and porridge made from cassava flour, drink beer at the company store, sleep on a straw mat, get jaundice and treat it with medicinal roots, I'd no longer believe in God, maybe the following Christmas I'd get some hand-me-down pants from Rui, since I'd mistakenly lived in the house on the plantation for a few years,

Maria da Boa Morte dragging her left ankle trying to get away from me

"Please child"

there were afternoons when some of the young crocodiles came up near the workers' quarters and you could hear the foxes mewing as they gathered their cubs, afternoons while they were burning the fields when hundreds of gledes flew toward the house frightened by the flames, my father set down his whiskey for once and went out on the balcony to protect his azaleas

(if Lena and I separated I'd buy a flowerpot and azalea seeds to remind me of Angola)

there were afternoons when pink masses of winged ants flew through the air, the tractor drivers were smoking at the little grocery stand, Maria da Boa Morte pouring beans into the setters' bowls shaking like she had barbed wire for nerves, me tugging and tugging at her apron not apprehensive or sad, just curious, the police chief dusting the ashes from his uniform advised my mother

"She'll stay out of trouble here under your watchful eye Dona Isilda if by chance she doesn't straighten up and this problem with your son continues we'll just solve the problem once and for all"

(Clarisse elated snapping her fingers telling her friends at school in the city

"Maria da Boa Morte says that Carlos is black Maria da Boa Morte says that Carlos is black")

"Is it true that I'm black?"

me to Lena who was looking at the clock and at me, waiting to clear the table, she went to the hair salon earlier, dyed her hair, did her nails, but instead of looking younger she turned into some strange person that I only half recognized, some distant cousin wearing mascara and stark lipstick, smoothing out the tablecloth, straightening the bowls of almonds, wiping off a streak from one of the glasses with a cloth napkin

"You always knew I was black didn't you Lena?"

wiping off a streak from one of the glasses with a cloth napkin without altering the movement of her hand or changing the expression on her face, when we got married my mother paid for a trip to Lobito for the two of us, two weeks in a hotel on the beach, I can still see the palm trees and the waves, the trunks of the palm trees against the lilac-colored sea, the police chief telling me good-bye with a meaningful nudge of his elbow

"Later kid"

the second my father left for Malanje to have tests done on his liver the chief would go into the study with my mother and lock the door, you couldn't hear a single noise coming from inside there, I'd stand with my ear to the door thinking but lacking the courage to say out loud

"They're dead"

I'd listen there for hours, worried, the only thing you could see through the keyhole was a corner of the desk and then there were the sounds of footsteps and voices, the door being unlocked, the police chief pointing me out to my mother, gesturing toward me with a nod of his head

"Were you waiting for us kid?"

the fan whirled around on the ceiling of the hotel room in Lobito, stirring the gelatinous, humid air, the sea generously left conch shells on the beach for us, in which other smaller seas whispered their secrets, Chinese boxes within Chinese boxes within Chinese boxes, moths with their wings folded together walked along the lampshade, my foot touched Lena's foot and Lena pulled her foot away

"Aren't you hot?"

the hotel orchestra was made up of three decrepit musicians who played mambos off-key, the police chief grabbed me by the throat and shoved me down the hallway, the same gesture he used to run off the Bailundos

"Beat it kid"

never Carlos, just "kid," him shoving me down the hallway and my mother silent, Clarisse was Clarisse, Rui was Rui, I

(*"You're black"*)

was just "kid" because Maria da Boa Morte had said

"You're black"

Lena set the glass on the tablecloth, folded the napkin back along its creases, made sure that everything was in order in the apartment

which would immediately get bigger were we to get separated

for when my brother and sister arrived, the lights strung on the Christmas tree, the decorations, the presents, the champagne, back in Angola Damião uncorked the champagne since my father's hands shook so much while my mother furrowed her brow and my father looked down at his fingers with the shock of someone looking at something that is part of him yet somehow does not belong to him, Damião poured the champagne into the flutes and my father, afraid that if he picked one up he'd spill it, smiling as though actually raising the glass that he refused to touch

a smile that would soon fall from his face with a splash and a bang and roll down the table

the rain at the window obscuring the port and the hills of Almada, everything except the two of us in the living room dressed like we're going to a baptism or a wake

one more wake

the two of us in the hotel room in Lobito below the fan blades that stirred the gelatinous, humid air

"You always knew I was black didn't you Lena?"

moths with their wings folded together walked along the lampshade, flashes of palm trees, of dawn, of music like the flashes of fruit bats on the night my grandmother died and they told us to play out in the back where the generator shook the ground rattling the shadows

rattling the shadows like dice

one against the others, the generator broke down every so often, its sickly lung coughing and the house vanishing in the darkness, house and no house in alternating spasms, the grass was there, the stars were there in between dark clouds but there was no place for us to live and we weren't there either, Maria da Boa Morte brought out candles and a different house, one that was insecure, now smaller now larger, now fat now skinny, began to emerge, began to take shape yet was shapeless, began to rise up off the ground in yellow flames, my father and mother danced upstairs on a floor that was now elastic, faces that were illuminated from inside the skull took on strange contorted expressions, my fingers became extremely elongated in the mirror, sediment of milky tears hardening on the marble tabletop and now the grass no longer existed, just our ghosts floating in a dark nothingness, if they cut off the electricity here in Ajuda they'd put an end to Christmas and this miserable little tree, it would just be Lena and me as it's been for fifteen years, the outline of the hills of Almada and the sound of tiny raindrops on the roof, Lena got up to shut off the lights in the hotel room and the two of us evaporated, the sea emerged through the window blinds, the whirring of the ceiling fan seemed nearer, the mattress creaked when Lena scooted over to my side of the bed and kept creaking as she moved her buttocks into her new spot, I realized that she was taking off her shirt because something dim and pale grazed against my side, her foot touched my foot in weary resignation

"Now"

her closed mouth, the wall of teeth that repelled me, the navel that eluded me, no joy, no shiver, no heavy breathing, no kiss, I bet she had her eyes open looking up at the ceiling fan and counting the revolutions of its blades, Lena quiet as I moved away from her, homesick for the little house on the edges of the slums regretful that she didn't just marry some random neighbor of her own race, the police chief grabbed me by the throat

"Beat it kid"

never Carlos, just "kid," Clarisse was Clarisse, Rui was Rui, I

"You're black"

was just "kid" because Maria da Boa Morte had said

"You're black"

and threw me toward the huts where I belonged, I went into the room in the morning and Lena was still in the same position, like a statue in a graveyard, like my grandmother on her bier, her eyes open and looking up at the ceiling fan without taking notice of me, the voices of the other guests went silent, I'm certain that the painting above the bed was staring at me that the clothes hung over the back of the chair were staring at me that the telephone was staring at me, just like Lena's family, relatives from Salazar, relatives from Narriquinha all stared at me during the wedding Mass, me with skin that was whiter than theirs, a nose that was thinner, hair that was straighter, if I could only just fall into oblivion and sleep, run away, take the bus to Malanje, tie a loincloth around my waist, ask the foreman for a sack, start picking a row of cotton, me in Ajuda trying to get the lights straight on the tree

"You always knew I was black didn't you Lena?"

and after straightening the lights getting the box that they came in out of the closet and putting the lights back in it, a string of lights and little figures

(angels, shepherds, sheep)

and comets, all made of glass, gathering the presents with their red ribbons and wrapping paper with little bells on it, pulling the tree out of its stand, taking the box, the presents, the tree, and the stand out the front door to the landing, dumping Christmas into the elevator, shoving it into the lobby next to the mailboxes along the wall, I went back upstairs to get my umbrella so I wouldn't ruin my new suit

with the trifle that the laboratory pays me

I can't afford to buy another, Lena remained at the table eating almonds from the bowl and straightening the locks of her new hairdo with her fingertips, the dumpster was a block away or rather a thirty-meter trek that was certain to give me a cold, with big puddles of rainwater underneath the branches of the mulberry trees, nobody out on the street, no cars, no taxis, no pastry shop with its lights on, the whole world feasting on codfish and turnip greens, in the windows you could see cardboard cutout letters, happy holidays taped to the windows, candelabra, the Pope on TV surrounded by cardinals removing their miters and putting them back on, dozens and dozens of cardinals and just one or two black ones who will never be Pope, I made who knows how many trips back and forth, getting more and more soaked, from the lobby to the dumpster and from the dumpster to the lobby, first the tree stand and the little rocks that anchored it down, then the lights and the gifts and then last of all the worthless tree until Christmas itself

thankfully

vanished from my life, my brother and sister, what a joke, family, what a scam, touching family get-togethers, what a lie, while the wind ripped at the ribs and fabric of the umbrella and a drunk spoke to me in his happy, honking voice

"Hello there sir"

a man more or less the same age as me, more or less my size, stumbling toward me enthusiastically with his overcoat unbuttoned, with a package tied with twine about to slip out of his arms, the streetlights and headlights on the bridge below lit up an invisible Christmas tree, the rain in the crown of light from the streetlights looked like the snowflakes inside the paperweight in the study back in the days when we had over four hundred Bailundos working for us, not counting the leprous ones in the huts down by the river, the medic came on Saturdays and rang a little bell so he could deliver their pills from a distance, the hills of Almada looked like the mountains made out of blotter paper in the Nativity scenes, the Tagus River was the shard of glass that stood for a pond, the drunk greeted me with his convoluted joy

"Hello there sir"

more or less the same age as me, more or less my size, holding the package against his chest as some sort of decoration on that night in Ajuda among all the trawlers disembarking

"Hello there sir"

he staggered along sluggishly, jovial and menacing, freshly emerged from some hidden tavern tucked away in the Monsanto forest, some hole in the wall filled with cheap prostitutes that serves rubbing alcohol sweetened with a drop of honey, he was a leper in Lisbon who hobbled along on his femurs as if they were a pair of broken crutches, sometimes when the Belgians invited my parents over I'd go down with Clarisse and Rui to the straw huts by the river and we'd see them shuffling along the riverbank, almost dragging their knuckles as they walked, stopping to scratch themselves or cry out in pain, Rui whispering in my ear

"Want to throw rocks at them?"

Clarisse in her gossamer voice

"Want to sic the dogs on them?"

you could tell where the huts were from the squawking of the sparrows, the falcons gliding through the sky, the close watch that the gledes kept over them, the eagles tugging out their entrails like I tugged on the cook's apron not apprehensive, not sad, just curious

"Is it true that I'm black is it true that I'm black?"

because if I was black I could walk around barefoot and no one would scold me, I'd be able to run faster than the others, I'd be stronger and no one would call me names or beat me up at school, Rui whispering in my ear

"Want to throw rocks at them?"

Clarisse in her gossamer voice

"Want to sic the dogs on them?"

ungrateful Clarisse and ungrateful Rui, whom I didn't kick out of here, I didn't throw them out of these two little rooms where there would certainly be more dust on the shelves and more dirty clothes in the basket if Lena and I separated but in recompense I wouldn't
· have to eat at set times or sleep with the window closed and the apartment would immediately get bigger I'd throw out the trinkets from Angola, masks, necklaces, little statues, rhinoceroses

(I don't want anything to do with Angola don't talk to me about Angola leave me alone with Angola it's been ages since Angola was dead to me I swear)

Clarisse overjoyed in Estoril with all its nightclubs, Rui over-joyed in Damaia with the liveliness of the market and the movie starlets on the posters, both of them

regardless of what my mother might say

much better off than with me hesitating over who should pass through the door first, retreating, advancing, retreating, advanc-ing in unison stepping on each other's toes and muttering insults under our breath

"Idiot"

"You're the idiot you fool"

always feeling someone's breath on the back of your neck, some-one on the couch every single time I feel like sitting on it, an ogre with an angry fist always huffing at the bathroom door

"Hurry up"

at the exact moment that I turn on the water in the shower and check the temperature with a cautious index finger, me at the window that I can't even open because she catches a cold at the slightest breeze, looking out on the hills of Almada, looking at myself down below under the pathetic mulberry trees standing next to the dumpster on the street, my presents, my pine tree, my wreaths, and my Christmas amid all the trash, kitchen scraps, and empty bottles, struggling with the ripped fabric and broken ribs of my umbrella, the drunk with his convoluted joy

"Hello there sir"

more or less the same age as me, more or less the same size, stumbling along enthusiastically with a dirty package tied with twine that was about to slip out of his arms accusing me with the honking voice of a seagull

"You're black"

repeating it with a maniacal insistence

"You're black"

still repeating it

"You're black"

and

"You're black"

and

"You're black"

(you always knew I was black didn't you Lena everyone always knew that I was black they always made fun of me they knew about the Cotonang cafeteria worker and that my mother traveled to Malanje to buy me your father your family my classmates

all of Angola knew it isn't it true that you knew that you always knew Lena?)

the drunk, whom the rain, spiraling in the crown of light from the streetlamps like the snowflakes in the paperweight, had driven down to the huts by the river, amid the whirling white specks, with Clarisse and Rui hidden around some corner in Ajuda, hidden in the tall grass, throwing rocks at him, siccing the dogs on him, waiting afterward for the medic to ring his bell and call out

"Kid"

not Santa Claus

"Kid"

"You're black"

and deliver the leper his pills from a distance.

Because I'm a woman. Because I'm a woman and women don't die like men because they lack the weight of fear that resides in the flesh of men, the density of innocence and solitude in their bones: women turn into ghosts, or maybe not even ghosts, they turn into something nebulous, phosphorescent beings that wander from room to room with the same movements and the same gait they had when they were alive, rustling the curtains, darkening the metallic surfaces of doorknobs and picture frames, watching us from the backyard or the kitchen, with their hair done up, fanning themselves with decorative fans, returning to earth when they wish to watch us, then returning to the sepulchre, where we buried them weeks or months before, with the ethereal speed of running water. Because I'm a woman. Because I'm a woman, I was never surprised when, for years and years after her funeral, I would find her knitting in the rocking chair on the back porch, I'd softly call her name, silently, inside my head

"Mother"

the setters never noticed her, neither did my husband nor the peacocks nor the azaleas, my children just kept playing underneath the golden rain tree, the shadow of the rocking chair looked empty as it swayed back and forth on the ground, and yet there was my mother, putting her knitting aside, setting it in a basket, smiling, holding out her hand to run her fingers along my clothes, pleased

"That dress looks so nice on you honey"

my cousin who was married to a farmer from Duque de Bragança came out from the house holding the tea tray looking all around, astonished

"Have you been talking to yourself Isilda?"

nodding toward the empty rocking chair, the vines that wrapped around the columns, the edges of the cotton flowers that seemed to wink in the blowing wind, while the smell of sweet perfume, like the ink from old letters, tenderly enveloped me, two fingers with rings on them touched my dress

"That dress looks so nice on you honey"

I felt happy, young, pretty like when she used to help me get ready to go with her to the dances at the Ferroviário Club, dressed in white, white gloves, white shoes, a white gardenia pinned to the neckline of my dress, the governor lifted my head up with his hand at my chin

"My how you've grown young lady"

and I was sure I'd never grow old or get wrinkles or gray hair or get ill and the band would keep playing up on the stage until the end of time. Because I'm a woman. Because I'm a woman and they taught me to be a woman, which is to say that they taught me to understand while pretending that I didn't understand

(all you have to do is feign detached amusement instead of talking)

the weakness of men and the sordidness of life, the emotional wounds that are resewn, the broken hearts that are cobbled back together, the sheaths that serve to protect the soul, they taught me to forgive the lies and restlessness of men, not to accept it or be blind to it, but to forgive it the way I forgave my father for his scandalous infidelities and forgave my husband for his pathetic indecision, they taught me the bright idea of paying very little attention to my children, until my husband died and I was forced to take care of them and the plantation both, taking care of them with the same pitilessness that I'd reserved for the servants, sending them off

"Angola is dead for you all do you hear me Angola is dead for you all"

on the ship to Lisbon, while I stayed here among the dead who watched me from the orchard or the back porch, cleaning the bullet wounds that killed them with the corner of a handkerchief. Because I'm a woman. Because I'm a woman and the government troops have overtaken my house, they stripped the shingles and rafters from my roof so they could make bulwarks to guard them against attacks from the Luchazesians, the Afrikaners, the mercenaries funded by the diamond money in Lunda, they stole all the cows and pigs and chickens and goats they could find and roasted them on spits made from broom handles, they let the sunflowers and the rice wither away in the cold during the dry season and let weeds choke their roots so that there's no trace left of the plantation that once belonged to my father, and to the man who sold it to him and then emigrated to Venezuela or Brazil, and to those who came before both of them, who for two or three or four generations cleared the forest and the animal dens with slaves and axes, with blood, and with blood they forced cotton to grow on the hillside, and to the south of the cotton they forced the slaves' huts to be built between the garden and the river, next to the speckled marbled skin of the crocodiles sunning in the sand, slaves that

even though they were still slaves

we called Portuguese people of color, living in my house, my room, my children's rooms, the study, and all the rooms that have been stripped bare of my furniture and paintings, with their guns, sleeping mats, and battery-operated radios, forcing me to sleep on a wooden bed frame in the kitchen with Josélia and Maria da Boa Morte, waking up every time they lurch in their sleep, enduring their constant presence, putting up with their smell, Josélia and Maria da Boa Morte telling me without saying a word

"Angola is dead for you ma'am do you hear me Angola is dead for you ma'am"

serving me the dried fish that was left in the company store, which they hid under the firewood, the canned food that was well past its expiration date, some birds that died out by the acacia trees, every now and then a chicken that the troop overlooked, after eating I always noticed my mother in the rocking chair, setting her knitting down in the basket, pleased, holding out her hand to run her fingers along my clothes, no longer a skirt or a blouse but a length of batik cloth that used to belong to Damião, tied around my waist the way the washerwomen wear it, my mother so proud of me

"That dress looks so nice on you honey"

touching the fabric with a leisurely contentment, me young and beautiful again for a few moments, walking arm in arm with my father to the sound of the music on the tile floor in our kitchen as if walking along the arcade of the Ferroviário Club, admired by uniformed officials and men in tuxedos, admired through the lenses of the governor's glasses, which reflected the lights and the shiny decorations in tiny geometric points

"Very beautiful indeed my good sirs very beautiful"

the governor asking my father's permission to dance with me, to hold my hand in his, to put his arm around my back and in the midst of all this the whole world spun around, not just the walls, the paneled ceiling as well, the guests, the buffet table, the city, the palm trees, Africa, Josélia, Maria da Boa Morte, the wooden bed frame in the kitchen, everything, the world twirled round in the reflections of the governor's glasses, now transparent now opaque, shining in time with the shiny medals around his neck

"Very beautiful indeed my good sirs very beautiful"

the lieutenant calling me in from the doorway

"Comrade"

my mother no longer smiling, vanishing, the music stopping, the governor's been dead for ages, the Ferroviário Club was destroyed during the civil war, the universe is suddenly quite narrow, there's no gas in the generator, the fridge is ruined, all that's

left of the dishes are five or six metal dinner plates that Maria da
Boa Morte brought up from the workers' quarters, I'd love it if my
mother were still here knitting in her chair, smiling

"That dress looks so nice on you honey"

I'd ask her to wait for me

"Mother"

Josélia worried about me

"Ma'am"

the wind covering the stems in the stubble fields with dust,
breaking off the ends of the azaleas, devouring the golden rain
tree branch by branch with Clarisse's hammock still hanging from
the trunk, the lieutenant combed his hair with my comb and sat
down in front of my mirror pointing his pistol at me as though I
were a rabbit or a hare

"Where'd you hide the white policeman comrade?"

the wind blew across the top of the water tank and the flower
boxes, the cracked columns supporting the front gate, the hinges
pulling out of the wall, what was left of the tractors

(twisted sheets of metal, cylinders, a wheel)

serving as a barricade to protect them against UNITA's cannons,
Josélia wrapping the batik cloth around what used to be my neck
and is now just a bunch of wrinkled ropes hanging from my head

"Very beautiful indeed my good sirs very beautiful"

"Ma'am"

the soldiers caught Fernando along the dirt road to Chiquita,
brought him back to the plantation with his ankles bound with
liana vines, his cheekbones transformed into bluish open wounds,
his mouth turned into a bloody pulp, another wound that ripped

open his pants and went all the way down to his leg bone, Fernando on his knees on the patio, soldiers' boots stomping his body, rifle butts smashing his face, belt buckles whipping against his kidneys, the first shot fired and he shuddered, a second shot and a cloud of bats shrieked in terror out in the barren fields, thrushes flying into the clapboard walls of the store wherein rats the size of partridges panted feverishly in the shadows, a soldier wearing corporal's stripes, my husband's spats, and one of the necklaces I bought in Europe, in Paris or Bologna, which I used to hang on the knob of one of the drawers of my dressing table and which they divided among themselves amid shrieks and shouts, the soldier wearing corporal's stripes

(I remember the smell of crushed azaleas and cheap tobacco and the more distant smell of clay and spring water, of the French woman's perfume on my father's sweater when he came back from the monastery whistling and the smell of my mother when she hugged me close to her making me cry

"I'll take our little girl and leave Eduardo I swear I'll take the little girl and leave and you'll never see us again"

a perfume that was tart and sweet and hot and made the carnations in the vases quake)

the soldier wearing corporal's stripes, two red crosses stolen from one of the European soldiers during the pandemonium of their departure from Angola when the battalions shoved and elbowed their way onto the boats, walked up from behind me, pushing Josélia aside, put a cartridge belt in the machine gun and pulled the butt against his shoulder, Fernando lying awkwardly and pliant began to jolt and jolt and jolt, with red circles forming on his armpits, his stomach, his chest, and he kept jolting on the porch and flowerpots were blown apart and pieces of the wooden handrail fell silently to the ground until the soldier set the machine gun down on the edge of the water tank, Fernando landed on the ground as if kissing it, finally at rest, the setters eyed him, half out of fear, half out of hunger, the vultures, all Adam's apple and claws, walked toward him like weary turkeys, flapping their filthy wings, the troops went back into the house that had neither windows nor doors, its walls destroyed by the bazookas, the house that by three in the afternoon began to withdraw into itself, insects creeping in, their sounds echoing at night, the house a mere cube being invaded by wormseed weeds, the geese that weren't devoured by the soldiers eating the drapery sashes and the fringe on the rugs, the guard dogs lying on the blankets, the wildcats panting as they drowsed on the insulation in the attic and the edge of the bathtub, Josélia, Maria da Boa Morte, and I shrouded Fernando in cotton sacks and buried him

(three women because I'm a woman or at least I was a woman before the acid from the tin cut these wrinkles in my face, three old women with shovels and pickaxes and rakes and knives made for butchering meat that we didn't have kindly helping each other with backs bent)

next to the generator, safe or so we thought from the vultures and the setters who still greedily dug up the ground with their paws while the troops laughed at us, leaving their beer bottles on the porch steps, Maria da Boa Morte to the dogs and birds

"Scram"

and as soon as we lit the candles in the kitchen there was my mother setting aside her knitting and caressing my batik cloth with two fingers and smiling happily

"Very beautiful indeed my good sirs very beautiful"

"That dress looks so nice on you honey"

confusing it with the satins and silks from the dances in Malanje, in Luanda, back when we went to Luso to the bishop's niece's wedding, a town with a dozen or so people and a dozen or so little lanes hidden in the savanna grass on a sandy plateau, the Marine airplane brought the cake in from New Lisbon, me kissing the smooth surface of the bishop's ring and the bishop

"The devil himself created you in order to tempt me young lady"

the savannah lit up with bonfires and unpolished lamps, a chain of *quimbo* villages even poorer than the ones in the north, children with pale hair and distended stomachs, a row of Cadillacs with muslin curtains in the windows parked in front of the mission, Spanish nuns as skinny as greyhounds peeking out from the cloister, sergeants about whom Lisbon had long forgotten wasting away from amebic dysentery on a public walkway made out of cane reeds, the bishop blessing me with his thumb, which smelled like the wine cruet and consecrated oil

"No doubt about it the devil himself created you to tempt me young lady"

coming back from burying Fernando my mother stood up from the rocking chair pleased with me as if instead of the batik cloth I was wearing a bow in my hair and my dress with lamé piping

"That dress looks so nice on you honey"

we heard the government lieutenant

"Comrade"

not to Josélia or Maria da Boa Morte, to me, singling me out from the servants with unerring animal instinct, precise plantlike tropism

"Where'd you hide the white policeman comrade?"

the Cabindan who took my garden, my tractors, my thresher, my granary from me

"Where'd you hide the white policeman comrade?"

he didn't call me lady or ma'am, he called me you, *tu*

I swear

he called me comrade and *tu* as if he were one of the guests I'd invited over back in the days when we had food served to us by Damião's gloved hands and formal uniform, my father at one end of the table and my mother at the other, a fog of perfumes and cigar smoke in between the two of them, platinum-blond locks, military medals and ribbons, exposed collarbones, laughter, the antelope horns on the wall above the furnace as impressive to me as the clock on the wall that my son Carlos considered

(that I'm sure he still considers

that fool

still considers)

to be the heart of the house, the Cabindan didn't address me like an equal but as a superior would address his subordinate, the owner of this plantation in ruins to his prisoner, which I was

"Where'd you hide the white policeman comrade?"

the police chief from Malanje whom the Portuguese refused to let onto the mass of boats that were fleeing Angola, going from one pier to the next, in plainclothes, looking for a measly spot in the hold, showing his papers, faded certificates, tattered citations, useless medals, begging, arguing, bribing, jogging to the next boat down and starting to beg all over again, the government detested the police chief, UNITA detested him, the Portuguese colonists detested him for the high-percentage kickbacks he'd taken for the sale of their crops, the people detested him for dragging them from one plantation to another in cattle trucks, but I was never able to detest him because he gave me something that neither my father nor my husband ever gave me in this life

(because I'm a woman)

my father too preoccupied with his lovers and my husband too preoccupied with the fear of being the person that he was and with his whiskey

"Spiders Isilda get the spiders off of me"

brushing those imagined animals off of his pants, spiders, grasshoppers, lizards, snakes, the police chief looking for any ship that would take him, sleeping on the pier in busted china cabinets or abandoned freight containers, finally realizing that he wasn't going to get out of Angola and coming back to Baixa de Cassanje on foot with a bindle filled with his citations and a box full of his medals, keeping clear of the South Africans' armored vehicles, the military patrols, the packs of beggars who mugged people on the highway, and the scattered groups of FNLA militants with the guns they stole from the white soldiers' barracks, so that when I went down to the river one afternoon in search of any scraps of food left over in the leper colony

(by which I mean those clapboard huts knocked over on their sides with a layer of ash covering everything)

I found him curled up in a hollowed-out tree trunk in such a state that when I first saw him I thought it was a dead child with patchy gray hair on its head, interred in a colorless shirt and policeman's pants, holding a cassava root in his hand, I was able to recognize him by opening a pathway in my memory that led me back to that tall man who wore spurs on his boots, who lynched Jingas in the mango trees and who waited for me in boardinghouses in Malanje without worrying about the scandal it would cause, never discreet, never cautious, calling me over to him from the bar where he played dice with the lieutenant governor and the men from the neighboring farms

"Isilda"

oblivious to their surprise, their embarrassment, their obvious discomfort, gesturing towards his companions, defiantly at ease

"You know everybody here right Isilda"

the neighbors who were dinner guests at my house and in whose houses I had been a dinner guest saying hello to me hurriedly, anxiously, leaving and giving excuses about appointments with notaries, dentists, bank managers, business meetings, while the police chief

"Your drunk of a husband didn't give you any problems did he Isilda?"

pretending to be shocked by the insulting, hasty departure of his companions, offering them cigarettes, a light, drinks, forbidding them to leave the boardinghouse, raising his right eyebrow ever so slightly and treating me like some ghetto scum

"Isilda will wait as long as it takes for us to finish our game"

offering me a cigarette as well and a light and drinks not as though offering them to a lady but as though offering them to some hotel masseuse, getting a kick out of the uneasiness of the lieutenant governor, of my neighbors, of the customs inspectors, one of whom was a friend of my husband, another one of whom was his cousin, the police chief ordering me to blow on the dice for good luck

"Isilda will wait as long as it takes for us to finish our game"

giving the bartender a tip, slipping a couple of bills into my purse

"Buy yourself a new pair of pantyhose"

showing off the key to his room to everyone as though showing off a trophy, his companions too scared to complain about
him to Luanda or Lisbon, worried that he'd retaliate and ambush
them out in the rice paddy, boardinghouse rooms that were so
cheap that it seemed like he brought me there to insult me, as if
he wanted to humiliate some other woman or all other women
through me, and nevertheless he gave me something that neither
my father nor my husband ever gave me in this life, some sort of

(what's the word)

hope, some sort of

(it's true, don't ask me why because I can't explain it but it's true)

joy, the police chief after taking off his boots and hanging his
holster on the nail in the door

"Come here"

he could have been our servant, never our friend, a shift foreman, a telegraph operator, a clerk, never someone who would've
been our guest, just someone inferior to us whom we wouldn't
treat poorly or especially well and whom we'd pay rather poorly,
somewhere between us and the blacks or better yet somewhere
between us and the poor white people like the family of my
daughter-in-law whom I accepted because it had to do with Carlos
and I thought that I should keep quiet when it came to Carlos, it
wasn't what I wanted for him but I kept quiet, obviously a woman
I would never have allowed to marry Rui or whose brother I never
would have allowed to court Clarisse, the police chief to whom
we wouldn't have paid the slightest attention if he hadn't been the
police chief, just like we wouldn't have paid the slightest attention
to the governor or the bishop

"Come here"

wearing policeman's pants curled up inside a hollowed-out tree trunk, so curled up that I thought he was a dead child with patchy gray hair, hiding in the leper colony where he used to train the native soldiers making them toss grenades near the huts and evaluating their aim based on the number of wounded, the police chief to whom I took a chicken wing or the dregs of a can of food under my batik cloth, my heart an enormous tear that ran down my chest, me, much older than my children or my mirror suspect I am, already starting to look like a ghost to myself at the end of a hallway or in the corner of a room, waving at myself before I evaporate and head back to the tomb whose location I don't yet know, me who was terrified of leprosy as if old age weren't another form of leprosy, another kind of shame and horror, walking over to the police chief

"Your drunk of a husband didn't give you any problems did he Isilda?"

who had come back to Baixa de Cassanje to die, not to be with me, not to kill anyone or hunt anyone down, to die and to beg them to help him die so that every night I understood him a little better and I finally understood him completely when the Cabindan lieutenant asked me from the doorway, singling me out from Josélia and Maria da Boa Morte out of animalistic instinct, plantlike tropism

"Where'd you hide the white policeman comrade?"

and since I understood him I mercifully led the troops down through the mist from rock to rock and from cement ditch to cement ditch toward the filthy stench of the river, I passed by the bell, the first few huts that had toppled over, the first bits of broken housewares, the first pieces of garbage, there were no dogs or chickens around the workers' quarters, not even hyenas had the courage to traipse into it, the workers' quarters with a lone vulture or glede or falcon circling with eternal patience above the tops of the leafless tress, for the trees had fallen ill, grown skinnier, and become smaller as well, I led the troops to the edge of the water that brackish bog full of frogs and insects that were the exact same color as the sky, the exact same color as the morning, if you can really call that water, I pointed to the hollowed-out tree trunk and the child inside it with his ridiculous medals and faded certificates, then I turned back home, to what was left of my home, to the pieces of my home that the government, UNITA, South Africans, and mercenaries had allowed to remain intact and only after I entered the kitchen and lay down on the wooden bed frame did I hear the gunshot and maybe it wasn't even a gunshot, maybe it was a branch that broke from a tree, only after I pulled the blanket over me and closed my eyes did I hear the gunshot and maybe it wasn't even a gunshot maybe it was a door being slammed, some final door being slammed.

24 December 1995

When I got back home it had already stopped raining, Lena was packing a suitcase in the bedroom

"What's going on Lena?"

"Don't talk to me just do me a favor and don't talk to me"

taking her dresses out of the closet, her earrings and costume-jewelry rings out of their little basket, tripping over a shoe left in the middle of the floor, rubbing her shin after hitting it against the table, the Christmas lights on the town hall sparkled like stars from across the street, lighting up the living room, the wind changed directions and blew toward the apartment, bringing with it a gust of music from the block up the street where there's a pool hall and the movie theater, it shook the limbs of the trees and blew them towards Alcântara, Lena screwed on the lids of her facial creams and put them into a Mickey Mouse bag, she gathered up the cup on the bathroom sink and her toothbrush, which really touched me just like I was touched at the sight of the shabby teddy bear with one of its glass eyes missing, one of her childhood toys that she grabbed from the mattress and threw into a plastic bag, the teddy bear that I usually wanted to grab by the arm and toss out the window and now

(how strange)

I was starting to miss it, I bent over to get a better look at it, to run my finger along its head, thinking

"What was your name when she was a little girl what name did she secretly give you?"

thinking, angry with Lena

"Why didn't you ever sew up its belly why didn't you ever buy a new eye for it?"

thinking about a little girl hugging a stuffed animal in a tiny house near the slums, thinking that I'm an idiot and not even caring that I think I'm an idiot, the poor teddy bear terribly lonely with no one to hold it close, the teddy bear that she would toss in the trash the moment she stepped out on the street if she had the chance, if she rented a house she'd just leave out in the rain on the front porch, Lena yanked it out of my hands as she walked over to the wardrobe, putting it back in the bag, a taxi stopped on the street outside, I felt butterflies in my stomach

"My brother and sister"

I could see myself running like a fool

"I'll be right back I'll be right back"

to fish the presents out of the dumpster, straightening out the ribbons, smoothing out the wrapping paper, pausing to think while I'm looking at the stains

"They won't mind a little smudge of grease"

me as though on death row waiting for the doorbell to ring but it didn't ring, waiting for Clarisse and Rui to call out to me from the street below but they didn't call out, waiting to hear footsteps on the staircase but I didn't hear them, the taxi started to speed off towards the Tagus confused about the street numbers in Ajuda, Lena came back from the wardrobe with a heap of blouses and T-shirts pinned between her chin and chest, the wardrobe empty, the empty hangers swinging on the rod, I was going to be terribly unhappy in no time flat, all alone with my hands in my pockets in an empty apartment, having to wash the dishes, put away the silverware, vacuum the carpet, dust the shelves, take the clothes from the laundry basket down to the dry cleaner, and the apartment, instead of getting bigger, would stay the same size only without the watercolors and the vases and even uglier than before, a bachelor's apartment that would smell like a bachelor's apartment

(sour milk, stale cigarettes, the stuffing in the couch cushions)

whereas the houses of single women smell like hand soap and family, it has nothing to do with furniture, decorative trinkets, money, it has to do with the way that sadness settles in, a dead man is just a dead man, but with a dead woman you never know when she's going to sit down next to you and start a conversation, Lena lifted up her chin, opened her arms, the T-shirts and blouses spilled onto the bed like a pot of porridge being poured out and they didn't seem like her usual tacky apparel, clothes that made me embarrassed to be seen with her if we happened to go out for dinner or to the movies, I saw one or two cute shirts in there plus one or two things that I didn't even recognize at first thinking

"Must be new"

and then later I remembered that Lena had worn them for a whole week, the wind blew down another gust of music from the block up the street, let it echo among the tree branches for a second, and then blew it away, gathering the music in its arms and leaving me behind, touched by a stupid teddy bear in a bag in the doorway, I remembered that as a child, in Luanda or on the plantation, lying on the bed looking out into the darkness, listening to the darkness and the sunflower stalks that rustled and suffered in the darkness, I used to be surprised by my own name, I'd say my name

Carlos

and I was different from that name, that name wasn't me, I couldn't be that name, when people called me

Carlos

they were talking to a version of Carlos that was just the me inside them it wasn't me and it wasn't the me inside me, and if I responded to them it was someone else who responded it wasn't me it was their version of me that spoke, the me inside me kept quiet inside me and so they only ever knew their version of Carlos, they knew nothing of me and I remained a stranger, a me that was two, theirs and mine, and since mine was just mine it didn't really exist, so I called it the same thing they did

Carlos

and their Carlos didn't exist for me, I remembered that the times in Luanda or on the plantation when I lay listening to the darkness and the silence of the darkness that was filled with the suffering of the sunflowers were the only times when I really slept with me inside me, the only times when I slept with myself repeating

Carlos Carlos Carlos

until the word Carlos was purged of all connections and no longer signified anything, just a sound like that of the rustling of the mango-tree branches or the unobtrusive panting of the setters as they sleep, until the word Carlos was transformed into a skin that could be shed, not the echo of an echo but a body that had no life outside of their lives, and then I could close my eyes, escape from their darkness, their worries, their plantation, and dissolve my own me into myself while the clock, changing its rhythm, aroused the interest of the peacocks, me in the doorway to the bedroom in Ajuda

(it had stopped raining and the raindrops appeared and disappeared on the window reflecting the Christmas lights on the town hall, no longer those long streaks of rain but stationary red drops, now red now black and stationary)

"What's going on Lena?"

"Nothing's going on absolutely nothing's going on tomorrow or the day after or next week I'll be sure to come back for the Lunda masks"

the wooden faces that we brought with us from Angola, five faces bought for a song from some street vendors by the beach who foisted them on one group of people after another at the restaurant tables along the boardwalk, they crossed the street to get some shade underneath the palm trees swapping insults and cigarettes, calling out to us in a thin, chirping voice

"Mister mister"

the second my mother saw those five masks in the jeep on our way to the pier she pulled over on the Salazar highway while cannons were firing to our right and left and glared at us in incredulous indignation like we were criminals or worse than criminals, stupid

"Who brought this junk into my car?"

cannons, machine guns, noxious defoliants, napalm raining down in flames of phosphorus, us exposed on the blacktop thinking

"We're going to die here"

thinking

"A mortar's going to land on us bam and we'll all die right here"

straw huts on fire, a trail of napalm flames falling from an airplane, my mother furious grabbing at the scowling wooden faces

(roundels with no eyes and no mouth)

"Who brought this junk into my car?"

staring at the wooden masks that at that moment had become the center of the universe, us vulnerable to land mines, the whims of UNITA, some stray bullet, as if the boat would just wait beside the pier for as long as it took us to get there, Clarisse at each explosion, each gunshot

"For the love of God let's go Mother let's go"

Lena set the masks on her lap, staring at my mother

"I did"

sizing each other up with the stubbornness of buck deer

"*What's going on Lena?*"

"*Don't talk to me just do me a favor and don't talk to me*"

until she started the engine again, the jeep bouncing past the smoldering ruins of the workers' quarters, two weeks later we had barely set foot in Ajuda and my wife was already hanging the masks up on the wall in the living room, in the little cubicle that we insisted on calling the living room, facing the window that looked out on the hills of Almada and the cranes in the port, perched on the wall like birds looking out at the water, Lena when we had barely set foot here, even before cleaning out all the grime, moths, and wasp nests in the place, she unwrapped the newspaper they were packed in, as cautious as though they were some great treasure brushing off Clarisse's complaints with the back of her hand

"You've lost your mind Lena hanging that shit up in the apartment"

and then I realized

"*What's going on Lena?*"

"*Nothing's going on absolutely nothing's going on tomorrow or the day after or next week I'll be sure to come back for the Lunda masks*"

that the masks were just like her father's tiny house at the edge of the slum, built on the weekends with bricks, sand, and cement that had been taken from an abandoned construction site, a little wall around it with arabesques of exposed mortar, a cheap metal gate with posts that were painted orange at the top, copper lions with no tails on top of concrete pedestals, a small garden with a flower bed full of daffodils, the canvas chair for reading the late-edition newspapers, the relatives praying to the rosary in front of ceramic figures of the martyrs, Saint Expeditus Saint Philomena Saint Mary of Egypt Saint Engratia, relatives who dressed the same way in Africa as they used to back in icy Minho, motionless with arms outstretched like a scarecrow, the masks were just like Angola before the war sent us packing for Lisbon, the smell of the acacias in the morning, the burning diesel fuel from the trawlers, the stones and old tires weighing down the corrugated cement asbestos roof panels, the masks were the poor white people in Angola on the outskirts of the slums, I understand my mother, I understand my father, I understand my brother and sister, I've never understood Lena

"What's going on Lena?"

"Don't talk to me just do me a favor and don't talk to me"

when I was a child I'd swat at the mango trees with a stick and as the bats flew off the branches the treetops grew smaller and you could see the sky and the clouds of the Congo through them, on my grandmother's birthday the Belgians filled our entryway with suitcases and spent a whole week with us drinking with my father on the porch, hunting crocodiles in Chiquita, the men wore tailcoats to dinner and the women put their hair up in extravagant hairdos, the clock became more significant, my brother and sister and I ate in a separate room since there was no place for us at the table and one day I realized that it wasn't because there was no room at the table nor was it because of Clarisse or Rui it was for fear of the foreigners noticing that I wasn't white, that I was black just like the field hands, all we had to do was set foot on the back porch where the seated ladies were taking their tea, wearing pith helmets and riding boots, looking at us with an expression of discreet aversion on their faces, and my mother would immediately jump up from her chair and hold out her arms to hide me, telling us to play under the golden rain tree while the clock resounded with clangs the color of the priest's purple vestments and the ladies looked at us with pieces of toast between their fingers and raised eyebrows, my mother who called Clarisse or Rui over to her if they came out on the porch alone, let them stay out there, showed them off to her guests but if it was me her countenance would fall as though she had no cheekbones and she'd shoo me away hurriedly before they could see me, Lena brought the masks to Lisbon for me as well since she thinks that there's no more difference between a rich black person and a poor white person than there is between two rich whites or two poor blacks, Lena on the plantation watching Rui chase quail with his pellet gun while Clarisse was leaving for a party in Dondo in the car of some friend we'd never met and who'd never been in our house, he just honked out by the pond, my father opening drawers propping himself up against the hutch

"Dear God how the hell did I get so thirsty?"

me in the study settling accounts with the exporters and the state customs agents, calculating percentages, consulting the ledgers, checking the invoices, summoning the man in charge of the company store lost in a sea of muddled excuses

"That's not exactly what happened Mr. Carlos that's not exactly what happened"

mixing up the numbers, Lena

(I just now noticed this)

brought the masks to force me to see that I wasn't born on our land like my brother and sister were, I was born in the neighborhood

where the Cotonang workers lived or rather not even in that neighborhood, in one of the shanties on the other side of the barbed-wire
fence that belonged to the servants who took care of the cleaning,
the cafeteria, the parking garage, the air conditioning in the administrators' offices, my mother following me down the front steps pulling at my jacket

"Where are you taking the van Carlos?"

"I have a meeting with a wholesaler I'll be back tomorrow without fail"

following me as far as the porch with the same sheepish apprehension with which she used to shoo me off the back patio
before the Belgians noticed me, longing to say something but
incapable of saying anything, getting smaller in the reflection of
the rearview mirror, disappearing behind a stand of eucalyptus
trees at a curve in the road, just as the house and the plantation
then disappeared in turn, a troop of mandrills in a balsa tree, the
bridge, the Mete Lenha store, the sculpture of a colonel on top of
a column of stone where the asphalt and the cattle fence began,
the Cotonang neighborhood on the outskirts of the city was made
up of dozens of cement tenement buildings among dwarf palms,
separated and protected from the black peoples' shacks by a row
of boards that served as a fence, women carrying pots and clay
basins full of water from a fire hydrant, clapboard houses with no
gate out front being overtaken by the tall grass so much so that
the last of them were nothing more than just frames of houses or
a few corners of walls and cornices that served as shelters for barn
owls and the ones that were even farther out were covered in a
fluff of lilies, the entire place characterized by the still air of village
cemeteries, a typist wearing a visor ran his weary pencil down the

length of a column of names and pointed me toward the tenements on the left, I began to sense certain smells, I saw chairs with missing legs, sick people at death's door, and I encountered the cafeteria worker wearing an apron and a hairnet in her miserable hole of a home that reeked of the sour damp smell of poor people, a black woman just like the black women on the plantation, the same saggy breasts, the same thin arms, she didn't raise her head, didn't greet me

"Sir"

identical to Lena's masks and staring at me, just like the masks, through two hollowed-out eyes without surprise or interest, accepting the money that my mother gave her and handing it out to cousins or wasting it on beer so fast that by the end of the week the money was no longer there to prove that I'd been there before, me in the alleys of the Cotonang neighborhood hearing the bell from the administrative offices that marked five o'clock and the trucks that constantly came and went, the generator providing light for the engineers' building, the mess hall, my father much younger than when I knew him heading over to the tenement building where the cafeteria worker lived walking without anyone's help, back when my father didn't traipse around searching for whiskey bottles in all the drawers and cabinets in the house tripping over his own feet knocking over baubles

(Dear God how the hell did I get so thirsty?)

the black woman was younger then too if indeed she was ever younger than she is now, almost an adolescent, almost a little girl, my father giving her sugar, cigarettes, beer, maybe you could hear the crickets, the rustling of the tall grass, a black woman just like

the Lunda masks that peer out on the port and the hills of Almada, me taking the pipe out of her mouth, forcing her to look
me in the eye, asking her softly with anger that grew and grew but
still kept me from hitting her

"Where's your son?"

*an adolescent, a little girl I bought from her family for a price I
named because a black woman can't refuse a white man, there are
always trains heading east and people who get run over and cut to
pieces on the tracks*

"Where's your son?"

*or you could do it right there and wouldn't need the trains, just a
branch of the baobab tree to hang a rope from, or a bullet in the neck
while your friends keep smoking, not saying a word, back before I
became a drunkard, a clown, back before my wife slept with the
police chief in the study below the bedroom without trying to hide
it from me or worrying themselves about me in the least, me grabbing the neck of the bottle on the nightstand pretending that I didn't
notice, me to whom the medic showed the results from the tests on
my liver and the X-rays of my bladder that cheered me up instead of
frightening me, the medic trying to stave off my death, keep me from
vomiting blood, from developing jaundice, stomach ulcers, pains,
fevers, me contentedly imagining the blooming of the azaleas and
acacia flowers, my daughter Clarisse visiting me on Saturdays in
the house that belongs to my mother-in-law, to my wife, to my wife's
children, but doesn't belong to my son, to me, since my real house is
a hovel in the Cotonang neighborhood in Malanje that I ordered the
Jingas to build next to their hovels, my house is the still-developing
body of a little girl who doesn't look forward to my visits, she puts*

up with them, no smiles or complaints, no displeasure, no pleasure, never a single word over two years to ask me where I've been when I hadn't visited her for a month or two, I'd show up unannounced with a bottle of perfume I'd bought at the company store, pull off her dress with a hastiness that wasn't quite haste it was my sense of shame and in the midst of all this I discovered the presence of my son Carlos, his presence startled me, I felt him stirring when I touched her belly, my son Carlos

"Where are you taking the van Carlos?"

"I have a meeting with a wholesaler I'll be back tomorrow without fail"

who went to Malanje and came back from Malanje without finding out anything more than that there's a woman there who's become embalmed in her own bitter stench, my son Carlos

she said my name

Carlos

and I was different from that name, that name wasn't me, when people called me

Carlos

they were talking to a version of Carlos that was just the me inside them it wasn't me and it wasn't the me inside me, similarly it was someone else who responded to them it wasn't me who responded it was their version of me that spoke, the me inside me kept quiet inside me and so they only ever knew of their version of Carlos, they knew nothing of me and I remained a stranger, a foreigner, a me that was two, theirs and mine, and since mine was just mine it didn't really exist, so I called it the same thing they did

Carlos

my son Carlos
Carlos
all alone on Christmas eve in the apartment in Ajuda that hadn't gotten an inch bigger despite the fact that the clothes in the wardrobe were gone the Lunda masks were gone his wife was gone, my son Carlos who despised me, despised Angola, despised Africa, despised the color of his skin and the weight of his own blood, holding the letters that his mother wrote him from the plantation in his hand without reading them, without ever having read them, without even attempting to read them until the lights go out at the town hall, until the river slowly emerges in the first light of morning, without taking notice of the chimneys, the cranes, or the mulberry trees on the street below, without taking notice of the rows and rows of buildings in the city or the streets or the city squares or a field of cotton waving good-bye in the depths of his memory.

26 FEBRUARY 1986

When was it, how many years ago was it that Maria da Boa Morte stopped calling me Isilda and started calling me ma'am? I remember her grandmother wearing one of my father's pith helmets on her head, drowning in an enormous hand-me-down jacket, I don't know whose it was, I remember going into the hut they lived in and sitting on a mat eating cassava-flour porridge and dried fish, refusing the fork that her uncle the native soldier insisted on giving me, always with his eyes on the door as if his superior were going to barge in there suddenly and punish him for having me over, I remember marveling at the dirt floors, at the lack of furnishings, at the doll that I'd thrown away because it was missing an arm and no longer said

"Momma"

in that small, disconcerting, bleating voice, something, maybe a heart, rattling in her chest, me only five or six years old, extremely worried and trying to calm her down

"I'm here"

the little thing monotonously persistent

"Momma"

the doll that Maria da Boa Morte or her grandmother or the barefoot native soldier, with that standard-issue serious look on his face and a joke of a rifle slung over his shoulder, fished out of the trash and placed on top of their only table as if they were putting a sacred image on an altar, that doll named Rosarinho

Rosarinho

with its arm outstretched in an attitude of benediction on the verge of yelling

"Momma"

reproaching me for having abandoned her in the trash can

(that's what I feel most guilty about in all my life a doll in a trash can)

Maria da Boa Morte didn't notice, her grandmother didn't notice, her uncle the native soldier who would've liked to be a toy soldier didn't notice, squatting around the dried fish and porridge, Rosarinho got very upset with me

"Momma"

me wanting to hold her in my arms before we both burst into tears holding each other tight swearing that from then on we'd never be apart, I liked being in the workers' quarters better than anywhere else because everyone there obeyed me and stood up when I walked in whereas up at the house I not only had to stand up when others entered a room I had to obey everyone else but I can't remember when it was or how many years it's been since Maria da Boa Morte stopped calling me Isilda and started calling me ma'am. Back in those days even the rain was different: there were coconut palms where the tool shop and the garage stand now

(or rather where they used to stand before they were hit by UNITA mortars)

and what I listened to at nighttime in March April May wasn't the water it was the tiled roof and the leaves that suddenly came to life, thousands of little footsteps, pecks, taps, drumming fingers superimposed over the sound of the clanging clock, I listened to the humming of the generator that grew louder when the wind blew, my mother pointing at a stain on my father's shirt

"Don't tell me you weren't with the French woman Eduardo don't try and tell me that you weren't"

back then Maria da Boa Morte didn't call me ma'am she called me Isilda and wore the clothes that no longer fit me

(they didn't fit her either and were always too short but she thought they were very beautiful)

she slept in my room on a mattress beside my bed, we used to wake up to the silk-flower rustle of the bats returning to the mango trees just before daylight, we'd go down to the workers' quarters, past the hut where her grandmother, the tribal chief, the witch doctor, and the men of the village crossed themselves in front of the doll that I'd thrown in the trash, and we'd come upon my father on horseback giving orders to the foremen and then heading off to the decrepit old monastery to wait for another horse to come trotting from the plantation to the right of ours carrying that woman who spoke in a foreign tongue, covered in perfumes and smiling at him from behind the veil of her hat which concealed her entire face except for a streak of lipstick that remained visible, the woman and my father whom we spied upon from the cloister, terrified of the wildcats, the woman who looked to me like a life-size version of Rosarinho, but with two hands and more hair, on the verge of batting her eyes and saying

"Momma"

there was something loose, maybe her heart, that rattled in her chest and I couldn't understand why my mother got mad when she pointed out the stains on my father's shirt, when, with her thumb and index finger, she pulled

"Hold still"

a blond hair off his lapel, threatening to take me and leave for Malanje or Luanda, I couldn't understand how she could be so jealous of a lowly doll with a cloth body and porcelain head, running away sobbing in her delicate, hollow voice, I couldn't understand that curious hatred she had for my toys, the screams, the tears, the cursing, the tantrums, Rosarinho, before whom the tribal chief bowed and then picked her up to display her to the crowd

"Momma"

I couldn't understand the threat that I would never see my father again, behind some locked door or another with my mother who was bawling, that I would never see Maria da Boa Morte again or sleep in the same room with her listening to the rooftop and the coconut palms on rainy nights, oblivious to the clock that propelled our lives forward through time in a direction that I didn't understand but that would eventually turn us into grown-ups, me playing cards on the back porch and her sowing cassava seeds out in the field although it seemed impossible to me that we would be separated someday, that someday we'd no longer catch eels in the river together and eat chicken *muamba* stew on the straw mats, me who when I was five or six years old used to wish that I were black, so I could pick my teeth with a piece of straw, comb my hair with a wire brush, spend whole afternoons squatting on top of a big rock, looking out at Pecagranja while the months passed by inside me as slowly as the drifting fog, it seemed impossible to me that we'd ever stop being sisters, whenever a she-goat lay down with something wiggling in her womb she would flag me down wearing one of my old long-sleeve dresses that was coming apart at the seam along the waist and with sleeves that didn't even reach her elbows

"Isilda"

her grandmother in the oversize jacket called me little girl, the native soldier in his ridiculous uniform called me little girl, Maria da Boa Morte flagged me down

"Isilda"

and a tiny wet goat emerged little by little from the big goat attached to it by a cord, it started walking and shivered from the cold each leg going in its own direction, fell, got back up, scrambled blindly to find the mother's nipple, the witch doctor shook a gourd filled with seashells, the doll with the missing hand reproached me for having forgotten about her, I tried to explain to her

"I'm here"

to ask her, I don't mean recently, I don't mean today, since Rosarinho has been gone for ages, to ask her then to

"Forgive me"

just like the woman of the house has been gone for ages, replaced by the woman I am now, not knowing what to do in a house that's been invaded by the soldiers, with no flooring no roof and no place for me

"Forgive"

the house that we left behind yesterday, making our way to Chiquita, Maria da Boa Morte, Josélia, and me or rather

it should really be

me, Josélia, and Maria da Boa Morte fleeing out the back like thieves in the night before a grenade put an end to us, three shivering women putting their fingers to their lips to remind each other to keep quiet, holding onto each other like cripples or invalids, led by the light from the eyes of the owls along the trail through the rice field, we heard a gunshot but maybe it was just thunder over the Cambo River, we heard voices but maybe they were just the yelps of wild dogs chasing after a hare, until we could no longer see the stubble of the cotton field and we realized that the plantation had ceased to exist for us we would never again see the house or the azaleas or the golden rain tree, the plantation had ceased to exist and all the other plantations had ceased to exist just like ours, overrun by the army, the Cubans, the mercenaries, the corpses, the gledes, the pallid barn owls, the faded gray mules, and the overgrown grass, me, Josélia, and Maria da Boa Morte trying to make out the mango trees of Chiquita in the darkness, the silhouette of black treetops that were darker than the hillside, in search of the trail that passed through the stand of eucalyptus trees and ascended toward the village, Maria da Boa Morte

"Isilda"

handing me a jar of glowworms that we kept hidden under the sheets and which emitted a halo like the one around the phosphorescent Virgin Mary that protected my godmother from trespassers and illness, as soon as we heard her snorting as she slept the way the peacocks snorted in their sleep we gently pushed open the door and there beside her nest of white hairs was the glowing icon, we put out our hands to touch it and our fingers became transparent, Maria da Boa Morte was frightened and drew back, knocking over a footstool, knocking over a tray of medicine spilling pill boxes and syrup bottles onto the floor, my godmother jolted upright and turned on the light in search of her shawl

"Get out, you and the repulsive little black girl"

and for the first time I began to suspect that Maria da Boa Morte and I weren't equals, since my godmother hadn't called me a repulsive little black girl, hadn't looked at me with indignant disgust, I began to suspect that Maria da Boa Morte was somehow my inferior, she didn't have carpet or rugs just two or three straw mats, metal dinner plates that didn't match, a battery-operated radio with a broken antenna, and a doll presiding over all this wretchedness in its porcelain innocence, painted face, its funnel-shaped mouth calling to me in silence as it blessed the native soldier

"Momma"

and so we rarely ever saw each other after that, or rather I'd spot her or believe that I'd spotted her carrying a gunnysack, spurred along by the foreman's whistle, in the midst of all the field hands in the sunflower fields, I'd believe that I'd spotted her on Sundays in the line of people buying beer at the company store, at one point she was pregnant, at another point she had a child with her, at another point she was pregnant again, at yet another point she had an entire retinue of children with her as she walked behind a man who didn't even look at her, but seeing as we can't tell the difference between one Bailundo and another, since they all look the same, it could have been a sister or a cousin or some brute who'd just come in on the last cattle truck from New Lisbon, lined up against the wall of the store while the shift bosses counted them up, while the medic checked out their leg muscles, my father paid the driver according to the number of people and how healthy they were, the workers' quarters were expanded toward the river and as a result there were more chickens, more incense, and more flies, three hundred and fifty or four hundred at the beginning of the harvests, half that number or less than half due to dysentery once the cotton harvest was over, trucks would come up the hill from the workers' quarters with seven or eight invalids covered in blowflies in the back, the same ones who stole my house from me, my silver, my pictures, the letters my father wrote my mother when he was courting her, if I went into the living room I'd find them lying on the ground smoking, if I opened the door to the study I'd come across the Cabindan lieutenant seated at the desk as relaxed as if he owned the place, if I tried to look at myself in the mirror all I'd see would be them, never taking off their hats or asking permission for anything, rummaging through my books, ripping the old necklace my aunt gave me off my neck

"Give it"

and I was suddenly naked, unable to escape, unable to speak, just like I was on the afternoon that the police chief from Malanje undressed me at the plantation, my children were playing in the sequoia grove, Damião was setting the dinner table, the gardener was pruning the creeper vines not fifteen feet from me, a female peacock ran in front of the window in a blur of blue feathers, the police chief

"Isilda"

but as he touched me it was no longer him it was Maria da Boa Morte who said

"Isilda"

who repeated

"Isilda"

who persisted

"Isilda"

holding my arm to hurry me away from the crocodiles in the Cambo River, not out of friendship but out of selfishness, so she could still have the luxury of sleeping in my bedroom

(that sly little girl)

instead of on a tattered straw mat placed between two other straw mats and the doll bugging her all night long

"Momma"

something loose and hard rattling in its chest, the doll incessantly tormenting her with its ominous whimper

"Momma"

my children or rather Clarisse and Rui along with the one who's not my child but whom I pretended really was

no, that's not right

my three children playing among the sequoias whose flowers made a glasslike tinkling sound when they blossomed, Damião closed the silverware drawer, prancing around the table as he set out the glasses

(my three children I repeat my three children because as strange as it may seem and it seems strange to me Carlos may have been the one)

the gardener, almost directly by the window frame, fixing the stem of one of the plants, fastening a piece of cane to it for support with a piece of twine, the police chief untied his tie and held it with both hands, together with the horsewhip with which he beat the locals

"Isilda"

but it wasn't the police chief who said

"Isilda"

it was my husband, rummaging around in the sideboard table for a whiskey bottle, unable to get mad at me, unable to leave, never making a scene, never getting angry, never telling me off, never complaining

(strange as it seems he may have been the one I liked the best)

"Isilda"

but it wasn't my husband, that poor humiliated wretch, who said

"Isilda"

it was Maria da Boa Morte showing me the mango trees of Chiquita, the silhouette of the mango trees that grew along the hillside, as little girls we lived together, played together, ate together down in the workers' quarters, Maria da Boa Morte showing me the mango trees of Chiquita next to the ashes of a dry-goods store, pieces of a wall, half a dozen shanties that had been knocked down, singed blankets, a woman the same color as me who'd been dismembered lying in pieces in the rubble, encircled by a crown of carrion birds, a breeze that came from nowhere in particular and rippled the grass, a four-wheel drive Unimog truck with bent rims, the cylinders and wires from its motor ripped out like a tangled mess of intestines, the defoliants had dried up the tree trunks and the cassava plants, Maria da Boa Morte showing me Chiquita

"Isilda"

and in the midst of all this a man who was also the same color as me lay with his body contorted on a plywood board talking to himself, Clarisse used to argue with her brothers

(Carlos my son Carlos in a scrap-wood crib in Malanje reading my letters and getting terribly worried about me)

"Let me have the pellet gun for just five minutes Rui let me have the pellet gun so I can shoot a dove"

the policeman paid no attention to my kids or to me, my husband unable to reproach me hiding his whiskey bottles, the rats and spiders all over the bedroom, rats and spiders and the fear of death

"Don't let me die"

the fear of a new suit, new shoes, the coffin lid, and a shroud over his face

"Throw out those new shoes Isilda don't put them on me"

trying to stand up, reaching for the iron rails of the headboard, Carlos in the doorway to the bedroom

(Carlos my son Carlos with his brother and sister in Ajuda asking the mailman for my letters tearing open the envelopes reading

them on the landing of the staircase slowly climbing the stairs read-
ing them aloud to Clarisse and Rui getting uneasy as he rereads
them unable to call me unable to write me unable to get any news
about me if my son Carlos had stayed in Angola I'm convinced we
wouldn't have lost the plantation or the house I'm convinced that
the Americans or the Russians would apologize for the situation and
would send soldiers here to keep watch over the field hands and
would buy our sunflower and cotton)

my son Carlos in the doorway to the study trying to comprehend what was happening, the police chief buttoned his shirt with
his right hand and struck him with his left subduing him the same
way he did when he carted people off to jail, with the same vehe-
mence and contempt

"What are you doing here kid?"

the same scorn in the Cabindan lieutenant's eyes when he glared
at me yesterday in the kitchen after the old government airplanes,
old single-propeller planes flew overhead toward Luanda, limping
along like wounded partridges, the kitchen thick with shadows,
the pale night clouds drifting outside the window, my father dis-
mounting from his horse by the back patio, wearing neatly pressed
pants and English cologne as if the week were composed of seven
Sundays, younger, more agile, much more charming

"Hey little Isilda little Isilda"

the kitchen thick with the shadows that the kerosene lamp projected onto one wall and the other, filling the room with the dead,
my mother, my godmother, my grandmother, the bishop, the governor waltzing around the room with the lights reflecting in his
glasses, Rui shaking the snow-globe paperweight, the whirling

white specks we called snow, a group of uniformed officials whispering about my good looks behind my back, the Cabindan lieutenant indifferent to the presence of the uniformed officials, the bishop, the governor, my grand success at the governor's palace, a woman with no wrinkles glaring at him with the same severity I used with the servants, Josélia whom I inherited from my mother the way one inherits a couch, Maria da Boa Morte whom I brought up to the house from the workers' quarters after I got married because she was the one servant we had whose name I still remembered and she no longer called me Isilda, she called me Mrs., she called me ma'am, just a Jinga who believed that a one-armed doll was a medium for the spirits of the dead, Rosarinho, to this day I don't understand

(kids like the strangest things)

how I ever liked her back then, preening in front of the mirror back before it, not me, became old and corroded, one side of the Cabindan lieutenant's body visible in the light from the lamp, then disappearing behind the kerosene smoke

"Comrade"

reappearing as the night and the silence grew and as always happens in the silence I started to believe that it was all still there, the river, the leper colony, and the fresh running water, the Cabindan lieutenant standing next to a shackled white man, a South African or a mercenary from UNITA which had been dynamiting generators and trying to surround Luanda by approaching from Caxito, a barefoot white man with a bandaged ear and eyes that looked like my husband's whenever the spiders and rats crawled up his thighs underneath his pajamas, I started to believe that it was all still there, the river, the leper colony with the invisible bell that no one ever rang anymore, elderly lepers crawling on the ground, the owls lighting the pathway with their luminescent eyes, and I could almost hear

in my imagination

the clock that my son Carlos believed to be the heart of the house but yesterday the heart of the house was that South African or Belgian mercenary looking straight through us the way I used to stare into my wardrobe dreaming about what I'd wear to the inauguration of the movie theater, to a reception in Malanje, to the charity bingo night that raised money for victims of tuberculosis in Negaje, the Cabindan lieutenant telling us to go out on the back patio where the soldiers were making a stew of crickets and snails

"I need to use your kitchen for an interrogation comrade"

the South African

(he must have been a major judging from his stripes)

vomiting blood after a second blow from a rifle butt, the mango trees came closer and closer to us you could make out the military post and the barracks with the ensigns of various battalions painted on the wall, the first-aid station on the corner, the cots inside it, the first few deserted buildings of the workers' quarters, the first emaciated watchdogs, the first corpses, the mercenary begged for water and the Cabindan lieutenant, lacking all regard for the presence of a lady, unbuttoned his fly and urinated in the man's mouth, the crickets in the acacias chirped incessantly, I thought about my hat down in the wardrobe in the basement, about the wide brim that could conceal my wrinkles and sagging eyelids, the other guests praised my beauty in hushed tones behind my back, the police chief putting his arms around me in front of the men who played dice with him

"Come here"

some field hands hanging from the eucalyptus trees in Chiquita, one or two sergeants with no legs and no place to go holding out their hands to passersby, the government troops camped in the clearing between the stands of mangos where the native soldiers used to count up the field hands to make sure no one had run away, the government troops wearing Russian berets, with cannons, mortars, barricades, crates, bottles, sandbags, Josélia tried to find some ants for us to eat, Maria da Boa Morte guided me by the hand the way one would guide an imbecile

"Isilda"

paying close attention to the demolished shanties, the gunshots, the cutlasses, the bazookas, the fires, I kissed the smooth surface of the bishop's ring

"No doubt about it the devil himself sent you here to tempt me young lady just imagine the lengths the devil will go to in order to torment a priest"

me in Chiquita slipping in the mud, holding fast to the arm of Maria da Boa Morte, to my father's arm, a freshly cut camellia pinned to his lapel, his neatly pressed shirt, his quiet dignity, the smell of aftershave and tobacco, the two of us motioning to the government troops, a Cuban captain astonished at the sight of us while the orchestra began to play a tango, the streets of Malanje were decorated, the servants opened the door to the tent where the refreshments were served, my father or Maria da Boa Morte

"Isilda"

showing me a tiny hovel with no windows and no door, a thatched-grass roof, a torn piece of a straw mat, a piece of a broken crate that served as a toilet seat, and through the holes in the dirt walls I could see the plantation owners seated in their damask-draped chairs watching me as I walked to the center of the dance floor and danced with my father, watching me as I entered the hovel that reeked of cassava, dried blood, soot, holding Maria da Boa Morte close to me as if there were something loose and hard rattling inside my cloth body, me with porcelain fingers and a porcelain head, facial features painted over my varnished skin, coarse eyelashes on eyelids that open and shut over my glass eyes, my father or Maria da Boa Morte wrapping an arm around my waist on the waxed wood of the dance floor, out on the dirt floor or the waxed wood of the dance floor

(either one)

while the tempo of the tango gathered speed, my skirt brushed across the hardwood floor, the murky May clouds danced with us far away from the plantation owners with their cigars and silver pocket-watch chains, far away from the amputees, far away from the deserted plantation houses in Chiquita with their tall front-porch columns, Maria da Boa Morte forcing me to settle down in this shack

"Isilda"

as if death

what an absurd idea

really existed, when everyone knows that only black people die, not us, that blacks are predisposed to dying the same way they're predisposed to have kinky hair and live in poverty, they arrive from Huambo in cattle trucks with a number written in charcoal on their necks, twenty-seven, two hundred and two, forty-nine, thirteen, and then they start dropping dead before the harvest really even gets started, Maria da Boa Morte forcing me to settle down

"Isilda"

when I've got foremen waiting for me and it's time to start harvesting the sunflowers judging by all the crows that are fluttering around the fields and two weeks from now it'll be time to harvest the rice and a few more weeks from now it'll be time to harvest the cotton, the exporters' boats waiting in Luanda Bay, me in the shack in Chiquita thinking about a doll that was fished out of the trash and used to bless me in a hut in the workers' quarters down by the river, thinking about the Cotonang cafeteria worker whom I never saw again, thinking about the rain on the palm trees, the dried-up creeping vines out in the orchard, thinking that it's about time for my children to come back from the apartment in Ajuda and move into this little room with us, my mother, my husband, Damião in his white uniform, white gloves, and gold buttons, me in Chiquita standing up to greet them, offering them food, a bite of grilled lizard or a bunch of ants in the palm of my hand

"Would you like some?"

while something loose and hard rattles in their cloth bodies and I try to calm them down

"I'm here"
reassure them
"I'm here"
promise them
"I'm here"
swear to them that we'll never be separated again.

2

Every time we went to the doctor in Malanje my mother would buy me a cream cake after the appointment and then drive us back home as she dusted crumbs off my shirt and cried. When we got to the plantation she'd take out her handkerchief, dry her eyes and face, plump up her hair, put some rouge on her cheeks, and tell me in an infuriated voice

"You're all sticky from the sugar"

she'd step out of the car near the flower beds, trampling the azaleas without realizing she was trampling them, Damião still in his gray robe would take the bags out of the trunk, the generator would start up, Clarisse and Carlos would appear on the porch with the setters running all around them, hoping for candies or chocolates, my mother would walk up the stairs without paying them any attention, the door to her room would shut while my grandmother walked down the hallway using her cane like an oar

"Isilda"

my father would wipe his mouth on his sleeve and grab the newspaper, the lamps made the house look sadder, my grandmother would pat me on the shoulder and quickly pull her hand away, as if my clothes were on fire

"You're all sticky from the sugar"

a quail would wail from its perch on a cedar tree, the water tanks and the golden rain tree moaned incessantly, the medic took off my pants and laid me down on the bed

"Stick your bum up in the air little guy"

Carlos begged him

"Let me give him the injection he won't get upset if I do it Mr. Guerreiro"

my father would turn the pages of the newspaper without reading them, crossing and uncrossing his legs, my mother, mad at the world, would scurry around the kitchen bothering Fernando and pecking at Josélia, inventing incidents when she'd been disobedient, made a mistake, broken something or made a mess, my mother would get mad at all the servants so that she wouldn't start crying again, a piglet appeared on the back porch for a moment, snorting, the cashier at the company store said good-bye to the last customers of the day and closed the shutters, Clarisse sorted through the medic's bag, pulling out a catheter, a rubber bulb syringe, a tongue depressor

"Rui's really sick and is going to die isn't he Mr. Guerrero?"

I felt important since I was sick and going to die, since the medic who set broken arms and sewed up cuts came all the way from Marimba to care for me, I was proud of the doctor who wore a white jacket that looked like a royal ermine coat to me and the reflex hammer that was kind of like a bishop's crosier as he carefully shielded

(which proved that there was bad news to come)

the results of my head exam from us and then handed it to my mother with the solemnity of a final judgment

"Epilepsy ma'am"

my grandmother beaming with disgust making her way up the stairs with her cane, shaking the bun on the back of her head as she went, my father dropping pages of the newspaper, Mr. Guerreiro bursting Clarisse's bubble, since she was looking forward to the flowers and coffins and a week of mourning without having to go to school

"Unfortunately that's not the case little girl"

Fernando would fix me a special dinner, as if it was my last meal, he'd take the little bones out of the fish, serve me my food before anyone else, my mother hugging me close against her new dress after she paid Mr. Guerrero, a new dress because she was going to a birthday party at some friends' house

"Rui"

and immediately lurching away from me looking down at the pleats along her neckline in horror

"This child's got so much sugar all over him it's almost like glue"

Josélia wiped me off with a sponge and washbasin full of water, Carlos grabbed the pliers the medic used for pulling out teeth and ran off with it to try it out on the setters, the village was just a bunch of dim lights you could see through the tall grass, Santo António just a plain dotted with tiny pale fires, my father couldn't get the knot right on his necktie, the headlights on the medic's car alternately lit up the cotton to the right and left of the dirt road, white plants that looked bigger than they really were, Carlos out in the garden with the dental pliers trying to coax Adamastor and Lady into coming over to him, my father started over with his tie like I have to do on Sundays when Clarisse comes to pick me up here in Damaia and takes me to have lunch in Estoril either in her little car or her friend's huge car with the windows that go up and down at the push of a button

Carlos saying to Lena, showing her makeup pencils and cosmetics with the lids off, holding up a see-through tulle bra the way someone would display the evidence of a crime

"That slut that slut"

her friend the same age as my mother reclining on the couch with a cigarillo and a glass of gin his jowls shaking as he gripes

"Where'd you get the bright idea to bring over your pest of a brother Clarisse?"

plants on the balcony that are different from the ones in Angola, rooftops, parasols, rectangular pools, the lighthouse, the sea, the sails, Clarisse would put a chair in front of the TV, turn the TV to the sports or cartoon channels, bring me a Coca-Cola, a package of vanilla cookies, popcorn, gummy candies

"I'm going to go talk with Hermano I'll be right back"

a photo of her in a bikini

beautiful

smiling at me from the shelf on the entertainment center, a flock of forty or fifty pigeons flew round and round the palm trees outside the casino, in another photo a group of men and women were dancing in a restaurant, unlike the pigeons, the seagulls lined up on the seawall, the cartoon was about a wily cat who's trying to eat a very clever bird, a canary or a chick that bats its innocent little eyelashes and turns the cat's tricks against it, hurting the cat so badly that it has to use crutches and wears a bandage on its forehead and a cast on its leg, in a third photo Clarisse was waving from the deck of a ship arm in arm with a different friend, not Hermano, who was wearing a captain's hat, the cartoon about the cat and the bird ended and another one started about a stocky bulldog who's constantly pestered by a pint-sized terrier, more fiascos, more falls, more collisions, more bandages, more crutches, the pigeons flew from the palm trees outside the casino to the church tower, I got up to get some peanuts and cream puffs in the kitchen, through the half-open door I could see clothes on the ground, an ankle and a bare foot, a stick of incense smoking in an incense burner, one figure hovering on top of another, a series of coughs, and the despondent voice of Hermano

"Clarisse how do you expect me to be able to perform with that idiot in the living room and all the racket from the TV?"

one afternoon when I was coming back with my pellet gun from the river where I'd been shooting at the washerwomen, watching them jump, rub their skin, catch sight of me, run off toward the workers' quarters, tossing aside their washbasins and soap, I passed by the sunflower storehouse while I was tracking down a she-goat who'd been attracted by the smell of the seeds, I overheard some giggling and the sound of a struggle in there with the sacks of seeds, I swung open the wooden door and pointed my gun at what I thought were two field hands stealing from our harvest so they could sell it behind our backs to the Pakistanis at the company store, the motor on the generator hadn't started up yet so you could still hear the earth undulating with great waves of leaves and birds' wings all the way to the very edges of Angola and they weren't field hands, it was Clarisse and the accountant who my mother swore wasn't white but descended from São Tomé blacks

"Just take a look at his nose and you'll see right away"

laying in a gap between two rows of sacks, I took aim at him slowly so I wouldn't miss, a bat was shaking dust from its wings on a rafter, at the very second I pulled the trigger the accountant saw me

"Clarisse"

the pellet pierced one of the burlap sacks just inches from his throat

"Clarisse"

and all the other bats let go of the beams above us and flew out toward the lampposts in the garden, each of which had a halo of mist floating around the lightbulb, a dewy wig of light that oscillated, Lady howled at some animal or another, scraping her claws on the cement, Fernando was perched on a stepladder fixing a light socket, the Sao Tomean guy shielded himself with his elbows, Clarisse threw the gun all the way to the back of the storehouse where the rats gathered and kept watch, the accountant's jeep sped away from us up the hill, my sister straightened her blouse, brushed off her skirt

"If you promise not to say anything to Mom I'll help you find the pellet gun"

the golden rain tree and the bees whispered about this and that, Adamastor joined in with Lady growling at the owls, Carlos must have been in the kitchen chatting with the servants, I felt like running back home, lying down on my bed, sitting on someone's lap

"Where'd you get the bright idea to bring over your pest of a brother Clarisse?"

and then it was time for dinner, my father looking at the sideboard table full of whiskey bottles, my mother catching his eye and giving him a reproachful look, my grandmother seated to the right of my father without looking at the bottles or reproaching anybody concentrating on counting the drops of her blood-pressure medicine, she squeezed her little contraption and fifteen drops fell into her glass while all of us, frozen, counted them in our heads one two three four five six seven eight in a silent chorus, all of us watching her drink it, grimacing the same way she did as if we were drinking it along with her and could taste the acidity and feel its effects, my mother changing her expression and putting down her fork

"Why you've even got sunflower seeds in your hair Clarisse where have you been?"

picking leaves, grains, and pieces of lint off her back, putting on her glasses to examine a hem that had come unstitched, looking closely at a red mark on her neck

"Where have you been Clarisse?"

the clock cleared its throat, gave off the impression that it was rolling up its sleeves like an orator preparing to speak, then gave a speech made up of a bunch of slow clangs, my father sneaked a sip of whiskey and became relaxed and gentle and all of a sudden Carlos's voice

("That slut that slut")

not accusatory or hostile, as if he wanted to ease my mother's
mind and keep her from being deceived

"At the storehouse with the Sao Tomean guy I saw them go in
there in the middle of the afternoon"

plants on the balcony in Estoril that are different from the ones
in Angola, rooftops, parasols, rectangular pools, the lighthouse on
the little island

(I like that little island, I could take my pellet gun, stay out there)

the sea, the sails, the motionless seagulls with their profiles to
me on the seawall like targets in a carnival game and me, unfortunately, without my gun, I bet the people on the beach would love
to watch the seagulls plop over into the sand, I bet they'd look up
here and they wouldn't see anybody among the creeping vines or
in the windows of the buildings, a guy carrying a cooler with a
strap on his shoulder was selling ice cream and cookies from umbrella to umbrella on the beach

"Gross you're all sticky go wash your hands"

Hermano came back to the couch in socks and with his shirt
untucked, looking ten years older than he did an hour earlier,
he grabbed his cigarillo from the ashtray, tried to light it with a
table lighter that was shaped like the Eiffel Tower but there was
no flame, just the sparks from the flint gleaming in vain, since I
naturally have good manners I politely offered to help

"Give it here"

he grumbled at me to change the channel, Clarisse came out of
the bedroom brushing her hair with a hairbrush that could have
belonged to a princess out of a fairy tale, with gems on it and everything, while Hermano, furious

"Nothing's working right in my bullshit life today"
threw the cigarillo across the room and glared at me angrily
as if I had purposely ruined the whole universe in order to humiliate him, Clarisse, afraid he'd have a heart attack, cuddled up
to him on the arm of the couch and started nibbling on his ear-
lobe, which was always much easier than calling an ambulance,
not to mention the wife the embarrassment the phone calls the
magazines, member of parliament suffers heart attack at lover's
apartment, I pushed the button on the remote control and the
cartoons were replaced by a struggle between two monstrous
Japanese men, trying to push each other out of a circle made of
flower petals and grains of rice, where a guy in a kimono tied at
the waist and who's a tenth of the weight of one of the wrestlers
waved about a lacquered fan, Clarisse winking at me over the top
of the head of the member of parliament, who had come to grips
with his troubles, squeezing

*"A slut I can't think of any other word to describe you except slut
I can't bear to have a common slut turning my house into a brothel
a woman with the same blood as mine running through her veins
insulting the memory of her father"*

*"At least I'm not black like you I'm a normal white person if Mother
hadn't bought you in Malanje you could have been my servant"*

who had come to grips with his troubles
(the pigeons were closer now flying in circles above the hillside)
squeezing her thigh with his hand
"You naughty little thing"
the pigeons flying out of sight towards São Domingos de Rana
or Alcoitão so they can sleep in the fields of olive trees, I never saw

an olive tree in Africa, tiny and lead-colored, with branches that were twisted by arthritis, the two Japanese men who looked like my grandmother's Buddha, which was just a big smile perched on a mount of fat in rolls, continued their struggle as stubborn as a couple of ivory elephants, Hermano

"Go get my jacket from the room young man"

opened his wallet and left a few bills between the glass tabletop

(*"Don't you insult me don't change the subject who were you with last night until five in the morning you slut?"*)

and a nickel-plated statue of a shark and on the next Sunday Hermano was there again or maybe a cousin of Hermano, the same age, the same clothes, the same cough that turned them both red and teary-eyed whenever their spit went down the wrong pipe, the two of us slapping them on the back, the guys with hoarse voices and watery eyes, fidgeting with their ring fingers, sometimes there were two bands on their fingers, sometimes one band and one ring covered in gemstones

"Thanks, I think it's over"

(*"In the storehouse with the Sao Tomean guy I saw them go in there in the middle of the afternoon"*)

ash-colored fields full of olive trees, balsa trees, crumbling walls, wild doves that you can spot more easily by watching the grass that shakes when they walk through it than by actually seeing their bodies, in Damaia I have the market and the movie theater, the director sitting behind a desk full of paperwork and bills telling me that Carlos invited me to spend Christmas with him in Ajuda

"Your brother, that thief, who I would have taken to court ages ago if it weren't for the respect I have for Dona Clarisse"

("In the storehouse with the Sao Tomean guy")

"who's on time with the monthly payments"

In Damaia I have the pastry shop full of retirees, with all the trophies and pennants from the soccer teams on a shelf in the display case, where I watch them play dominoes after dinner, after my epilepsy checkup at the hospital

("Do you wet yourself during your attacks after you've blacked out?")

where they prescribe pills for me, which I never take because the director of the home thinks they're too expensive, if I just eat well and keep my mind off Africa I get by just fine, it's not an illness at all, fainting isn't an illness, everyone faints, it's just a daydream, nothing that a rich girlfriend couldn't fix, why don't you find yourself a little lady here in Damaia, not a gold digger, one of those women who are only out to get nice things at our expense, but an honest young lady, someone like Dona Clarisse for example, someone with that same kindness, that same lack of vanity, the same elegance, I just can't understand why your swindler brother holds such a grudge against her, or rather I know exactly why, he's jealous, when a person doesn't get anywhere in life he gets jealous of others

in the storehouse with the Sao Tomean accountant, I saw them go in there in the middle of the afternoon, my mother put her glasses in their case, put her case in her purse, put her purse on the floor by one of the table legs, my father shrank down into his pajamas, his little girl, the sharpest, most beautiful little girl, whose absence he wouldn't be able to bear if she ever got married, whenever she paid him a visit while he was bedridden his pain would disappear, he'd sit and talk with her, they'd take a walk around the farm, he'd start to make plans again, planning trips, noticing the cotton, calling out to the foremen, promising not to drink anymore, stupid whiskey, take the whiskey bottle out of the drawer and throw it out I don't need whiskey at all, my mother as calm as if she were dead, picking the napkin up off the tablecloth and folding it on her lap, motioning to Damião to serve the food

"You were in the storehouse with the accountant Clarisse?"

not shocked, not angry, not sad, my grandmother raising a handkerchief to her mouth

"Not a Sao Tomean it can't be I don't believe it"

because there couldn't be a second mulatto in the family, never, even with Carlos, whom no one thought of as a mulatto, who didn't look like a mulatto, my grandmother would completely shrink away from him when he kissed her, she'd sniff her clothes, disgusted that she smelled like the workers' huts, and take out her bottle of perfume, she never gave him presents on Christmas like she did with my sister and me, she avoided him, she pretended not to hear him when he spoke to her, my grandmother, to whom the Africans weren't just a different race, they were a completely different zoological species who were able to imitate people up to a certain point, but who still thank God bore no relation to us, it's obvious just look at what they eat, they even eat cockroaches, just look at how they walk, look at how they carry their babies, just like baboons, my grandmother crying out in anguish the way she would years later with the priest standing over her, the priest looking like a witch doctor but without the face paint and feathers, tracing crosses on her forehead and muttering the words to some polka in Latin, my grandmother looked at Carlos as though he was nothing but a liar, those thieving mulattoes, repulsive, *dirty, why did you bring him here from Malanje, why didn't you just leave him in the village to starve to death like he should have so we could get him off our hands*

"It's not possible I can't believe it a Sao Tomean I refuse to believe it I don't believe it"

Damião took away the roast and brought out dessert, fruit, coffee, my mother asking about this or that, excited, smiling, ordering the servants around, locking herself in the study then to make a phone call to Malanje, you couldn't hear her voice you could only hear my father struggling to open the drawers, the sound of the generator, the sound of someone crying out at the workers' quarters, the sound of the river whenever a crocodile, whenever a fish, whenever the burbling muddy water, whenever a little goat slipped on the rocks

the director of the home sitting behind a desk full of paperwork and bills telling me that your brother, the thief, what nerve, that guy's got a lot of nerve, invited you after all these years to spend Christmas with him in Ajuda, he must want to steal your inheritance or take all your money or something, the employees of the movie theater perched on a stepladder to put up new posters out front, replacing the picture of a blond actress with one of a dark-haired actress, who's much less attractive than Clarisse, caressing a man with curly hair and a mustache, who's much more attractive than Hermano, the domino players abandoned the pastry shop, one of them used to use a crutch with an arm pad that had been reinforced with medical tape

my mother came back from the phone as calm as the sea at low tide, she settled down in the armchair, picked up her basket of yarn and needles, the azaleas rebelled with loud voices, the bodies of the dead dissolved in the dirt in Angola, one time on a judge's orders they exhumed a corpse in the cemetery one town over from ours, but there was no corpse, the coffin was still varnished and intact, the metal parts were still shiny, the satin lining was flawless, the handles didn't even need to be cleaned, but there was no dead body inside, no trace of it, no bones, no scrap of cloth, Josélia said that right after the dead are buried they leave the tomb and walk through the petunia fields, she said that if you peek out the bedroom window you can see them by the water tank sipping water and lichen out of their cupped hands, Carlos said

that's a lie

Josélia said

if you don't believe me then open up my coffin after I die

Fernando was shooing a peacock out of the kitchen with a broom, I never shot pellets at the peacocks or geese because I was afraid of their screams, which sounded like the screams of living people, and because my mother would spank me, Carlos said

I can't open your coffin after you die because you're black and blacks aren't buried in coffins they're just buried in the cotton fields on top of a wooden plank and that's it

and Josélia said

if blacks were buried in the cotton fields and never came back to wander around the workers' quarters the color of the cotton would change

Carlos said

and who says it doesn't change there's lots of black cotton it's just that it's worthless and the Americans and the Swedes won't buy it *from us the same way nobody except us ever buys a black person what good would it be to have a black person in Sweden*

my grandmother walked through the kitchen to sneak a spoonful of jelly and said, as she scooped some jelly out of the jar with her spoon

what good is a black person anywhere at all except for insulting us and stealing from us

a week later Clarisse had started to get distressed, impatient, she wouldn't eat, she was mean to everyone, walking out to the front gate sometimes, or peering into the storehouse, asking the mailman questions, interrogating the brokers that came to the farm, making phone calls with her mouth so close to the receiver that we couldn't hear her, turning down invitations to parties or to take a spin in someone's car, my mother watching her from behind her crochet with a look of satisfaction on her face, my father

"Clarisse"

and Clarisse pushing his arm away

"Let go of me"

without worrying that my father would lose his balance and knock over a bottle or a glass or the flower vases where he hid his whiskey, one afternoon when my father couldn't get out of bed, my mother and the police chief locked themselves in the study and the threshers bounced along the rows out in the fields, Clarisse came in on the ground floor with a telegram in her hand pounding her fist on the door over and over

"You had him killed it says so right here you murderers"

Carlos standing on the steps leading out to the garden with his mouth wide open, the curtains producing a gust of wind that would then blow through the orchard, the UNITA soldiers setting fire to

the workers' huts, we could see the flames but we didn't hear a single
scream, just ashes floating through the air, the smell of burnt wood,
burnt flesh, burnt trash, like when you light a scrap heap on fire, my
grandmother looking for her rosary, Carlos standing on the steps
leading out to the garden, Clarisse

"It says so right here you murderers"

not to mention the hypocrisy of it, what nerve, it really takes a
lot of nerve

the door to the study swinging open, the police chief with the
jacket of his uniform unbuttoned, grabbing Clarisse, my mother
in the tone of voice she used to scold us when we were little if we
brought a grasshopper or a beetle onto the patio or if we snuck a bite
of dessert before the guests came

"Clarisse"

the sound of footsteps in the bedroom upstairs, my father propped
up against the handrail at the top of the stairs, his fingers brushing
back his hair, making it even more disheveled, his potbelly supported
by two spindly thighs, his lips trying to form a word of comfort that
never left his mouth

father my father my dead father buried in Dondo, the medic
checking for breath with a piece of a mirror and my father's toothy
smile, it wasn't a grimace, it wasn't a look of fear, it was a smile,
Carlos covered his face with a handkerchief and took off running
past the flower beds, Christmas at your swindler brother's house
in Ajuda, it must be some inheritance, must be for some money,
his wife's name is Lena and she treated me well

Carlos

the police chief letting Clarisse go when he saw my father, his pa-
jamas, his slippers, not really slippers, but what was left of a pair of

slippers, two pieces of tattered cloth full of holes, his unshaved face, his shortsightedness, feeling his way down the stairs with his finger- nails running along the wallpaper, my father beside Clarisse, facing the study, that poor devil as Carlos used to say, that old scarecrow as Carlos used to say

Carlos, my brother Carlos

Carlos

that defenseless old fool thinking he was capable of protecting his daughter, of keeping them from doing her harm or hurting her feel- ings, calling out her name, kissing her, holding her hand, walking side by side with her, almost proud, can you believe it, almost happy, consoling each other out of what seemed to be affection, out of what seemed to be love, walking towards the leper colony from which

as Carlos used to say

creatures as worthless and idiotic and weak as those two should never have returned.

1 SEPTEMBER 1987

One afternoon soon after we brought Carlos home from Malanje, I was sitting on the terrace with my husband, Amadeu was reading a newspaper from Lisbon that the mailman delivered a month after it was published and I was pregnant with Clarisse, waiting for night to fall, wishing it was already nighttime so that I wouldn't be bothered by a single voice, a single presence, alone on my bed with the pendulum of the clock swinging in the nothingness, the branches from the golden rain tree projected through the window onto the carpet, the hinges on the gate squeaking in time with the wind, the gledes disappearing into the forest, my husband set down the newspaper on the edge of the half-wall of the balcony and looked at me, the edges of the pages fluttered, begging me

"Pick me up"

and at that moment Clarisse moved around in my belly, I took the wedding ring off my finger, threw it into the flower beds below, the grass and the creeping vines that nobody ever trimmed, I saw the white glimmer of the ring and became furious, Clarisse moved around inside my belly again and I became furious with her as well, regretting that I hadn't listened to my parents and stayed put in my spouseless bedroom, with the body of a fifteen-year-old, balanced between two parts of life, free of the weight of Clarisse who was growing inside me but never belonged to me, free of the blood of some stranger mixed with my blood, I could stay in my room, go for a ride on my horse, run the plantation, sell the harvests, argue with the exporters, and at the same time my mother was lying on the couch in the living room with the shades drawn and a damp towel on her forehead, Josélia preparing her herbal tea, sometimes threatening to leave and at other times begging us to let her die in peace

"I'm in your way here one of these days I swear I'm going to get up walk down to the workers' quarters and throw myself in the river"

a minute later she'd set the towel aside and leave Josélia standing in front of the empty couch with the tea in her hand, she'd go upstairs stomping around above our heads, turning on faucets, swinging open doors, rummaging around in drawers, and I'd think

"She's going to find the revolver and put a bullet through her chest"

I'd walk over to the staircase

"Mother"

my father would relax with a game of solitaire at the card table in times past, far away from the drama, the corpse, the blood, the last words spoken by pale lips, and while he played my mother appeared in the doorway, beaming, one of her hands on her waist and the other fine-tuning her coiffed hair with the quick little gestures of a turtledove, walking over to us slowly, haughtily, hovering around my father like a planet, holding his face between her hands and shaking her head to show off her earrings at the very moment that he moved one of the jacks to a different spot

"Aren't I still attractive Eduardo aren't you still attracted to me?"

the thrushes on the branches of the cedars watching us with that air of insulted idiocy that large birds have, Fernando walked across the garden with a can of gasoline for the generator, my father chewed on the corner of the jack, torn between a queen of spades that would open up one of the rows and a queen of clubs that wouldn't open up anything, but would free up an ace

"Of course I still do my dear"

her suede shoes, the gemstones in her earrings matching the ones in her necklace, the ring with a coat of arms on it that my father promised he'd ordered from a catalog and was custom-made by a jeweler in Benguela, the lavender water that a friend had brought from Europe, the fake beauty mark on her cheek, the lipstick that bled beyond the outline of her lips, my mother grateful, sneaking glances at me as though she'd defeated me

(I felt sorry for you Mother for as far back as I can remember you I've felt sorry for you so foolish ridiculous melodramatic)

leaning over my father and kissing his neck, suddenly noticing how she could finish his game, forgetting about the kiss, moving the victorious cards around faster and faster, transforming the whole deck into four piles arranged by suit deuce trey four five six defeating him as well

"You didn't see any of those moves Eduardo"

and him desperately trying to stop her from moving the cards

"This is my hand of solitaire don't you dare mess with it it's my game"

my father who detested it when someone read over his shoulder or solved his crossword puzzles

"Nine across river in France Seine what are you waiting for write down Seine seven down to rob to pilfer I've never seen anyone so slow give me the pencil you're getting on my nerves"

she'd yank it from his hand, fill in Seine, to pilfer, the lightbulbs in the lamps grew brighter, like gleaming apples, revealing a frayed Arraiolos needlework rug that I hadn't noticed, an insect on the wall, flaws in the varnish on a part of the molding, a piece of cardboard wedged under the foot of the wardrobe, my father standing up from his chair ready to strangle her, my mother running out of energy, kicking off her shoes, taking off her clip-on earrings which were pinching her, developing wrinkles, her back hunched over, slumping down onto the couch, asking for a damp towel, ordering Josélia to draw the shades and bring her an herbal tea, begging us to let her die in peace

"I'm in your way here one of these days I swear I'm going to get up walk down to the workers' quarters and throw myself in the river"

the thrushes on the branches of the cedars with that air of insulted idiocy that large birds have, Fernando walked across the
garden on his way back from the generator any day now one of the
tribal chiefs would come knocking at our door, the whole village
would be at the river's edge, the foreman and the tractor driver
would pull something out of the water with a rake and we'd spot
a corpse wearing a gemstone necklace and a ring with a fake coat
of arms

*(but in the end it didn't happen that way Mother, you spent years
prancing around the house turning all the pictures of my father toward the wall*

*"I'm going to pull one over on your friend the French woman you
bastard I'm going to raise a scandal with her husband"*

on your deathbed asking me to put on my blue hat

"You look so beautiful Isilda"

you could have almost liked me if it weren't for my first son

"Holy Mary why do we have this mulatto child living with us?"

*you could have almost been happy with your diets, your drops of
blood-pressure medicine, and the earrings that we buried you in so
you could seduce my father under the ground)*

the foreman and the tractor driver using rakes to pull a body
out of the water that was wearing a gemstone necklace and a ring
with a coat of arms, a face staring at us from the mossy water
frozen in an expression of pure terror. Thus one afternoon soon
after we brought Carlos home from Malanje, I was sitting on the
terrace with my husband, Amadeu was reading a newspaper from
Lisbon that the mailman delivered a month after it was published,
crumpled and missing its postal wrapping, with pages cut and torn

out by the censor in Luanda, the shadow of the golden rain tree on the tiles, the leaves wasting away as though they were in a stagnant lake, I was pregnant with Clarisse, waiting for night to fall, wishing it was nighttime already so that I wouldn't be bothered by a single voice, a single presence, alone on my bed with the little fires in the forest shining through the windowpanes, the pendulum of the clock ceased its unvarying monologue, yes no, yes no, yes no, a pause, a rattling sound from inside the case, a succession of clangs, a breath, a change in the rhythm, no yes, no yes, no yes, and in the midst of all this my mother appeared on the porch with an empty suitcase and an ancient umbrella, who knows where she dug that thing up, its ribs dangling in pieces

"Since your shameless father doesn't want to go I'm leaving with Josélia because I need her to cook for me in Moçâmedes"

Josélia wearing a dress for the first time, wearing sandals for the first time, walking behind my mother like a gosling, with her own empty suitcase and an even older umbrella, just two or three feet of decorative fabric sloppily glued to wire rods, a new batch of field hands had arrived from Huambo the week before and they were all putting up new huts in the village, carrying clay bricks, dry grass, sticks, poles, Maria da Boa Morte who never mentioned the doll or showed any signs of knowing who I was and who now called me

"Mrs."

or

"Ma'am"

was rattling pans around in the kitchen, the foremen handed out sickles, burlap bags, a plate, and an aluminum mug for each shift boss, my shameless father who didn't want to go and who burst through the door to the study and rushed straight over to my mother

"Where did you hide all my crossword puzzle books Eunice the ones that came from Portugal the day before yesterday?"

my mother turned toward him, her eyebrows raised with the hauteur of a queen in exile

"I burned them"

and it wasn't just the games of solitaire and the crossword puzzles

(the acacias, I just remembered the acacias, the pollen in my hair, on my fingertips, on the mirrors, waking up in the morning with hundreds and hundreds of little yellow dots throughout the room, I remember the scent of verbena during the rainy season, even here in Chiquita I can remember the scent of verbena, when I was little I would break off a stalk of it and rub it on my back where there should have been a pair of wings and I felt

it might seem stupid but I felt

like I could jump off the ground and fly like the flamingos and the toucans but above all I remember the acacias, there's not a day that goes by that I don't remember the acacias and the river that shattered mirror which reflected my face back to me in crooked fragments pieced together in an arbitrary, incongruous order)

it wasn't just the games of solitaire and the crossword puzzles, it was my father starting to tell a story and my mother interrupting him

"You're so slow"

and finishing the story, my father starting to recount an anecdote and my mother

"That's ancient history"

changing the subject, me grabbing her by the arm

"Where do you think you and Josélia are going to go in Moçâmedes you must be out of your mind"

an arm that was barely there inside her sleeve, the damp smell of mildew from the suitcase, the pauper's umbrella, Josélia in a state of submissive stupefaction ready to follow my mother to the south pole in the back of a pickup truck even though all those clasps and zippers on her dress bothered her, Moçâmedes where my mother didn't know a single soul except for her own family, a row of corpses that might very well hear her out although it was unlikely that they'd respond from under the weight of the crosses at the head of their graves, my mother walking through the streets of Moçâmedes underneath her parasol talking to the façades of the buildings, conversing with the dead

"Hello Uncle hello Aunty"

with a little luck perhaps she'd find a palm tree against which she could lean back and fall asleep, with a little luck perhaps they'd diagnose her as insane and admit her into a hospital, if in fact they have hospitals in the desert, all I remember about Moçâmedes are a bunch of naked brutes with pieces of wood stuck through their noses, sand and more sand, not even any dunes, just sand, a tiny stretch of coastline, old women whom my mother kissed and forced me to kiss as well, taking in the fresh afternoon air beside the ceramic columns on the porch, the head of a lion stuffed and mounted, a cousin who'd been a quartermaster in the army and had fought against Gungunhana in Mozambique

(so they said)

showing me his collection of faded and tattered postage stamps from Italy and France, my mother walking down the streets of Moçâmedes with her parasol

"Hello Uncle hello Aunty"

positive that the dead would reply to her, that something aside from the sea itself would talk to her

(just like the clock, yes no, yes no, yes no)

the sea, which never spoke to anyone, the selfishness of the sea always made me mad, with its incessant monosyllable

"I"

in every wave, every foamy band of surf, every little echo in every conch shell

"I I I I I"

my mother and Josélia going in and out of homes with ceramic columns on the front porch, rummaging through steamer trunks, herbariums, purple postage stamps, moldy crackers, bodies of dead beetles, ghosts with eyes wide open taking in the fresh afternoon air in canvas chairs, a dusty, mournful gentleness to everything, the quaking of the wistful curtains, women in long cloaks with bonnets and guys in bowler hats roasting in the heat, blending in with the crowd in the streets on Sundays accompanied by their servants who carried trays of lemonade and plates of cookies, the first car ever in Moçâmedes

and I bet it was just a little lunch box with wheels

belonged to my mother's father

"The first car ever in Moçâmedes belonged to your grandfather Isilda"

my mother neglected to mention that the little lunch box on wheels only went about two hundred yards before it broke down, spurting oil, catastrophic mechanical failure, the radiator boiling over, screws sent flying, one of the front wheels, as wide as a bicycle wheel with the same tires and spokes, was blown off in the euphoria of the explosion and is still slowly disintegrating up in the top branches of a tree, piquing the interest of the birds, my mother and Josélia with their empty suitcases and their skeletal umbrellas quick to cross themselves as they face the ruins of the car crumbling to dust in the sun

(a crooked crank, a rusty fender, a Medusa of wires)

as if they were facing my father's mausoleum, my mother and Josélia

me grabbing an almost nonexistent arm

"To Moçâmedes you must be out of your mind"

positive that the guys in bowler hats and the aunties in long cloaks were still living there, pounding away on out-of-tune pianos, gluing postage stamps into albums, losing track of time on calendars whose pages no longer turn

"At least my family appreciates us that's right they treat me with respect"

my mother and Josélia in Malanje waiting for a bus that didn't exist or crawling into a cavernous, broken-down train car at the station, a train coach from a century before, so old that it has the feel of a carriage, overrun by the tall grass, trees outside the windows, roofs and telephone poles that would never disappear in the distance, my mother and Josélia thinking they can hear the chugging of the locomotive and the rattling of the rails, thinking they can make out the sound of the train whistle that used to terrify me when I heard it in the middle of the night, it was like a human scream, a bloody wail, my mother and Josélia looking out the window for flag stops that weren't there, the skeleton of a bridge spanning a river, my mother and Josélia in Moçâmedes without ever having left Malanje, searching for the palm trees, the homes with ceramic columns on the porches, and the quartermaster who fought against Gungunhana, in the cafés, ringing doorbells, opening doors, greeting people on the sidewalks of the town square who look at them with derisive grins

"Hello Uncle"

my mother and Josélia with their empty suitcases and upraised umbrellas, me with Clarisse in my belly, infuriated with her, infuriated with my husband because of her, the Cotonang cafeteria worker, the son who wasn't mine even though I'd bought him, the son who was mine because I'd bought him

(Carlos, my son Carlos, the scent of verbena)

my son Carlos in Ajuda asking after me, leaving for Angola so he can take me back with him, my mother's arm as rail thin as Josélia's

"To Moçâmedes you must be out of your mind"

Carlos here in Chiquita with me, not Clarisse, not Rui, Carlos, paying little attention to Maria da Boa Morte, I never understood why he liked her so much, why he preferred her, Carlos paying complete attention to me

"Come here"

my father incensed about the loss of his crossword puzzles, the stories that she never let him finish, the anecdotes that made him beam as he started them but which he never managed to finish, the games of solitaire that she solved for him in a split second, he who allowed himself to cheat three times during a single hand, to no avail, claiming that cheating three times wasn't really cheating, it was a constructive collaboration with fate, it was the duty of a gentleman to lend luck a helping hand whenever it stood in need of it, my father whispering in my ear with a note of hope

"If only she'd leave and make it quick"

and a foretaste of being a happy widower, left in peace with his deck of cards, his rivers in France, his synonyms of to rob, my father lending luck a helping hand by sneaking a peek at the answer key on the penultimate page

"I promise I didn't see anything my sweet girl I didn't see anything"

putting the pencil in his mouth and pretending to think hard, pretending to figure out the answer, trying to prove his skill to me jotting down Seine for nine across, to pilfer for seven down

"I could do this with one hand tied behind my back why would I need to look at the answers"

(father)

sitting on the terrace with my husband, Amadeu reading a newspaper from Lisbon that the mailman delivered a month after it was published, me pregnant with Clarisse wishing it was already nighttime so that I wouldn't be bothered by a single voice, a single presence, alone on my bed with the branches from the golden rain tree projected through the window onto the carpet, the hinges on the gate squeaking in time with the wind, my husband set down the newspaper on the edge of the half-wall of the balcony and looked at me and when he looked at me Clarisse moved around in my belly, I took the wedding ring off my finger, threw it into the flower beds below, the grass and the creeping vines that nobody ever trimmed, I saw the white glimmer of the ring and got angry, Clarisse moved around inside my belly again and I got angry with her as well, me, fat, swollen, deformed, my mother appeared at my side, happy, proud

(the scent of verbena, I remember the scent of verbena and the scents of other plants, linden trees, lemon verbena, basil, chamomile)

one of her hands on her waist and other fine-tuning her coiffed hair with the quick little gestures of a turtledove

(the acacias the scent of verbena my dead father Carlos my son Carlos Rosarinho Carlos)

shaking her head to show off her earrings

"Nine across Seine aren't I still attractive six down to pilfer aren't they still attracted to me."

Sometimes at night the trains wake me up. It's not my housemates having seizures, not the little boy they tie to the bed after dinner screaming for a glass of water, not the orderly who goes from room to room and leans over the beds

"Hurry up let me know you're still alive so my boss doesn't fire me"

until we groan and she's satified, not the Cape Verdeans from the slums getting into drunken arguments on the street outside the bar, it's the trains that wake me up. The train whistle floats down from the station to ask how I'm doing, it comes looking for me, passing through abandoned mansions and courtyards, passing through streets, town squares, the gypsy market, the fire station, knocking on the wrong doors, apologizing, turning around and then coming back again

"Rui"

creeping up to the building and whirling around in the entry-way, climbing the steps, hesitating at the doormat, peering at the canopy over the entryway, the kitchen, eventually finding me

"Rui"

like my mother would say whenever they told her that I'd had one of my fits, unbuttoning my collar, holding my head up, making me drink some water, me coming to my senses down on the rug where you're surrounded by the little tufts of fabric, which we never even notice from up above, chipped chair legs, and piles of dust and dirt that the servants, instead of vacuuming up

("It's the principle of least effort"

said my mother angrily and my father replied

"The principle of least effort what an odd expression")

just swept under the furniture, my mother pinching my cheeks

"Rui"

me without the least desire to get up, fascinated by a world made up of talking shoes and ankles, the stray threads of rugs, the smell of wax and dried mud, cracks in the ceiling above, cockroaches scurrying across the floor, a whole universe at ground level where you can find pencil stumps, coins that blend in with the color of the floorboards, burnt matches, little pieces of paper, a scurrying infantry of ants, me with my ear against the ground listening to water flowing through the pipes and the sounds from the earthen basement, the grass, the sedge, the roots of the trees, to the house below the house, my mother convinced that I'd died

"Rui"

just like the whistle of the train on its way to Sintra, on its way to Lisbon, away from all the streets and plazas in Damaia, in relief against a background of docile pine trees, she thought that I'd died

"Rui"

the train arriving at Amadora or Benefica, at stations where the glow from the lamps makes the cement platforms look enormous, the whistle right next to my bed, sounding apprehensive

"Rui"

headlights shining through the window, lighting up the wall, moving from the wall to the rosettes on the ceiling, from the rosettes on the ceiling to shiny sheets of metal and then evaporating, the little boy tied to the headboard like the goats we used for hunting, tied to a stake in order to attract cheetahs, screaming for a glass of water, the orderly tired of gamboling from room to room

"You've already proven that you're still alive now shut your little eyes and get to sleep"

fragments of boleros wafted over from the dance club at the end of the street, the owner of the bar yelled at the Cape Verdeans, threatening them with a cudgel, someone on the third floor above me flushed the toilet, sending me down through the sewers and out to the Tagus through tunnels where the wailings of rats and echoes resounded, my father looked at me from under the arch on the patio without coming near me, unable to hold me, to bring me back

"How's Rui doing now tell me how's Rui doing now?"

the fragments of boleros slowly getting softer, replaced by the rustling of the sunflowers, the rain on the eucalyptus tree and the oilskin tarp on the generator, knocking the creeping vines loose from their moorings, extinguishing the light of the lantern on the porch, a wet bird taking flight from the porch, bumping into the flowerpots, me suddenly important, set down in the big armchair like a little viscount, my mother and my grandmother straightening my shirt in between sobs and kisses

"Rui"

the Cape Verdeans raising their fists to the bartender, the bartender's wife, who was bigger than her husband, storming out of the building with big, masculine steps ready to bust heads with a second cudgel, the train whistle returning to the station, climbing over mansions and courtyards, asking the way at street corners and forgetting all about me as it blew across the Dom Pedro IV plaza, Clarisse with a morbid desire to touch me the way one touches a terrible wound, worried that she'd catch my disease

"What does it feel like when you have one of your fits Rui?"

she wanted to faint too so she could get more dessert after dinner, take trips to Malanje every week, stay up until eleven o'clock with the grown-ups, draw with my father's new pen, listen to music on the radio and turn the knobs from station to station without anybody getting mad

"Poor child"

the grown-ups feeling sorry for me, happy that I was still moving around and talking, as if I'd been miraculously resurrected from among the ranks of the dead, Clarisse petrified to go to bed by herself, the moment Josélia appeared to brush her teeth and put on her pajamas

"If you make me go to bed right now I'm going to faint just like Rui"

petrified that the peacocks would peck her eyes out and that the people from the workers' quarters would abduct her and make her work the rice fields and carry children on her back, Carlos

(your brother the swindler who doesn't care about you at all except to cheat you out of your money)

walking upstairs angry with me, angry with my parents, without even saying good night to them, his hands in his pockets, stomping up the stairs, my grandmother putting the drops in her glass

"I'll be damned if I've ever in my seventy years seen a child so ill-behaved"

the entire slum revolted against the barkeep, with shrieks from children and dogs, lights in the windows, shutters flung open, people rushing around, a neighborhood with brick and mortar homes in the middle, porches decorated with shards of glass bottles, stolen *azulejo* tiles, and pieces of colored glass, cars that had bottomed out on the hills, kitchen gardens filled with rosemary, stray mules, the big shack that housed an evangelical church with a placard that said

Christ Awaits You

anguished sounds from an organ coming from inside and a Chinese pastor who sold lingerie in the market when he wasn't preaching, the bartender looking for his hunting rifle amid all the casks of wine, a new train shook the abandoned mansions but didn't creep up the steps or bother me, blurry square windows rushing by, one after another, visible through a gap in the shrubs, one of my housemates suffering another attack, the bed rattling like those toys

felt teddy bears, plastic ducks, penguins, giraffes

that have a little string that you pull, the ones that shimmy in store windows, their eyes wide open and staring at us with such looks of surprise that a strange feeling came over me and I wanted to bash them in with a hammer, when I used to live in Ajuda I saw a metal frog the size of a rabbit hopping up and down in a shop, hopping and convulsing while it glared at me with a look of delight on its face, the saleslady turned a key in its back, set it on the counter, and that annoying frog shook and squirmed, belittling me, so of course I stomped on it as hard as I could until it settled down, I kept stomping the pieces of it, screws and springs that fell out of its belly, the saleslady

"What are you doing?"

an old woman in gloomy mourning clothes accompanied by a grandson in short pants, a skittish fat kid who was fascinated by the frog, hobbling away from me, knocking over Monopoly games and tricycles

"Call the police Ms. Graciete he's crazy"

I scoured the whole shop searching for more frogs, more teddy bears, more ducks, more giraffes, more animals that dared to annoy me, rudely, shamelessly annoy me, I crushed some cap guns, shattered shelffuls of little tea sets and toy kitchens, strangled winking pandas, wailing mechanically, in English

"My name is Jimmy"

coming from their stupid mouths

"My name is Jimmy"

can you believe it, me strangling them wondering who their mother was, who was the woman who carried them for nine months and then sold them in boxes with a cellophane lid, wondering, squeezing their necks all the while, what woman would want to be the mother of such monstrous creatures, when she was little Clarisse had a stuffed cat named Sandokan that never got along with me, not only did it never get along with me but it wouldn't stop egging me on and I finally had to rip out its eyes to show it who was boss, my sister walked into the sewing room and caught me cutting its eyes out with the scissors and if I hadn't gotten the hell out of there in a flash to yell for help she would have cut my own eyes out, my blue plastic eyes pretending to be innocent just like the cat's eyes when they fell onto the rug, I strangled six or seven animals, one of them a sea lion balancing a ball on its snout, the saleslady watching the executions with an anxious look on her face, exactly like one of those gargoyles in public fountains

"What are you doing?"

or the owls that the headlights of the jeep used to reveal in the darkness of the forest trail, the saleslady with her plush cheeks, scarlet ribbon, and her naughty little paws, a doll that would send me into a frenzy just like the rest of them and say awful things about me

"My name is Jimmy"

word of honor

"My name is Jimmy"

there's not one bit of fantasy in what I'm saying, not one bit of exaggeration

"My name is Jimmy"

the saleslady, a doll surrounded by a bunch of strangled dolls, dolls that lay dead, thank God, in a pile like the Israelites you sometimes see in the movies or the field hands whenever the police chief in Malanje, with me at his side helping out with my pellet gun, had to clean out the workers' quarters, unleashing his men on the field hands who fell under their blows, the saleslady drawing back with a little hopping motion like the metal frog

or the teddy bear or the duck or the giraffe or the panda

shaking and writhing on the counter

"My name is Jimmy"

continuing to insult me

"My name is Jimmy"

not

"I'm sorry"

not

"Forgive me"

not

"It was an accident"

just

"My name is Jimmy"

the hills of Almada behind the barracks, the cranes, the tiled rooftops, ships heading to Panama or Turkey, the flag went up in the morning and came down in the afternoon to a fanfare of drums and bugles with the troops lined up in rows, sparrows would whisper in the mulberry trees in Ajuda and then fly away leaving the treetops mute because the branches were made up of beaks and wings and the drawn-out noises coming out of their throats, they'd fly away and we'd notice the leaves didn't sing anymore, the mulberry trees are nothing more than a bunch of birds grouped together pretending to be trees, trees that the city workers swept into dustpans come autumn

good-bye

the old lady in gloomy mourning clothes escaped out the door to alert the city

"Call the police Ms. Graciete he's crazy"

her fat grandson took the opportunity to speed away on the bicycle he'd been sitting on, an idiot, plump as a brooding chicken, I don't remember if there were any pigeons but there certainly were some between Monsanto Park and the school, in the three years I lived in Ajuda they never tired of fluttering between Monsanto Park and the school, women with a little purse over their shoulders, squatting on the curb, going up to talk to truck drivers or disappearing into the forest with them, even in winter, even in the rain, even after dark, you could spot them by the light of their cigarettes, a match protected from the wind by a cupped hand, lighting up a face, school dismissed with the sound of a porcelain bell at three o'clock and then a mass of backpacks and pinafores racing down the street, women that didn't look like dolls at all, they looked like the scarecrows from our orchard, right down to their clothes, their arms outstretched, their straw hair, children that looked like the geese from our farm, always in groups, their chins sticking out, dusting themselves off in anger, the saleslady with plush cheeks and a scarlet ribbon, just another toy that insulted me, surrounded by the wreckage of all the other ones and me beside myself with rage strangling her as well, hearing that little mechanical voice, faintly, a kind of bleating sound that got softer as I crushed it with my fingers but that stubbornly kept on

"My name is Jimmy"

me thinking that the police chief from Malanje, who was used to criminals and thieves and who knew the true value of certain things, would be happy with me, would congratulate me

"If we didn't kill the teddy bears and the penguins they'd do us in"

the soldiers would dig a grave with pickaxes in Ajuda for the saleslady and the rest of the dolls, they'd bury all those dolls in the hillside by the Tagus, the police chief would pin a medal on me while I stood with the pellet gun resting against my shoulder

"The government saw fit that the two of us should band together and together we quickly rid this country of cats and frogs"

it took hours for Carlos to clear up everything at the police station, showing the guards the results from the tests they'd run on my head, promising that there'd been something wrong with me ever since I was born, that I was a sick person, that I had a problem with my brain that couldn't be fixed, not even by the surgeons in London who can easily remove all sorts of guts from people and then put healthy guts in their place like someone replacing parts on a sewing machine, the guards were impressed with the example of the sewing machine and of guts being removed they looked at me with a mixture of astonishment and respect, me handcuffed to the bench

"It's a lie I'm not sick at all I'm normal"

Carlos had to pay for the broken metal giraffes out of his own pocket not to mention the bicycle that the fat kid rode off on, the saleslady arguing that none of her customers would buy the corpse of a duck, much less one that had been murdered, it was quite obvious they'd been murdered, just look at the frightened expression on their faces sir, a duck like that can bring bad luck, Carlos paid for the animals, stupefied

"To me they're alive and well Dona Graciete I don't see a difference" the saleslady, the last toy that was still breathing because they'd wrested her from my hands, rubbing the tendons in her neck

"A doll that can no longer say My name is Jimmy and you sir have the nerve to say that it's still alive so you can save a few pennies?"

pushing the buttons on their bellies and to my comfort they remained mute, no more

"My name is Jimmy"

or any hopping or twitching or those blank stares that made my blood boil, mute and perhaps even pale if you looked closely, if you think about it I didn't kill them well enough and left them hovering between life and death like my father during his last two years, I should have started all over and been more careful, more precise, more aware of my responsibilities, Carlos tried to be sneaky fixing a tennis racket so that he wouldn't have to pay for it too, shaking the penguins and teddy bears in hopes of some sort of reaction though some of them just make a laughing noise

"Ha ha"

and some sing hymns or Christmas carols

"If the only problem is that they don't speak English well I don't speak English but that doesn't mean that I'm dead"

a number of people outside were spying on us through the window their hands on their foreheads to shade their eyes and at that moment the saleslady's boss arrived, he had the face of a saleslady's boss, a brute that was twice the size of Carlos and at least three times as heavy, covering my brother's shoulder with his enormous hand in a friendly gesture that didn't bode well

"You don't speak English and you aren't dead yet but since you're a gentleman just as you should be you'll gladly pay for the toys that your poor bastard of a brother damaged won't you?"

the rustling of the sunflowers, the rain loosening the grip of the creeping vines, extinguishing the light of the lantern on the porch, Carlos with his hands in his pockets, stomping up the stairs, my father quiet like always, behaving like a guest or a servant which didn't make you feel sorry for him it made you feel nervous, Lady scratched at the windowpane with her claws, my grandmother holding the pipette over her glass, irritated that none of us were paying attention to the drops of her blood-pressure medicine

"I'll be damned if I've ever in my seventy years seen a child as ill-behaved as that boy Isilda"

the rain drip drip drip in my room as a result of the broken roof tile that they were always promising to fix and always forgot about just like they forgot about the top drawer of my dresser and the warped latch on the window, the house slowly crumbling, smelling musty, the walls leaning out toward the patio where nettles were growing in between the cement slabs, my mother

"Carlos"

the house transformed into a hut where nothing worked especially the things that didn't even exist, dead cousins arguing about politics, operatic arias on the crystal set, a sister-in-law of my great-grandfather's playing a zither in the living room, the workers' quarters down by the river getting closer and closer to us, with its squealing piglets and malaria-ridden mire, Carlos stopped on the second or third step, illuminated up to his waist by the lamp in the living room and from the waist up by the dimmest lightbulb upstairs, staring at my mother, still kicking his sandals against the metal rods of the carpet runner on the stair and the detached baseboard

"What?"

the boleros from the dance club came wafting back from time to time, the pigeons kept flying their inevitable route between Monsanto Park and the school, Carlos to Lena sitting on the only couch in the apartment in Ajuda, with the sharp end of one of the springs poking out of the upholstery and other springs that were broken, gesturing toward me with his chin while I amused myself watching the cranes in the shipyard, completely quiet, reasonable, not hurting anybody

"My paycheck this month was just enough to pay for the junk that this nutcase destroyed I should put a ring through his nose and chain him up in the kitchen"

my mother straightening my shirt, tying my shoelaces, kissing me

"Since when do you go to bed without saying good night to everyone Carlos?"

my father smoked his cigarillo with guilty gestures, guilty movements like a child who's done something wrong and is afraid the grown-ups will find out, you could smell the scent of the corn in the fields, Damião was setting the table, Carlos came down the stairs, twisting the carpet under his feet as he went, and drew near my mother, who was combing my hair with her fingers, without even looking at her, he went over to my grandmother who recoiled from him with a grimace, looked around for my father who was busy brushing ashes off his pants, who never spoke to anybody and with whom nobody ever spoke not even the foremen, not even the brokers, not even the exporters, signing wherever they told him to sign, next to a little X marked in pencil, pretending to be engrossed in his whiskey and newspaper, if the police chief happened to come by he'd lock himself in the bedroom with two or three bottles and only come out after the jeep had sped away, scaring off the quails, Carlos once again started to climb the stairs, there must have been a flash of lightning out by the eucalyptus trees because the outline of the house and the golden rain tree were suddenly backlit and the dogs and geese all started barking at once in a panic, and when the lightbulbs, dishes, and furniture finally settled down Carlos bent over the railing, waving his arms like a field mouse in a henhouse

"I'll see you all in the cemetery with Grandpa"

and then nothing save the rain on the roof tiles and the plants on the patio

azaleas

nothing save Damião with his kinky hair slicked back with pomade, his white jacket, white gloves, and gold buttons waiting for us with a platter of meat and a platter of rice, nothing save us walking in a procession to the table, Clarisse, my grandmother, my father, my mother, and I walking down the hallway like pull-cord toys

"My name is Jimmy my name"

teddy bears, ducks, frogs, plush giraffes, pandas

"is Jimmy"

strangled dolls smiling at one another without even knowing who killed them.

6 JANUARY 1988

It isn't true, it can't be true that this is happening, I'm still at the house on the plantation with my husband and my children, the Bailundos are staking down scarecrows to keep the birds out of the rice fields, my mother's in her bedroom upstairs yelling for Josélia, I'm not wearing a batik cloth tied around my waist, I'm wearing a dress, I've never lived in a thatched hut especially not one in Chiquita, the village we used to pass through on our way to visit my godfather, its shops all abandoned, the columns of the regional administrator's house reduced to metal girders, two or three trees, a circle of huts that disappeared in the dust that trailed behind the jeep as chickens squawked in fright, I never went around barefoot with chiggers burrowing into my toes, wherever I am I need my pillow to be able to get to sleep and so it isn't true, it can't be true that this is happening, Josélia, whom I inherited from my mother, used to drink rubbing alcohol on the sly, my mother showed her the empty bottle

"Josélia"

Josélia befuddled knocking pieces of silverware off the counter with limbs that wouldn't obey her will, trying to gain control of her own hands as though they were a pair of butterflies that she couldn't catch up with

"I'm sorry ma'am"

she filed her teeth down into sharp triangles and came back to the house from funerals or days off on Easter Sundays with traces of pigments on her face, sucking the meat out of the bodies of crickets, grabbing my arm and urging me to

"Swallow"

after urging me to

"Lie down"

she'd urge me to

"Wake up"

and lead me down to the river, wash me, bring me back from the river, argue with the soldiers and stand in front of me, protecting me from them, her, a woman who was just as weak as I was

"She's not my boss she's my godmother"

warding off their advances, shooing them away, hitting them with the mango-tree switch that she used to stir the fire, while they laughed at her

"She's not my boss she's my godmother"

the soldiers pretending to be maimed by the blows from her switch

"Godmother"

the toucans took wing northward in anticipation of the dry season, the lights from the Marimba workers' quarters, at the Macau
workers' quarters, not from the people who lived there but rather
lights from the fire, from the camps of the UNITA soldiers, from
the sheen of the feathers of the gledes, from the lapping flames of
the burning villages, from the helicopter that grew as dark as an
owl as it flew away, Josélia shielded me from the rain with a piece
of canvas from the top of a jeep

"There you go"

not out of respect, not out of deference, but for the pleasure of humiliating me, back when her movements started to disobey her will
and she tried to gain control of her own hands as though they were a
pair of butterflies that she couldn't catch up with, my mother became
very serious, very solemn, very deliberate, lining up the empty bottles
of rubbing alcohol, three or four empty bottles of perfume, an empty
bottle of my father's aftershave on the marble tabletop, whispering

"Josélia"

warning Fernando, Damião, Maria da Boa Morte

"No one leaves the kitchen"

the acacia trees blew in the wind, casting light and shadow by
turns through the window frame, rectangles of light, the teardrop
shadows of bees, the button-shaped shadows of beetles that the
setters spit out when they barked, my mother raised the long-han-
dled bath brush with missing bristles up in the air, I tried to sneak
out to the patio but she froze me with her glare

"I said no one leaves the kitchen"

the crows perched on the scarecrows gently swayed as they
devoured the chaff out of their chests, squawking at Lady, who

drew back, scampered around in a circle, barked at them from a distance, the patio just a meter away from me, the creeping vines, the azaleas, if I could just run to the infirmary, if I could just run up to my bedroom and cover my ears, I tried to take an imperceptible little step towards the stairs and her voice stopped me in my tracks

"I said no one leaves the kitchen Isilda"

like every time the foremen

(my father holding me close to him

"Stay by my side Isilda")

strung a thief up in a eucalyptus tree, they'd pull the stool out from under him and the body would swing around and around and kept swinging around all night long inside my sleeping head, all night and the next night and even the night after that

"Little girl"

I remember the feet tied together with a piece of rope, the distended stomach, the twisted jawbone, the foreman firing his rifle to scare off the gledes, and the sound of their wings like someone flipping furiously through the pages of an almanac

"Little girl"

my mother presenting the empty bottles one by one

"Rubbing alcohol aftershave perfume"

lining them up again on the marble tabletop brandishing the brush handle, if only the acacias, which made the rectangles of light appear through the window frame and then took them away again, could take me with them as they blew back towards the patio in the next gust of wind, if only I knew nothing, saw nothing, if only I were deaf, the scarecrows' hats were alive

(the only thing that was left alive on the crossbeam that had come unhinged from the stake)

and rolled along the ground, hobbling towards the Cambo River

the crown

the brim

the crown

the brim

some random harvesters would pick them up, stick them on top of their heads, and start dancing in the company store, strutting proudly, as if they were white men, slobbering on one of my father's cigarette butts, which they'd found along the trail, demanding another beer and owing even more money, the company store, with a shop counter at the back, crystal radio sets for sale on the shelves, enormous, purple, no spring motor and no batteries, the stench of rotting fish and misery that whetted the appetite of the suckling pigs, the trucks bounced up and down over the bumps and hollows of the dirt road, rolling back and forth like a boat at sea

"Palms up Josélia"

it isn't true, it can't be true that

and even without looking I could see my mother amid the rectangles of light that shone through the window frame, the teardrop shadows of bees, the button-shaped shadows of beetles, I could see the brush handle crash down from the ceiling onto Josélia's hands and then rise from Josélia's hands back up to the ceiling, the brush handle that wasn't straight but was curved like a switch or a willow, I could see Damião's eyes, Fernando's eyes, I could see the flecks that splattered against the wall tiles, Josélia inside my sleeping head all night long holding her hands under the faucet, anointing them with lard, showing me the swelling

"Little girl"

this is happening

this is happening, the government soldiers making haste to leave Chiquita with their rifles and cannons, the chaos of a quick retreat, leaving behind their maps, compasses, mutilated soldiers who dragged themselves around the roofless house of the former regional administrator, squealing like piglets, around the hollows of the old columns, through the grass, through what had once been a vibrant creeping vine with little blue flowers but was now just a few struggling, paralyzed tendrils, snakes, geckos, stems, the arrival of a disorderly throng of UNITA mercenaries, South African Belgian French Spanish German mercenaries, maybe friends of the friends of my father, who went hunting with him and slept in tents with him next to the river, who crossed paths with me at dinner parties in Cassanje, or who, when I was little, played tennis in white linen outfits beside shrubs with white blossoms in front of a crowd of officials in white uniforms and ladies in white shawls under white parasols, in Luanda, Carmona, Silva Porto, Lobito, at a time when almost all the cars were white, just like the bow in my braided hair, the houses, the walls of the gardens, the metal bars of the front gates, white horses, white greyhounds, white porcelain leopards set on the rugs by the entryway, the arrival of the UNITA mercenaries, the last heavy rainstorms, the first early morning fogs, my heavy bones saturated with water, Josélia, Maria da Boa Morte, and me without a white bow in my braided hair, squatting on the ground on a torn piece of straw mat with bits of tobacco between our lips and teeth

it isn't true, it can't

while the dogs, frightened by the gunfire, disappeared into the forest and a Frenchman

or a Spaniard or a German or an Italian

sprayed a stream of gasoline at them, like Rui when he crushed the begonias, when he crushed the azaleas

my son Rui with Carlos in Ajuda

chasing the mutts until the gasoline reached them and they burst into flames first their backs, then a paw, a tail that turned red, then black, then gray, and then vanished into the earth, the mutilated government soldiers crawled out of the regional administrator's house, slow as caterpillars, pointing to their scars, their scabs, their stumps, dragging themselves out of the house in jerking motions while the fire died down amid the crispy remains of the dogs

"We're friends we're friends"

it can't be true that this is happening: I'm still on the patio of the plantation right now, not with my husband and children, but with my parents on the afternoon when my father's brother came to visit us in Baixa de Cassanje, the only time I ever saw him, my father's brother looked different than he did in the photograph in the living room that my mother tried to hide behind all the trinkets and photographs she could find, he looked skinnier, more hunched over, and much older than that smiling, out-of-focus young man who was waving his hat from the step of a train car or what looked to be a train car in what looked to be a train station in Portugal, I think, Coimbra Lourinhã Lisbon, that motionlessness of everything, that scentless light, the gloomy smoke, my father's brother, for whom the police were searching in Cuíto, in Zenza do Itombe, in Mariano

Machado, constantly in and out of jail for spending day after day trying to convince the Africans that they were equal to us, the Africans were suspicious of him and made fun of him, respectfully

"What a joke you sure do like to joke around sir"

they'd steer clear of him, afraid of the police, the second they let him out of jail he'd be up on a platform giving a speech to an audience of baobab trees and little children, animated, fervent, comical, my mother very distressed

"That brother of yours Eduardo I swear"

her friends shocked if they ever saw that smiling young man waving his hat in the picture frame, my mother opened a cupboard and buried it deep inside

"Oh I pay so little attention to that man that I didn't even know that was there imagine that"

"Your husband's brother is the one who gave land to the blacks I refuse to believe it"

land that nobody planted nobody harvested where nobody had the courage to build even a hut, inhabited by hyenas and wildcats, my father's brother in São Nicolau giving a speech to the security guards, my mother's friends

"They spotted him in Luso in Gago Coutinho in Henrique de Carvalho demanding that all the Portuguese regional administrators return to the capital for good they spotted him in Luanda preaching in the slums"

my father's brother thrown into jail one minute then out of jail the next, in the prison camp one minute then out of the prison camp the next, traveling the highways of Angola in a van with a loudspeaker tied to its roof, my mother forbidding me to talk about him, at some point starting to respond to her friends' queries

"It must be some mistake or someone with the same name my husband never had any brothers"

throwing that youthful smile and hat into the trash can and yet that smile and that hat still irritated her like a skin disease

"That brother of yours Eduardo I swear he could show up here any day to threaten us with a machete and cut all our throats"

the UNITA mercenaries, the South African Belgian French Spanish German mercenaries inspected all the thatched huts with the barrels of their machine guns, the shops, the regional administrator's house, sending everything flying papers pieces of plaster shards of roof tiles a bust of the symbol of the Republic that was missing its nose and that served as a makeshift nest for a chaotic swarm of wasps, they felt along the ground with sticks looking for land mines, they killed a lamb, bashing its skull in, they made calls on a telephone, I couldn't tell where they were calling or to whom they were speaking, Josélia standing beside me with a switch from a dried-up mango tree in her hand, ready to protect me from them just like she'd protected me from the government soldiers

("Godmother godmother")

not out of friendship but for the pleasure of humiliating me, exactly as though she were brandishing the brush handle in the air, demanding

rubbing alcohol aftershave perfume

"Palms up Isilda"

the mercenaries launched mortars toward the forest

a tumult of beating wings and screeches, maddened fluttering of hawks

they didn't pay any attention to us or even look at us just like they hadn't looked at us up to that point or actually it was impossible to tell whether or not they were looking at us since they were wearing dark sunglasses and the brims of their hats covered their eyes, mercenaries who were white like me who would give me white-people food to eat, not beetles, not ants, they'd give me money, compensate me for my losses, hand me over to the Americans, they take me to a real house even if it wasn't my own a house with real walls and real floorboards, beds, mattresses, shower-heads, couches, plates, tables, carpet runners, towels, people I'd understand and who would understand me, whose ideas and feelings I could comprehend instead of this logic that's completely illogical, the mercenaries didn't even look at the mutilated government troops who had gathered together near the columns and the struggling, blind tendrils of the creeping vines on the porch of the house

"We're friends we're friends"

the leaves of the eucalyptus trees vowed

"We're friends we're friends"

the young saplings, the bark on the trunks, the green needlelike leaves that were beginning to develop, brown needlelike leaves, butterflies the size of sparrows that fluttered about the treetops, blown by the wind like the pages of a letter

"We're friends we're friends"

and then Josélia's hands

("Palms up Josélia")

covering my head, Josélia's body covering my body, her legs covering my legs, the dense fog blowing in from the south and covering the forest, transforming it into a grassless, treeless plain, a veil of shadows that had concentrated into a single shadow that stretched from Malanje to the Congo, concealing the fires, the villages, the bridges, the burial grounds of the Jinga kings in Dala Samba, the uplands in Marimbanguengo straddling the border and cut in two by the river full of diamonds that separates Angola from the country that belongs to the Belgians, brutes sifting the sand through a sieve, trying to sell shards of cruets and specks of charcoal to the Jews in town who were outfitted with acids, reagents, scales, jeweler's loupes, headlamps on their foreheads like miners and doctors examining the tiny stones on a lilac-colored velvet cloth, going in and out of the service-entry doors then turning out the lights in the alleyway with the timid quickness of conspirators, I remember the tree-lined avenue with the pastry shop, the well-trimmed bushes, the woodpeckers with orange beaks strutting along the grass while my father, smoothing out a wrinkle on his pants or brushing a tiny speck of dirt off his linen shirt, talked with a group of men about the cabarets in Luanda, and then Josélia's hands on my head, her body on my body, her ankles on mine, the eucalyptus leaves, the mutilated soldiers leaning against the columns of the regional administrator's house foreseeing something or other, fearing something or other, asking the mercenaries to spare them something or other that I couldn't

"We're friends we're friends"

that I, squatting on a straw mat like a dead Jinga king, motionless like a dead Jinga king, who lie still for hours or days or weeks on end and never notice anything or complain about anything since time and duration and age don't exist for them, the only thing that exists for them is death, not the end that comes to all people but the end that comes to rivers and villages and memory, insignificant corpses laid out on planks, fertilizing the rice fields, me smelling like the Jingas, eating crickets and larvae like the Jingas, if I worked for my mother maybe I'd even drink rubbing alcohol aftershave perfume

"Palms up Isilda"

or I'd be in the kitchen acting out the customs of the white people, neither rejecting them nor accepting them, forgiving them or, rather, not even forgiving them, tolerating them the way they unashamedly tolerated their fear of Europeans, usury, and death, the mutilated soldiers asking for something or other that I was unable to comprehend or didn't want to comprehend or couldn't comprehend, something that I could comprehend in white people out of instinctual compassion but that I could never comprehend in black people, they were so different from us, something I could never comprehend in animals or black people, the mutilated soldiers

"We're friends we're friends"

the mutilated soldiers of the government forces

"No one leaves the kitchen I said no one leaves the kitchen"

with their forage caps on backwards and their uniforms with missing buttons, moving about frantically, trying to stay alive, calling out to the South African Belgian French English Spanish German mercenaries who worked for UNITA just as they'd work for the government forces if the government paid them enough, they'd have the same calm competence, the same efficient patience, the same lack of enthusiasm, lack of compassion, lack of anger, calling out to the mercenaries who didn't even see them, who hadn't seen them since they arrived and who hadn't seen us either, Josélia, Maria da Boa Morte, and me no, me, Josélia, and Maria da Boa Morte

Josélia who I inherited from my mother just like I inherited her costume jewelry and the pile of rags that were her clothes, Maria da Boa Morte who stole Rosarinho from me, which even though I didn't want it still belonged to me, the two servants and I chewing moldy tobacco in Chiquita, the little backwater village we used to pass through

(the shops, the administrative building, a ring of wretched thatched huts, the forest on the horizon, the workers' quarters off in the distance, the blue hillsides)

on our way to visit my godfather in Dala Samba, the mercenaries didn't sit down, didn't eat, didn't set up the cannons, didn't clear the ground to set up their tents, they merely destroyed the maps and the radios that had been left behind, set off colored rockets, pointed toward the dense fog of the dry season that hung over the area where prospectors sifted sand through sieves so they could sell diamonds to the Jews in Malanje who examined the stones through a brass microscope, every one of whom had a mulatto lover who was even more dressed up than my daughter-in-law, who sat smoking cigarettes in cigarette holders and reading their tabloids about princes and actresses in the neighborhood near the high school, the dry-season fog that obfuscated peoples' movements, the huts, the lone wall of the grocery store, the eucalyptus trees, Josélia, the report of the firearms, the voices of the mutilated soldiers

"We're friends we're friends"

who looked like they were trying to flee, trying to ask for I don't know what from I don't know who, hands on my head, a body on my body, legs on my legs, my shoulders being pushed backward

"Lie down"

the mutilated soldiers who one by one seemed to be going limp, it looked like a South African

or a Belgian or a Frenchman or a Spaniard or a German

went over to them with a knife, it looked like he was pulling their heads back by the hair the way you pull a young goat's head back by the horns to expose its neck, it looked like the knife, it looked like a sudden shudder, it looked like the flight of a toucan up by the mango tree or even lower down by Josélia and me, Josélia took her hands off my head, her body off my body, her legs off my legs

(a Jinga whom I inherited from my mother just like I inherited her costume jewelry and the pile of rags that were her clothes and whom I kept in the house not so much out of pity but out of inertia, out of laziness, out of convenience, out of habit, out of having grown accustomed to seeing her pace back and forth whenever she happened to drop a teacup, shattering it, or happened to over-salt the food, or burn my husband's shirt with the iron, or forgot to help Rui when he had one of his attacks, to put a handkerchief in his mouth)

when she moved away from me I was sure that the mercenaries had left, heading down the trail to Marimbaguengo, the same way the government soldiers had gone, and the same way the inhabitants of the workers' quarters had gone before the troops arrived, when she moved away from me I realized that we were alone, squatting

"Sit down"

on pieces of a straw mat, looking for crickets, ants, beetles, insect eggs, digging with our fingers, our fingernails, the end of a fork, a sharp piece of wood, all alone in Chiquita amid the ruins of the regional administrator's home, the ruins of the shops, and the ruins of the thatched huts, which were so badly burnt and torn apart, so covered in grass, roots, and weeds that if I were traveling through right now with my parents on our way to Dala Samba we wouldn't even notice that the village was there, we'd just see the eucalyptus trees, the mango trees, the ashes that the wind and the forest fires would soon scatter, just as they would soon scatter the mutilated government soldiers with their shirts with missing buttons and forage caps on backwards, fighting with us over scraps of food, water that was almost black from being mixed with oil, which we got from carburetors, and torn pieces of canvas from the jeeps, which we used to cover ourselves on cold nights, Josélia acting as if nothing had happened, as if my husband and children were still with me, as if it was time for the cotton harvest, time to ready the sunflowers, for the foremen to build new structures in the workers' quarters to make room for the field hands from Huambo, to write the brokers and exporters, charter the ship, Josélia acting as if we were back on the plantation, in the hallways, in the bedrooms, in the study, on the patio, in the dining room, Josélia

"Ma'am"

as she should be, as she always should have been, as I should have forced her to be always

"Ma'am"

as if my batik cloth had turned into a blouse and a skirt, as if I were wearing earrings, shoes, necklaces, rings, as if I weren't scratching at the ground with my fingernails, a bent fork, a sharp stick, hunting for larvae and insect eggs, Josélia

"Ma'am"

laying out an oilskin tarp from the jeep with the same care that someone would take in making a bed, securing a sheet of zinc in place like someone closing a window, shooing away the gledes the way she used to shoo the peacocks to the back of the patio so that no screeching birds would interrupt my sleep, keeping watch over me all night long so she could come to my aid in case I got thirsty, or hungry, or needed a handkerchief, or my robe, or my afghan shawl, or if I happened to reach out my fingers and not find the lamp, if I awoke in a panic thinking the mercenaries were killing me the way they killed the amputee soldiers, pulling my head back to expose my neck, feeling the steel on my skin, hearing the cartilage snap, the knife diving deep into the bone, frantic that I wouldn't be able to get free, that no one could hear me

"Josélia"

Josélia at the plantation, in Chiquita, I think she was in Chiquita since the leaves sung in silence, they sung and they sung in silence, Josélia coming near me but not daring to touch me because a Jinga doesn't touch her boss, nor does a Jinga ask permission to do so, Josélia at the plantation, I think, since you can hear the commotion of the quails outside or rather the gurgling of the throats of the mutilated soldiers whose necks were slashed in the dark, Josélia coming near me so I don't frighten my husband, my children, my mother

"Ma'am"

softly

"Ma'am"

waiting for me to go back to sleep in my bedroom, to go back to sleep on the canvas oilcloth from the jeep as if it were possible, my good sirs, as if I'd been left

can you believe it?

alone and lived

can you believe it?

without anyone to take care of me, to worry about me, to look after me, me who at that moment found myself in Baixa de Cassanje with my parents, dressed in white, with a white bow in my braided hair, ten twelve thirteen years old if that

(you can tell by the smell, you can tell by the sight of the river and the storehouse over there, the cotton bolls that were opening, the sunflowers, the corn, you can tell since I don't have a single wrinkle, a single liver spot on my skin, a single gray hair, a single trace of old age in the mirror)

me on the patio with my parents on an afternoon when some random creature, hair disheveled, chewing tobacco, wrapped in a tattered batik cloth swung open the door with glass windows that led to the living room, tripping over the flowerpots, my mother distressed

"That daughter of yours Eduardo I swear"

the guests finding a photograph among all the picture frames filled with my grandparents my godfather my cousins, of a young lady smiling as she gets ready to dance at the governor's palace, amid government officials in uniform and gentlemen in tuxedos, a photograph of a young lady with her hair done up at a lunch with the bishop, my mother opening a drawer and burying it deep inside

"Oh I pay so little attention to her that I didn't even know that was there imagine that"

the guests taken aback in disgust

"I refuse to believe it"

me in Baixa de Cassanje, on the patio with my parents, dressed in white, with a white bow in my braided hair, ten twelve thirteen years old if that, my parents holding me close to them to protect me from that disheveled, barefoot, emaciated creature, chewing tobacco, wrapped in a tattered batik cloth, whom I could never believe was really me, I had no clue who it could be but it wasn't me what idiocy, how could it be me, I've never gone hungry, I always take baths, thank God

what a foolish idea

I've never smelled like a black person, me hugging onto my mother and staring at the rail-thin woman who looked at me from the doorway, in agreement with my mother, ready to scream in unison with her, with the same delusion, the same terror

"That daughter of yours Eduardo I swear she could show up here any day to threaten us with a machete and cut all our throats."

24 December 1995

As my sister Clarisse always says deep down I feel sorry for him, always stuck in the apartment in Ajuda looking out at the river through a gap in the curtains, thinking about Angola, waiting for Maria da Boa Morte to call him

"Child"

to give him a bath, serve him lunch, give him the sweets she made for him on the sly, mango compote, papaya jelly, coconut candy, my grandmother suddenly appearing in the kitchen treating him the same way she treated the Bailundos, with the same exasperated impatience

"What are you eating Carlos?"

and me not understanding the reason she was furious, my grandmother saying to my mother one night, when she thought that we were all in bed and couldn't hear them

"It's an embarrassment to the family to keep him here in the house Isilda only God can know how embarrassed I am"

my father entrenched in his newspaper, the clock pendulum dangling in silence, the trees that became enormous in the dark, the peacocks and owls perched in the branches, Carlos quickly tossing the mango or papaya or coconut sweets into the trash can next to the stove

"I'm not eating anything ma'am"

us upstairs in our pajamas, leaning over the banister on the landing, jealous of the grown-ups whom no one sent to bed, no one demanding to see their fingernails

"Your hands let's see your little hands"

who only brushed their teeth if they wanted to, and could even have removable teeth if they wanted, watching the quaking newspaper and my father invisible behind it, he crossed and uncrossed his legs, a strip of skin showing between the bottom of his pant leg and his sock that looked exactly like the skin of a chicken, his cigarette smoke floating to the ceiling, my mother knitting faster and faster, Clarisse showing off her new slippers and whispering like we did during Mass, in a mocking, excited voice

"Grandma's embarrassed of you Carlos why is Grandma embarrassed of you?"

grown-ups don't know their multiples of nine or the capital of Albania and they don't conjugate verbs but no one scolds them for it, they like turnip soup, they hate turtles and frogs, they don't chew gum, they wear shoes that are the right size and not three sizes too big, they don't care about those little chocolate umbrella candies, if they happen to have brothers or sisters they don't have to dress in identical outfits, they can cough as much as they like without anyone making them drink cough syrup, they can leave their potatoes and salads on their plates without it causing a huge scandal, they can turn out the lights before they fall asleep because witch doctors don't abduct them in the middle of the night they only abduct us, Clarisse stuck out her foot to show off her new slipper

"It's an embarrassment to the family to keep him here in the house Isilda only God can know how embarrassed I am"

the slipper fell off her foot, somersaulted in the air, and landed down below with a dull thud

thunk

between the couch where my mother was sitting and the couch where my grandmother was sitting, my grandmother clutching her hand to her chest, forgetting her embarrassment

"Oh that scared me"

my father completely invisible except for his legs, the swatch of chicken skin that separated his pant leg from his sock, struggling with the pages of the newspaper which had suddenly come to life, twisting, leaping from his hands, scattering themselves on the ground, the hands on the clock taking little turkey steps around the dial marking the time as it passed by, the generator slowly pulling morning toward us like someone pulling a toy with warped wheels by the end of its string, my mother mad at my grandmother, you could tell because her neck changed colors, not raising her voice or even looking up from her crocheting

"Back to bed kids"

my grandmother still holding her hand to her chest, clutching the fluttering sparrow that was her heart as she looked down at the slipper, frightened, as if she were staring at the devil himself, us rushing off to our bedroom, Clarisse limping along in her one slipper, curious

"Grandma's embarrassed of you Carlos why is Grandma embarrassed of you?"

us hearing the pages of the newspaper fall to the floor, my mother saying to my grandmother, I'd bet she was standing, I'd bet she was pointing with her index finger

"You'd better pray to all the saints you know that the little guy didn't understand anything because if by chance the little guy understood anything I'm going to put you away in an old folks' home in Malanje until the day you die"

the clock jiggling like cellulite, the generator tuckered out, dragging the morning toward us, struggling, grimacing as it burned through its gasoline, my grandmother afraid that they'd put her in a wheelchair and feed her through a tube that would go from her nose down to her stomach, picking up the slipper in order to make herself seem useful and avoid getting sent to the old folks' home, making excuses and citing evidence for what she said.

"Since when is it acceptable for mulattoes to live together with whites Isilda since when is it acceptable for a mulatto to eat at the table with us?"

a tree branch beat against the window over and over again, Maria da Boa Morte tucking us into the sheets, Clarisse tugging at her apron

"Why is Grandma embarrassed of Carlos?"

with Maria da Boa Morte there the tree branch that was beating against the window pane was harmless, just a tree branch nothing more, unable to scare me, Carlos's shoulders in that bright darkness, a sort of reverse moonlight that doesn't exist in Damaia, in which the furniture, drapes, and pictures all come to life, breathe, shake themselves from top to bottom, his teeth were shining, his cheeks were shining, his chest was sunken

"Don't cry Carlos"

in my opinion it was only fitting that he was crying since he kept me from catching grasshoppers and burning them with matches

"Rui"

acting like an idiot, always thinking he was in charge, even in charge of me, one day I'll be a grown-up and I'll go up to him and tie him to a tree trunk and stab a nail through his tongue

"Take that"

my father came up the stairs and looked at us from the doorway, about to talk to us, but then changing his mind, deciding against it, trading a conversation with us for a bottle of whiskey, the doctor underlined parts of the results of the tests

"You're just going to keep at it until you've destroyed your liver and turned it to mush aren't you sir?"

and my father just kept at it, going from one bottle to the next, his body getting skinnier and skinnier and his belly swelling up, he looked at the newspaper without really seeing it, using the news as a way to be alone, muttering slobbery phrases and wiping his mouth on his sleeve, one afternoon I put my ear next to his mouth

and, as if floating on a oil slick of delusion, I heard him repeat and
repeat and repeat

"Holy sacrament"

wandering around the house with a pliant, cautious gait, the
same as those long-legged birds from Egypt that aren't used to
walking, the floor rocked back and forth like the deck of a ship,
my grandmother paying close attention to the drops of her blood-
pressure medication.

"Pardon me Amadeu but I didn't understand you"

who liked him just as much as she liked Carlos, the same expression, wrinkled in indignation, the same repulsion, the same disgust

compelling me, in my forgetfulness

"Pardon me Amadeu but I didn't understand you"

*to rummage through rusty old things in my memory, half a pair
of scissors, thimbles, rusty broken tin picture frames with little roses
on them, a bracelet, but who did it belong to my God who did it
belong to, photographs in enamel frames, tie tacks, tubes of glue, a
piece of sealing wax, a bucket attached to a pulley over a well, me on
someone's lap, my mother-in-law rejoicing as she tortured me*

"Pardon me Amadeu but I didn't understand you"

*me on the lap of someone I can't seem to remember, a chicken
coop, a vineyard on a terraced hillside, straw hats bent over the vine
leaves, the train cars filled with goods that passed by at noon, the
mail that arrived at six, me on the lap of a woman wearing a robe*

(a relative, a friend, a neighbor?)

who was comforting me, caressing the nape of my neck

"There there, there there"

"Pardon me Amadeu but I didn't understa"

my father opening a cupboard door, looking inside as if peering down an endless tunnel, disappearing into a twinkling penumbra, knocking over glasses, clanging bottles against each other, his lip quivering, his fingers turning to leaves in the wind, no whiskey, no gin, no wine, nothing that could help him respond, that could help him speak, that could help save him from the contempt that others felt toward him, if he could only go ten years back in time, and if Cotonang were to hire him once again, my father locking the cupboard, standing up straight, smoothing out his shirt, his jacket, his hair, raising an imaginary glass toward my grandmother

(a piece of sealing wax, a bucket attached to a pulley over a well)

"To your health ma'am"

watching us from the doorway to the bedroom, then changing his mind, turning out the light, going down the stairs, stumbling on a faulty step that was missing a floorboard under which you could see an abyss of rats' nests in the basement, Carlos's shoulders moving up and down, the radiance of his teeth, the radiance of his cheeks, always stuck in the apartment in Ajuda looking out at the river through a gap in the curtains, thinking about Angola, Carlos expecting me for Christmas Eve dinner, looking down at the avenue lit up by streetlamps on either side of the sidewalk pouring their light out on the shrubs and making the façades of the buildings look sad, Carlos skinnier and weaker than I am, unable to stop me from burning grasshoppers with a match or breaking the necks of the pigeons that circle from Monsanto Park to the school and back, I used to put corn or day-old bread out for them on the balcony then pretend to be a statue, letting them strut around the flowerpots, then I'd throw a towel on top of them and presto, Lena would come out from the kitchen, with a jar of mayonnaise in her hand, as upset as if the pigeons belonged to her

"Let those birds go Rui"

the two of them never let me do anything, getting mad at me for no reason, not letting me have any fun, a pigeon that was half exhausted, half woozy rejoined his companions and evaporated amid the school-yard recess, it wasn't just Lena and Carlos who wouldn't let me do anything it was also the neighbors with their little complaints, you'd better keep an eye on him because your brother was throwing rocks at the canaries all morning long, it's the third time this week that my cockatoo has gotten loose, as if I had nothing better to do than climb up the sycamore tree, wearing gloves, because the bird will peck at me, just look at all the work he's cost me, there were people who'd take off running

"Look it's that idiot"

if I went out on the street to torment the street vendors and stray mutts, they'd pour water on me with a watering can just because I pulled the folded clothes off their stands or unscrewed the cover plate of their doorbell with a really wonderful screwdriver, those morons who painted the façade of the Dockworkers' Union building swore they'd kill me if I messed with their tethers or took away their ladders, here in Damaia at least, the Cape Verdeans from the slums wearing a red ribbon on their wrists and a Moroccan fez on their heads, living in a wasteland of sugarcane fields and carcasses of old cars, a drunkard sweltering on the busted upholstery of the backseat, the Cape Verdeans ask me politely, courteously

"Hey idiot hey you nutcase"

to help them catch cats to cook for dinner, the Cape Verdeans' children, also wearing a red ribbon and a Moroccan fez, which they must be born with, like my belly button, frighten the cats by banging on pots and pans and send them running toward us, we hold out a net and wrap the cats up in it, then start the cooking process by killing the cats with a few customary blows from the cudgel, here in Damaia at least, the gypsy merchants who sell nightgowns that shrink to half their original size the first time you wash them and wonderful radios that are displayed on countertops or hang from pegs floating like space stations, it's just that these don't have music or news reports coming out of them, just the thundering roar of a comet, the hissing sound from an alpha star, martian messages from beings with antennae and pointy ears, the gypsies politely asking me, from under their hats and mustaches, to stand guard in exchange for a polyester American T-shirt with a picture of an eagle and silver letters surrounding it

San Francisco

which could last for months as long as we never wear it

"Hey you bum"

asking me to stand guard in the by-lane by the police station, an alleyway of small houses with figurines of saints displayed in niches

Saint Philomena Saint Therese of Lisieux Saint Barbara to guard against thunderstorms and troubles of the heart

stick two fingers in your mouth and whistle loudly at the first sign of a patrol car, it's coming it's not coming I whistle even if there's no car, just to watch the spectacle of dozens of hunched figures in long skirts carrying baskets on their shoulders, bleating like sheep, leaving behind sandals and suckling children as they run off down the block, accompanied by the martian messages on their radios, here in Damaia at least, if I could, I'd set the cockatoos free and strangle pigeons, just like anyone else would, and nobody here scolds me or gets annoyed with me, for instance, after lunch I go out and earn an honest living watching the retirees' domino game at the creamery because the barber pays me ten percent of his winnings if I show him, by making signs

a little scratch of my nose, a discreet cough, a yawn

then the faces of the other players, grimacing when they lose

"Damn"

and threatening me with their canes, wrongly claiming that I'm bringing them bad luck, the barber, always a gentleman, calming them down convincing them otherwise

"How do you suppose this epileptic fool how do you suppose this poor bastard 'cause you can tell right away he's an idiot can really bring bad luck on someone come on buddy?"

the barber acting paternally towards me, his arm around my waist as we walked to his ship, jingling the coins in his pocket, dark, sticky coins, counting them out one by one on the manicure table

"There you go you brought me luck"

with a greedy stinginess

"Don't scratch with your whole hand 'cause everyone will notice just use the fingernail of your little finger that's enough and most importantly don't clap your hands and jump up and down when a round ends"

my salary, which I'd won by translating dots into coughs and yawns, would go straight into the purse of the young woman with sandy-colored hair who always had the sniffles and who set herself up in an old wine crate on the corner where the curve in Buraca St. meets the road by the campgrounds where I wait my turn, in the rain, in that waiting room of weeds and donkey excrement, wait in line after a blind accordion player playing mournful fados who always went around with his chin upraised

"Are you alone Irene?"

searching for her in the pine needles without setting down his concertina, which intoned a random, whining note every now and then, the D flat of pleasure, I guided him back to Damaia, holding onto his arm, which extended all the way to the ground if you count his cane

"Are you by yourself pal?"

the blind man wearing a raincoat that was as long as a priest's robe and dragged along the ground, I warned him

"Watch out for the step"

and he raised his boot for the nonexistent step and tripped over the empty space

"Damn you damn you"

he lived in a van with no wheels just past the fountain with a goldfinch in a birdcage by the pistons of the engine, surprised when he stuck his fingers in between the bars of the cage

"I don't hear the bird"

not realizing that I'd opened the door to the birdcage ages ago, that the bird, now orphaned by his father, was warbling on the edge of a roof somewhere in Queluz or Brandoa, the blind man felt around the perches, the birdseed, the hardened lumps on the bottom of the cage, then searched for me all over the van

"Damn you damn you"

the morning light illuminated the limestone fountain that bore the coat of arms of a king or a duke or from the can of some brand of olive oil that I used to poke holes in with a nail, the gypsies' mules with their sores covered up with grease or gray paint lapped up the water with the sound of a bubbling broth, old women wearing kerchiefs and shawls during the hottest part of the day held their pots and bowls out toward the spout, the blind man with his cane upraised, me running off in front of him, joking

"Watch out for the step"

an unbuckled sheepskin boot pedaling in the nothingness, his hand tracing an arabesque in the air, arms flailing

bang bang bang

like ice skaters when they lose their balance, the morning light, scarlet blue green brown yellow on the chimneys on the rooftops on the crochet drapes on the ceramic swallow perched on top of the ironwork railings of the balconies, the morning light sending the sparrows into the branches of the trees by the lake, an unbuckled sheepskin boot pedaling, a second, soleless boot slipping on a cobblestone, the accordion groaning, an unstructured, unmusical sound, as it hit against the sides of a boat, keys and silvery inlays breaking off of it until it disappeared altogether.

plop

into the canal, the blind man

"Damn you damn you"

he's probably still in his van, I guess, getting upset whenever he feels the birdcage

"I don't hear the bird"

or he's flailing along the boggy banks of the canal, swept down toward the mouth of the river by the rushing water, the blind man with his chin upraised, asking the seagulls

"Are you by yourself pal?"

me perfectly fine in Damaia with the movie star on the poster and Carlos wanting to ruin my night, waiting for me to come to Christmas Eve dinner, determined to yell at me because of my table manners, the napkin that I tuck into my collar instead of spreading it out on my knees, the rim of my glass that's dirty because I don't wipe my mouth, the olive pits that I spit out onto my plate instead of politely puckering my lips, taking them out of my mouth, and placing them on the edge of my knife, Carlos, who for three years made me swallow pills that made me tired and took all the fun out of inventing new steps for the blind man and letting cockatoos out of their cages, staggering like a willow from the bed to the living room and from the living room back to bed, sleepy, only able to keep my eyes open with great effort, like someone trying to raise wooden blinds with warped slats, having to use both hands to open them, the slats at last crashing open, Carlos, who for three years dragged me from hospital to hospital, doctors handing us X-rays, test results, and letters with annoying flicks of the wrist

"If I were you I'd send him back to Africa where everything is more or less epileptic he can get away with his mischief in the backlands entertaining the blacks, he can even shoot them through the eye or the guts and nobody will get mad at him"

Carlos worried that I'd turn on the gas, that I'd forget to turn off a faucet and flood the whole building, that I'd throw the furniture and the Lunda masks out the window, everything in the apartment was old, faded, worn-out, full of holes and turned to lace by the appetites of woodworms and moths, we'd sit down in a chair and the chair, one of its legs mended with a piece of twine, would start to wobble like a loose tooth, sobbing

"Aww"

we'd sit down on a cushion and the sick cushion would vomit up vegetable silk, the sink clogged, the toilet clogged, the doors to the service hatch in the kitchen so swollen with rust that they were impossible to open, Carlos waiting for me to come to Christmas Eve dinner, different from us, with different hair, different cheekbones, different skin color, lips that were thicker than ours, which embarrassed my grandmother and made Clarisse feel sorry for him

"Deep down I feel sorry for him Mom bought him in Malanje the way she used to buy brooms made with piassava fibers and baskets"

"So that means Carlos isn't really our brother that means Carlos likes dried fish and cassava porridge"

my father looking at him from the doorway without daring to speak, Maria da Boa Morte not calling him

"Child"

like she called us, but

"Carlos"

calling him

"Carlos"

sitting down to eat in front of him without asking his permission, treating him even worse than she treated the native soldiers, since she called the soldiers

"Mr. So and So Mr. This or That"

out of respect or deference or fear, I think it was out of fear

"Mr. So and So Mr. This or That"

me in Estoril eating vanilla cookies, drinking Coca-Cola, changing the channel from cartoons to sports, turning up the volume on the TV until I can't hear the waves, surrounded by photographs of Clarisse and her friends

"So that means Carlos isn't really our brother that means the lepers are Carlos's brothers and sisters right?"

the cat chasing after the tweety bird, the stocky bulldog chasing after the little dog, the coyote after the bird that runs really fast, the short little man after the respectable panther who smokes out of a cigarette holder, Clarisse's bare foot dangling from the armchair, laurels, tea roses, rich peoples' houses, boats, palm trees like the ones in Cassanje waving good-bye without a hint of sadness when we left

"Good-bye Rui"

a skunk in love with a cat, the pair of magpies who are always arguing, bears dressed like people, the old duck with glasses and sideburns, the little island with the lighthouse, water roiling as if it were in a saucepan behind the trawlers as they wait for high tide, my father didn't drink whiskey because of me like they always told me, it was his own fault, he made himself sick, stretched out in a chair on the patio, in a daze, bony

"So that means Carlos isn't really our brother that means the lepers are Carlos's brothers and sisters right?"

Carlos expecting me for Christmas Eve dinner looking out at the river through a gap in the curtains, thinking about Angola, not about Clarisse, not about my mother, not about me, thinking about his real family in Malanje, on the plantation, in the company store, in the cotton fields, in the workers' quarters, Carlos's shoulders moving up and down, his teeth shining, his cheeks shining, his sunken-in chest

"Don't cry Carlos"

and it was only fitting that he was crying since he was acting like an idiot, always thinking he was in charge

"Rui"

stopping me from catching grasshoppers and burning them with matches, it's only fitting that the Cape Verdeans should catch him the way they catch stray cats calling me over to help them

"Hey idiot hey you nutcase"

me wrapping my brother up in the net, throwing him into the canal and watching him float down toward the Tagus together with a bunch of trash

("Are you alone Rui?")

unable to stop me from strangling pigeons, unable to stop me from being happy.

10 MAY 1988

I should have known that Angola was over for me when they killed the people who lived two farms to the north of us, the man lying upside down on the stairs, or rather pinned to the stairs by a curtain rod that had been thrust through his stomach, the woman naked, facedown in the messy kitchen, even more naked than she'd have been if she were alive, her hands gone, her tongue gone, her breasts gone, her hair gone, chopped to bits with a butcher knife, the neck of a beer bottle sticking out from between her legs, her older son's head staring at us from a tree branch, his body had been cut into slices by a chainsaw and scattered about the flower bed, the younger son out back

(where we used to take tea with them in the afternoon, eating dry little cakes and cooling ourselves with fans made of palm leaves)

his entrails intertwined with those of the dog, bloody fingerprints on the walls, trinkets knocked to the ground, picture frames broken to pieces, the curtains of the open windows sweeping the silence and the smell of guts out of the house, a flock of geese flying over the burning company store, the tractors, and the fields of sunflowers, in which the foremen were curled up on the ground, made to chew on their own ears and noses with swarms of flies buzzing around their wounds, my father and the native soldiers searched through the fields but didn't find anyone except the wild dogs who would tear at the bodies of the dead and then draw away from them to breathe, the fur on their backs bristling, disgustedly setting aside any bones or scraps of clothes, my father not finding anybody except his own shadow, with a handkerchief over his mouth ordering them to bury the bodies, for the first time in his life with no safety or authority or certainties, I don't care where you do it doesn't matter where you do it dig a hole and put them in it, the diamond-mining Dutch patched up the asphalt road that had been destroyed by the rain with small stoves that spit stones and black teardrops onto the blacktop, the wild dogs returned to sniff the torsos, my father to the native soldiers with the handkerchief constantly covering his mouth and nose, drawing away from the bodies to breathe, just like the dogs, crosses man you're talking about crosses forget about crosses we're not going to waste our time making crosses, and as he spoke the rustle of footsteps, the sound of someone running off, the mad dash like a fuse burning toward its end, a group of sparrows taking flight, a struggle in the tall grass, the corporal blocking the path to the forest, bullets from the guns of the native soldiers striking the ground and forcing the footsteps to head toward the barn, the burning fuse and the harrowed flight coming to a halt in the driveway where the pickup trucks were parked, revealing an eight- or nine-year-old Bailundo standing motionless in front of us, holding a stolen sack of beans under his arm, while a leafy tree whose name I can't quite recall

I can almost see it in front of me but I can't recall the name of it

shook with the frightened movements of the crows in its branches, the curtains in the open windows that had neither window frames nor windowpanes, skeins of dingy fabric that continued to sweep the silence and smell of guts out of the house, the corporal turned toward the Bailundo with the butt of his rifle pressed against his chest and my father

"No"

a barefoot kid, eight or nine years old, with his back against the barn and a stolen sack of beans under his arm, looking at the rifles, looking at the native soldiers, the wild dogs digging up the graves of the dead, my father breathing through the handkerchief over his mouth and nose the same way the dogs panted for fresh air, once again feeling in possession of his safety, authority, certainties, forgetting about the boy's head up in the tree branch, the woman facedown in the kitchen even more naked than she'd have been if she were alive

"No"

the farm north of ours, a small farm with a small house, which had no corn or cotton or rice, barely any farm equipment, and that was worked by people from Luchazes who were bought for next to nothing in Moxico and so were even worse and more prone to illness than the specters who worked for us, my father would pay them a visit every so often, before teatime, striking them with his walking stick, not believing their excuses about malaria and dysentery, rousing the ones who pretended to be dying showing him their dry lips, that they were shivering with fever

"Look sir"

and yet we'd no sooner turn our backs than they'd suddenly be all better, smoking and drinking palm wine, my father with his boot upraised

"Get up you fool"

because he felt sorry for the woman with her cracked teapot and threadbare sweater out on the patio behind the house offering us faded canvas chairs and stools to sit on, offering us cookies, handing my mother and me palm-leaf fans that she used to fan the fire, apologizing for the tea, for the sugar, for even existing, calling my mother and me ma'am, calling my father sir, humble, ugly, sad, in her defeated little voice

"Do you need anything more ma'am need anything more sir?"

her children were also humble, also ugly, also sad, a couple of rats dressed up like people, quiet and skinny, so pale they were almost green, scratching their backs on the corners of the walls, admiring the cookies from afar, my mother holding out the platter to them unfurling her smile like the tail feathers of a peacock

"Want some?"

you could tell that the rats were hesitant, blinking in embarrassment, their knees bent slightly, giving the slightest indication of frightened acquiescence, and then their mother, intense, brusque, grabbed the platter from my mother and put it back on the table, which was covered by a tablecloth that had a big tear in the middle

"They already ate ma'am don't just stand there leaning against the wall go outside and play"

the rats sluggishly, silently obeyed, giving the cookies one last sidelong glance, and when we left we found them checking out our new jeep, with that smell of fresh varnish and napa leather that brand-new cars have, with additional headlights on the roof, comparing it with their car, which had no windshield, no paint, its fenders replaced with antelope horns, which I bet had never run, the whole car slanting to the right the way parrots and watercolor enthusiasts slant their head to get a better look, the rats taciturn and monotonous as they climbed up and down from the running board with a proprietary pleasure, their mother enraged

"If you've damaged the gentleman's jeep you don't even want to know what I'll do to you"

the rats, glued to each other's side like Siamese twins and sucking their thumbs headed back to the house, the woman cleaned off the running board with the hem of her skirt, shaking with uneasiness, irritation

"Forgive me sir forgive me ma'am they're a couple of pests you can rest assured that they didn't scratch anything"

as we drove off toward the front gate that didn't really exist, just a block of stone with a rusty metal ring sticking out of it and a piece of wood, once white, clamped within a broken piece of an old hinge, and while the woman and her husband, with a straw hat on his head, bowed at the waist in a respectful farewell, the rats suddenly became energetic, flying around with their mouths wide open, enormous, terrifying mouths, mouths as deep as wells, capable of swallowing the entire world, the cookie platter, the sugar dish, the teapot, ready to devour the torn tablecloth and the canvas chairs along the way, two little frail rats the size of the tiny Bailundo who stood against the wall of the barn with a stolen sack of beans under his arm, trying to protect it from the corporal who pressed the butt of his rifle against his chest, turning toward him, my father unfastening the holster of his pistol

"No"

the shabby house where they used old yogurt containers for cups and had armchairs that looked like they'd been salvaged from a shipwreck, the shabby farm, no water no river nearby no generator, smoke from the gas-burning lanterns that blackened the ceiling, sunflowers gnawed to bits by parasites, which no exporter would ever buy, the workers' quarters made up of half a dozen thatched huts with no wire fence around them to keep the Luchazes from going back to Moxico like a stampede of cattle, the yogurt containers and the gas-burning lanterns all shattered, a photograph of their wedding ripped up, the shabby house, the shabby farm, the sunflower crop chewed up by mice, overripe and rotting, the woman facedown in the kitchen, her hands gone, her tongue gone, her breasts gone, her hair gone, chopped to bits with a butcher knife, the neck of a beer bottle sticking out from between her legs, much more naked than she'd be if she were alive, offering us weak tea and cheap cookies that we begrudgingly held between our fingers

"I've got to put this in my mouth what a pain"

the woman who called me

"Ma'am"

the way the hairdressers in the city did, I should have known that Angola was over for me when the Bailundo kid, a stolen sack of beans under his arm his back against the wall of the barn with the barrel of the corporal's rifle pointed at him, killed dozens and dozens of white people in Luanda, in Salazar, in Dondo, passing through outlying neighborhoods, slums, and suburban streets, sneaking in through the backyards, setting homes on fire, decapitating chickens as well as people, bunches of heads hanging from trees, garlands of intestines, children who were eviscerated by cats next to the dahlias in the flowerpots, the woman hurriedly hiding the tear in the oilskin tablecloth, setting the sugar dish on top of it

(the sugar dish was in worse shape than the tablecloth)

hoping we wouldn't notice, that we wouldn't pay attention, that we wouldn't see it, the woman in a state of agonized politeness, thinking that she could hide their wretchedness and their lack of money and their hunger together with the tear in the tablecloth

"Ma'am"

my mother opened her purse with a sharp metallic sound

tic

(I liked that sound so much that if I had my way I'd open and close the purse over and over so I could hear the little chrome balls as they snapped together

tic

then separated from each other

tic

snapping together

tic

then separating once again

tic)

looking for her coin purse amid all the sad little coffee sweetener tablets that made the coffee taste of widowhood, my father and I looked away as if something fascinating vital irresistible were going on in the other direction, my mother whispering something about a loan, a gift, held out a few bills toward the pocket of the woman's apron and the woman jumped back, pushing her fingers away

"Don't insult me ma'am don't insult me"

her husband with a scythe on his shoulder wiping the sweat from his cheeks with a handkerchief

pinned to the stairs with a rod that had been thrust through his stomach

moved his ears as if agreeing with one of them I don't know if it was with his wife or with my mother, he reminded me of a lifeless, luckless peasant who'd been abandoned by the rains, abandoned by the rector, abandoned by the sun on the steps of the church, waiting for alms, neither begging for them nor refusing them, floating through life in his straw hat in a vague state of despair, the two rats watching aloofly buoyed up by their fearful hopes, sharing a tricycle with bent wheels that was too small for them, the house was missing roof tiles, a cover on the chimney, walls on the outhouse, a septic tank, a well, there was no soap, the tree

one of those really well-known trees I just can't remember its name

no, not a mango tree, what a stupid guess, I'll remember it in a minute

mourned together with us, the clouds stretched out above the plains by the Diamang company, floating eastward, the company store

cashew tree?

was closed

acacia damn that's not it

in the distance, an obligatory blue spot on the horizon, the woman jumping back, offended, red-faced, her hands gone, her tongue gone, her breasts gone, her hair gone

"Don't insult me ma'am don't insult me"

so very naked

Holy Mary

so very naked

her buttocks, her thighs, the nape of her neck, the depression at the back of her knees, I've never seen anyone so naked in my life, so very naked, how can I explain it, it wasn't really just that she was naked what's wrong with being naked, it was that she was naked in such an obscene manner, me with a handkerchief over my mouth and nose as well, not horrified, not nauseated, surprised rather by the neck of the beer bottle sticking out from between her legs, the complete lack of decency, of shame, her immodesty, imagining her with her husband in his straw hat, the two of them lying together, distracted, sleepy, weary, imagining the birth of those two rats, the sickening liquid discharge, the mucus membranes, my mother was surprised

"All right then Dona Matilde let's not speak of it then"

and put the bills back in her coin purse, put the coin purse back in her purse with the metallic snap of its little chrome balls snapping shut

tic

baobab tree, that's it baobab tree, quiet down now

the little balls resisted snapping shut and once they were closed they resisted coming undone, from the first pressure until the

tic

and then they'd separate, without any desire to come back together until we pushed them closed again, pushing them against
each other, building up a delectable pressure between the index
finger and the thumb, the little balls rubbing their rotund bellies up against each other, determined to disobey me, and then
came the

tic

intertwining the two fasteners that bound them to the purse

tic

every time I asked my mom to let me do

tic

that, she'd look at me as though I was an idiot, placing a protec-
tive hand over the clasp

"You're never going to grow up are you?"

so that when

(the clouds over Diamang, scarlet-colored like a robe or blood,
bloody fingerprints throughout the house, on the stairs, in the
kitchen, on the oilskin tablecloth where we'd been served tea

blood

the bloody clouds floating eastward, the clouds and some birds
from the same genus as doves but not doves although they were
bleeding as well, they were bleeding blood, blood

blood

disappearing into a stand of trees behind the company store)

so that when

"All right then Dona Matilde let's not speak of it then"

she snapped the two little balls closed

tic

I grabbed her purse, snatched it from her lap so I could open and close the clasp, overcome its inertia, hear the sound it made

tic

the woman, thinking that I was going to insist she take the bills, that I was about to stuff them into the pocket of her apron, grabbed my wrist with her sweaty fingernails, her sweaty nose pressed against my nose

"I don't need anything from you I don't want anything from you I just demand that you show me some respect you hear?"

me, who should've known that Angola was over for me and left it for good the day the eight- or nine-year-old Bailundo boy with a stolen sack of beans under his arm, his back against the wall of the barn with the barrel of the corporal's rifle pointed at him, my father to the corporal, holster unfastened, trying to lessen the stench of the corpses by holding a handkerchief over his face

"No"

on the day the Bailundo boy killed dozens and dozens of white people in Luanda, in Salazar, in Caxito, in Dondo, going around at night, passing through outlying neighborhoods, slums, even the neighborhoods in the center of the cities, the houses along the blocks near the citadel and the government building, the eight- or nine-year-old Bailundo kid nothing but two enormous eyes, enormous pupils, pulling the sack of beans away from the corporal, decapitating chickens and people with a blow from his machete, hanging their heads from trees with twine, or hooks, or leaving them to the appetites of the dogs, dozens and dozens of white people with their testicles, ears, and noses shoved down their throats together with the silence of the butterflies and the buzzing of wasps, the larvae and flies in their rotten stomachs, the fetuses of the pregnant women ripped out and cast to the cats like trash fish, in Lobito, in Benguela, in Sá de Bandeira, in São Salvador, in Luso, in Carmona, in Tentativa, in Huambo, it wasn't a bunch of savage drunks or some groups organized by Russian or Hungarian or Romanian or Yugoslavian or Bulgarian communists, or a coalition, or a movement, or a political party that wanted to gain control of Angola, make the decisions in Angola, replace us white people in the companies, the branches of government, the office buildings in Angola, take over our houses and farms, round us up on the pier, holding tight to our worthless belongings, and deport us, it wasn't hatred or vengeance

(oh why, Father in Heaven, why would they want vengeance?)

or a feeling of impotence or a revolt against us, no it was just an eight- or nine-year-old Bailundo kid with a sack of beans under his arm, a single kid with faded kinky hair hiding out in the forest like a badger, like a baby ferret, like a hedgehog, a single kid at the end of the barrel of the corporal's rifle, my father with a handkerchief covering his face

"No"

confirming that Angola was over for me, not just Baixa de Cassanje, and our cotton, our rice, our corn, Angola, all of Angola

all of it

the land the rivers the cities the beaches of Angola including the deserted streets and deserted homes of Moçâmedes, the aunts that I never met dressed in fancy clothes like the great-grandmothers in our photographs, the quartermaster who fought Gungunhana, whose eyes had seen the eyes of Caldas Xavier and Mouzinho de Albuquerque, collecting stamps

"Isilda"

the palm trees shrouded in sand complaining and griping like living beings

"Isilda"

the shabby house, the shabby farm, the canvas chairs, the tea table with the tear in the oilskin tablecloth now on display, no sugar dish to cover it up, the corporal pulled back the hammer of his rifle and I put my hand out to stop him

"No"

not my father with a handkerchief over his face, tortured by the smell, it was me, putting my hand out to stop him

"No"

heads, garlands of intestines, pieces of leather, of metal, of rubber shoved in between their buttocks, napes of necks that had been crushed by stones, eyeballs that had been scooped out with a spoon, a fork, the end of a knife, the native soldiers creeping toward him panting heavily like wild dogs, the naked woman with no hands no tongue no breasts no hair

blood

I don't need anything from you I don't want anything from you I just demand that you show me some respect you hear, the tea that tasted like brackish water, the cookies that tasted like plaster, the car with no windshield, with antelope horns on its radiator, slanting to the right the way parrots and watercolor enthusiasts slant their head to get a better look, the Bailundo kid staring at the corporal staring at my father staring at me, the kid who stole a sack of beans the same way he stole Angola from us, I never imagined that Angola was just a sack of beans in the hands of a little kid and yet it was just a simple sack of beans, it wasn't made up of mountains or hills or oil rigs or factories or plantations or that cloud that looked like a cloud with the shape density width and movements of a cloud yet was really just a group of ducks figuring out which way the wind was blowing, Angola was nothing more than a stolen sack of beans under a little kid's arm, a sack that I couldn't quite understand, I couldn't understand if it belonged to him or to us, just like this country this land this shabby house with its furniture and dishes that were missing handles drawers decorative metal plates with encrusted jewels and embossed designs, this plantation with its grayish sunflowers that the brokers refused to transport to Luanda

"Hold on pal"

overripe and rotting, chewed to bits by field mice, the company store or rather the angular cubicle box chicken coop that we called the company store locked up with a padlock that could be wrenched open by the slightest breeze through the reeds, the slightest exhalation from the grass, the company store with no tobacco no fish no beer none of those big shiny things that the field hands liked, the man in the straw hat pinned to the stairs with a curtain rod pierced through his navel smiling at us next to the teapot wiping the sweat from his cheeks with a handkerchief while the Bailundo kid set fire to the half-dozen huts that made up the workers' quarters and the slaves

workers peasants laborers not slaves

purchased from the regional administrator

contracted through the regional administrator, a friend of the natives who defended their rights and encouraged them to take jobs, the workers who were employed through the regional administrator, unaccustomed to the humidity, unaccustomed to the heat, wasting away from malaria and dysentery

contracted with wages that were perfectly fair free medical attention free medication free school free lodging a company store that was just for them complete freedom how could they be called slaves, can you please tell me how they could be called slaves

the two rats, happy, clambered up and down from the running board of the jeep, the walls of buildings in Marimba in Marimbanguengo in Chiquita in Santo António of the workers' quarters in Macau all damaged by fire by gunfire by bullets, our porch, our orchard, our patio, our azalea garden, our guesthouse, the Bailundo kid knocking over our dressers, our corner shelves, our armchairs, our clock, the Japanese tureen in the china cabinet that only my mother, with the care of a jeweler polishing his stock, was allowed to clean, the Bailundo kid with sun-faded kinky hair and a stomach swollen from hunger, a stolen sack of beans under his arm, coming up to my mother with a broken bottle neck, ripping her clothes, pulling her clothes off, leaving her even more naked than if she'd been alive, shamefully naked, obscenely naked, the corporal pulling back the hammer of the rifle and me holding out my hand to stop him

not my father with a handkerchief over his face, feeling the urge to sit down, to run off, the two little chrome balls

tic

and

tic

and

tic

and

tic

my dead father fending off the stench of the dead, my father with testicles shoved down his throat, his head staring at us from the branch of a tree, not my father who'd been sliced to pieces by a chain saw and scattered about the flower bed, his body his legs his knees his cartilage the color of milk his very fingers, my cotton crop on fire, my rice crop on fire, my corn crop ruined, the generator drooling its gaslike blood

blood

the corporal pulling back the hammer of the rifle and me holding out my hand to stop his movement

"No"

the kid who killed me, who tracked me down in order to kill me and tangle up my guts with the dog's, the Bailundo kid with his back against the wall of the barn or what was left of the barn with a stolen sack of beans under his arm looking at me as if he accepted

no, not as if he accepted, but rather truly accepting

without a word without a gesture without a sign that he'd try to run off, accepting the fact that I was taking the pistol out of my father's holster, that I was taking off the safety

tic

that I was aiming it

tic

that I was squeezing the trigger

tic

the eight- or nine-year-old kid who kept looking at me while he slowly slid down the wall of the barn, the way a drop of wax or resin slides down a smooth surface, the way a tear slides down a cheek until it falls to the ground.

24 December 1995

My sister Clarisse to me
   "It's over there"
   in a part of Luanda that wasn't really the city and wasn't really
the slums or it was both of those at the same time or neither of
those, there were still houses and buildings but they were all unfinished, more like shacks although they had the appearance and
intention of being buildings, half-brick half-wood structures with
small dusty gardens, dreary rooms, workmen's clothing hanging
on clotheslines, a line of people in front of the public fountain
or rather a metal faucet set in a cement block with a tiny meager
stream of dirty water dripping from it onto the ground, driving

the honey bees mad, half-brick half-wood structures inhabited by white people who were poorer than the rest of the white people which is to say they were poor, and black people who were richer than the rest of the black people which is to say they were one step away from being indigent wretches, houses and buildings that the builders left unfinished so they could go work on vacation homes for the Americans from the oil company and the Portuguese from the beer company, or work in the neighborhoods where the government workers lived, or the places where the government was hurriedly erecting monuments, or work on buildings for insurance companies, banks, hotels, factories, or work on infirmaries, mess halls, and barracks for the soldiers, houses and buildings with no chimneys and no roofs, windows that were drawn on the walls but never cut out, crooked doorways, iron beams at the top of pillars where storks liked to perch, houses and buildings to which were added little shacks constructed from planks and cheap mortar that were used to complete unfinished hallways living rooms kitchens bedrooms, Clarisse to me

"It's over there"

as if there could possibly be a doctor's office somewhere in all those narrow alleys and lanes like the twisted branches of baobab trees and old men aiming their crude rifles out toward the sea, as if a kidney doctor would set up shop amid concrete mixers and the long spines of construction cranes, stray goats wandering up to him, sniffing at his legs, my brother Carlos in the house that faced the sea in the Alvalade neighborhood in Luanda, the little men who exchanged Angolan coins for Portuguese coins in Versalhes square ten percent twelve percent sixteen percent twenty-five percent, the house in Alvalade rented from some friends of my parents, with antelope and zebra pelts all over not just as rugs on the floors of all the rooms but also draped over the backs of all the divans, bows, spears, and shields covered in leopard fur on every wall, stuffed cranes and pelicans on every shelf not to mention the monkey in a cage out on the balcony that started shrieking the moment he heard us open the door, a tamarin monkey that I tortured with a firebrand from the kitchen, Clarisse, when she saw it on the floor of the cage

"I wonder what's wrong with that animal"

little lights walking along the sand at night, my history teacher in school stood up on his tiptoes in the middle of the room, surrounded by all our desks, his arms outstretched as if he were going to fly

"And Caesar said"

all of us with our heads down in our notebooks while our teacher grew taller, he grew taller and his chest swelled, grew taller and taller and taller even the stripes on his suit grew taller his coat his vest his pants, his pocket-watch chain that drooped down to form a smile made of little silver rings right at the height of his belly button, the chain sparkled, his shiny shoes sparkled, every part of the teacher sparkled as he struck the pose of a diver on the high dive, bellowing the decisive phrase

"And Caesar said"

suddenly jumping off the platform and holding the chalkboard eraser in both his hands, holding the chalky sponge over his head like a trophy, not just a sponge but a whole continent that sullied his suit with chalk dust, our teacher coughing up little white puffs of chalk dust

"I have taken you Africa"

sprawled out on the floor unable to get up or stop coughing, his pocket watch crushed, lying below a poster that read We are the beacon of civilization and the terror of all atheist communists, Clarisse found monkey fur and the smell of burnt meat on the firebrand in the kitchen

"Honestly Rui"

the tamarin would make a great rug to add to the antelope and zebra ones in the house my parents rented in Luanda

(little lights from ghosts from dead people from soldiers on leave looking for a woman walking along the shore of the island all night long)

so that Carlos and Clarisse could go to the high school, under the pretext of sending them to school they could be free, I mean my mother could be free of the scandal of having a mulatto son and a daughter who dressed like a cancan girl and wore as much makeup as a clown, who was the biggest disgrace in all of Baixa de Cassanje

(sometimes the little lights floating on the sea)

so that Carlos and Clarisse could go to school and I could, on the advice of a specialist, breathe in the iodine-rich air on the beach

"Iodine is good for the nerves and will alleviate his attacks ma'am he'll be as good as new after he breathes in that iodine for a few months"

so that my mother could be alone with the police chief in the study, without any witnesses, while my father drank his whiskey upstairs pretending not to hear them, the police chief would have made a great rug next to all those antelope and

zebra rugs, and I'd stomp on it and stomp on it and then stomp
on it as hard as I could, my father smiling at us as he wiped his
chin with his sleeve and I'd stomp on my father too just the
same, me, furious with him, how could anyone think I'd ever
really liked him, I don't like him, how could I like him, stomping on him just the same

father

if I could only explain what I'm unable to express, if I could
only touch him, or something, rather than stomp on him, I've
never touched anyone, people have touched me, but I've never
touched anyone

and one or two or three months after we arrived in Luanda,
Clarisse waking up pale, her eyes bulging out, throwing up, holding herself up on the backs of chairs, her stomach getting fatter,
grabbing at her ribs and complaining of pains in her kidneys

(sometimes the little lights floated along the sea searching
for me and they weren't bugs or animals or people it was my
father perhaps

father

it was Josélia Fernando Damião getting worried about me

"Child")

Clarisse in the house in Alvalade grabbing her rib cage

"I need to go to the doctor my kidneys hurt"

lying on her back on the couch, uninterested in everything not
responding to anybody, only paying attention to her own body or
whatever was happening inside her body as if her nerves and veins
were speaking to her, Clarisse, who didn't put on any makeup,
didn't comb her hair, didn't smell like perfume, didn't giggle and

whisper sweet nothings into the phone motioning for me to leave her alone

"Scram"

with a few quick gestures, Clarisse, moving slowly and very carefully, from one armchair to the next, as cautious as a waiter holding a tray of food, Carlos

"Your kidneys hurt what a joke"

hesitant to write to Malanje, you know what'll happen if I tell Mom and Dad, Mom will go upstairs to the bedroom and blame Dad and that'll make him drink double what he does now, become even more ridiculous, kill himself even faster, or should I pretend that I haven't noticed, that I don't know anything, and not write to Malanje, and then perhaps those pains in her kidneys, this little problem

"What problem Carlos what problem?"

those pains in her kidneys will go away by themselves, and if they don't go away by themselves perhaps she'll have the good sense to go fix what she's done

"What did she do Carlos tell me what did Clarisse do?"

in a hospital or a clinic or a pharmacy or at the office of some kindly doctor or some witch doctor or some underground clinic in Mutamba or Cuca, all she'll have to do is spend a few days laid up in bed and when she gets out of bed she'll just put on her makeup and perfume, comb her hair, whisper into the phone for hours on end, go downstairs in a new dress, a dress the size of a handkerchief, if I might be allowed to exaggerate, going out to meet someone who's outside whistling for her, running his car engine, honking, the house in Alvalade with two sycamore trees out back, beetles quietly waiting for the lamps to be lit to come out, the house in the shade of those two sycamores, which were too big for the small backyard, the house that got dark earlier in the evening and felt the brightness of dawn later in the morning than the rest of the neighborhood, the sea would still be shining outside our window and we'd be floating, not moving, but floating in a jar of darkness, the stuffed and mounted cranes and pelicans following us with their eyes

"Why would our parents die if Carlos wrote a letter to Baixa de Cassanje Clarisse?"

Lady died, my grandmother died, tons of blacks died, my grandmother died in her bedroom and Lady and all the blacks died on the ground, I remember that they all looked the same with the same green flies going in their noses and ears and they were all buried in the ground with a sack of quicklime dumped over them

(you could hear the quicklime which sounded like it was boiling and burning on their chests)

in the plantation cemetery with all the moss that no one ever cleared away, the headstones with writing in Latin, the stone crosses, the metal fence that had fallen over, I remember the motionless lizards drawing back their feet, their necks stuck out, ready to run off, I remember my mother saying on our way back from the cemetery

"I'm going to send someone out to fix it up it would be disrespectful not to send someone out to fix it up"

and then forgetting about it soon after, as soon as she took off her linen mourning clothes, so the headstones with writing in Latin almost invisible under the mosses and the grass were still broken, the stone crosses were still worn down by some sort of leprosy or canker, the crowns of thorns around them wasting away, the metal fence still didn't protect the dead from wildcats and dogs, the plastic tulips in glazed porcelain pots still disintegrated into little colored granules if you so much as laid a finger on one, the priest, Damião, and Fernando would lower the casket while my mother stood under her umbrella even when there was no rain, wearing glasses so she could follow along with the prayers, which she never said, in her missal, which was shut, her index finger in between the pages, marking the prayer for the dead, glancing around at the cemetery, vaguely remorseful

"I swear I'm going to send someone out here to fix it up it would be disrespectful not to send someone out to fix it up"

the house in Alvalade smelled like crab and gutted animals, the monkey suffered his misfortunes beneath his white beard, Carlos would leave for school and come home from school in a strange angry mood, his brow furrowed, never talking to Clarisse whose belly kept getting fatter and fatter while her face got skinnier, getting up at two or three in the morning, her face pale because of her upset stomach, going to the fridge, eating the paraffin rind of the cheese, not the cheese itself, eating the mold on the jelly jars, not the jelly itself, I'd find her in her nightshirt standing next to the fridge, her body dark in the murky light, looking out at the lights on the island, laughing, with an expression on her face that I'd never seen before, me feeling worried about her

"Your kidneys hurt right Clarisse don't they hurt?"

the same lights that sometimes floated on the sea and they weren't bugs or animals or ships it was Damião carrying a lantern

"Child"

Clarisse standing next to the fridge just laughing and laughing

"Such an idiot such an idiot"

me feeling worried about her, holding her chin and turning her face toward me

"Your kidneys hurt right Clarisse don't they hurt?"

a piece of the cheese rind in her hand a smudge of mold on her tongue, a procession of little city ants disappeared through a gap between two tiles, Clarisse laughing, laughing incessantly, her shirt bouncing up and down as she did

"I'm such an idiot I'm such an idiot"

if I was back at the plantation I'd hear the rustling of the sunflowers, even if there was no wind, not to mention the clock, which Carlos swore was the heart of the house, Carlos was afraid that if it ever stopped ticking we would all stop ticking too, if I was back at the plantation I'd grab my pellet gun, open the window, and, in spite of the heavy fog, in spite of the scolding I'd get from my mom and the heartache it would cause her, I'd shoot the peacocks, troubled by bad dreams as they slept in the branches of the golden rain tree, if I was back at the plantation Fernando would turn off the generator and the house would stop shaking and trembling, the filaments of the lightbulbs would fade until they became nothing more than a thin pink line slowly disappearing, the azaleas would shudder from the cold, the cotton, awakened from its slumber, would start to sparkle, the sycamores were watching us from the backyard, Clarisse set down the cheese rind, stood up straight, smoothed out her hair, and suddenly became serious, Clarisse, talking to the beetles and the moths in the darkness, talking to no one at all

"I'm such an idiot"

Clarisse sweeping the floor, closing the cupboard doors, turning off the light, saying good night to me at the door of her bedroom, the harsh neon light making her look especially gaunt, as it would with a statue, Clarisse looking as lonely as my father

"Tomorrow you'll come to the doctor's office with me Rui tomorrow the doctor's going to take out this kidney stone and I'll be all better"

the doctor in a part of Luanda that wasn't really the city and wasn't really the slums or it was both of those at the same time or neither of those, in a part of Luanda where Luanda came to an end, there were still buildings but they were all unfinished, more like shacks although they had the appearance and intention of being buildings, half-brick half-wood structures with small dusty gardens, crooked doorways, workmen's clothing hanging on clotheslines, a line of people in front of the spigot of the public fountain, a metal faucet set in a cement block with a tiny meager stream of dirty water dripping from it onto the ground, driving the honey bees mad, half-brick half-wood structures inhabited by white people who were poorer than the rest of the white people which is to say they were poor, and black people who were richer than the rest of the black people which is to say they were one step away from being indigent wretches, buildings to which were added little shacks made out of planks and cheap mortar that completed unfinished hallways living rooms pantries bedrooms, the part of Luanda where Luanda came to an end and turned into rows of cashew trees, uninhabited huts, and the ocher of barren lands, there was a railroad car and to the left of it what had once been a grocery store, a store run by Indians, a shed for storing seeds or wagons or tools or cattle back when Luanda was still full of swamps and tents and cows were herded along the beach, a roof with no crossbeam, bare walls in need of a paint job, a recently added balcony that would end up getting knocked down by the impending rains, impending heat, or merely the unstoppable passage of month after month, my sister

"It's over there"

as if there could be a doctor's office or a doctor or a nurse or even a lowly hospital worker in a storeroom full of sacks of seeds and harnesses and saddles, with the cracks in the plaster covered up with blankets, chickens running in and out of the hole in the wall that served as a door, a second room that was walled off by a bedsheet and smelled like gasoline, like disinfectant, with some sort of sink, some sort of bed, some sort of washbasin with the enamel cracked and falling off, with a corner of a towel, a piece of soap, and a bucket underneath it, a little kid leading a live frog along by a leash made of string, pulling back the bedsheet and disappearing behind it, dragging the frog behind him into the stench of disinfectant, a whistle of flowing propane, the sound of rattling aluminum, of lids being removed and replaced, the little kid appeared again from behind the bedsheet, her kinky hair gathered into two wirelike braids, followed by a woman in an apron wearing what had once been a surgical cap, which sat lopsided on her head, slanting down toward one ear, me speaking softly, fearful like I always was in church, holding on to Clarisse, standing next to a pile of baskets full of broken bottles, the type of junk you pick up along the beach at low tide and then sell by the pound

"Is that the kidney doctor Clarisse?"

Clarisse disappearing in turn behind the bedsheet curtain, seagulls from the bay perched on the railway car, well within reach, and me with no pellet gun, what a drag, with no stone to throw at them, the seagulls waited a little while longer, looking at me with one eye and then the other, wanting me, begging for me, but then they ended up getting tired of it and headed back to the coconut trees and the puddles of gasoline of the bay, just as disappointed as I was, the little kid made the frog jump by pulling on the string, a bunch of stray dogs were following around a bitch that would stop to sniff at the lampposts, like the police chief, the governor, the lieutenant-governor, and the town administrators who followed my mother around like a pack of dogs, lighting her cigarettes, bringing her drinks, offering her ashtrays, trying to put their arm around her, caress her hand, kiss her, I saw her in a mirror kissing the bishop's nephew and then I smashed it with a bronze candlestick, the kiss fell to the ground in a waterfall of pieces, and it was no longer a kiss at all, just shards that reflected the ceiling, my mother and the bishop's nephew were no longer inside the mirror frame so my father could look at it without drinking, without rummaging through all the snifters the glasses the bottles in the buffet, Clarisse and the kidney doctor were talking to each other on the other side of the bedsheet or it looked to me like they were talking or the doctor was talking and Clarisse was laughing like she did in the kitchen the night before with the wax rind from the cheese falling from her hand

"I'm such an idiot"

laughing and laughing and laughing with traces of makeup still lingering on her face, her hair disheveled, and her eyes dead, her eyes staring straight ahead and dead, above her mouth, which was still alive and trembling

"I'm such an idiot"

the two sycamores merging together in the darkness, the lights from the island floating atop the waves, me taking care of my sister without hitting her, without pouring her perfume down the toilet, without breaking her necklaces, without tossing drawers full of her blouses out into the street, putting my arm around her without really putting my arm around her shoulder because I hate it when people touch me and I hate touching anyone no matter who it is, ever since I saw my mother in the mirrors, ever since the mirrors, ever since the key turned in the door to the study and they locked themselves in there, I don't touch anybody unless it's with pellets from my pellet gun, with a broom handle, with a fire-brand, with my own feces, and I've noticed that everyone makes the same face and the same sounds, a scrunched-up grimace, their eyes wide open, weird whining sounds coming from their throats, when it began to get dark and the buildings and the shacks

(the unfinished buildings that were like shacks and the shacks that looked like buildings and were intended to be buildings joined together stuck together with plywood boards cement as-bestos panels zinc panels pieces of canvas of oilskin tarps or un-treated cloth palm fronds held up by screws hooks tape clothes-pins twine, the buildings and shacks of poor white people and rich black people as miserable as sickly mules or stray animals)

started to dissolve into a coagulated mass on which the flicker-ing light of candles and oil lamps conferred an intermittent vi-bration, a diffused restlessness, Clarisse pulled back the bedsheet,

walking really slowly along the dirt road holding herself upright as if her body didn't belong to her and she was just holding it up by the armpits, forcing it to walk, she looked for me in the dark but didn't see me by the pile of baskets full of scrap metal and broken bottles, by the sleepy chickens, by the crumbling walls

"Rui"

like a blind person, just like a blind person, her feet, her hands, her torso leaning forward, her head, her flared nostrils gauging the echoes, measuring the sounds

"Rui"

Clarisse whose kidney stones had been cured by the doctor holding herself up against the plaster columns while the streetlamps of Luanda were being lit, an army jeep was patrolling the silence, the trash, and the oil lamps, all the exact same

(the desistance the abandonment the wastefulness the resignation the stench)

as the workers' quarters on the plantation but bigger, even more wasteful, probably with even more lepers, probably even more dilapidated, more broken down, more like my father, even closer to death, my father preferred Clarisse to us, he never drank in front of her, never complained, and pretended he was all better

"I'm almost back in tip-top shape tomorrow I'll be in tip-top shape if you'd like to go for a walk with your old man the two of us could go for a short stroll"

raising his head off the pillow, smiling, covering up his emaciated neck with the collar of his pajama top, shriveled up, unable to get around on his own

"The two of us will go out for a short stroll"

the next day he asked the servants to dress him, shave him, put on his shirt, his tie, some pants that danced around his waist, some shoes that were now much too big for him, he asked them to set him down on the chair next to the bed to wait for my sister, not my father but a caricature of him, a half-erased memory of him, a scornful sketch of him, and then there'd be a whistle, the sound of a car engine, a woman's laughter, someone's voice calling out, someone honking out in the driveway, Clarisse with her hair done up, her makeup on, wearing a low-cut blouse like the movie stars on the posters in Damaia, wearing a red skirt, red sandals, carrying a red purse, yelling from the hallway, the sweet breath of her perfume arriving in the room long before she did

"I'm going"

adjusting a pleat, a strap, a piece of lace, the seam of her stockings, walking past us as she put on her earrings, not even thinking about my father, her womanly laughter annoying the quails in the garden, the setters barked when they heard the car horn, feverish with rage, then there was more giggling, more whistles, more voices, footsteps out by the flower beds, the clanging protestations of the clock, the trembling of the azaleas, the acidic squeal of the doorbell, my father, or the worn-out creature that my father had become, plopped down in the chair wearing his enormous suit, shoes that were a few sizes too big, the golden cuff links he reserved for the inaugurations of generals, meals at the Ferroviário Club, and the galas in Luanda

"Clarisse"

the peacocks, enraged, hopping from one mango tree to the next, their wings sounding like the rustling of silk sheets, the clock unleashing a slew of hours that then flew off like a bunch of turtledoves, hours that pecked at the window panes trying to get outside, out to where the golden rain tree was, the sunflowers, the rustling of the cotton, Clarisse slipping on the second earring, looking for a polished surface where she could admire the curls in her hair, her lipstick, her bracelets, saying good-bye to my father, lightly brushing her cheek against his so she wouldn't rub off any of her face powder, so she wouldn't mess up her hair, so she wouldn't smudge her foundation, spurred into action by another whistle, another flock of hours flying off, another squeal of the doorbell

"We'll take a stroll around the plantation next week I promise"

Clarisse in a part of Luanda that wasn't really the city and wasn't really the slums or it was both of those at the same time or neither of those, no makeup, no perfume, no low-cut blouse, no jewelry, propping herself up as if her body didn't really belong to her and she was just holding it up by the armpits, forcing it to walk, gauging echoes, measuring sounds

"Rui"

just like my father used to do, an exact copy of my father

"Clarisse"

certain that my sister would take him for a walk, talk with him, amuse him, entertain him, staving off his death, strolling out to the gate or the crossroads just outside the gate where the highway to Malanje began, and it would all be gone, the fevers the palsy the injections the police chief and my mother in the study downstairs, an exact copy of my father

"Rui"

certain that I'd take her home, talk to her, entertain her, stave off her death, that I'd take her back to the house in Alvalade that looked out onto the bay and the coconut palms on the island, and the pains in her kidneys were gone, no more nausea, no more swelling, no more vomiting, Carlos could write to our parents in Baixa de Cassanje if he wanted to, he could write whatever he wanted to because ever since I pulled back that bedsheet and took off my skirt and slip and laid down on the cot there was nothing absolutely nothing nor would there ever be anything that could ever worry my parents.

13 AUGUST 1989

I honestly don't know what my mother saw in that woman, but
she was the one my mother asked for when she was dying, not
me, she was the one my mother asked to help her when she was
trying to catch her breath, it was her hand that my mother held on
to, and just imagine me there in the room, the priest there saying
his prayers and blessings and instead of the daughter he finds a
Bailunda wearing plastic sandals acting like a part of the family,
whereas I was shoved into a corner like some old piece of junk
next to that fool husband of mine, that worthless bum to whom
no one ever paid attention, just imagine what a shameful scene
that was, my ungrateful mother replacing her loyal family with

a servant, replacing me with a little old lady from the workers' quarters in front of everyone

(and if she could just replace me with a little old lady from the workers' quarters then what am I after all?)

my guests and friends completely scandalized, the poor priest pretending not to notice as best he could raising his eyebrows at me

"Shall I go on Dona Isilda?"

me there in the back of the room, what could I do about it, wanting to strangle Josélia, raising my eyebrows as well

"What else can we do please continue Father"

hoping that idiot would come to her senses, move away from the bed, and go back down to the kitchen, if not out of a sense of decency, which is something she lacks completely, then at least out of fear of what I'd do to her after the wake, after the burial, after the reading of my mother's will, which she changed every-day, locking herself in the study, seated with us at the dinner table staring at us one by one, a silent threat, wordlessly telling us Since I can't interfere with the plantation or the house when it suits me I'll leave the building in Henrique de Carvalho to the Franciscan priests, I'll leave the land in Benguela to the Red Cross, and I'll give our stock in the railroad to the poor people in our diocese who are almost starving to death, and me wordlessly telling her, while I instructed Damião to serve her more soup, If you're not going to think of me at least think of your grandchildren, wanting to smash her face in yet smiling all the while, humiliated, tying the bib around Rui's neck, perhaps a little too forcefully due to how angry I was, since the little guy stopped breathing and his face turned purple, Damião made the rounds with the serving trays, Fernando uncorked the wine, Maria da Boa Morte appeared with the cream, my mother looking at my children, frowning in contempt My grandchildren, you say, what grandchildren, a mulatto, an epileptic, and a shameless hussy who, from the looks of it, is going to end up in a gutter in Luanda, are those the ones you're calling my grandchildren Isilda, they aren't my grandchildren, they've never been my grandchildren, they've got the blood of your husband and father in them, they didn't want a single drop of blood from my side of the family, the wind changed directions, silencing the rustle of the sunflowers and making the room seem bigger, my mother hidden behind her drooping eyelids as if she were behind a wall, dripping her blood-pressure medication into her glass with the sound of rain dripping from gutter pipes on a sleepless night, the most important ritual in the world, so important that we couldn't help but concentrate intently on it one two three four five drops forming little clouds in the water, each little cloud repeating My grandchildren my grandchildren my grandchildren, a mulatto, bought from his mother in Malanje and who isn't even really my grandchild, using the same silverware I use, eating the same dinner I eat, an epileptic writhing around during his fits, and a hussy who'll end up living in one of those shacks out on the island, half naked like all the other hussies out there, heating up a pan over a fire in the sand, grinding cassava roots, receiving soldiers in the evenings

the soldiers' slut the soldiers' slut

an adult at twelve years old, an old woman at thirty, a cup of acid thrown at her face or a knife to her throat at thirty-five during a brawl between a bunch of derelicts in Sambila, my children in Ajuda somehow getting along without me, God willing he's getting my letters and reading them aloud to his brother and sister, my mother with no grandchildren calling Josélia to her side to help her catch her breath, holding her hand so tightly that as soon as the priest finished and we draped a handkerchief over her face we had to wrench her fingers off of Josélia's hand one by one, so we could comb her hair, wash her, dress her, Josélia standing motionless beside the bed.

(you could hear the blows from the hammers of the carpenters who were building the new storehouse and the new barn, scaring away the doves who were perched on the roof, as well as the calf-like whimpering of those diurnal owls that I hate and were always looking for hedgehogs along the rows of cotton)

Josélia wearing an apron, not a blouse and a skirt like us, holding her hand out to my mother as if the dead woman, with a crucifix on her chest, might actually reach out and grab it, talk to her, bequeath her the building in Caxito, we wrapped her in damask silk and brought in the oratory from the hallway and some chairs from the living room, Fernando closed the drapes, which by the way were quite expensive, brought there from Malanje back when my father was still alive, and that idiot Josélia just stood there among all our guests, all our friends, all the people from the neighboring farms who hadn't even had time to put on a fresh shirt and still had crease marks in their foreheads from the felt lining of their hats, tracking dust and dirt upstairs on their boots, that idiot Josélia didn't even notice we were there, focused instead on keeping my mother away from her coffin, away from that death that only starts to feel real the moment the pallbearers appear and the coffin is closed and they screw down the lid and we all feel each screw as it sinks into the wood, as it bores a hole through the wood, through its nerves and flesh, when it's no use to plead

"Wait"

when it's useless to plead

"Wait"

because the screws are driven into us, the lead has been welded, we can't get out, we can't hear anybody calling out for us, my husband who despite everything miraculously retained a vague notion or two of how to act civilized, put on his tie and combed his thinning hair, the generator started to rumble, thus convening the night, the beetles and moths appeared, dancing along the furrows of the walls, tiny yet casting enormous shadows as they ran along the stucco, that idiot Josélia standing among her employers and all the white people, tending to my mother, listening to her, the way all our guests, our friends, and the farmers with their hats in their hands, getting my floor dirty with the grass and mud from their boots, the way all these people listened to her as she told all of Baixa de Cassanje, even the barracks, the government palace My so-called family, my so-called grandchildren what grandchildren they've never been my grandchildren, you're telling me a mulatto, an epileptic, and a whore are my grandchildren

the soldiers' slut the soldiers' slut

you're calling them my grandchildren, these people I'd never, not for anything in this world, load into the car and introduce to my aunts and my godfather in Moçâmedes

"These are the children of my daughter Isilda Aunt Benvinda" (or Aunt Lúcia

or Aunt Encarnação)

my grandchildren

and Aunt Benvinda or Aunt Lúcia or Aunt Encarnação would be mortified and run off to the pantry with a rustle of velvet silk organdy skirts, their decorative fans fanning incredulously back and forth, like a flock of birds taking flight

"I don't believe it it can't be true I must be dreaming it can't be"

"This is my mulatto grandson Aunt Benvinda"

"This is my epileptic grandson Aunt Lúcia"

"This is my whore granddaughter Aunt Encarnação"

the grandchildren that my daughter Isilda gave me, wearing black ribbons, black coats, black buskins, red-faced from the heat, walking in procession behind my coffin under this stormy sky, this March rain, my mulatto grandson at the end of the procession mingling with people of his own race, my epileptic grandson who tortures animals and pokes out their eyes with nails, hanging onto his mother, my prostitute granddaughter checking out the neighbors with a measured, lingering stare that's mature beyond her years, going up to them with an air of distracted casualness, using the rain as an excuse to rub her body against theirs under their umbrellas, standing on her tiptoes to whisper in their ears and smile at them, and in Moçâmedes Aunt Benvinda Aunt Lúcia Aunt Encarnação are all devastated, offering me a glass of coffee liqueur and a stool to sit on while I take in some fresh afternoon air

"Stay here with us don't ever go back to the northern lands my child"

Josélia who stayed out in the cemetery in the rain by herself after we all left, holding her hand out to the grave as if my
mother were searching for her among the headstones, calling
out to her, saying
"Help me"
saying
"Don't let me die"
which is what everyone says with their eyes when they're no
longer able to speak, when they start to slip away from us, growing
smaller and smaller as they fade into the distance
"Don't let me die"
my husband coming to the surface, then sinking, struggling
beneath the surface of life itself, able to reach the surface once,
I'm sure of it, because I clearly saw him scream don't let me die, I
don't know whether the medic, or my children, or Damião, who
was bringing syringes and bedpans in and out of the room, saw
it or not but I saw him sinking, even though he was motionless,
inhaling water, choking, able to come back to us for just a second,
even though his expression never changed I could make out his
grimaces, his pleas, his fear, finally slipping away after waving his
arms at us for I don't know how long, slipping into the depths
while we just stood there, getting smaller and smaller, more and
more indistinct, harder and harder to see, and then when we finally take a good look at the bed we're confronted with some object lying there that's no longer them, something that's similar to
them or that's pretending to be them but isn't them, something
lying on the bed in imitation of them, and that's the thing we bury,
as if it really were them, although it isn't really them since they

no longer exist, they've already vanished into the dark recesses of a deep abyss, their appearance even changes in old pictures of them, a photograph of someone who's dead isn't the same as a photograph of someone who's still alive, they follow us around the house timidly or they don't even follow us but still search for us throughout the house like a meek, rejected puppy, Aunt Benvinda Aunt Lúcia Aunt Encarnação out on the patio to get some fresh afternoon air, Moçâmedes buried in sand, the ridge of the rooftops where the houses used to be, the tops of the palm trees where the park once was, the sea wiping its fists off on its knees like a peasant in the noonday heat, stay here with us never go back north my girl, when we returned from the cemetery Josélia stayed behind with her hand held out to the grave amid all the broken headstones, crucifixes, little vases filled with artificial flowers, what was left of the wrought-iron fence, waiting for an entreaty, a request, a command, our friends, neighbors, and the other farmers all left in a procession of headlights that shook the cotton, cotton, cotton, more cotton still and the rain derisively pounding the windshields like little stones and playing on the branches of the golden rain tree, leaving, returning, the next morning the tractor driver came to tell me that Josélia was still standing next to the stone that marked the gravesite would be standing there until they delivered the limestone angel from Luanda that was chosen out of a catalog full of angels of varying prices depending on their pose, melancholy angels, angels reading a book, others playing trumpets

(or harps with real strings ten percent more expensive)

who pointed to the heavens with a joyful index finger, I chose the one with the book because a book, even if there's nothing

written in it, takes a while to leaf through, and always keeps one
entertained for a while and would keep her entertained during
the few years she'd remain there before the weeds and ants devoured her, so I told Damião to bring Josélia back to the house
and he didn't come back until it was almost noon, after having
gone to drink a few beers I'm absolutely certain of it, judging
from the smell of his breath, a whole case of beer at the company
store, confirming that Josélia, acting as though she were her own
master, refused to leave the grave so that she could attend to my
mother, so I told Fernando

"Go get her"

and before those two went and got lost in the cemetery forever,
keeping the angel company, I got up on my feet and headed out
after the Bailundo, a real seducer, an aesthete who took a detour
past the workers' quarters, veering off the path that led to the stone
angels so he could check out the women who'd arrived the night
before to work the rice harvest, I caught him red-handed, bowing
languidly to introduce himself, leading a lively young thing into
the tall reeds on the bank of the river, the gallant smile disappearing from Fernando's face

"Don't hit me ma'am"

what those idiots always repeat when they do something foolish

"Don't hit me ma'am"

more afraid of the lash than the cattle trucks they rode in on the
weekends en route from Huambo to Luanda and from Luanda to
Malanje in order to have a gunnysack thrust into their hands and
be forced to pick rice from six in the morning to six in the evening
for five escudos per day, while they themselves paid ten a day for

food and fifteen for lodging in the huts not to mention the state taxes, Fernando trotting over to the cemetery while Aunt Encarnação eyed me from behind her fan, severe, nodding in approval, your grandfather never let a native misbehave, my girl

my grandfather in his store in Luso

in his general store

in his shop

in his dry-goods store of sorts

there we go, in his dry-goods store in Luso which was neither very big nor very prosperous, articles of clothing medicine assorted utensils knickknacks, a man who was always snorting in anger at the counter, leaving burning cigarettes all over the store and forgetting about them, just three or four streets, a half-dozen houses, a detachment of soldiers who'd lost their way at that end of the earth some twenty or thirty years before dragging their gaitered legs from hut to hut, baobab trees, tiny emaciated trees, my Aunt Encarnação engaged to a corporal who spoke of Viseu to her as if it were paradise

"Ah Viseu my love"

singeing her cape with his cigarettes, her pointing accusingly at the tobacco while she rubbed a piece of margarine on her singed elbow

"Ow that hurts"

the corporal confusing the past with his memories, forgetting all about those potato and cabbage lunches, the shale rooftops, sleeping outside with the sheep, his stepfather taking swigs from a jug of liquor, the cold

"Ah Viseu"

the dry-goods store in Luso, a store that, let's admit it, was ab ab-surdo *quite modest, a store that, let's admit it, for instance lost more than it made, although what business could ever prosper with thirty or forty penniless customers, the soldiers, to whom the government owed decades of wages, all they could do was sell their forage caps and rifles with no butts and wrench a few small, stubborn vegetables from the dirt, my grandfather and his daughters closing the dry-goods store, drawing the cretonne curtains over the window so no one could see them, eating cassava roots in secret, looking all around warily, my grandfather foisting lengths of fabric on people in hopes of some future payment*

"You'll pay later don't worry about it take it you can pay me back in May with a little hen"

craving a grilled chicken wing, a thigh, some rice with chicken innards, a nice Easter chicken soup, my aunt Encarnação saying to the corporal, imagining Viseu as something other than a city, cities, I've got more than enough cities here, humph, all cities are the same and they all get on my nerves, but Viseu was more like a never-ending tablecloth chock-full of platters of ram's meat on spits and pigs' ears with coriander sauce

"And what about tripe Celso do they at least have tripe there?"

a grilled chicken wing, half a chicken wing even one that was withered, measly, chewed up by beetles, sometimes the Luchazes would hook a frog at the end of their cane fishing poles, they'd fish for eels or a tiny bitter-tasting fish no bigger than a finger and my grandfather would be on the lookout, tossing his cigarette aside, jumping to his feet to run out of the store, a blur of mustache and teeth, grabbing hold of the guy from Luchazes, not forcefully, not authoritatively, but humbly, distraught from hunger

"You can have all the quinine if you want it just give me the fish you can have the quinine but hand over that fish"

my grandfather hoping they'd hand him an eel, some bitter-tasting fish they'd caught out in the savannah, a frog ready to be seasoned at the end of a fishing rod

my grandfather going into the cemetery with me where Josélia waited for a voice that was indistinguishable from the other thousand voices of the dead to beg her from below the weeds

"Don't let me die"

my grandfather

your grandfather my girl, a serious man who knew how to get his way and never allowed the natives to laze around or misbehave

a miserable wretch with his pockets full of stale bread, biscuits, grains of rice, little sugar cubes, speaking from my lips that morning in the dense fog of the dry season that hindered the smell of the cotton from spreading all across the plantation, suspended in droplets of water above the plants

"Josélia"

my grandfather in Moçâmedes, always prowling around the kitchen even after he received an inheritance from his cousin, the house where the sea echoed, the certificates of the stock options in the railroad and in coffee from Uíje, the hectare in Novo Redondo where the school is now located, my aunts' luck had changed, they bought nail polish, fine china, decent clothes, they volunteered at the church, they lost sight of the platters of pigs' ears with coriander sauce, the corporal still lives in Luso, hobbling

around using his rifle as a cane longing for those shale rooftops,
the bad breath of the cattle, and his stepfather taking swigs from
the jug of liquor, hauling his malaria-ridden body from the dry-
goods store to the barracks

my grandfather in the cemetery speaking from my lips

"Josélia"

the sand must have buried the family vault in Moçâmedes a very
long time ago, the one right near the entrance, to the left, the one
with a colonnade, cornices, and muslin windows as if it were a real
home, a granite roof carved to mimic gables, roof tiles, and eaves,
a little garden behind it full of hyacinths, I'm not sure if they were
hyacinths I've never seen a hyacinth but I like the name hyacinth

hyacinths hyacinths hyacinths

my grandfather, my aunts, the quartermaster who fought Gun-
gunhana all nicely stretched out inside it until the end of the world
when they'll be resurrected in that desert by the sea

here I'll await the end of the world

a few petrified rushes here and there, a basalt wind blowing at
full speed through the park

Josélia looking like the angel with the harp as she parted ways
with my mother

my grandchildren what grandchildren show me that there's even
a single drop of my blood in them

"Yes ma'am"

with the howls of the wild dogs out behind the workers' quarters, when Clarisse was little she'd scream whenever she heard
them and demand to sleep in our bed, how many times did I
wake up in the middle of the night to see my daughter in her

nightshirt and barefoot in the dark tugging at our covers, as persistent as regret

"Mom"

that little darling tugging away at the covers, my husband used to sleep on the side of the bed by the door and she'd walk across the hallway in the dark, walk across the bedroom, feel her way along the edges of the mattress until she suddenly appeared by my side

"Mom"

her teeth came in earlier than her brothers' did, she started walking earlier, speaking in sentences earlier, holding a fork earlier, she looked at us as though we were looking at ourselves through her and we didn't like what we saw, so there are times when I think that if I, there are even times here, inside what's left of me, in what's left of Chiquita, a fragment of a woman in a fragment of a hut among fragments of ruins, when I think that if I'd allowed her to, to put it that way

as persistent as regret

and yet what good does it do or what can I fix now, Josélia returned home with me herded along by Fernando who was also frightened of the wild dogs, Fernando tugging at my covers in the middle of the night

"Ma'am"

until we arrived at the kitchen, where Maria da Boa Morte

Carlos didn't look at us like that, Rui didn't look at us like that, my husband of course didn't look at us like that, but with Clarisse it was as though we were looking at ourselves through her and didn't like what we saw turned on the stove to start lunch, Josélia looking like the angel with the harp, certain that the dead spoke to her

if they ask me if I believe in God I haven't the slightest idea how I'd answer them but if God exists he's white and therefore there isn't enough God left over for the blacks from which it proceeds that if I were black I wouldn't believe in God or better yet the idea of God wouldn't even cross my mind for a second since it would be so preoccupied with leprosy and hunger and malaria and the like

the smell of the wild dogs grew stronger out in the grass behind the generator which I'd forgotten to remind them to hoe and since I forgot to remind them it's only logical that they also forgot to do it, although they sure remembered to steal and run off and get sick they never remember anything they should

your grandfather my girl was a serious man and never allowed the natives to laze around or stood for any misbehavior from any of the

the wild dogs howled on the porch looking down from the terrace, sticking their snouts in the azalea bushes, making the peacocks readjust their positions uneasily in the branches at the top of the golden rain tree just like me and Josélia and Maria da Boa Morte when we moved to evade the war, to evade the government troops who traded places back and forth with the mercenaries from UNITA, to evade the napalm bombs and the decapitated soldiers, to evade squalid Chiquita, which no longer really existed, and head to Marimba, which if you really think about it no longer exists either, thirty kilometers to the north traveling past Pecagranja and the surrounding hills, past the queen's shanty, me and Josélia and Maria da Boa Morte fleeing from the stabbings, the trip-line explosives, the bandits with their swords and pistols, the mines planted under dirt roads, at present following the first river where we started to smell them, hear their heavy panting, see a slight movement in the bushes, Josélia searching for a fallen branch and brandishing it at the shadows

"The wild dogs"

their cries and their eyes like those of malevolent children, their phosphorescent tails in the gaps between the trees, what looked to me like mouths, what looked to me like paws, the wild dogs looping around in a circle to block our path to the river, the sentry box that marked the edge of the plantation and stalks of corn that had been scorched by controlled burns, Josélia pulling the leaves off a tree branch, not a thick trunk but a branch, a thin switch which would break against the first knee it hit

"The wild dogs"

placing herself in front of me as if the government troops or the South Africans or the Belgians were trying to slit my throat with a single slash of a knife, explaining to the wild dogs

"She's not my boss she's my godmother"

the first river behind us, and the second, the one with the raft, was too far off, there was no hut, no house, no mango tree we could shimmy up, which we'd have done even at our age, even as worn-out as we were, our bones heavy-laden with the dense fog, and transformed into hard, gesso-covered crocheted fabric, and in the middle of all this I saw the dogs sizing us up, assessing us, approaching at an oblique angle, then running away from us, bounding over an exposed root, then coming back toward us, ten twelve fifteen dogs stalking us, not going for our heads or our necks, but our legs, the tendons of our legs, the way they do with cows until the cows fall down and only then do they go for the throat and only then do they go for the chest, the cows with their mouths gaping would still drag themselves along the ground and the dogs together with the vultures would open up an entryway through the skin and the rib cage ripping out chunks of lung of muscle of liver, emerging from the flesh and scurrying off dripping fat, blood, nerves, amid clamorous barking, Josélia standing in front of me shaking her branch

"She's not my boss she's my godmother"

Josélia, I honestly don't know what my mother saw in her yet she preferred her to me

preferred her to me

since as she was dying it was the Bailunda woman she demanded to have at her side, holding her hand, and just imagine how angry I was, just imagine what I was going to do to her once the wake was over, once the burial was over, what I'd do to her once the wild dogs ran off, she was happy to see Maria da Boa Morte tug at my arm, tugging and tugging at my arm pulling me toward the raft on the second river where the wild dogs couldn't reach us, she was lucky that Maria da Boa Morte forced me against my will to go with her, separating me from the yelps, the teeth, the paws, the eyes like those of malevolent children, the phosphorescent tails glimpsed in the gaps between the trees, she was lucky that I was in the raft while Maria da Boa Morte pulled on the pulleys and ropes that connected the two riverbanks, the clapboard platform moving forward on the surface of the water *if you ask me do you believe in God if you were to ask me out of the blue like that without giving me time to think it through do you believe in God*

while Josélia looked over at us to verify that we'd gotten off the balsa and were heading toward Marimba, Josélia hitting the wild dogs with the branch so much that it broke, hitting the wild dogs with her fists, the dogs sizing her up, approaching at oblique angles, then running away from her, bounding over an exposed root, ten twelve fifteen dogs stalking us, not going for our heads or our necks but our legs the tendons of our legs, the way they do with cows until the cows fall down and only then do they go for the throat and only then do they go for the chest, the cows would try to gore them with their horns, still dragging themselves along the ground, Josélia was happy that I couldn't go back to scold her, put her in her place, punish her, Josélia was happy that there was a river between us, or something that was a river in the rainy season and was at this point just a swamp a slushy mire in which even the crocodiles couldn't find shelter

if you asked me do you believe in God
hyacinths
I haven't the slightest idea of how I'd answer

Josélia was happy to fall down the instant one of the dogs latched on to her ankle, a second dog latched on to her thigh, happy to keep swinging at the dogs with the broken branch, first from her knees and then on her back, happy to finally disappear under the chaos of barks and howls, the chaos of claws, paws, phosphorescent tails, and the swarming backs of the dogs, Josélia was happy that

if you ask me do you believe
the wild dogs tore a path through her skin and rib cage, ripping out chunks of lung of muscle of liver, looking at me
in God I haven't the slightest idea
one last time as if she wanted to say something that I couldn't understand, that the sound of the river kept me from understanding, trying to apologize for something that I wouldn't forgive her for because just like my grandfather I never allow the natives to laze around or misbehave, I'd never tolerate laziness or misbehavior in some woman who means nothing to me.

24 DECEMBER 1995

When my mother used to take me to the doctor in Malanje and then after the appointment buy me a cream cake at the pastry shop, instead of going straight back to the plantation on the Diamang highway she'd drive the jeep over to a little neighborhood made up of identical houses out behind the barracks, she'd fix the collar of her shirt, straighten up her hair, dab the stopper of the perfume bottle on her neck, and ask me, with a cheerful look on her face, her whole expression different

"Stay here and behave no monkey business I'll be right back"

she'd cross the street with a different sort of gait, prettier, slower, and it made me take notice of my mother as a woman, she stopped being my mother and turned into a woman, so much so that I wanted to get close to her, the way I did with the Bailundas, to smell her, touch her, treat her badly, me sitting in the jeep with a cream cake watching her cross the street with a jaunty skip in her step that stopped a whole slew of men in their tracks and altered the rhythm of the blood flowing within me, watching her turn the corner of one of the houses and come back ages later, no longer a woman, back to being my mother once again but with her makeup smudged and her shirt buttoned crookedly, watching her realize that she's missing an earring, putting the remaining one away in her purse, someone's silhouette drawing back the curtain, revealing the light fixture on the ceiling, it seemed to me that I could make out an arm waving, it seemed to me that my mother or rather my mother once again the way I knew her responded to that arm, raising her hand off the steering wheel, she'd pull on the knob to turn on the headlights since it was nighttime both inside and outside the jeep, inside the jeep the blue glow of the gauges on the dashboard made us look more solemn, outside the jeep the city was replaced with fields and more fields and cattle fences that stretched into the darkness, the outline of my mother's face, frowning as if driving a jeep at thirty or forty kilometers per hour along an empty highway required all the concentration and attention to detail of a watchmaker

"Did you behave Rui?"

and me with no desire to get close to her, smell her, touch her, or treat her badly because it wasn't any sort of real woman, I mean like the ones out on the island in Luanda or the governor's nieces, who was there in the car with me, it was just the person who scolded me morning to night, told me to brush my teeth, to not be rude to my brother and sister, to go to bed when there was still interesting stuff going on in the living room, young ladies, card games, people pounding their fists on the table, arguing, it was just the person who took me to the doctor's office weeping while she spoke to him, wringing a handkerchief in her hands

"He'll get better isn't it true that he'll get better promise me that my son will get better"

and then we'd leave the examination room after more tears and wailing and melodramatic kisses that suffocated me

me wanting to get away from her and breathe and not being able to

then she'd head to the little neighborhood back behind the barracks as if nothing had happened, having forgotten her sorrows, while I died of boredom locked in the jeep with nothing to keep me entertained not even a measly fly whose wings I could tear off and during the trip back to the plantation my mother's scent caught my attention, not her perfume, another scent that combined with the perfume, one that smelled like our bedsheets after a guest had slept in them, after the cattle fences came a desert and lights in the distance that intermingled with the stars and a round moon, half blue half gray, mimicking a plate of fine china, the kind that you fasten to the wall with three little bits of wire beside the sideboard table and that nags at our dreams, my mother sniffing at her blouse, sniffing at her shoulders

"What smell Rui?"

a little less mother and a little more woman

"What smell Rui?"

looking for hairs on her clothes, rubbing the palm of her hand against her neck and then holding it up to her nose while the potholes in the asphalt shook us and there were no more lights, just the stars and the plate of fine china with a thin veil of nimbus clouds, spiderwebs, gauzy vapors floating through the air

"What smell Rui what smell?"

a little less mother and a little more woman like the farmers' wives when they brought their children over to our house, they didn't tell me what to do, they didn't forbid me to smash the teacups or send me to bed, they looked at me warily and looked at my grandmother respectfully

"Your grandson must be getting better with that treatment he's undergoing he's behaved himself splendidly the entire day"

the farmers' wives, whispering to their children to stay away from me, pretended not to notice when I screamed, even the skinny one, the one with the chestnut brown hair, whom I'd let kiss me if I let anyone kiss me

"Your grandson must be getting better with that treatment he's undergoing he's behaved himself splendidly the entire day"

out on the balcony complaining about their servants, their husbands, their irregular bowel movements, the heat, their kids, who wouldn't leave their mothers' side, even if they wanted to play, to borrow my tricycle, my toy cars, frightened by me or just frightened by how much their mothers were afraid of me for their sake, my grandmother saying to the skinny woman after giving her a look of disappointment, resuming her crocheting with a sigh

(the skinny woman was fanning herself and her hair was glistening and her teeth were glistening)

"Seizures and seizures and more seizures Cacilda he's even had four or five on me in a single hour I just don't know if I can take it anymore"

we all have our cross to bear and mine is my grandchildren, my son-in-law and my grandchildren, how many times did I tell my husband

"Eduardo"

how many times did I warn my husband

"Take notice Eduardo"

yet my husband didn't listen to me

"Don't you worry"

too busy thinking about his lovers in Luanda, the French woman who made me suffer until the day I died, my husband ignoring me, debasing me, humiliating me, wanting nothing to do with me for months on end, not weeks, months on end, if I ever spoke to him affectionately

"Eduardo"

he'd recoil as if I'd stuck him with a pin as if he were suffering from some painful skin condition

"Let's wait until later in the week because I've got a toothache that's just killing me"

me lying awake listening to the clock, listening to the silence inside the clock and feeling sorry for myself, a daughter who was just like her father, grandchildren who were just like their father, if they'd just let me leave, if they'd just leave me alone, if it weren't for Josélia, tell me is there anything sadder than taking comfort in the company

of an African woman, anything sadder than chatting with an Afri-
can woman who
   naturally
   doesn't get it, asking her
   "What do you think about it Josélia?"
and the African woman nodding her head in assent
   "Yes ma'am"
looking for my handkerchief in one of the dresser drawers, hand-
ing it to me with those grotesque fingers they have
   "Don't cry ma'am"
tell me is there anything sadder than crying in front of a servant,
anything sadder than hugging a servant and crying on her shoulder,
I swear I went so far as to hug Josélia and cry on her shoulder
   "Sit down here beside me"
Josélia sitting on the edge of the chair feeling what for them passes
for shame
   "Yes ma'am"
looking at me with what for them passes for compassion
   "Yes ma'am"
so when I was dying I asked her to help me breathe, to hold
my hand, to take me to Moçâmedes, far away from my daugh-
ter, from my son-in-law, from my grandchildren, from the friends
and neighbors of my daughter and son-in-law, far away from this
plantation where the devil dwells, I asked her frankly the way I al-
ways addressed people, and maybe that's what my husband didn't
like about me, my sincerity, my candor, maybe he'd prefer me to
be dishonest and deceitful like the others, nothing but sweet to
your face but once your back is turned you better watch it, I never

resorted to deception, to lies, I just asked her frankly to take me to Moçâmedes where my family lives, I didn't ask a white woman to take me, I asked an Angolan, because white women ridiculed me, belittled me, I asked right in the middle of all the prayers the tears the blessings

"*Take me to Moçâmedes Josélia*"

my family thinking I was dead, washing my body, changing my clothes, combing my hair, calling to order marble angels, carelessly carrying the oratory in from the hallway knocking it against the side of the door, putting the images of Christ out of order and shattering a statuette of a saint

"*Damn it get that saint out of the way and the other saints as well I've never seen so many saints together on a single shelf*"

my daughter brought some glue and reattached the saint's head saying to her friends

"*Poor thing*"

with a sympathetic, melancholic smile and her friends listened to her with sympathetic, melancholic smiles as well

"*If my mother knew that I broke her saint why she'd be insufferable*"

thinking I was dead, placing a crucifix in my hands, flooding my bedroom with flowers, transparent drops of candle wax dripping on the floor, bringing in chairs, heating up soup, fixing sandwiches in the kitchen, and me going downstairs to catch the bus to Moçâmedes with Josélia, me in Moçâmedes with Josélia, each of us with a suit-case and a parasol in hand saying hello to people left and right on the way to the house

looking for hairs on her clothes, rubbing the palm of her hand against her neck and then holding it up to her nose

"What smell Rui what smell?"

when we turned off onto the dirt road the exhalation of the plants came in through the window, the exhalation of the river, the village, the company store, the barn, the lamp out on the patio, my father, my brother and sister, and my grandmother waiting for us in the living room, the whole world in order once more, my mother

how nice

no longer a woman, just my mother, different from all the farmers' wives, going up the front steps with me, going in the entryway with me, everything in its proper place, everything easy, everything simple, confirmed by the clock, which promised me that, yes, my mother was just my mother fixing one thing or another that needs to be fixed, telling me what to do, leaning over the balcony to yell at the setters, my brother and sister rummaging around in her purse hoping to find caramels with chocolate filling

"There's an earring in here Mom"

my grandmother stopped crocheting for a moment and gave my mother a pointed look, then gave my father a pointed look

my stupid son-in-law who lucky for him is blind and doesn't realize what all of Malanje already knows

going back to her crochet, my mother following my grandmother's look and becoming alarmed, turning into a woman for a moment then calming down, going back to being a mother, taking the earring from Carlos and putting it back in her purse

"Well I guess there is"

the setters got quiet out in the garden, except for Lady who was growling at the owls (the next morning I happened to trip over a pile of bloody feathers covered in ants among the weeds in the flower beds that Damião gathered up with a rake swearing that for every owl that died a person died too little boy, Damião kissing his thumb and crossing himself

"For every owl that dies a person dies too little boy")

my father who didn't drink so much back then smiled as he sat on the sofa, calling Clarisse over to him, sitting her down on his lap, he helped her open the caramel wrappers, beleaguered by my mother's voice, her voice accompanied by a wagging index finger and that was higher pitched than usual the way it always was when she got mad or was starting to get mad

"I don't want any dirty pinafores or any wrappers on the ground or any trash or sticky couch cushions"

my father putting the wrappers in the ashtray, checking to make sure the rug was clean, wiping off Clarisse's hands with his handkerchief

me putting the wrappers in the ashtray, checking to make sure the rug was clean, wiping off Clarisse's hands with my handkerchief because I don't want any dirty pinafores or any wrappers on the ground or any trash or sticky couch cushions, because I've got to pay the price for what happened in the shack that belonged to that Co-tonang cafeteria worker years and years ago, pay the price of offending Isilda, when I arrived at her shack I'd have to shoo the chickens away blindly so I could lie down on the straw mat, you could see a sliver of the sky, tiny distant flames that shimmered in the darkness, I never talked to her, I swear I never talked to her, I just stared at her body on the other side of the counter as I came down the cafeteria line toward her with my tray in hand and watched her serve lunch and dinner, I just asked for the street number of her little hovel back at the front office and the typist

"Twenty-six"

we never talked, I never knocked on her door, I never asked her permission, I just went in and found her there in the smell of the chickens, I mean my hand, the one that had brought a six-pack of German beer as a gift, found her there in the smell of the chickens, an arm, an elbow, what seemed to be a breast that neither recoiled from me nor encouraged my advances, she stayed quiet, she breathed quietly, her legs stayed still and quiet

I don't want any dirty pinafores or any wrappers on the ground or any trash or sticky couch cushions

quiet the way I am here at home because I have to pay the price for what happened at Cotonang, pay the price for Carlos, for bringing a mulatto son into a white person's home, the next day she served me my food in the cafeteria the same way she served everybody else, us with our trays in hand at the counter and her not paying any attention to us dishing the food out onto our plates, she wore a gold chain, a gold-plated metal chain, I invited her to go out on the town in Malanje with me on Sunday and she refused to go, it wouldn't have bothered me to show up with her at the movie theater or the café

Carolina

yet she refused to go, she was outside washing clothes and wasn't wearing her work apron and she refused to go the same way she refused to take the money I tried to give her, a little necklace made of seashells, a new pillow, yet she nonetheless let my wife give her a

check, just like she let them take away her child, thinking that it was
a fair price for the son of an engineer or thinking that the son of an
engineer didn't really belong to her unless

   given that she was black

   I allowed for it, I left her washing clothes outside, at the end of the
alleyway, when I turned around she was still putting clothes into the
water of the clay washtub all alone, like me in my room listening to
the people below, the conversations, the furniture being dragged to
block the door, the footsteps, the door of the study being closed when
my wife and the

   I don't want any dirty pinafores or any wrappers on the ground
or any trash or sticky couch cushions

   laughing in the doorway, unperturbed by my presence upstairs,
slapping his riding crop against his own backside, sitting down in
the armchair judging from the sound of that one loose spring, his
voice, hearing him clap his hands together, bossing my kids around
knowing that I could hear him and getting a kick out of the fact that
I could hear him

   "Go play outside in the garden kids because I've got an important
matter to settle with this woman"

   I overheard my wife, worried that her mother would notice, not me
   "Quiet"

   more laughter more joking more anecdotes, the sound of boots
on the tile floor, the sound of the key in the lock, noises that sounded
like whispers, secrets, the desk knocking against the wall, me tak-
ing the whiskey bottle from the nightstand drawer with all the ac-
companying noises that bottles make knocking against this and
that, alarm clock, slippers, pill bottles, and even though I'd taken

the bottle out of the drawer my wife saying in a breathy voice like someone blowing out a candle worried about my mother-in-law not me

"Quiet"

so there are times when I think it's a pity that whiskey can kill a man but can't ever make him deaf, the medic assures me that alcohol can destroy the liver the arteries the stomach the esophagus the nerves the legs the memory and yet

"Quiet"

every Monday and Thursday that breathy voice like someone blowing out a candle

"Quiet"

my wife and the

no trash or sticky couch cushions

who marched upstairs to pay me a visit without even going to the trouble of disguising what he'd done or smoothing out his wrinkled clothes or straightening out the shirt of his uniform, the

no thanks

helping me pour whiskey into the glass without spilling it, wiping my mouth, pouring more whiskey, wiping my mouth again, giving me a few little slaps on the cheek, commenting to Isilda and winking at her as he straightened out my pajamas

"This husband of yours is too good to be true Dona Isilda"

and Carlos infuriated with the

dirty pinafores wrappers on the ground

infuriated with me, pointing Rui's pellet gun at him, shooting, the pellet breaking a windowpane without hitting anybody, Carlos who was barely waist-high, charging toward him threatening him with

the butt of the gun, Clarisse arguing with Josélia about the golden
rain tree, my wife
   "Carlos"
   the
   (*a gold chain, a gold-plated metal chain around her neck, when*
it was my turn in line I held my tray out to her and she served me
my food without even looking up at me, it wouldn't have bothered
me to walk into the movie theater or the café with you, I didn't
care if they saw us together and pretended not to see us, I didn't
care that they called me into the front office, not to forbid me from
being with you far from it that's not the problem here Mr. Engineer
sir far from it everyone's free to do as they wish slavery ended a
long time ago, I'd just like you to think for a moment about your
position as a high-level employee of the company and what this
means for your future, promotions research grants trips to Europe,
think for a moment about your image, one that's neither prejudi-
cial to you nor embarrassing for us the shareholders in Luxemburg
are quite different from we Iberians so fussy and persnickety we
shouldn't be afraid to speak some hard truths here I'm sure I've
made myself clear Mr. Engineer sir I'm sure you've understood me
quite well)
   he took the pellet gun from Carlos
   "You little shit"
   me unable to get up off the bed spilling my whiskey on the bedsheets
finally deafened by a shriek from one of the peacocks, me feeling no
pain or uneasiness spilling my whiskey on the bedsheets and smiling
   my mother with a certain smell about her, which my father, my
brother and sister, and my grandmother didn't notice

("Do you smell that Clarisse?"
and Clarisse sniffing at the air all around her
"What smell?")
a smell that combined with her perfume, my mother shocked
that my father had eaten as many caramels as we had
"Really Amadeu"
grabbing the bag of caramels and putting it away in a drawer
"No more sweets or you won't be hungry for dinner"
the Christmas Eve dinner in Ajuda that my brother or Lena
called to invite me to so they can scold me the whole time for getting into everything, for not sitting still, for making the TV go out
of focus, for turning up the volume, for turning down the volume,
for changing the channel in hopes of finding some cartoons or
sports, Christmas Eve dinner in the apartment in Ajuda with the
African masks and little knickknacks that I'd send crashing to the
ground by just barely moving my knee, Lena bent over sweeping
up the broken pieces
"Oh Rui oh Rui"
Christmas Eve dinner with my sister-in-law at the head of the
table just like my mother once she was back on the plantation,
when she was my mother and nothing more, not a real woman,
nothing more than the smell of her perfume, doing nothing more
than scolding us and telling us what to do, at night the pigeons
don't fly between Monsanto Park and the school, nor do they
come to rest someplace where I can call out to them and toss little
pieces of bread on the ground to attract them, they sleep on the
façade of the church, perched up in the niches, tucking their heads
under their wings the way motorcyclists carry their helmets under

their arms, at night you never see any stray cats or dogs out on the street and the rustling of the mulberry trees frightens me, those soft, unknown voices

"Rui"

I was never afraid of what the mango trees, the baobab trees, and the golden rain tree said but the mulberry trees along the street, even in the daylight, with sparrows in them and people walking along the street, no thank you, how many times did I hear them as I lay on the couch where Clarisse and I used to sleep, and whenever I heard them I'd cover my ears with the pillow, Clarisse talking in her sleep

"Let go of me"

lying there in the morning she thought she was still in Malanje, she'd complain about the fog, which gave her a fever, she'd yell out to Maria da Boa Morte to bring her breakfast, and then all of a sudden she'd open her eyes and see the dilapidated ceiling, the wallpaper with its stains and cracks, the cranes in the port, the Tagus, then she'd realize she was in Ajuda

"My God"

she'd notice the sofa bed that took up the whole living room and made it so that we had to fold up the table and scoot it over by the hall along with the rattan chair where Carlos sat and stewed, noticing the dirty dishes in the kitchen where flies were breeding, noticing the lofty adobe-colored hills of Almada standing before us, separating us from my parents' house, Clarisse in Ajuda

"My God"

with Carlos always on my case, quick to forbid me to do one thing or another, Lena walking over to me to examine my skin with the look of a cannibal on her face

"Stay still"

taking hold of me, holding my arms down, digging her fingernails into my cheeks, my forehead, my cheekbone, my ears

"This doesn't hurt now does it?"

since the greatest pleasure that life has to offer women is picking
at the blackheads on my face, my mother, my grandmother, Lena

"Stay still"

picking at the blackheads on my face

"Oh my"

showing them to me on the tips of their index fingers

"Look at this one Rui look at the size of this one"

then they'd get back to their explorations and procedures with
a sense of joy that I never understood

"An enormous one don't move right now don't move"

my mother, my grandmother, and Lena with their pupils di-
lated, observing me, looking at me from the corners of their eyes,
waiting for me to get distracted, to forget they were there, to sit
down, then putting their hands on me with ferocious speed the
instant they saw me in a vulnerable, convenient position, holding
me down so I couldn't defend myself

"Stay still"

and then out would come those thumbs that pierced my skin
down to the bone

"Don't make a face Rui don't be a sissy there's no way this is
hurting you"

then came the delighted gasp

"Oh my"

the victorious pride, the tip of the index finger, the demand that
I admire their handiwork before they scraped the blackheads onto
the edge of the ashtray

"Look at this one look at the size of this one"

so if I were to accept Carlos's invitation to have dinner in Ajuda it wouldn't just be the knickknacks that would break, and Lena bent over sweeping up the broken pieces

"Oh Rui oh Rui"

my brother raising his voice at me, a damp towel diligently wiping off the stains on my jacket, the absence of pigeons during the night, the mulberry trees on the street, those voices

"Rui"

those fingernails watching me, circling me, looking at me out of the corner of their eyes waiting for me to get distracted, to forget they were there, to sit down, holding me down so I can't defend myself

"Stay still"

and so when the director of the home said that Carlos

your brother

called to Damaia to ask them to put me on the Monsanto bus I convinced him that Clarisse

Clarisse, who took no pleasure in the blemishes on my skin

was waiting for me in Estoril together with the rest of the family, that is, my mother, Josélia, Maria da Boa Morte, Damião, and Fernando, one of the workers bought me a ticket and left me on a train bound for Cascais, he didn't leave me with the passengers in the train station but inside an empty train car, in a seat next to the window where I could see the Tagus, leaving me there after talking with the conductor who looked at me while scratching his head through his cap

"And what if he gets it into his head to start hitting people or jump down onto the tracks?"

my reflection swayed in the glass window, traversed by buildings and trees and every now and then by the abyss of the water, it smiled if I smiled, yawned if I yawned, shook in its seat if I shook in my seat, making a little game out of mimicking me, which frightened the conductor who nervously snapped his hole-punch, feeling uneasy about the two of us, sometimes the tracks ran alongside the waves and you could make out tide pools, rocks, floating docks, sea foam, at other times they moved away from the shore, passing through some uninhabited neighborhood or an abandoned farm while the two of us, both transparent, with tree trunks and rock walls passing over us, communicated with each other in the windowpane moving our mouths at the same time saying the same words, interrupted by islands of illumination at the railway stops that wiped our image from the glass with a rag of fluorescent lighting, we reappeared when we were once again next to the waves, which tried to reach us by leaping over the sea, and then I recognized Estoril from the casino, from the arcades and the boardwalk and shops, the pedestrian boulevard, the conductor terrified that I'd strangle him like a pigeon, if the police chief in Malanje were a pigeon I'd scatter some bread crumbs on the balcony, hide behind the creeping vines, catch him in a net, and squeeze his neck really tight and my father would stop drinking and would take me and my brother and sister on trips to Duque de Bragança, to Salazar, to Luanda, my father searching for a bottle in the nightstand while my mother and the police chief argued in the study, it almost seemed like they were fighting with the desk banging against the wall over and over

"Why are Mom and the police chief arguing Dad why are they fighting?"

the whiskey spilled down his neck soaked into his pajama top, Lady barked out back on the patio

"Why are Mom and the police chief fighting in the study Dad?"

my father hugging the bottle against his chest, a second stain growing on the sheets beneath his buttocks, my mother yelling down to Damião

"How disgusting"

"Why are Mom and the police chief"

there were Christmas decorations in the streets, wreaths, bows, balloons, blinking lights, music, decorative cutouts in gold paper, white-bearded men riding sleighs in shop windows, women and men coming and going in spite of the rain, Clarisse's apartment was just past the casino along an unfinished dead-end street, unpaved and with no streetlights, where I almost maimed myself tripping over bricks, boards, piles of sand, pieces of scaffolding, but I didn't care about the rain and didn't get upset because before long my sister, beautiful, dressed up like the movie stars on the posters in Damaia, would be handing me a Coca-Cola, pine nuts, almonds, candies, she'd hand me the remote control, would sit me down in front of the TV and let me turn up the volume and change the channel so I could watch sports, so I could watch

"What a burden what offense to God did I commit to have to bear this burden"

cartoons, forgetting that Clarisse was in the bedroom arguing and fighting with a man my father's age who looked down at me from the couch, fed up

"How am I supposed to concentrate in this situation how can anyone concentrate in this situation"

who looked down at me from the couch with the cigar of his defeat burning bright, sweaty, red-faced, furious, wishing I was dead.

11 October 1990

My father used to say that the thing we came in search of in Africa wasn't wealth or power but black people with no wealth or power to speak of who could give us the illusion of wealth and power, and that even if we actually had those two things we wouldn't really have them because we were merely tolerated, begrudgingly accepted in Portugal, looked down upon the same way we looked down upon the Bailundos who worked for us and thus in a way we were blacks to them the same way that blacks owned other blacks and those blacks owned other blacks still, in descending steps that led all the way down to the depths of misery, cripples, lepers, the slaves of slaves, dogs, my father used to explain that the thing we came in search of in Africa was to transform the revenge of ordering other people around into what we pretended was the dignity of ordering other people around, living in houses that aped European houses and which any European would despise, looking down on our houses the same way we in turn looked down on the straw huts, with the exact same repulsion and the exact same disdain, bought or built with money that was worth less than European money, money that was good for nothing except for the cruelty by which it was gained, money that for all intents and purposes was nothing more than seashells and colorful beads, because

as my father used to say

they saw us as primitive, violent creatures who had accepted exile in Angola as a sort of punishment for some obscure crime, a sentence to be served far from our family, far from whatever little villages on craggy cliffs we'd come from, living among all the blacks, almost living like them, breeding like them in piles of hay, in piles of trash, in piles of excrement in order to produce an odious, hybrid race that the Europeans tried to keep locked up far away from them in Africa by means of a shady web of official decrees, government mandates, absurd exchange rates, and false promises in hopes that we'd die from some plague in the backlands or that we'd all end up killing each other like animals, yet all the while forcing us to fill their coffers with tariffs and taxes on things that didn't belong to us anyway, us stealing from the blacks in Uíje and Baixa de Cassanje so that they could steal from us in Lisbon until

my father used to explain

the Americans or the Russians or the French or the English convinced the blacks, in the name of liberty, which they would never have anyway, arming them and training them to use those arms against us, until they convinced the blacks

my father used to explain

to substitute the conditions that we imposed on the blacks for conditions the foreigners promised not to impose on them once they'd driven us out of Angola and settled in themselves, with their machinery for mining minerals and their oil rigs set up from Cabinda to Moçâmedes, taking more from Angola than we ever thought or wanted to take from it, not just out of pure ignorance but because of our love for Africa, since

my father used to explain

we ended up liking Angola, with the intense affection that an invalid has for the sickness that devours him or that the beggar has for the cardboard box that humbles him, we ended up liking the fact that we were blacks to them back home and owning blacks who were blacks to us, accustomed to the violent weather and the violent people and the merciless rain, accustomed to settling things with the barrel of a gun, be it a disagreement or just a whim, and one day, not during my lifetime since I don't have much time left but probably during yours

my father used to explain

those who haven't become fertilizer for the cashew trees, sliced to pieces along the forest trails and on the front steps of houses, will return to Portugal, exiled once again, exiled by the Angolans on behalf of the Americans, the Russians, the French, the English who don't accept us here only to arrive in Lisbon where they also won't accept us, sending us on a wild goose chase from one government office to another, from one department to another in search of a government pension, sending us out like packages in the mail, from one room for rent to another on the outskirts of the city, us and the mulattoes and the Indians and even the blacks who will come back with us out of submissiveness or fear, not out of fondness, not out of respect, don't think that it's fondness or respect especially when it starts to seem like fondness or respect, they'll come with us out of submissiveness or fear, holed up with us in abandoned hotels, hospitals, convalescent homes, stores, far enough away from us so that they won't get too tired of us being there

the requests, the protests that transformed into requests, the anger that first transformed into protests and then transformed into requests, my father used to explain

and therefore don't agree to leave, don't leave Angola, let your children go but don't leave Angola, just become a Bailunda for the Americans and the Russians, a Bailunda for the Bailundas, but don't leave Angola, me in Marimba with Maria da Boa Morte, in what was once the government office building, what was once the town administrator's house, what was once the first-aid station, what was once the Portuguese barracks during thirteen years of war with coats of arms and ensigns on the cement walls, the first general store, the second general store, the adobe chapel, what were once the workers' quarters, the row of mango trees still intact on the edge of town, and the hills of the Congo on the horizon, no government troops, no UNITA mercenaries, no suckling pigs, no chickens, no corpses, nobody, the dust devils of the dry season raising up a universe from the soil, scorched earth to the south, scorched earth to the west, falcons flying off in the sky, Maria da Boa Morte in the town administrator's home looking for food, bedrooms, hallways, more bedrooms, a porch that gives out onto the grass in the backyard

the town administrator's wife showed me the new furniture she'd ordered from Luanda, napa leather couches, lace-covered tables, a painting of a stampede of buffaloes, she showed me plants she'd brought back from Rhodesia to put in the flowerpots in the backyard, not the grass that's there now, but nice little squares of sod, flower boxes, and flowerpots

"Isn't it lovely, Dona Isilda?"

the row of eucalyptus plants, the native soldier who guarded the house with his crude rifle, the nurse was black, the store owners were black, the schoolteacher was black, the local government employees were black, at six or six thirty they'd turn on the generator for five hours, one smaller than ours, older, with more mechanical problems, the town administrator and the town administrator's wife, snugly seated on the napa leather couches and deafened by the crickets, stared at the painting of the buffaloes until they became nauseated, until the native soldier with the crude rifle shut off the generator and the house and the painting dissolved, we stopped in Marimba the following July on our way back from the Congo, the town administrator's wife got up off the couch and without ever leaving off talking started to slash the stampede painting with a pair of sewing shears

bedrooms, hallways, more bedrooms, the place where the painting used to hang between two windows, marked by a hook and a rectangular area whiter than the rest of the wall, the place where the furniture used to be recognizable by the thickness of the dust, a pearl from a necklace, not a real pearl, a fake pearl, forgotten in a crack in the flooring, Maria da Boa Morte pointing to the pantry, paper towels on the shelves

"Ma'am"

the white people in Lisbon are right to laugh at us, to look at us the way they look at blacks, with the same indifference or the same repulsion

my father used to explain

since our lives are a sort of caricature of their lives, in houses that imitate their houses, the way that the least poor of the poor people, ashamed of the poorest, imitate rich people, accomplishing nothing, just becoming more like themselves, never getting close to what they wish they could become, the white people in Lisbon

my father used to explain

they'll be right to not take us back after the Americans, the Russians, the French, and the English force us to return, dispossessed of our pride in our farms, our couches, and the paintings of buffaloes we looked at until we became nauseated

"Isn't it lovely, Dona Isilda?"

our pride in our money which is worth less than seashells and colored beads in Portugal

Maria da Boa Morte standing in front of the empty pantry

"Ma'am"

in front of the paper towels that they forgot to take with them when they fled to Malanje or Salazar or Luanda, waiting in the airport or on the docks for weeks and weeks, stretched out on blankets, shawls, bundles of clothes, waiting for some impossible plane or ship, bartering among ourselves with pencil and paper in hand, engaging in ridiculous transactions, houses, properties, and automobiles that we no longer had, offering the entire harvest and all the land we owned out in Cuíto for a place in the hold of the ship, while behind our backs soldiers shamelessly stole our blankets, shawls, bundles of clothes

one day

my father used to explain

it won't be during my lifetime since I don't have much time left, but during your lifetime, you'll see the airport and the docks with no lights, birds out in the bay fascinated by the lack of trawlers, fires in the slums, a general commotion in the city, the dead in the morgue overflowing into the plaza, the sick stabbed to death in their beds, and you won't understand it

my father used to explain

because we don't understand Angola, even having been born in Angola, we don't understand the land, the different smells, the fluctuation from the dry season to the rainy season, from submissiveness to rage, from laziness to violence, Angola, this present with no past and no future, in which the past and the future are completely bereft of any relationship to the hours, days, and years, those arbitrary measurements of the calendar, when the only true calendar is the coming and going of the wild geese and the permanence of the eagles crucified on the clouds

the eucalyptus trees in Marimba, a fake pearl in a crack in the flooring, Maria da Boa Morte in front of the empty pantry

"Ma'am"

the town administrator's wife suddenly got up to slash the painting of the buffaloes with the sewing shears

"I can't stand this"

she slashed her own life, not the painting, with the sewing shears, just like my father slashed his life with his lovers out on the island, and my husband slashed his in a Cotonang hut, and my children will probably slash theirs in Ajuda, and I slashed mine in the downstairs study, if I could only go up to the attic and dress up in the old clothes in the trunk, the raggedy hat, the petticoats, then go into the bedroom, show it off to my mother

"Mom"

my mother caressing the fabric with her fingers

"You look so pretty Isilda"

me with bare feet, my hair in a kerchief, digging under the grass with a piece of metal in hopes of finding beetles, ants, asking my mother, as if I could touch her, as if she could respond

"I'm white aren't I white Mom?"

it wasn't eucalyptus tea, as my daughter Isilda thought, there was sediment from the tea leaves at the bottom of the teapot, in Moçâmedes the quartermaster who fought against Gungunhana read my future in the tea leaves, separating them with a spoon, pushing them together, separating them, my Aunt Lúcia restless while waiting to hear

"What was it?"

my Aunt Encarnação turning her attention away from her needlework

"What is it?"

the quartermaster who fought against Gungunhana setting the flower-print teapot back on the tray, going back to his album of

*postage stamps with tweezers and magnifying glass while the waves
wiped the coast clean and he wiped his hands on his knees*

"Says she shouldn't live in the north she shouldn't marry"

*predicting that Eduardo, for whom I only existed a half-dozen
nights during those many years, would come into my life, predicting
the existence of my daughter Isilda, wearing a batik cloth around
her waist, digging up earth in hopes of finding beetles, ants, aided by
the servant who at times called her*

"Ma'am"

at others called her

"Madam"

at others called her

(on my honor it's true)

"Isilda"

*setting up makeshift beds in the local government offices or just
one bed for the two of them as if they were sisters just like when they
were children when my husband, against my wishes, used to let her
stay the night in the workers' quarters and let her bring Maria da
Boa Morte to stay the night with her, the doll with a missing arm
that Maria da Boa Morte's grandmother enthroned in their straw
hut, blessing the river with its remaining hand, her grandmother at-
tending her own funeral tied to a bench, sitting upright with her pipe
on her knees while her family pounded drums all around her shoving portions of cassava porridge in between her gums, offering her
tobacco, eggs, fermented sap, the blood from a decapitated chicken in
a little cup made of leaves, the head of the same chicken, which was
still twitching, the family members marking her forehead and wrists
with ink made from wood and aniline and ash, Eduardo and Isilda*

at the chief's side, Eduardo who educated Isilda as if she were a savage, how many times did I try to stop it, I told him that he shouldn't be surprised at what his daughter would eventually become, married to some random idiot and that uniformed man who comes in here like it's a barracks, walking across the room with complete disregard for me walking across the room without any regard for me not to mention the torment he's putting my grandchildren through

("What grandchildren?")

how many times did I warn Eduardo, how many times did I ask him to send her away from Baixa de Cassanje, to send her to school in Europe, so she could forget Africa, never return to Angola, and Eduardo

"Do you think we're better than all this, that we don't belong here, do you think I don't realize that they'll throw us all out eventually?"

Eduardo, who wanted to get even

(and wanted his daughter to get even for him)

I don't know with whom he wanted to get even, or how, transforming

he used to say

by means of the illusion of money and power, the revenge of giving orders into the dignity of giving orders, transforming contempt into a sort of pride, although a pathetic sort, one made of seashells and colored beads, even if it cost us the misery of the lepers, who would give us leprosy, and the slavery of the Bailundos, who would enslave us one day, or just restrict themselves to killing us, either because they don't have the time or just out of malevolence, or else out of a simple need for more space, how many times did I ask him to send her to school in Europe, to live in Europe, never to return to Angola,

not even to Moçâmedes, where the seaweed floats like the leaves in
the teapot, even if I never saw her again for the rest of my days, con-
demned to Baixa de Cassanje, to the cotton, to the sunflowers

(it wasn't eucalyptus trees in Marimba it was the golden rain
tree where the peacocks slept their breath floating up against the
curtains)

a husband who preferred the guest room so he wouldn't have to
lie down with me, trading me for all the shameless women out on
the island and the neighboring farms, without even the modesty to
do it in secret, talking with them, laughing with them, getting an-
noyed if I ever said anything to him, asked him anything, showed
any interest in him

"What?"

not even a smile not even a glance not even a gesture, not out of
tenderness, not even out of respect

my mother stroking the fabric from the trunk in the attic, not
noticing the lack of color, the unraveled weave, not noticing, above
all else, the batik cloth, my mother, content

"You look so pretty Isilda"

while we walked north or toward what we thought was north,
judging from the color of the shrubs, the deserted workers' quarters and after the workers' quarters the haphazardness of the
jungle, searching for a city full of white people like me where I
could be white, where Maria da Boa Morte could be black, where
the world could regain the order of days gone by, with a clock
on the wall that could bring me a sense of security, a sense of
peace derived from the way it shimmied like a fat man, back
when there were tractors, planting seasons, and harvests, not to

mention a mirror about which I could be certain that only acid had corroded it leaving yellow stains, turning it old, giving it wrinkles, silvery hairs, teeth that were falling out, creases in its lusterless skin

"You look so pretty Isilda"

a city full of white people at a time when there weren't any white people, they were disappearing from the airports and the docks, heading for Lisbon, Maria da Boa Morte and I running into government troops and UNITA troops who were as destitute as us, staring at fields that had been poisoned and bridges that had been destroyed, abandoning the sick beside the nearest tree, a soldier or a peasant lynched with a doubled-over strand of rope, troops with no rifles, no bullets, no mortars, Cubans yearning for the brothels in Luanda, where they never paid for the sparkling wine, giving orders to the employees like someone demanding something that rightfully belongs to them Bring me Clotilde Berta Alice Alda, giving the women cigars and martinis that were merely colored water, climbing up the stairs to the bedrooms, stairs my father

stairs my husband had climbed so many times

the red satin sheets, the decrepit grandeur of a bed with dragon claws at the base of the legs, a hand-carved headboard, pillows with no pillowcases, sheets that needed to be changed, Clotilde Berta Alice Alda all of them the same age, whether they were twenty or fifty years old, brought to Angola on government ships for the use of the farmers in Uíje and Cassanje

in the opinion of the Portuguese in power in Lisbon they were the women we deserved

("You never deserved other women Eduardo you never even deserved me")

teaching them to ask us for money and dance on a stage, not their own daughters or their friends or their wives, since we were black
my father used to explain

since we'd accepted exile in Africa in order to suffer through our obscure penances, punishments, and condemnations feeling less humiliation and less shame than if we were in Portugal, the Portuguese in power in Lisbon hoping that we'd die of a plague in the backlands or that we'd all kill each other like animals, forcing us to make them rich with tariffs and taxes on things that didn't belong to them, the same way we became rich from coffee and cotton that didn't belong to us either, women whose passports were confiscated so they couldn't return to Europe, prisoners of the little huts out on the island, of the buildings on the outskirts of town, of the slums, of police inspections where they were asked questions about me

"Did Eduardo talk about politics?"

"Did he speak ill of the regime?"

"Did he speak ill of the President of the Republic?"

"What did he talk about afterward?"

helping themselves to the women and still asking questions

"Did he talk about politics?"

"Did he speak ill of the regime?"

"Did he speak ill of the President of the Republic?"

"What did he talk about afterward?"

insulting them, beating them, stealing their wallets, bursting in on them in the morning while they were still sleeping, not knocking on the door, not calling out for them, breaking the lock with the butt of their guns, two or three policemen, not just one, in order to satisfy a judge who already has more informants than he knows what to do with, smashing the dirty dishes, tearing apart the bedrooms, the pasteboard suitcases, the prayer cards and stuffed animals with which they surrounded themselves in an attempt to recapture a childhood that, although it might not have been anyone else's either, certainly wasn't theirs, an invented childhood, like all childhoods

my father used to explain

which gave them a true feeling of nostalgia and was touching to them, a reason to live even though their reason to live was merely to keep going, given that our great misfortune

my father used to explain

was to have been born in God's old age, the way that others are born in their parents' old age, to have been born when God was already too elderly, too selfish and tired to worry about us, listening closely, anxiously to the sound of his own organs, the autumn of his stomach, the moaning of his liver, a heart made out of concentric teardrops like an onion or a chrysanthemum, a God who was losing his memory of himself and his memory of us, staring at us from a sick man's easy chair with startled bewilderment

my father used to explain

just like the Cubans in the jungle between Dala and Marim-banguengo when they came upon the UNITA mercenaries or the platoons of Katangans who didn't know for sure for whom or against whom or for what reason they were fighting just as they didn't know who was giving them orders and who was paying them, expressing themselves in a language that was some species of French, a French that sounded like a dog's bark, marching through the grass in a wild confusion that frightened the crows, killing anyone who got in their way, running them through on a roof beam from a straw hut, I remember the queen of Dala run through, along with her children, on a flagpole with no flag that the Portuguese had set up at the entrance to the village, I remember a South African pilot run through on a helicopter propeller that had been half buried in the ground, a war in which it was the dead themselves who fought, not the living, knocking each other down with their nauseating, rotten smells

the smell of the cabarets in Baixa de Cassanje, the smell of women waiting at the side of a highway for truck drivers who would never come, and who, if they came, would never stop, never stop, me squatting next to Maria da Boa Morte on a small hill, identical to the creatures who looked at us from the gate on the afternoon when I was married, when we arrived from the church in Malanje in a procession of cars, vans, jeeps, the bishop's car, the governor's limousine accompanied by motorcycles that had been decorated with feathers, me in my white dress, white gloves, white veil, a bouquet of flowers in my closed hand, asking myself

"Why?"

my husband paralyzed in a double-breasted suit that was too short and missing a button and he barely noticed the missing button, that missing button summed him up "Why you?"

the tables underneath the colored canopies, Damião and Fernando with trays, platters, bottles, casseroles, the bishop and the governor talking nose to nose like a couple of parakeets on the same branch, my mother looking up at the sky, afraid that it would rain, one of those unexpected torrential storms in May that would tear up Baixa de Cassanje like the blade of a knife, a pianist my dad had scrounged up who knows where in Luanda

"I don't know anything else I don't know anything else"

bent over the keyboard as if it were a sewing machine, turning out waltzes that nobody listened to, with the concentration of a seamstress, the workers hoping for a beer, some leftovers, some spare change, a day off, the company store opened at my father's orders, giving out dried fish and cassava flour, me seated at the table with the wedding cake, with the bishop, the governor, the best man and maid of honor, and my nobody of a husband, asking myself as I looked at that stranger

"Why you?"

as I stood up to cut the cake I noticed Maria da Boa Morte squatting near the gate the way that years later in the jungle between Dala and Marimbanguengo, with God much too old, hobbling among all the dead who'd been run through on pikes and all the unarmed Cubans, Maria da Boa Morte

no, the doll

no, Maria da Boa Morte looking exactly like the doll, raising her hand in some sort of blessing, bidding me farewell forever.

3

When I returned to Portugal the thing I liked best in Ajuda were the electric streetcars and the fat men who leap from the platform their movements identical to vultures when they land: they'd jump down, gliding along the running board with their torso leaning back, balancing with their outstretched arms, take a few quick, short steps, and then gather together with friends, bellies bouncing, very dignified, on the sidewalk outside the café, crowding together around the corpse of a table, an antelope with metal paws and a Formica body around which they quarreled amid shrieks over the scraps of meat that were dominoes. Every time I walked down the avenue, in the morning and the afternoon, I'd find them perched on branches, chairs, with their heads sunk down between their bulky shoulders, patient and bald, staring at me from under their white eyelids, waiting for me to die. Down below them, in the savanna of the town square, hyenas, schoolkids trotted in a circle, hunchbacked with their backpacks, with the fur on their coats bristling from the cold and drool from their gummy candy dangling from their jaws, sniffing around the street vendors' carts, jumping to one side, growling out nicknames, disappearing into the jungle, garden, where hippopotamuses, ships could be seen flashing their eyes in the Tagus as the afternoon began, forest buffaloes, mechanical cranes drinking in their wake, raising their iron horns against the backdrop of the hills of Almada a flock of shipping containers sleeping on the tarred decks with seagulls walking along their backs, picking parasites off their hides, wild dogs barking all night long in the gypsies' neighborhood, Rui wanted to bring the pellet gun that was left behind in Africa and hunt them down in the dark, Damião, Fernando, Josélia, and two or three native soldiers smiled from the wall where Lena had hung them up, with hollow eye sockets and hollow lips

"Don't mess with my masks Clarisse"

if Rui had shot the dogs their bodies would have jolted, electric, and they'd have run off, surprised at the tiny threat of death lodged in them, from which they'd try to free themselves by outrunning the pain, Damião, Fernando, Josélia, and the native soldiers, all made of varnished wood, changed their expression when we turned on the light on the ceiling, as though they were going to get down off the wall and talk

"Young lady"

and bring me a glass of milk, turn down the bed for me, kneel before me and pull off the boots that got stuck on my feet, I went up to Damião, who was telling secrets, some amusing tidbits about Lena

"I thought I asked you to leave those masks alone Clarisse"

for example, that she married a mulatto because she thought that the mulatto's father

"How many times do I have to tell you to leave those masks alone"

had more money than her father and a plantation that was better than her house in the slum, never supposing that the mulatto's father, who never let go of my hand, smothering me with kisses

"Clarisse"

had nothing more than liver disease and a bottle of whiskey hidden in the cupboard, and that when he died the mulatto wouldn't inherit a thing, not even a single sunflower corolla or a lone cornstalk, the lady of the plantation was the stepmother of the mulatto who would just as soon have sent Lena back to the filth of Marçal and the pennies counted out one by one in the little store, back to the chicken so tiny it was almost still a chick, served on Sundays and divided up between six or seven relatives with rosary beads wrapped around their wrists, Lena convinced that she'd one day spend a fortune on dresses, rings, and fashionable chests of drawers with wide midsections and legs that curved at the bottom near the ankle, just like the relatives with the rosaries, but with drawers and extra faces, hand-carved ones, but she ended up in a two-room apartment in Ajuda, with me and Rui on the sofa in the living room, with blinds that were stuck open and woke us up at seven in the morning, the sun in our eyes and a breeze blowing on our necks, not to mention the bedsheet, which gathered up in painful bunches beneath my chest, I'd wake up more tired than I was when I first went to bed, Rui tickled me with his breath and Carlos on the other side of the paper-thin wall in a small, plaintive voice

"Why don't you want to Lena tell me why you never want to?"

forgetting that he was a poor mulatto, that he wasn't from the city but from the jungle, born in a straw hut in Malanje with a bunch of raucous chickens, forgetting that instead of fashionable chests of drawers with inlaid decorative flourishes and bronze ring pulls what Lena really got was secondhand furniture that had to be balanced out with pieces of cardboard under the legs and that only opened if you really yanked on them, rain leaking through the ceiling, keeping out the draft in winter with newspaper stuffed under the windowsills, mismatched plates and silverware, forks with crooked tines, Rui disturbing the whole building with his fits and annoying the neighbors by breaking their windows, the neighborhood drafted a petition and sent it to the council president and the council president appeared in our doorway, chest puffed up like a pigeon's, wearing a ring with his initials on it, a handkerchief in his jacket pocket, accompanied by a delegation that was ready for a fight, looking less well-off and less puffed up

"What do you have to say about this disgrace?"

catching sight of me, modifying his expression, chest no longer so puffed up, straightening his tie, wiping his shoes on the doormat, the delegation waiting, the council president putting the petition away in his pocket, his eyes climbing up my body from my legs to my hair as though I was naked

a silver ring with interlinked initials on an oval-shaped coin

"Please excuse us barging in like this, young lady"

after dinner we'd take the cushions of the couch, unfolding the accordion bellows of the couch until it transformed into a bed, Lena moved things around in the bedroom knocking things against the warped doors, calling them names, bringing a blanket out of the closet, one that smelled like mold, the way it used to smell in the slum during the deep fogs of the dry season

I'd sit on my father's lap, the quails coughing in the backyard, the setters coughing on the porch, my father's breath had little needles in it, the medic pulled a medicinal syrup out of his bag, his bag which frightened me since it also contained syringes and pliers for pulling teeth

"You shouldn't smoke, sir"

my father's hand moved slowly up and down my back, the world went out of focus and then without any transition at all I was upstairs and it was daytime, if we've only slept for a second then why do the hands of the clock, I've never known anything to be so slow, why do they go round and round, it was daytime, my father was talking to a tractor driver, he wasn't Carlos's father or Rui's either, he was my father

"You're not Carlos's father or Rui's either are you Dad?"

my father because Carlos's father is a black man and Rui's was that policeman from Malanje

Lena would bring the blanket, which was smaller than the sofa bed and which Rui would pull over to his side of the bed when he rolled over, leaving me exposed to the cold, before they turned off the lights the room was bright and the window was dark and after they turned off the lights the room was dark and the window was pale with blinking, multicolored spots on it, Damião, Fernando, Josélia, and the native soldiers couldn't be seen on the wall, but from the feeling of a certain weight on our shoulders you could tell that they were still in Ajuda, with their hollow mouths and eyes, though you couldn't make them out on the wall, the rustling of Carlos's clothes as he undressed, Lena fidgeting with the cord to the alarm clock, footsteps in the apartment above us, sounds of water swishing to rinse teeth, the neighbor pulling back his lips to examine his gums, running his hand over a mole, thinking of cancer, pulling his hair back to see how much his hairline has receded, the woman removing her makeup with a white cream, the cotton ball turning black, putting her foot on a lever, the top of the trash can popping open, tossing the remains of hygiene products into the trash can, taking her foot off the lever, the top clamping shut as quick as an oyster, Carlos reached his arm out to the lamp and what was left of the apartment disappeared, Ajuda disappeared, the multicolored spots went dark, the whole world began to flow with the river, to Almada, with its lamplights in the dockyards, a lifeless world, with no noises except for the wild dogs in the gypsies' neighborhood and the fat men who leapt down off the platforms, gliding along the running board with their torso leaning back, who balanced with their outstretched arms, took a few short steps, and then gathered together with friends, bellies bouncing, very dignified, when we arrived in Luanda, where we were going to depart for Lisbon, they were already there with their little tiny skulls sunk down between their bulky shoulders, perched up in the palm trees along the coast, on the tile rooftops of houses, or hopping around in the street to escape machine-gun fire from the soldiers, they were there perched on the masts of the ships and the cranes in the shipyard, attracted by the rosy-colored blood that the soldiers sprayed toward the sea with blasts of water from fire hoses, blood, chunks of people, children who floated for a moment in the bay before conger eels pulled them into the mysterious chasms below the waves where debris from ships collected and gathered dust, I didn't feel bad about leaving Angola where as soon as you leave the city everything is exaggerated and places are much too distant from one another, hours and hours from one plantation to another, where ladies drink their tisanes, frightened the moment they saw me, as if they desired me

how silly

their husbands who suggested, in low voices, Saturdays at a little place in Dondo that looks out over the water, water that flows backward, the way it does in rivers when it begins to suspect a waterfall's ahead, what I mean is that it seems that the water's flowing backward, yet it's still flowing forward, like on trains when it seems the earth is shifting backward, not us moving forward, telephone poles, trees, houses, Saturdays in Dondo with their husbands who hurriedly tucked in their shirttails

"We're about to arrive in Malanje damn it"

back in the jeep driving over the rocks of the dirt road, straw huts, a family of mandrills in the ruins of the old mission, fingers that hesitated along the edges of bills in a wallet, seeking a middle ground between too much and not enough

"Buy yourself something special to remember me by"

as if I ever remembered them, what a joke, I never remembered them, I only remembered the water flowing backward away from the falls, husbands who, in Europe, would have been shopkeepers or handymen, but who in Africa had horses, servants, English furniture, German automobiles, dinners with the governor, holidays in Durban, their daughters' wedding cakes brought all the way from Negaje, sets of fine china, crystal figurines of roosters in fighting poses

"We're about to arrive in Malanje damn it"

I didn't feel bad about leaving Angola, maybe Carlos did since he's a mulatto, maybe Lena did since she's used to living in the slums, her forehead wrinkled up like she was holding back tears and the package with the masks in it on her lap, Damião, Fernando, and Josélia, and two or three native soldiers with hollow lips and hollow eyes, Lena never let go of the package, not even for a second, her father read magazines wore shorts and stuttered in front of my mother out of shyness

sometimes it makes me sad that my father didn't

fourteen days sitting around aimlessly on the deck of the ship, no toilets and no room to lie down, soup and beans at noon and night, a bucket in which to relieve ourselves, thrown overboard to the delight of the dolphins, the propellers stirring up the food in our stomachs, there were even people in the pool, even in the life rafts there were people, bags, trunks, suitcases, a broken-down piano, parakeets, Luanda getting smaller and smaller until the coconut palms on the island evaporated and there was nothing left of Africa, just some algae and a bunch of weepy creatures, and Lena shading her eyes with her hand, her father wearing shorts in the little garden full of marigolds and turnip leaves, holding himself up by his smile as if it were a cane, one of those smiles that once let go disappears immediately, they didn't say anything, didn't hug each other, didn't kiss, the roar of bazookas and cannons, the unrelenting fire of a machine gun, a conflagration growing in the Roque neighborhood, the body of a dead woman on the sidewalk, Lena and her father standing in front of each other as if they had all eternity to stand there, my sister-in-law and that poor wretch, holding himself up by his smile, his cane, while his daughter held onto the wooden masks, which were her smile, her cane, bullets from the machine gun clanged against the rain gutter and scarred the façade with pockmarks, when Lena got back in the jeep her father took off his hat, the same gesture country folk make graveside, at burials, when we looked back at him from down the street he was back in his canvas chair and was reading magazines in the middle of the clamor of war, of the dead, of crows flapping about, of mercenaries placing bets on little boys the way people bet on hares or partridges, one of the boys stood frozen still for what seemed like centuries before he fell, limbs splayed out on the ground, as we got closer to Portugal the clothes of a brigadier general who was all dressed up as if for a ball, convinced that Europe was a nonstop party, got more and more wrinkled, slowly turning into a pile of rags, the people in the pool asked every half hour if we saw any seagulls, the way Rui did when he was a kid right after we left the house to have lunch with the Belgians, covered in dust in the backseat, pulling on my mom's arm

"Will it take much longer?"

I feel like I can still hear it as I bounce around in my seat
"Will it take much longer Mom?"
until he fell asleep curled up between us, I didn't feel bad about leaving Angola because I never liked the plantation or the house, Malanje was like a provincial town where they sold diamonds in the market instead of cabbages and eels, for instance I never met a man who didn't try to whisper in my ear and ply me with dozens of bracelets, even the officials, even the governor, tacky corsages made of flower petals at the dances at the Ferroviário Club, old ladies watching carefully from their chairs at the edge of the dance floor, taking one of their shoes off to scratch their toes against the seams of their socks, they'd put a ribbon in my hair that matched the one around my waist, and I'd hide out in the ladies' room and smoke, dispersing the smoke by waving a towel, my mother knocking at the door, worried she'd find me in there with some boyfriend, the county clerk for instance, she got it into her head that I was interested in the county clerk

"What are you doing in there Clarisse?"

the most tiresome creature you could ever imagine, and on top of that he had a speech impediment, his tongue always sticking out, always trying to pull me aside to explain the vital importance of the county records, full of words like

"Eventually"

like

"Necessarily"

like

"Basically"

with my father all it took was for me to sit on the edge of his bed for his expression to change and for him to be happy again, he

wouldn't touch the bottle on the nightstand, he pretended that he
wasn't drinking, his eyelids almost didn't tremble, he'd button up his
pajama top the way he used to button up his suit coat, ceremoni-
ously, before speaking to an old woman

    "Give me a week to rest and I'll be just fine I just had a little bout
with malaria that's all you see?"

a little bout with malaria or amebic dysentery or jaundice like
the refugees on the boat

    "Will it take much longer Mom?"

holding tightly to their miserable bundles of possessions terrified that someone might steal them, the way Lena never let go of
Damião, Fernando, Josélia, and the native soldiers all wrapped up
in paper, their hollow mouths and lips unable to respond

    "Yes ma'am"

unable to obey any orders, for as simple as they may seem, hanging from nails in the living room, the mercenaries picked a kid about
a hundred yards away looting a burning store, they put all the cash
for the bet into a hat, nestled the butts of their guns against their
shoulders and their cheeks up against the butts of the guns, rested
their elbows on a tabletop, spread their boots apart, an index finger
released the safety, the barrel moved just a hair to get the boy in its
sights, before you even heard the sound the kid was on his knees,
his friends surrounding him, the back part of his head nothing but
a whitish pulp, not red, not black, whitish, the store cleared out in
a flash, once again the shoulder, the cheek, the boots spread apart,
the index finger, a second kid limping, touching his pants with his
hand, checking his hand for blood, limping even faster, dragging his
lame leg behind him toward a ditch, the mercenary reprimanded
by his sergeant, ordered to clear the breech, line up his sights, sup-

port his elbow on the table better, then the same strange silence, the limping kid leaning forward, bent over at the waist, trying to take a step or two, collapsing into a crumpled heap like an overcoat slipping off the hook of a coatrack, a helicopter up above the rooftops, the baobab trees at the Cuca-beer plant ablaze, the county clerk pulling me aside, his tongue sticking out of his mouth

"Eventually"

"Necessarily"

"Basically"

sometimes it makes me sad that my father didn't

soup for lunch, a plate of beans for dinner, one bottle of water to last the entire day, we pushed our noses against the portholes of the grand ballroom, guarded by marines carrying pistols, where a line of servants entered with flaming desserts, gold-colored sticks that shot out sparkles, provincial cabinet members, factory managers, priests, bank presidents, the marines ordered us to get back to the deck while the music was playing, and then the first albatrosses appeared, circling the ship and screeching, you could see the malice in their glassy pupils

my mother swore that if my father were alive and healthy enough to set me straight I wouldn't have turned out this way, it was a question of authority and example, the authority and example set by her lover whenever he came prowling around me, she thought there was no one better than her lover to straighten out her children and that's the reason that we always seemed to be running into our instructor at every turn

more albatrosses, seagulls, the women in first class clapped as Lisbon came closer and closer, it was no longer the sea, it was the

Tagus River, the smoke from chimneys, storefronts could be made out in the grayish drizzle, a train receding along the wall, Lena's father quivering above that smile of his the way oil lamps do right before they go out, they gave us a number with which to collect our bags five months later, transported us to the outskirts of town where there were no mercenaries or burning slums, so they could vaccinate us, take a blood sample, and measure our blood pressure, terrified at the possibility that we were carrying contagious black-people diseases, leprosy, rabies, foot-and-mouth disease, goiter

it's not that the Africans aren't our equals of course they're our equals but those poor things they don't even speak Portuguese I've seen wonderful documentaries the most objective ones there are about Africa that show them half naked and eating spiders you all are basically white thank God you all are different you take showers with those funny little buckets with tiny holes in the bottom I would love to experience what it's like to take a shower in the middle of a field of banana trees and have a chimpanzee or a domesticated lion there was this film once with a domesticated lion and it was just like a little puppy it ate out of its owner's hand and would lie down belly up you all fortunately use rubbers and have enormous rhinoceros horns in your houses they must be worth a fortune Pedro promised me that we would go on a safari next year sleep in a tent with a kerosene lamp for light converse with cockatoos hear tigers at night know what I'd really like to put in our bedroom a tiger-pelt rug from a tiger I'd kill myself then in the middle of this miserable life we lead every time I'd step on it I'd remember the backlands and I wouldn't need sedatives for anything fortunately your tests results came back normal see ya later

the apartment in Ajuda locked for I don't know how many years
if my father were alive and didn't drink I wouldn't be here
the lock was stuck, the furniture was falling apart, we turned on
the water and not a drop came out, we flipped the switch in the
fuse box and the lights didn't come on, we found some candles in
the back of the cupboard, an employee from the utility company
messed around with the pipes and for a steady hour there was nothing but a dark liquid mixed with dirt, which clogged up the bathtub, an apartment in an old building with missing *azulejo* tiles on
its façade, even before unclogging the bathtub and sweeping up all
the garbage Lena grabbed a hammer and hung Damião, Fernando,
Josélia, and the native soldiers on the wall, three on one side of the
mirror and three on the other side, facing the hills of Almada, the
mirrors in which my mother used to admire herself, straight ahead
and in profile, running her hands along her body, satisfied with her
breasts, her figure, the lack of a gut, her backside, the hairdresser
in Malanje who called all his female customers precious dyed her
hair, applied an antiwrinkle product to her forehead

"It's the one I use precious how old would you say I am?"

the UNITA troops came storming into his salon, not through
the door but through the storefront window, knocking over hair
dryers, tools from manicure kits, lacquers, dyes, fingernail polish, faux-marble shelves, they cut the hairdresser's throat with a
pocketknife and left him spinning in a rotary chair amid shards
of glass, the way they did with the Jewish diamond merchants,
their safes forced open, lying facedown in their offices, just like
the unarmed police squad and the security guards lying on the
ground with their bellies sliced open, they drilled down through

the dentist's molars one by one and he came crawling out of the consulting room bawling, the slum-dwellers looted the stores despite the mortar fire, they'd disappear into craters in the road, then reappear farther down the road with a stove in their arms, then they'd end up disappearing in a sudden explosion and the stove would be stuck up in the fork of a tree, crushed, the mulberry trees in Ajuda, as soon as I without a second thought got the stupid idea in my head to take a new outfit off the hanger and wear my hair down, Carlos would be in the doorway, blocking my way to the taxi

"Where do you think you're going in that getup young lady?"

convinced that I had to obey him, that he'd received a mandate from my mother to impose certain manners, curfews, and friends on me, to keep me from sending letters or using the telephone

"Hang up this instant"

to keep me from going to the movies with my friends, to birthday parties, on trips, on strolls

"Don't even think about it"

I think he did it because Lena rejected him, because at night I clearly heard his little mournful whisper

"Why don't you want to tell me why you never want to?"

blocking my way out to the street even though there were no mercenaries hunting him down with rifles, a mulatto who was bought for a trifle, the way you buy a suckling pig or a baby goat, the cafeteria worker at Cotonang happy to be free of such a burden, always alone, sullen, quiet, staring at the clock as if adding up all the hours that passed, running off to the pantry, always tugging at the servants' apron strings, so quiet in the evenings it was like he was dead and I yearned to open up the windows so the fat men would leap down from the platforms of the electric trolleys, gliding along the running board with their torsos leaning back, balancing with outstretched arms, taking a few quick, short steps, moving toward us with their bellies bouncing, very dignified, their heads sunk down between their bulky shoulders as they come through the living room, tripping over each other as they surround my brother together with the wild dogs from the gypsies' neighborhood until all that's left of him is a scrap of flesh and a pile of ribs, which Lena, finally at peace in her bed, no begging, no whimpering, no complaining, would hurriedly sweep into the trash can the following morning.

How do you go back home when there's no home, there's a hunting
shelter that my father had built for him close to Marimbanguengo,
a little hut built on stilts in a clearing in the jungle for sleeping and
playing bridge when he was out with friends hunting antelope,
deer, and forest buffalo and took me along with him, I remember
the hooks where we hung the animals in order to flay them and
the barrel of salt for curing the meat, my father strung up a hammock between two tree trunks and I sat watching Damião bring
firewood from a second little hut that was surrounded by yellow
butterflies, a smaller hut with no porch where he kept his straw
mat and his oil lamp and his tobacco, we spent half a week going

around in the jeep and the pickup truck, dancing over the loose planks of bridges, putting boards down on top of the mud, fixing the holes in the radiator with tape, my father, my godfather, the regional administrator, the government veterinarian who approved our ailing cattle with certificates and stamps, which the slaughterhouse couldn't refuse, the people from the workers' quarters stopped doing nothing for a moment to take a look at us, seated in a circle, passing the calabash pipe from one person to the next, shocked that we were moving around so much and with so much energy, homes of settlers forgotten in the tall grass, inhabited by a vegetal silence, a girl's bicycle with no tires still leaning against the useless water pump, my father let me go from room to room in search of lifeless objects in dresser drawers, a belt on the back of a chair, photo albums, thimbles, the remains of curtains against the windowpanes, I placed my fingers over the extant fingerprints in the dust, my feet walked over the footprints of people long since gone, the bell on the bicycle still rang, calling out to nobody after so many years

Filomena Dulce Fátima Margarida Idalina

mine had fenders and a metal basket in the front, on my very first try I rode round and round in the garden and on the patio without falling down, all they had to do was hold on to the seat just a bit, running alongside me for five or six meters

"Watch out for the flowerpots"

I never broke a flowerpot, never rode over a flower bed, never bent the handlebars, I steered from right to left, I traced a figure eight, I called out with my eyes on the ground in front of me, concentrating, not daring to raise my head

"Mom look"

Maria da Boa Morte admired me in silence, holding her doll close to her chest, I offered to let her ride the bicycle and as soon as she sat down she got too afraid to ride it

"No no"

in May and October we'd go to Marimbanguengo, Damião would unload the pickup truck, clean the hut, set up the beds, he'd build a tiny hut the size of a beehive to appease the spirits

"Be careful young lady"

he believed in spirits the way I believed in the movies, if the actor in a movie didn't end up marrying the actress it made me want to cry, movies where they like each other but get divorced and then by chance run into each other in a restaurant accompanied by the new husband and the new wife and are left speechless, remembering the time when they were together

(then we'd again see soft-focus scenes of their former happiness, kisses, strolls along the beach, embracing each other in a taxi)

with the new husband and the new wife just standing by, waiting, I'd fidget in my seat feeling the urge to climb up on screen and arrange their lives for them, implore them to not be fools, I'd leave the theater sniffling into my handkerchief, indignant over the injustice of the world, my godfather shuffled the cards, mad at my father for not paying attention

"Did you discard an ace Eduardo did you discard an ace?"

holding back bad words for my sake, the thing we came in search of in Africa wasn't wealth or power but black people with no wealth or power to speak of who could give us the illusion of wealth and power, and even if we actually had those two things we wouldn't really have them, the regional administrator and the veterinarian won every hand, you could hear the soft buzz of insects, the sound of thunder following the lightning striking way off in the Congo, the rustling of the tall grass, Damião secured a searchlight on the jeep, because we were no more than tolerated, accepted with disdain in Portugal, they looked at us the way we looked at the Bailundos who worked for us and thus in a way we were their blacks, just like the blacks have their own blacks, and those blacks have their blacks and so on going down from one level to the next to the absolute depths of disease and misery, cripples, lepers, the slaves of slaves, dogs, Maria da Boa Morte and I in Marimbanguengo walking up the steps of the front porch, if we happened upon a little girl's bicycle leaning against the water pump I wouldn't be able to steer from right to left, trace a figure eight, even ride it, the searchlight on the jeep created a colorless daylight from scratch in the middle of the night, specks of screech owls and rabbits that appeared and then disappeared, road signs in disrepair, the jeep's motor jolting its way toward the river, a pair of horns, a puff of air blown through the nostrils, a grayish boulder trotting about, the regional administrator got up from his seat, the boulder moved out of the light, my father drove down the hillside wanting to cut off its escape farther below, you could feel the damp branches and the nearby water, the whispers of water running past the rushes, Maria da Boa Morte and I in Marimbanguengo in the midst of horns, pelts, empty gun cartridges, playing cards on the table, I placed my fingers on top of fingerprints, stepped on footprints, the antelope motionless about ten yards away from us, frozen by the searchlight

"Stop the jeep Eduardo"

smaller than I'd imagined, skinnier, the remains of curtains against the windowpanes, my father's belt over the back of a chair, I picked up the belt and just like in the movies

the movies how silly

I realized the energy it takes to not

I hope that my children in Lisbon never

the energy it takes to not cry, I wouldn't give her the satisfaction of it, not her, the one who stole my doll, who stole my Carlos, I quickly bit down on my fist, my teeth sure noticed my fist but my fist didn't notice a thing, the regional administrator and my godfather fired at the same time, at the very instant I closed my eyes, when I opened them the antelope was still motionless, its head raised as if it were already one of the trophies in the living room, the veterinarian fired, my godfather and the regional administrator fired, the animal's legs gave out from under it, its chin slowly fell to the ground in high relief against the grass, I rested my chin on the windowsill in between pieces of glass, Damião wasn't bringing us firewood, the beast stared at the regional administrator, my godfather, and the veterinarian before it departed yet remained in the same spot, they hoisted it up into the trailer with a winch, hanging up in the tree its eyes that followed us everywhere, not red anymore, dark, I'd pedal around for hours on end on the patio because I didn't know how to get down without running into something and I didn't want to admit that I didn't know how to get down, ask for help, tell her to grab hold of the frame or the handlebars, the veterinarian

Doctor Mendes or Doctor Nunes, some plural-sounding last name, Nunes, Doctor Nunes, no, Mendes

hung the lantern on a hook and shadows descended from the wall all the way down to our feet, my godfather huffing and puffing, impatient with my father, who wasn't watching out for mud puddles

Doctor Mendes

"Are you asleep Eduardo"

the antelope that was too young for us to be proud of killing it and Damião looked at it with pity, we didn't keep its pelt or its horns, just buried it in a pit where wild dogs couldn't get at it and sprinkled quicklime over it but even so the vultures pecked at its lime-covered abdomen and the regional administrator ran toward them revolver in hand, the vultures that were keeping an eye on Maria da Boa Morte and me with drunken patience, gliding into the living room with beaks wide open and then retreating in a halfhearted flight to the roof of the smaller hut as soon as I threatened them with a stick, when Lady disappeared we found her a week later in the cemetery, vertebrae and ribs strewn about, a piece of the snout, skull fractured and pecked at, Clarisse swore that some Bailundos had done it in retaliation for some punishment they'd received for stealing cassava from the company store, someone had been lynched, I think, and she proposed sending the native soldiers to the workers' quarters to do the same to another four or five of them before we lost the dignity of giving orders that my father used to talk about, but whether it was vultures or Bailundos we'll end up just the same as Lady in a month or two when the government soldiers or the UNITA troops or deserters from the government troops or UNITA troops find us in Marimbanguengo, if anyone even remembers that Marimbanguengo exists, all of a sudden I wanted to forget who I was and embrace her, not because I liked her but because there was no one else to embrace, but thank God in the nick of time I remembered the sorry figures of my mother and Josélia, embarrassing all of us, and I immediately turned my back on her, I'd grown sentimental with age, Damião filled up the tank and cleaned the insects and mud off the searchlight, my father let me hold the rifle until we got to the part of the jungle near the river where we discovered droppings, hoof tracks, and broken branches

who is finding all the signs left here by me and Maria da Boa Morte, our tracks and broken branches, who is going from one clue to the next until they stumble upon us, wild dogs, vultures, mercenaries, soldiers, the searchlight freezing us in our tracks, who will shoot first, who will shoot second, who will hoist us up with a winch, stuff glass eyes into our sockets, stuff our heads full of straw, bolt our necks to a varnished wooden base, between other glass eyes, other heads, other varnished wooden bases with dates inscribed on a metal plate, who will dump a bucketful of quicklime on whatever is left of us, and yet for all that I won't touch her, I won't embrace her, I won't say

"Help me"

I'll say

"Get to work"

I'll say

"Find me a decent straw mat"

I'll say

"Maybe they happened to leave behind some preserves some-where go look"

I'll say

"Find me something to eat even if it's just ants"

and I think I'm being too generous by keeping her with me, saving her from the army, the UNITA troops, the laborers who can't get back to Huambo and who are running from the army and the UNITA troops just like we're running from them, not a single farm, not a single store, not a single plantation that's still in working order, the missions deserted, my godfather, the regional administrator, and the veterinarian down by the river, waiting, the searchlight on the jeep turned off, passing around the bottle of cognac, passing it to me as well and nobody giving it much thought, the regional administrator pressing his ear up against a tree trunk, walking out of sight, returning to the jeep announcing in a low voice

"Nothing"

except the gurgling of the muddy water, the screech owls, the drab-colored presence of the rain, the lowly beasts creeping through the grass, I missed my mother, a piece of paper and a pencil to doodle with while lying on the rug in the living room, a sibling to play with, the underbrush started to move, my father handed me the bottle reached for the switch on the searchlight, the veterinarian

"Not yet don't startle them"

Doctor Mendes

the sound of hooves on the grass, not the sounds of an animal that you see first and only then begin to hear, but the invisible rustling of its horns, my godfather and the regional administrator sitting upright, the veterinarian to my father

"Now"

a white-gray radiance, trees upon trees, not real ones, painted on paper, leaves and owls printed on a screen, the noise of animals hesitating, standing up straight, running away from us, monstrously large flowers, invisible birds, a tissue of tangled fibers, caves filled with echoes like the ones in mineshafts, frightened bats, the regional administrator pleading, crazed

"Start the jeep get going"

Doctor Nunes, Doctor Mendes, Nunes, Mendes

(Barros?)

lived in Malanje in a building with a pastry shop where men in hats sat and conversed, there were two bronze horses, a silver ink-well, and a roll of green blotting paper on his desk, his wife would offer me honey-flavored candies and tousle my hair and say to my mother My how big the little one is these days how big the little one is while the veterinarian put stamps on documents concerning my father's cattle, he'd pour out some glasses of port wine and my father would hand him an envelope that the vet would slip into his jacket pocket as if it was only his hand accepting it not him, and he didn't notice that I noticed

"A little something for your troubles as always"

his wife not noticing either, gathering up the candy wrappers and tossing them in the trash

"My how big the little one is these days"

my mother would ask after an old woman who was always coughing in a back room, a cough that sounded like bricks tumbling down into a pile, the veterinarian's wife who'd been cheerful up to that moment gestured down the hallway with her chin, resignedly   .

"She's not going to get better poor thing"

then becoming cheerful once again, placing on a book on my lap, one with clasps that scraped my skin

"Here you'll enjoy looking at these photographs young lady"

gentlemen with mustaches, wearing pith helmets, standing next to dead lions, and at the same time the old woman opened her gullet and out tumbled some more bricks, in my opinion down the hallway there were only ruins, dust, debris, in no time the chandelier would fall off the ceiling, the paintings would crack down the middle, we'd cross the border into the Congo, we'd board a ship that would take us to Lisbon, even if we didn't have a cabin or any other comforts, get Maria da Boa Morte a job as kitchen help in a restaurant in the Baixa neighborhood and take her paychecks, a little something for our troubles as always like the something the veterinarian slipped into his wallet as if he didn't even notice it, she'd have to help out with the expenses, when we left the place where we got the stamps I'd sneak countless looks back at the building, certain that I'd see it collapse, the searchlight wavered as it shone across the trees made of painted paper, following the forest buffalo, forest trails that mimicked real forest trails, rushes that mimicked real rushes, a chapel that twirled around and disappeared behind us, a niche that housed a bell with no clapper, the priests' humble vegetable garden, the forest buffaloes galloping diagonally through an open field, the regional administrator holding onto the windshield, beating against the side of the jeep

"Faster"

my godfather tried to get his bearings with a compass, the tires on both sides dipping in and out of potholes, stomachs now up in our throats, now down at our feet, shoulders jostling against other passengers' bouncing shoulders, one of the fenders snapped and broke loose, flying up near to my face, then lost in the air behind us, straw huts that swerved around us and flew past, the regional administrator tapped the butt of his gun on my father's back

"Faster"

things that looked like clouds, things that looked like lights in the distance, a tomb underneath a crumbling tile-roofed awning supported by columns, the trailer bounced in the air above us, the cork fell out of the bottle of cognac, alcohol ran down my legs, burning, my father tried to drive the forest buffalo back into someplace where they could be cornered, where the searchlight could capture them, even if it was only two of them, even if it was only the oldest one, the adult male, whose death would disorient the females, with the money Maria da Boa Morte would make we could move from Ajuda to a bigger apartment, a bedroom for Carlos and Lena, a bedroom for Clarisse, a bedroom for Rui, a bedroom with a view of the Tagus River for me, a decent living room, a kitchen, a little area out back for the servant's sleeping mat, and those things you hang from the ceiling that eliminate odors, I'd occupy myself as I should with Rui's illness and Clarisse's marriage prospects because children, inasmuch as they ever grow up, never grow up enough, a troop of mandrills made silver in the bright light came running out in front of us and then scattered in every direction like beads from a broken necklace rolling under the couches, cupboards, bookcases, which even if we moved all the furniture and got down on all fours with a flashlight we still never found, sometimes I would end up touching one with the very tip of my finger, way in the back, which would roll off, mocking me from some little hole in the floor or another, months later by chance I'd slip my hand in between the cushions of an armchair and bam the cap of a pen, a matchbook, and the pearl, or else in the pocket of a winter coat that I hadn't worn in years, the spitefulness of inanimate objects, their cruel little lives, forks that poke you on purpose, the heater that won't turn on and just looks at you with that air of innocence, feigning ignorance, lightbulbs that turn off as if they'd burned out and then later after spending hours rooting around for a lightbulb in a basement full of everything except the one thing we need they light back up again

those mocking objects

glowing weakly the second we touch the fixture in order to put in the new one, if only objects had a neck that could be throttled, skin that could be pinched, clamped down on, twisted, some tender spot, the mandrills bared their teeth at us and screeched like wild kindergartners on the playground, we ran over a row of box-tree shrubs that got jammed in the motor, the jeep slowed down, hiccupping along, the searchlight revealed the forest buffalo standing in the mud, a spindly legged calf, two females, and a male up to its ankles in the water, their silhouettes cut inch by inch by the scissorlike searchlight, offering themselves up to the crocodiles in the river in their tremulous innocence, the way my family and all the other farmers in Cassanje offered themselves up without complaint to the Angolans, here you go, kill us if you like, here you go, we've been here for twenty or fifty or one hundred or two hundred years, but here you go, here are my sunflowers, my cotton, my corn, my house, my hard work, the hard work of my parents, the hard work of my parents' parents before them, the place where my dead are buried, here you go, the people in charge in Lisbon decided that my life, and more than just my life, the whole reason for my living, belongs to you because the Americans and the Russians say that it belongs to you and they obey them the same way you used to obey us, with the exact same passivity and the exact same submissiveness, so here you go, take all of this that cost me an arm and a leg and cost my family an arm and a leg, my cattle, my coffee, my tobacco, my farm equipment, my money in the bank, here you go, cut our throats or drive us onto the ships bound for Lisbon, steal what little we have left on the docks, stuff our testicles in our mouths, wear our intestines as accessories, here you go, a spindly-legged calf, two females, and a male up to its ankles in the water, their silhouettes cut out inch by inch by the scissorlike searchlight, the searchlight slowly got dimmer and dimmer and the regional administrator started shaking it

"This is the last thing I need right now"

the regional administrator with the lover he'd brought from Dembos years ago and never introduced to anyone, locked up in the house far away from the windows so that no one would ever even catch a glimpse of her, she never went out shopping never enjoyed the breeze on the balcony never went to Mass or to the movies whenever the projectionist set up a white sheet as a screen in town, never put clothes on the line in the backyard, we never heard her voice or her footsteps, if she ever happened to get sick he was the one who went to the doctor, describing his fever or a pain in his side and then he'd bring her the medicine, just like he brought her food, bleach, starch, a jacket or shoes purchased in Salazar for Christmas, it was said that they had children but we never knew anything about them either, the same secretiveness, the same absence, the door that was always closed, which he'd enter sideways, concealing the interior with his body, even after he'd made sure there wasn't anyone peeking into the entryway, a tiny house with a neglected garden and a native soldier squatting out in front, on the way home from school I caught sight of her, her hair up in a kerchief, warily dumping out a basin of water and running back inside, I was startled

"Why?"

my father thrilled by the story when I told him, my mother looking up from her knitting and sending me to brush my teeth and wash my hands the way she always did when she didn't know what to say

"You just took a bath yesterday Isilda I've never seen anything like it"

a calf, two females, and a male up to its ankles in the water, my godfather and the veterinarian moving away from us as the jeep's motor went quiet, reduced to a meager whistle, the searchlight went out, the regional administrator

"This is the last thing I need I swear this is the last thing I need"

examining the battery, the fan belt, the clamps on the battery terminals, and the trees became real again, and the marsh, and the river, insects took off from the surface of the water in a chorus of echoes, the calf and the two females started to walk off, unafraid, because we were nothing to them, we were worthless, we told the blacks here you go, cut open my veins, here you go, twist your machete around in my child's guts, in my husband's guts, in my wife's guts, set my thresher on fire because of the Americans the Russians the English the French, the people in charge in Lisbon who offer us up to you, here you go, the calf and two females, walking slowly at first, then trotting, the grass trembled and then stood still, the calf stumbling as if caught up in wire, with the imperfection of a beast not fully formed, the regional administrator

"I swear this is the last thing I need"

unscrewing the distributor cap, cleaning off the sparkplugs, it was said that his father had a business in Lunda and was an informant for the police who worked with the diamond mines, he'd purchased land in São Salvador and Bié, and would never accept mulatto grandchildren, work your whole life for mulatto grandchildren who would betray your son and burn down his house with barrels of oil, here you go, what can I possibly do in Lisbon, sit down beside Carlos on that rattan couch that barely holds one person and stare at the dockyard cranes and the hills of Almada through the window while Rui tortures the neighborhood pigeons and Clarisse disappears down the stairs to meet up with the first idiot who honks at her in the street, the regional administrator's father with his hands on his hips in front of the windows with lowered blinds, as if the native soldier who guarded the house were one of those bronze statuettes that turn gray and crumbly over time

"Act like a man and come out here Arménio"

the whole town looking on, my mother and I in a store peering out the window at an angle, the store owner climbing up on a shelf with a pretext of straightening some cans in order to see better, the regional administrator's father taking his pistol out of his vest, pushing the native soldier aside with the tip of his boot

"Get out of my sight you clown"

my father trying to start the engine, my godfather

I offer this portrait dating from the time I spent in the military as farrier corporal in Santarém to my dear goddaughter Isilda Maria with affection from her friend and godfather António Cândido Felício, not yet fat, not yet authoritarian, not yet rich, trimming abscesses off of mules' hooves in a military barracks in Santarém, what did an old farrier corporal who wasn't even a commissioned officer, who was born poor, matter to the people in charge in Lisbon, take all the farrier corporals you want, do whatever you want with them, here you go

my godfather and the veterinarian returning to the jeep with a crown of fireflies and beetles flying swarming around their heads, the regional administrator's father firing at the house

"You coward"

he fired all the bullets in his clip at the façade of the house, got into his van and circled around the plaza, slowing down next to the native soldier and screaming at him as if he were screaming at his son

"You cowardly piece of shit you clown"

knocking over a wire fence, spooking the billy goats, my godfather

I offer this portrait dating from the time I spent in the military as farrier corporal in Santarém

searching for the bottle of cognac in the jeep, the veterinarian took the bullets out of his rifle, the regional administrator to my father, pleading, the voice of a drowning man, oil roiling in his throat

"Now"

the engine crackled, quivered, gave the impression that it was going to start up through sheer brute force, the cylinders pounded, found their rhythm, vibrated in unison, the regional administrator's face appeared and then evaporated in the glaring searchlight

"Speed up"

erasing high-relief images, shadows, transforming the real trees and underbrush into theater-prop trees and underbrush, there where the muddy banks had been, the tangles of reeds, the ripples in the water of the river, the male staring at us, ankle-deep in the water, still staring at us while my father turned the steering wheel back toward Marimbanguengo, found the trail that wound around the jungle, picked up speed going downhill, still staring at us with disdain

"Clowns"

while I fell asleep on my father's lap, squeezed in between defeated men and dreaming of a poor farrier corporal with no future and no hope trimming abscesses off of mules' hooves in a provincial military barracks.

24 DECEMBER 1995

When he called about the Christmas Eve dinner of course I said I
would go, for the pleasure of imagining him waiting all night long
in Ajuda where he made my life miserable for three years. Carlos, the same as when I saw him last, with a pine tree in a stand,
a fresh tablecloth, a little bowl of almonds, fruitcake, a present
for Rui and one for me, wrapped in fancy wrapping paper, with
pink ribbons on it to make it look like it cost twice what he really
paid for it, getting up to peek out of the curtains, worried about
the reheated *caldo verde* soup and the codfish getting cold, going
downstairs to the street to open the door with a hopeful smile
on his face, fooled by the echoes of some drunks talking out on

the street or the sound of the rain on the mulberry trees, finding nothing but a row of trash cans overflowing with garbage bags, the only imaginable Santa Clauses in that impoverished neighborhood that flees down the hill toward the river, houses scampering along, their open windows like flared nostrils and chimneys like tails waving good-bye, waiting up for me all night long going back and forth between the balcony and the couch, should I cut the codfish or not, should I take down the tree or not, should I go to bed or not, noticing something

"What was that?"

pacing between Lena's wooden masks and the marble elephants on the shelf, pausing with his nose pointed at the clock I'll give her another half hour, another forty-five minutes, one more hour, thinking, after that hour has passed, I'll give her twenty more minutes and then those twenty come to an end, and another twenty, and another twenty still, the final twenty, and after the final twenty minutes five minutes and another five and another five and another five, and no doorbell ringing, annoyed at the speed of the hands of the clock, which move so slowly when you have time and so quickly when you're in a hurry, waking up freezing on the couch in the living room, watching them turn off the lights on the trees and wreaths at the town hall, deciding to count to one hundred and at one hundred, if they haven't come, I'll give up, trying to give up at four hundred and seventy-five and really giving up at nine hundred and thirty-six when the rain suddenly shoves open the window shutters, startling a few pigeons and revealing a full ashtray, congealed oil on the serving platters, potatoes that have turned black, Carlos stumbling to the bedroom where Lena is asleep with her makeup still on, a necklace around her neck, asking from the depths of her sleep as he sits down on the edge of the bed to untie his shoelaces

"Are they here?"

Lena, without waking up, stretching out her unsure hands to straighten her skirt

"Come in"

Carlos and Lena greeting us from the bed, facing the cold December wind

"Come in come in"

like on the docks in Luanda while we waited for the ship, talking without knowing what we were saying, getting up without even noticing that we'd stood, looking around for the sunflowers and cotton from the plantation and finding only people and children and chests of drawers with vanity mirrors and whimpering dogs, looking around for the flower beds with azalea bushes and the back porch and finding only wooden crates numbered with chalk and policemen and soldiers pushing us aside with their rifles

"Papers"

toward the black peoples' buses, Carlos hidden among us, scared that they'd find him among the whites and call each other over, call out to him, beat him with the butt of their guns

"Mulatto mulatto"

take him off to Grafanil or Caxito to dig ditches, Carlos the mulatto with nobody to persecute him in Ajuda, determined to be my master, waiting for me on the couch, switching on the lights when I arrived, coming toward me with his hand upraised, where did you go, where have you been, don't lie to me, what did you do, with whom, startling the hideous masks on the wall that treated me with respect, called me young lady, walked away pretending they didn't notice if they ever found me with the tractor driver or the accountant in the storehouse, with owls and bats perched on the crossbars of the roof, and God as well, who doesn't exist, up there with the animals, watching me, the tractor driver and the accountant doing whatever I told them with hesitation, uneasy, terrified that my parents would find out, that someone would tell or that I'd tell them myself on some regretful whim and they'd lose their jobs, convinced that they were important to me when they weren't, or that I was going steady with them when I wasn't, Carlos calling me in Estoril after fifteen years, speaking in a ceremonious voice that felt its way around, carefully weighing each word out of shyness

"Clarisse"

a voice that brought Ajuda back to me, and Baixa de Cassanje and Angola as well, everything that I didn't want to remember, the tractor driver made up an excuse about work so he didn't have to go to the storehouse with me, not knowing that he wasn't really with me even when he went with me, Carlos, fifteen years later, as humble as Damião, as Fernando

"Clarisse"

and underneath his

"Clarisse"

was his humble mulatto entreaty

"Young lady"

Carlos, and along with Carlos every other man, except for that trembling bedsheet upstairs, we heard the sound of something falling, my mother held her fork still for a moment and then started eating again

"Your father never lets up"

Rui would pretend to fire his pellet gun, making gunfire sound effects with his mouth, my grandmother would count the medicinal drops she added to her cup, the sound of footsteps coming down the stairs, one stair at a time, with childlike difficulty, all brought back by Carlos's voice on the telephone, tormenting me, trying to make me cry, a voice that felt its way around, the way those sandals felt their way down each stair

"Clarisse"

and if I were to cry my face would transform, it would become like the walls of old houses, dark-colored streaks running down them, I'd have to restrain my eyelids with a handkerchief, hold back my eyelashes, I have the life I want, health insurance, friends, apartment, car, a little safe filled with jewelry, a line of credit at the bank, the doctor handed me the test results last week with a cheerful expression

"Nothing showed up on the mammogram congratulations don't worry about the lump"

the globe with a sleigh and reindeer and a chubby little figure in it on the desk in the study, you could turn it upside down and make it snow inside, which was really

I don't know why, I'm silly

touching to me, it wasn't really snow it was hundreds of white specks that whirled around and around, my mother bought a cardboard picture of the nativity scene, which had one little door to open each day and inside the door was a shepherd or a wise man or an angel, and when there was no one around I peeked inside the biggest door, number twenty-five, in the middle of the picture, and it was baby Jesus, blond with a multipointed halo, I never understood why all baby Jesuses are blond and chubby and have blue eyes and all the adult Jesuses are dark-haired and skinny and have brown eyes, similarly I never understood why there was never an adult Jesus without a mustache and goatee, never a clean-shaven Jesus, and why he was never shorter than anyone else, always the tallest, the handsomest, with a gash in his side and the cheeks of a starving man, one of his hands upraised in a gesture somewhere between a warning and a blessing, his other hand on his chest, I closed the little door and on the twenty-fifth my mother opened up again and gave me a long-sleeved dress to wear on Sundays, which I wasn't even remotely interested in, and a tricycle, which Rui quickly damaged, knocking off one of the pedals with a hammer, Carlos and Lena waiting up for me in Ajuda with a new tricycle for me, when the doctor handed me the test results last week she didn't say

"Nothing showed up on the mammogram congratulations don't worry about the lump"

she said, while holding the X-rays up to the light, two ovals, light and dark, a bunch of long streaks that looked like spider legs

"We're going to request some more tests I don't like the look of something on here"

me, convinced that they'd mixed up the names, laboratories are always mixing up peoples' names, I've heard of many such cases, I look great these days, I have a healthy appetite, I don't feel tired at all, and furthermore I always give a few bucks during the cancer drives, I put the little sticker of a crab on the collar of my jacket so that the well-dressed ladies who hold out the cans won't ask me for another donation at traffic lights or crosswalks, come visit us at the hospital, holding out pamphlets, an understanding psychologist, a priest saying compassionate prayers, because it's not the doctor who has something in her breast that she doesn't like the look of, it's not my sister-in-law, not my coworker at the store in the shopping mall

a tricycle

I don't want tubes in my nose, an injection of serum in my arm, that medicine that makes your hair fall out and forces you to wear a kerchief, a new tricycle that could whisk me far away from the cancer, the street outside the doctor's office full of people with no diseases, I felt a lump while I was taking a shower, a hard egg-shaped thing, and another one in my armpit, and not just on the street outside the doctor's office, in movie theaters, on sidewalks, in houses, one morning during the trip from Luanda to Lisbon we woke up and the man beside us in the boat was dead, my mother used to say that the year I was born she saw hundreds of corpses in Baixa de Cassanje and none of them were us, the doctor put the test results in an envelope with my name on it, the wrong name, a mistake, instead of calling the laboratory to confirm that there'd been a blunder she started to write something as long as a letter on a prescription pad, What do you mean you don't like the look of something on there? the sea off the coast of Estoril outside, the palm trees in front of the casino, the palm trees in Angola, Carlos peeking out of the curtains the lights from town hall reflected by the rain, not in the trees but in the puddles on the ground, the doctor holding her pen still without looking up at me, Before we get the test results back it's hard to say, I put on the long-sleeved dress, sat down on the tricycle and as I raced past her, missing pedal notwithstanding, one of the secretaries took her fingers off the buttons of the multiline telephone, with a compassionate look on her face, Good-bye Clarisse, why did you smoke so much? you're going to die, good-bye, my grandmother putting drops into her cup, my mother who would talk to the police chief without interruption, she never had to worry about tubes in her nose, vials of serums, hair falling out by the fistful, Rui pointing the pellet gun at me making popping sounds with his cheeks

clack

my father's bottle

I don't have a father, I don't have a father

on top of the nightstand, something different about the furniture in the apartment in Estoril all of a sudden, knickknacks that belong to some stranger, in the closet the clothes of some strange woman who was going to come in any second and kick me out, they put the man who died on the boat in a fruit crate and nailed it shut and I could still smell him, if I accepted Carlos's present and ripped open the wrapping paper I'd find that dead colonist staring at me, the doctor licked the adhesive on the envelope with her enormous tongue, We're going to take some pictures of your skeleton and perform a little biopsy with localized anesthetics, it doesn't hurt at all, I remembered two hyenas latched onto the throat of a forest buffalo, and one that had clamped down on its snout, I remembered the buffalo taking a half-dozen steps with the hyenas hanging off it, Luís Felipe stopped calling, stopped showing up, stopped making payments on the car, his secretary explained to me, as though she didn't recognize my voice, that she had been instructed not to interrupt the meeting, but give me your contact information and I'll give him the message, hours and hours next to the phone, but nothing, if I called his home his wife would answer Hello hello hello in the cackling voice of an old woman older than my mother and me silent on the other end, I tried again, Luís Felipe, Yes, also in the cackling voice of an old person, impatient, irritated, I'm completely distraught I really need to talk to you, and Luís Felipe, You have the wrong number, he spent months chasing after me with bouquets of flowers, lingerie, rings, invitations to spend the weekend with him in Madrid, promises that he would get a divorce, a four-bedroom place in my name, a car, a boutique, the doorbell rang, one of his employees with a piece of a paper from a little notepad, written with such force that it tore holes in the paper if you dare harass my family you'll be out in the middle of the street in three seconds, my grandmother, who measured out her life in medicinal drops into her cup, reproaching me with a sigh, Rui running after the peacocks with pockets full of rocks

fortunately there are times when I forget Africa, forget the plantation, the layout of the rooms, the open parasols on the patio, the endless dirt roads that led to nowhere, just more cotton fields, more villages, more mango trees, more workers' quarters with the company store off to the side, more sick people, more misery, the Indian daughters of the manager of Cotonang, silent and rotund, used to play with me in the garden with an air of solemn idleness, the manager, in the study, assessed taxes on my mother, delivery deadlines, costs, percentages,

they strung up the chief's grandson by his feet and cracked his head
open against a tree, the lynching tree where they never let anyone cut
the ropes, the rain slowly stripping the victims of their clothes, hands
bound with a length of wire, Rui running after the manager's daugh-
ters the way he did with the peacocks, Carlos to Rui

"*Rui*"

the surgeon handing me a typed report I didn't understand a
word of, the wild dogs backed off, disillusioned, and there wasn't
a single vulture on the roof of the storehouse

"False alarm"

so I no longer needed the tricycle or the long-sleeved dress in
order to pedal far away from the cancer, the secretary at the doctor's office in her rubber-soled shoes guided me down the hallway
with cheap prints of paintings on the wall and a door marked Reserved where it's possible that they create monsters in secret using
body parts from different people, faces with one eye socket higher
than the other because they cut them out separately and added
them to the face double checking

"Please come in Ms. Clarisse"

a folding screen covered in frilly fabric that hid the examination table from view, the same frilly fabric covering the windows
blocking my view of the sea, the doctor also dressed in frilly
clothing, this time with no pen and no prescription pad, maybe
younger than me but looking more worn down than me, with a
wedding ring on her finger, symbol of a marriage in which there
were no lies because there was no more truth to be told, enduring each long day in pragmatic acrimony, the furniture salesman,
taxes, schools, vacations

"It seems like we can"

can we?

breathe a sigh of relief

I breathed a sigh of relief when we arrived in Lisbon where the alleys and avenues all have a reason for being, a beginning, an end, death was far removed from us, in other streets, in other neighborhoods, latched onto necks and snouts that didn't belong to us, squatting in the grass, its ears trembling, protected by the direction and force of the wind, the hobbling lion surrounded by gledes, biding their time, the police chief asking the native soldier to hand him the machine gun, machine-gun shells popping out like popcorn, the guy who smuggled Bailundos got out of his truck to show his counterfeit licenses, dozens of laborers breathing through the slats in the crates, even with the motor turned off the truck kept shuddering and spewing exhaust, the police chief tore up the man's licenses, the native soldiers removed everything from his pockets, coins, a pocketknife, a butane lighter, the key to the ignition, a crude sort of map drawn in pencil on butcher paper, they tore off his shirt, his shoes, his pants, the police chief fired off a series of shots at the crate in the back of the truck and we left them there in the rain for the leopards

while the doctor with a wedding ring on her finger congratulated me with a hint of enthusiasm

"It seems like we can breathe a sigh of relief"

in November the leopards prowling around the house, we could hear delicate little footsteps outside, someone trying to save the azalea bushes, Carlos saying to me

in a faint voice that barely whispered the words, as if walking along a sidewalk trying not to step on any of the cracks

"Clarisse"

Carlos and I lying in the bedroom upstairs wishing we could get out of bed and go downstairs where my mother and grandmother were because when I was little I thought that grown-ups could keep us from doing it

speaking of Christmas as if after all these years Christmas were still important for us, a Monopoly board game, a cap gun, a tricycle, Carlos saying he's sorry without saying he's sorry or even assuming that I'd guessed that he was saying he was sorry, as if apologies meant anything to me after he kicked me out of the house, presuming I wasn't my father's daughter, getting revenge on my mother and on the man he was certain was my father by taking it out on me, since he was unable to take it out on them, Carlos hating them through me as though every time he looked at me he could see them in the study, the whispers, the giggles, the demands

"Wait a minute"

the desk knocking against the wall the wall the wall, the desk knocking against the wall without respite for weeks months years centuries on end, my mother caught him hammering nails into the desktop, the police chief caught him letting the air out of the tires of his jeep and ripping open one of the seats with a knife, then held him up in the air

"What's going on here?"

and Carlos in the tone of someone proposing they settle the matter as adults

"I'm going to kill you when I grow up"

Carlos to me

"Clarisse"

lying in the bedroom upstairs wishing we could get out of bed and go downstairs where my mother and grandmother were, Damião serving them verbena tea, because when I was little I thought that grown-ups would never let anyone harm my brothers and me

even though the man had pushed him up against the jeep just like he pushed the desk up against the wall

"Kill me huh?"

his right hand on his holster and his left hand on Carlos's neck, Carlos, whose voice hadn't changed yet, who couldn't grow a beard yet, kicking his legs like a suckling pig

"Kill me huh?"

dropping him into the flower bed, raising his boot up over Carlos's head

"You black piece of shit"

so it wasn't me he hated, it was my mother and the man and my father that he hated in me, my father who never went for his shotgun, never went downstairs, never let the bullets fly at them, hugging his bottle close to him, destroying himself instead of destroying them, Carlos grabbing at the collar of my father's pajamas, deafened by the whispers, the giggles, the entreaties, the desk knocking against the wall

"Why don't you go down there for the love of God explain to me why you don't go down there?"

my father feeling around with his hand on the nightstand, opening the bottle when he could have sat down on my tricycle and caught up with them in an instant, I never let Carlos or Rui or the manager's daughters borrow it but I'd have let him

"Do you want me to get my tricycle for you Dad?"

Carlos, who wouldn't talk to my mother, he talked to Maria da Boa Morte, when he heard the engine of the police chief's car he'd run off to the workers' quarters, my mother would point to the serving dish

"Do you want some more Carlos?"

Carlos, not to my mother, but to Fernando, as if it was Fernando who'd asked him

"No"

keeping a close watch over me the way he did with her, analyzing my eyebrows, my gestures, the way I walked, searching for something in me that I never understood, and finding it or believing that he found it since he wouldn't talk to me either, he tormented me without opening his mouth, threatened me without articulating a single sentence, comparing me with the police chief on those Saturdays when he used to have lunch with us, the way he held his knife, his fork, his expressions, his smile, the way he spoke, barging into my father's bedroom to save me from him, forbidding Rui from going out on the back porch with me, from holding one of Lady's puppies that I held out to him, Carlos setting the laboratory results down on the couch where he'd entrenched himself all night long, waiting up for me so he could kick me out of Ajuda, since he couldn't kick me out of Baixa de Cassanje and now his soft, humble voice on the telephone, feeling its way around

"Clarisse"

wanting to go downstairs with me to find my mother and my grandmother, to whom Damião was serving lemon verbena tea amid all the flowers and mirrors

"Clarisse"

running down the stairs to find the avenue deserted

"Clarisse"

not in Lisbon, in Angola, in the police chief's jeep driving along the dirt road, pulling up to the house with the horn honking, a native soldier with a machine gun riding on the running board

"Clarisse"

holding my father's rifle, which was too big for him, pulling on the bolt-action, which wouldn't move and stayed stuck in place, Carlos in the living room surrounded by the Christmas tree, the reheated *caldo verde* soup, and the codfish that was getting cold, pointing the rifle at me, shooting, a branch of the golden rain tree came tumbling down, knocking against the tree trunk over and over as it fell, the desk stopped knocking against the wall, the sounds of whispers, giggles, entreaties, and sounds of things on top of other things all stopped, the faux-bronze trash can rolling on the ground on its side, the police chief holding him up in the air

"You black piece of shit"

throwing him down in the flower bed and holding his boot above his head, Lena running toward Carlos to keep him from hitting me, or hugging me, or hitting me and hugging me at the same time

"You're just like Mom you're just like Mom"

or hitting and hugging me and starting to cry, hitting me because he started to cry and hugging me because he hit me, Carlos unhappier than I was, more hopeless about himself and about me than I was, even though the doctor in the examination room with the folding screens that blocked the view of the ocean and the casino and the boats anchored in the bay, even though the doctor guaranteed

"It seems like we can breathe a sigh of relief"

we couldn't breathe a sigh of relief because of the people who were lynched, because of the lepers, because of the trawlers heading out to fish, surrounded by corpses and seagulls and those rail-thin birds, because of the man who was rotting in a fruit crate on the boat from Luanda to Lisbon, because of the hyenas hanging from the forest buffalo's neck, from my neck, because of the unopened letters from my mother in the drawer, because it wasn't so much the lies but the truths that ceased to exist and so sometimes I woke up in the middle of the night in Africa and could hear the land could hear the land sighing with the clock guaranteeing

no no no no no no

with each swing of its pendulum, sensing my own body without touching it, Carlos sleeping beside me and Rui sleeping with Josélia at the end of the hallway, I'd wake up in the middle of the night and the lights from the workers' quarters, the lights in Estoril terrified me, in the middle of the night when new laborers from Huambo arrived at the plantation the managers at the casino would turn off the neon lights, I'd bring a chair out on the patio so I could breathe a sigh of relief, thinking of Rui out in Damaia, of the actresses on the movie-theater posters who looked like me

"You're just like Mom"

but the word mom no longer meant anything, like the word Clarisse or the word Carlos, when my brother called me on the phone he wasn't calling me, the rifle too big for him, the police chief's jeep driving along the dirt road, pulling up to the house with the horn honking, a native soldier with a machine gun riding on the running board, the sunflowers silently spying on us and it wasn't necessary for my brother to shoot, it wasn't necessary for a branch of the golden rain tree to tumble down, knocking against the tree trunk, I never let Rui or Carlos or the manager's daughters borrow my tricycle but I'd let him borrow it, the tractor driver avoiding me

"Young lady"

the foreman avoiding me

"Young lady"

Luís Felipe hanging up the phone

"Wrong number"

it wasn't necessary for my brother to shoot since as soon as the police chief hopped down out of the jeep the hyenas latched onto his neck, and another one clamped its teeth down on his face, and another severed the tendons in his legs and the police chief surrounded by wooden masks with hollow eyes and hollow lips tumbled to the floor in the living room in Ajuda, facing the hills of Almada and the pigeons from the schoolhouse roof, with the little white specks from the glass globe swirling around him until they completely covered him in gold-tinted snow.

When I asked him one day in the study why he'd come to Angola he replied that if he had stayed in Portugal he would still be churning out reports on a typewriter in some random police station and pestering street vendors along the alleys in the Castelo neighborhood while in Malanje he was in charge of a bunch of whites and native soldiers who passed for policemen and he never had to report back to anybody except for higher-ups in Luanda, which was too far away for them to require anything more of him than to ensure that the quantities of cotton and sunflowers that arrived at the port didn't drop off, ensure that the Dutch diamond companies didn't complain about ambushes, and ensure that the Spanish

priests from the mission didn't write letters to the governor exposing imaginary abuses and made-up stories of massacres

*the priests I hurriedly transferred way out to Cazombo because
of their subversive sermons and conspiracies against the regime on
top of their sexual problems about which I have appended declara-
tions written and signed by the victims before witnesses who therein
identified themselves and signed their names as well even though it
seems important to me that at the very least we maintain the confi-
dentiality of this report in light of the fact that it is not my intention
to damage our relationship with the hierarchy of the Catholic Church
merely keeping the report here with me as a record in case there is
some minor show of apostolic zeal from the Vatican since these things
require diplomacy and discretion I personally went around to five or
six churches in Cassanje to give them forty-eight hours to clear out of
the district or else I'll come back here with the boys and we'll demolish
everything and there won't be a single finely bound book or statue of
Saint Philip left not to mention the Russians whom you all instruct in
catechism to guillotine us I'll come back here with the boys and offer
a parish full of obedient dead souls to every deacon souls with no demands and no doubts quietly seated at their desks all very intelligent
just with a hole in their ear that's a little wider than usual on that very
night I sent men to burn down the nursery school to underline the
speech I'd given in bright red ink and on the following morning there
they went like a traveling circus a caravan of vehicles with a bunch
of clowns wearing fake beards inside convinced that a few shakes of
the holy-water sprinkler would make the world better this world that
doesn't want to be better it wants to stay the way it is absurd and cruel
and selfish and violent and unjust and utterly meaningless*

with me thinking that we had dug ourselves a plantation, inch by inch, out of twenty thousand hectares of swamplands and jungle with machetes, hoes, tractors, and formerly exiled murderers and thieves who stole from us, that we'd dug it up by the strength of our bones and our flesh as shown by the cemetery out back and the graves that have been swallowed up by the cornfields, and they kicked us off of it for no other reason than a word whose definition is unknown to me, freedom, the quails squawked about freedom in the garden, the setters barked about freedom on the porch, the Jingas went to sleep freely in the workers' quarters, the freedom to send my children to Lisbon their fortunes tied to those of some miserable boat, the freedom to imprison me with Maria da Boa Morte in this old hunting shelter with just three walls, a portion of the roof intact, and pelts and horns and skulls of antelopes falling off the walls because the nails have rusted through, a tomb in Marimbanguengo with a wraparound porch, or what of the porch the tall grass had allowed to remain, where there was still the faint sound of spoons, laughter, bets, debates

"Did you discard an ace Eduardo did you discard an ace?"

Damião hanging an animal's neck up on a hook, hanging me and Maria da Boa Morte up on a hook, upside down, paws dangling, eyes that stared without staring, tell me the reason why you traded your police station and the street vendors in the alleyways of the Castelo neighborhood for Angola, to live in a musty barracks on the outskirts of a city that's as desolate as a provincial village, where the world only reaches it, if it ever does reach it, through newspapers with missing pages that show up two weeks late with their pages striped up and down with censor's ink, Maria da Boa Morte, no, my mother shaking me, waking me up on a straw mat, get up Isilda get up and it's not my mother it's the wind through the cornstalks, my godfather infuriated

"Did you discard an ace Eduardo did you discard an ace?"

it's a finger that lightly touches the fabric of the dress from the attic, the hat

"You look so pretty Isilda"

the burial of my father in the rain, the burial of my mother in the rain, the burial of my husband in the rain, all my burials in the rain, the water discoloring the sopping wet flowers, the quicklime fizzling on the wood of the coffin, get up Isilda get up

when I entered the police station in Malanje for the first time three months before the cotton pickers' revolt the guards were playing quadrille among the turkeys out back, with a piglet with its leg tied to one of the table legs, there was no interrogation room, there was no meeting room, there was no jail cell, there was no dentist's drill to jog a suspect's memory, the Jews trafficked diamonds almost out in the street with no laws regulating their business and after some violent robberies, no one knew who committed them, of course they asked us for help, the plantation owners didn't pay a tax for protection for the idiotic reason that there was no protection tax but after a second case of arson and the realization on the part of the esteemed governor that he needed to remodel his palace it's obvious that a protection tax went into effect, I've always held that the first obligation of the police is to make itself wanted, the way we were wanted in January of nineteen seventy-one when the Bundi-Bângalas refused to work the harvest, robbed the company stores, destroyed the workers' quarters, wandering along forest trails, present even when they weren't there, absent when they were there, and never having been there at all once we were done and had returned to the city, the lookout planes flew off and in order to harvest the cotton we transferred Jingas and Chokwes over to Baixa de Cassanje with promises of work, shelter, and pay, which we made good on even though the priests maliciously maintain that we didn't hold up our end because of the simple fact that the indigenous people foolishly wasted too much money on dried fish, cassava, and tobacco at the company store, dried fish, cassava, and tobacco, which the priests, who had no idea about the real price of anything, said were too expensive the same way they unjustly accused us of practicing a captious sort of slavery, dried fish, cassava, and tobacco that they agreed to pay for after the next harvest and the next and the next, increasing their debt instead of paying it off and becoming entangled in a web of fiscal commitments, which is their own fault, just like it was their fault when they were overcome with fever, I met the epileptic kid's mother when she asked me to help resolve a dispute between her and the regional administrator who demanded an absurd percentage for the transfer of a dozen truckloads of laborers, a woman who was neither pretty nor very young, who didn't accept the chair I offered her, preferring to stand beside the desk with her hand on mine in order to stress the gravity of her arguments, a few Luenas whom the priests had poisoned with strange theories were pulling weeds out in the station's reeducation camp, the acacia plant I'd had planted turned everything a shade of yellow, a crucifix on the wall and a picture of the commanding general with a smashed mosquito over his nose, it turned the two of us yellow as well, a dishonest woman, the regional administrator had explained, sir, the way people are in the northern

part of Cassanje, people who took their plantations by force from
packs of hyenas not from the jungle itself, and who cut off our legs
before they take the knife to our jugular because they don't even
know how to kill properly, what I asked for on top of the price of the
healthy laborers, you see that I didn't bring along any cripples and
just one or two children who work as much as or even more than
the others since they haven't yet fallen victim to the vice of laziness
not to mention that for now they eat less drink less beer and can't get
pregnant, was the payment for the driver and his helper, who kept
everyone in order, and the gasoline for the trip from Nova Lisboa to
Chiquita, since it's almost all the way to Chiquita, that little village
with its forgotten mango trees where that bitch, excuse me, this lady
here and her family live

not Chiquita

"Get up Isilda get up"

or Marimba or Dala, in the old hunting shelter in Marimbanguengo, hung up on a hook by Damião, unable to respond
when, as a child, my mother called for me in the doorway of my
bedroom

"Get up Isilda get up"

because my father, my godfather, and the veterinarian were
waiting for me in the jeep

"Get up Isilda get up"

so we could head out in search of the Bundi-Bângalas who
were dancing their way from one plantation to the next instead
of working in the fields, me already grown up, already married,
carrying a Mauser rifle like a grown man, the governor advised us
to bury the bodies

"Above all that the newspapers don't find out above all that this news doesn't get abroad"

bodies, rotund bodies that slid down into mass graves with a rotten languidness, the way Maria da Boa Morte and I slid down off the hooks

and when the regional administrator left full of excuses and apologies and more excuses and even more apologies, afraid that a letter would be sent to the district administrator

(who pulled the same scams he did but couldn't admit that he did)

recommending he be banished to Ninda or Chiúme, out there among the eucalyptus trees and the sand, the woman to me

"*I guess you sleep here at the barracks where's your room*"

that's word for word, I haven't altered it one bit, sitting on the edge of the desk with her knees touching mine

"*I guess you sleep here at the barracks where's your room*"

a tiny room, a nook, a closet, a uniform on a coatrack, a straw mattress, a lightbulb hanging from the ceiling with an enamel light fixture, a suitcase underneath the bed, an alarm clock with a brass ringer, and a photograph on top of a wooden chest that he wouldn't let me see

maybe it wasn't a hotel room but it was a decent, clean place, at any rate it was better than the dormitory room in Lisbon with a window that looked out onto other rooftops and a tiny bit of sky above the barbed wire at the top of the wall, not to mention the bathroom, a bucket and a rubber hose connected to the faucet that served as a showerhead, a decent, clean place that the officers on cleaning duty swept on Sundays and saved me the cost of renting an apartment where I lay down with him on shabby bedsheets that smelled like cheap soap

(my mother at the door without noticing us

"Get up Isilda get up Isilda don't you hear the jeep?)

the same way I would have lain down with anyone driving along the street, pointing at random with my index finger

"You"

and would have driven to the study and ordered

"Take your clothes off"

feeling his surprise, his embarrassment, his hesitation, listening to the rustle of the sunflowers

"Take your clothes off"

and would have lain still staring at the ceiling, suffering under the weight of a body without even noticing the body, the swollen stomach of a Bundi-Bângala, rotund, rotund, sliding into the mass grave with a rotten languidness, realizing that he was getting dressed without watching him get dressed, realizing that he'd left without watching him leave, that he paused at the door with the doorknob in his hand without caring that he was looking at me, staying in the study like an animal being flayed by Damião, the sound of a hide being ripped off

"Get up Isilda get up Isilda"

since even though he was looking at me he didn't see me, or he only saw the remains of the ancient airplanes that had been given to the government by the Germans, flying in circles over Baixa de Cassanje, gravity keeping them aloft out of spite, and in the windows of the airplanes were people tossing armfuls of bombs that were as old as the airplanes themselves onto the forest, onto traditional native villages, onto granaries

the woman saying to me, wondering at something I didn't un-
derstand, examining the bathroom, the bucket, the bed, the rubber
hose that served as a showerhead, arranging the felt roses in the little
vase, straightening one of the pleats of the curtain where a bee was
in its death throes, surprising me

"I thought that guys like you took your clothes off the second you
found yourself in a bedroom with a woman aren't you going to take
your clothes off sir?"

he only saw the airplanes that almost scraped the treetops, with
the bronchitic sputtering of their old engines, he didn't see me or
only saw me with my neck crushed and one of my legs ten meters
away from my body, no blood no fat no tendons, just cracklings
and ash

as if I were from a different species or a different race

"I thought that guys like you took your clothes off the second you
found yourself alone with a woman aren't you going to take your
clothes off?"

to me, who, if I felt like it, could have locked her in a cell without
a judge's warrant for a month or a year or as long as my stubborn-
ness would allow, and there wouldn't be a single colonist, bishop, or
governor who would dare to ask questions about it

"I thought that guys like you took your clothes off the second you
found yourself alone with a woman"

brushing off her hands, worried that there was dust in my
bedroom, or maybe something else, bedbugs, microbes, ticks that
would give her some skin disease, looking for spots on the pillow-
case, running her hand over the pillow, hesitating before lying
down on the bed, checking again with the same surprise in her
voice from earlier

"Aren't you going to take your clothes off?"

as though I were a dog, as though she or any other woman had the right to turn me into a dog, moving toward the mattress with her rear end shaking and her mouth open with sad, intense desire, I remember my mother sewing in the kitchen and my stepfather coming in from the garden, knocking into the furniture, guided by the smell, guided by the smell alone, I remember the expression on his face, his mouth open, his knees shaking, my stepfather not even noticing me and leading her by her arm like it was a horse halter, I remember that there was always a pot that would fall, shattering on the floor, and then there was nothing, a pause, the droplet of water dangling at the edge of the faucet before it fell, my mother returning to the kitchen, my stepfather returning to the garden, time started up once again and nothing had happened, nothing at all, he weeded the rows of beets and used clothespins to hold his pant legs tight against his shins when he rode his bicycle to the café

and as soon as the German airplanes had disappeared, limping through the air, one foot on one cloud the other foot on another cloud, as slow as an invalid shuffling along in slippers, as soon as we got out of the jeep to finish off the wounded lying in gaping holes in the earth, a soft, childlike rebuke, like a little kid

"You're the one who asked me to show you my room"

the police chief straightening up the bedspread and the brass knobs on the bed, turning his pillow over, turning the bucket around to hide a rusty streak on it, waiting for me to load the rifle, slowly take aim, start to pull the trigger

("Get up Isilda get up")

and he, the man, the police chief

"You're the one who asked me to show you my room"
the suitcase under the bed, a suitcase under a bed always left a strong impression on me

time started up once again and nothing had happened, absolutely nothing, my mother was the same, my father was the same, nobody touching the broken pot

a suitcase under a bed always left a strong impression on me, the way the fact that the women in my family were always buried in their wedding veils left a strong impression on me, veils not white but gray, so delicate that the mother-of-pearl buttons would fall off at the slightest carelessness, and the orange blossoms were preserved in a bell jar so that they never fully opened, how many times did my mother climb up into the attic to look at it, how many times did I come upon her unawares, in front of the mirror the wedding dress draped in front of her, in a jubilant mood that disturbed me, the shoulders of the dress on her shoulders, the fitted bust over her bust, the tiara of the veil tucked into her gray hair, not straight, crooked, like a caricature of a virgin, a cruel reflection

"I want you to put makeup on my lips and cheeks Isilda"
exactly like the dead people we'd find out in the garden, looking at themselves in the well but with no reflection rippling in the water, there was the reflection of tree branches though, of the bougainvillea plant, of the golden rain tree, but no reflection of the dead, my mother curling her eyelashes with a little comb, walking toward me floating through the junk in the attic, then sitting on a rocking horse that could take her nowhere, even though it never ceased moving, rocking back and forth with its wooden rigidity

"Isilda"

no, not the man, not the police chief, but the wounded Bundi-Bângala crawling away from the rifle on his elbows, without any fear of dying, without asking forgiveness, without promising that he'd work, merely crawling away from the rifle on his elbows and buttocks, no, not the Bundi-Bângala, but my mother, dressed as a bride, rouge cascading out of her wrinkles, embracing me in a little cubicle in the police station in Malanje that smelled like clutter and insomnia the way the bedrooms of single men smell, my husband's little hut along an alleyway full of drunks near Cotonang, the airplanes with German crosses painted on the wings returned the next morning and the next and the next dropping bombs out of their open windows, confusing the plantation manor house with the company store, confusing our desperate attempts to signal them with the threatening gestures of the blacks, destroying the balcony, the garden, the greenhouse, the storehouse, the granary, replacing the trucks that hadn't been stolen from us with ones that were now destroyed, stolen *de facto*, my mother

"Oh dear God"

kneeling before her altar, kissing her saints, one of the airplanes slipped on a cloud and crashed into the Franciscan mission, turning into a pile of charred aluminum, the little martyred saints knocked against each other with each explosion, my father searched for a flag that he could wave out on the porch

I embraced her without taking off my clothes

"I thought guys like you took your clothes off as soon as you"

not like my stepfather embraced my mother, nor like a dog, which is how she thought of me, embracing a bitch, which isn't how she

thought of herself, me, unable to take off my clothes, the way a black
peasant in the city

(to call Malanje a city, just a secondary school, a police station, a
hundred buildings, excuse me, half that, fifty buildings, excuse me,
twenty buildings and a slum filled with idiots who live off scraps)

would show respect to a white woman for fear of being lynched

so I had to urge him to lie down, a frightened little child who couldn't undo his necktie or unbutton his sleeves, even lacking the courage to ask for my help, with a suitcase under the bed in his little bachelor's nook, the suitcase of a poor immigrant like the colonists from Cela, in their hats and vests, plowing fields in Africa as though they were still in Minho, confused by the lack of seasons, the soles of the shoes of one of the policemen scraping against the cement floor

"Sir, lieutenant"

a dove flying above the palm trees, two doves, three doves, the man straightening his shirt, extremely relieved

"Excuse me"

he showed up in Baixa de Cassanje five or six months later, face shaved, wearing cologne, hair combed or rather his locks slathered in brilliantine like Damião, he parked the jeep in the courtyard out front, climbed the front steps of my house with fierce determination, stubbed out his cigarette on the stone flowerpot that held the hyacinths, not worried about my children, my husband, my parents, the police chief, a white man who seemed almost black to other white people and a black man who seemed almost white to other black people, so much so that he could have lived at the edge of the slums in Luanda where my daughter-in-law used to live, reserved for those unhappy people who won't admit that they're unhappy and poor people who won't admit they're poor, surrounded

(like me, why delude myself, like me too, offering up expensive furniture, in the solitude of the jungle, to the woodworms)

by the gloss of plastic and pathetic bookshelves, the police chief demanding of Fernando, tossing his cigarette butt into the fish pond to humble me, just as he could have dumped a mug of coffee onto the tablecloth or ripped a chair covered in damask silk

"The lady of the house"

in an authoritative tone that could be heard in the living room, in the kitchen, and upstairs, and which my children noticed, Rui distracted, Clarisse curious, and Carlos furious, searching for his brother's pellet gun, the pocketknife with a broken blade, a rock, so that he could kill the intruder the same way we killed the Bundi-Bângalas on the cotton plantations

"The lady of the house"

determined not to be the dog she thought I was, determined that she would be the bitch that she was certain she wasn't but which I knew her to be, me to the fool who opened the door, whose owners had taught him to behave like a person in order to turn themselves into people, as if I didn't know these plantation owners, just as miserable as me, so important here where no one else existed except for us and the Africans and so worthless in Lisbon where there was everything except for us, Africans who were nothing more than Africans and us who were nothing more than some intermediate thing between the Africans and them, yet closer to the Africans than to them, I tossed my cigarette butt into the fish pond to show them

that I was the boss, the man in charge, paying no mind to the two
or three kids playing around the golden rain tree who stopped play-
ing when they saw me, a simpleton with a plastic revolver, a little
girl with pigtails on a tricycle with a missing pedal, and a mulatto
dressed the same as them, standoffish, with a look of hatred on his
face, me paying no mind to her husband if she had one or to her
parents if she had any

"The lady of the house"

hearing Fernando say

"Sir"

my mother curious, closing her crocheting basket, looking
around to see that everything was tidy, straightening out her bangs

"Could it be the French woman Isilda?"

the woman who'd continued to consume her with jealousy
many years after she'd died in the Congo and many years after my
father had died, certain that at any moment she'd invade the house
on horseback, wearing a low-cut blouse, elegant, informal, laughing, wearing bracelets made of European gold, bejeweled rings on
her index fingers and thumbs, my mother all of a sudden like the
old women from the village by the river, ashamed, defeated

finally exactly like me, finally turned into immigrants from some
small village in northern Portugal just like me, a village squeezed in
between oak trees and cliffs by hoarfrost pincers, people who'd obvi-
ously retained all the apprehension and mistrust typical of the day
laborers they really were, quick to address others as

"Sir"

or

"Ma'am"

anybody who lived in the county and wore shoes, quick to address them as

"Sir"

or

"Ma'am"

anyone who came to their doorstep, and without a good morning or a good afternoon for anyone if they addressed them with the informal tu, me in Baixa de Cassanje with the mulatto kid prowling around me with a plastic pistol clenched in his fist, Fernando disappeared down a hallway where veneer floors, umbrellas in vases, and the pupils of taxidermied animals glistened, a house that smelled like my stepfather's house, perhaps with a garden, a bicycle leaned up against the side of the wall, an outhouse with a reed fence around it to protect the washbasin, the servant from off in the distance

"Ma'am"

a distressed sigh unsteadily chasing after each syllable

"It can't be the French woman of course not tell me it's not the French woman"

a pause, renewed agitation, a silence in which whispers could be detected, another pause, more renewed agitation, more whispers, the retard and the mulatto fighting over the revolver, two cranes screeching at each other up in the acacia tree, the little girl on the tricycle pedaling over to her brothers

"If you don't let go of Rui I'm going to tell Grandma Carlos"

now an agitated voice

"A policeman from Malanje what could a policeman want at this hour Isilda" without responding to my mother I told Fernando to take him to the study, I stood up and asked myself why he didn't come through the service entrance like the foreman, the kitchen door where Josélia and Maria da Boa Morte, busy cooking dinner, would let him in without paying him any attention, getting angry at his lack of etiquette, a person who lives in a little nook of a police station with a rubber hose for a showerhead and a suitcase underneath his bed, not to mention the bathroom, the bucket, the felt roses, that same person making himself at home in my study, lighting a cigarette and throwing the match on the floor, looking at the bookshelf, the invoices, the inkwell, holding up the photograph of my husband, setting it aside and pointing at me with his riding crop as if it were a finger

"I thought women like you took your clothes off the second you found yourself alone with a man aren't you going to take your clothes off ma'am?"

24 December 1995

Today I'm not leaving the house. I'm going to pull Rui's chair in front of the television and sit here the whole day eating popcorn, drinking Coca-Cola, and flipping channels, sports, cartoons, a ventriloquist conversing with a duck, Italian Dutch Belgian Spanish Moroccan news channels, the lights in Estoril out of focus because of the rain, boats dripping down the window-panes, Luís Felipe's hurried whisper on the telephone, covering his mouth with his fingers because of his wife, his children, his grandchildren

"I have to hang up dear you received my present didn't you merry Christmas merry Christmas" a bouquet of flowers wrapped in cellophane, with a greeting card and a check, a bracelet in a jewelry box, a box of chocolates, a dress, all of it over there in a pile on the couch, the bracelet too long, the check for too little, the dress a size too big, the flowers a wreath you'd get out of respect for the deceased, maybe he got himself another girlfriend, at work, a secretary, a typist, the new economist, maybe I've died, me on the bed and my brothers and my sister-in-law standing around me, Carlos with his eyes lit up as he estimates the value of the apartment and turns it into parquet floors in Ajuda, Lena turning the furniture into a cruise to the Canary Islands, Rui not turning the apartment or the furniture into anything, looking for yogurt and strawberry ice cream in the fridge, calling me

"Clarisse"

so I would bring him comic books, peppermint candies, the Snow White puzzle in an old rice can in the pantry that's missing the pieces with the witch and half the dwarves but that he loves anyway, if my father were here he'd put his hand on my shoulder and smile, what I remember of him is a tiny man in pajamas, smiling, today I'm not going to leave the house, I'm going to pull the chair in front of the television

(that's not true I remember other things too for example that he used to push me on my tricycle with his cane, cutting out paper dolls for me holding me up in his arms so I could reach up where no one else could up to the top of the lampposts the curtain rods the tree branches Carlos envious

"The tree branches that's not fair")

I'm going to spend all day flipping channels until the sleeping pill takes effect, it never takes effect on the head first, it starts at the feet and rises, if the doorbell rings, let's say, I can hear it just fine, I look at the clock, ask myself who it could be, I want to get up but I can't walk, I wake up on the couch, centuries later, at eleven in the morning, feeling the sunlight on me, very still, curled up between my knees like a cat, then jumping down onto the carpet, sulky, I start to stretch and rouse myself, my feet awake, the rest of my body waking up as well, except that the match hasn't lit the stovetop burner where the coffee pot is waiting, the sun perched atop a countertop paws at the plates and cups, plays with me, spurs me on, if I try to catch it in my hands it illuminates my wrists with its little tongue, how cute, if the doorkeeper lady were to ask me

"Do you want a cat young lady?"

I'd respond that I do, it's just that I'm afraid of the armchair and the rugs getting ripped to shreds, afraid of Luís Felipe's reaction

"What's this?"

(up to the tree branches if we wanted to, to the clouds if we wanted to, Carlos, who loved it when my father picked him up but he never did, he only picked me up, fidgeting with the glass globe with snow in it, pretending he was a frog

"Not fair"

I caught him many times jumping up and down trying to touch the leaves

"It's not fair is it Dad?"

my father, who wasn't always sick, offering him the leg I wasn't attached to

"Come on let's all three of us go out to the golden rain tree"

Carlos with his arms crossed, holding back tears, obvious because his face was turning red

"I don't want to"

if it weren't for Africa and whiskey I wouldn't live here)

the problem with the cat is that Luís Felipe can't stand animals, the only weekend we ever spent in Algarve, when his wife had gone with her sisters on a shopping trip to London, a horsefly landed on his tie and he sat motionless, moving his body away from his tie as much as he could, I've never seen anyone, much less a fat person, suddenly make his body so concave, his chest as concave as a washbasin, his chin tucked under his collar, his eyes crossed, staring down at the bug, out of a tiny corner of his mouth

"For the love of God get this off of me"

at no other time had I ever heard him utter the word love, sweetheart, yes, my little baby, yes, darling, yes, but love was never used, he was afraid that I'd ask him to live with me and divorce his wife, similarly he never wrote letters or signed the cards that came with the flowers, he signed the checks because I always cashed them and couldn't use them as evidence, he never took me to the movies or the opera or to any of his usual restaurants because wives will stop at nothing, hiring lawyers and causing scandals, they'll demand alimony, damage their husband's business, and make their husbands' lives a living hell of contention with all the newspapers looking on, as such it took a worthless little bug on Luís Felipe's tie, drawing back his shoulders

(my father held Carlos by the waist, lifted him up very high, and Carlos reached the branches of the golden rain tree, my dad tousling his hair

"Silly little guy"

Carlos with his arms in the air, his face red, a different shade of red than when he cried

"Higher"

if it weren't for Africa and whiskey we wouldn't live here)

Luís Felipe four or five meters behind his necktie, or rather, the necktie decorated with a horsefly and him far away from it, down at the end of the balcony, which was all of a sudden extremely long

"For heaven's sake get this off of me my love"

the sea at Algarve, the beach, the rows of fishing boats on the horizon, shrubs like the ones in Angola, hundreds of insects wafting in on a sweet breeze, the horsefly disappeared with a flick of my finger and Luís Felipe started to come alive again, his caved-in chest swelling back up, recounting stories of dozens of close friends who'd been killed by bees, wasps, locusts, dragonflies, holding his tie between two fingers, examining it closely, worried there might be some venomous spittle on it, wavering, should I disinfect it with alcohol or not, I can accept the doorkeeper lady's cat and lock it in the kitchen on Tuesday and Sunday afternoons with a saucer of milk and the cat food you see on commercials that transforms cats into happy little creatures with such intensely green eyes, if I saw a man with those eyes I'd faint, during the dry season the wildcats would prowl around the workers' quarters because of the chickens, Josélia told me that they dragged a child about my age out into the jungle and divided up the body parts between them, an ear for you, an ear for me, a nose for that one, toes for the kittens, I didn't dare leave the back patio, afraid they'd tear me to pieces, my father lowering his newspaper

"Silly little girl"

pushing me on the tricycle around the pond with his cane, pushing Carlos, pushing Rui, the wildcats, out of consideration for my father who didn't even carry a slingshot, never did us any harm

(if it weren't for Africa and whiskey we wouldn't live here)

the blacks drank beer on the steps of the company store, a frog leaped from one puddle to the next, my mother appeared on the windowsill, angry with my father, and along with my mother appeared the house and the sound of the clock

"You're not going to stop until the little ones all catch colds because of the damp are you?"

the house, the sound of the clock, and the dark hallway where the sunflowers whispered, the way they whispered in the pantry

"Clarisse"

I'd stop to listen and the sunflowers would go silent, I'd start moving again and the sunflowers

"Clarisse"

I'm not making it up it's true, I told my mother about it and my mother laying cards down in her game of solitaire

"Nonsense"

I told my father and my father grabbed a flashlight

"Let's go listen for it"

sunflower stalk after sunflower stalk, taller than me, with eyelashes the size of tongues, scarecrows made of large, empty bottles and strips of fabric for hair, which the foreman perched atop sticks to frighten away the gledes, the sunflowers didn't whisper, there was only the wind on the dry leaves and the wings of owls hunting for rats and small rabbits, a humanlike shriek close to the ground, shadows that the clouds carried off to the south or the moaning of the whole world, identical to the hazy smoke of the cemetery at night, little blue flames moving from one stone to the next, my father didn't smell like alcohol he smelled like my father, my grandmother smelled like an old person, when he gets out of bed with no cologne or deodorant on Luís Felipe smells like an old person too, his hand next to my face smells like an old person with its brown liver spots and the soft skin on his fingers that old people have, the tuft of hair that he has left combed over from the back of his head in strands hardened by hairspray smells like old people, his thin, hairless legs and arms and his thick, soft torso smell like old people, one time I caught him brushing his dentures with a toothbrush and he looked like the oldest old person I've ever seen, I felt something inside me and thought how repulsive my God I can't kiss him, if my mother had ever dreamed of such a thing she would have fainted, if my father had dreamed of such a thing he would have grabbed the flashlight and we'd have headed out into the middle of the sunflowers together the dampness notwithstanding because if it weren't for Africa and whiskey I wouldn't live here, where I'm going to spend the whole night in front of the muted television, eating popcorn, drinking Coca-Cola, and flipping channels, sports, cartoons, the Pope, a ventriloquist conversing with a duck, Italian Dutch Belgian Spanish Moroccan news channels, listening to the sunflowers

"Clarisse"

the wildcats, the screech owls, a hare disappearing into its burrow, if there were visitors Josélia would come looking for us out in the garden, we'd go in through the back door, have dinner at the table in the kitchen, Maria da Boa Morte tucked our napkins into our collars, Carlos could feed himself and didn't get dirty, I could feed myself but I'd get a little bit dirty, Maria da Boa Morte fed Rui his soup and wiped his chin with a napkin after every swallow, Damião and Fernando carried out gravy boats, tureens, pitchers of wine, cakes that we could only eat the next day, when the Chantilly cream had hardened and was covered in cracks, crumbling, tasting like sweetened plaster, Josélia cut the cake into three pieces, it stuffed our bellies, my mother looking elegant and younger, happier, would take me and Rui into the living room with the two chandeliers lit up, a room that was ours and at the same time wasn't ours, where there were a dozen ladies as luxurious as she was and a dozen gentlemen smoking, people who during the day, compared to their nighttime selves, were poor and ugly and suffered from headaches, Carlos remained in the kitchen with Maria da Boa Morte and Josélia, the ladies acting as though they'd never seen us before

"They're so big"

Damião would bring us back into the kitchen with Carlos who knocked his plate off the table on purpose, spaghetti and meat mixed with shards of china on the stone slabs of the kitchen floor, Lady, who seemed to be asleep, leaped up from her corner and came over to sniff at it, from the open window you could see the candlelight from the workers' quarters and the bales of hay burning black where they stretched out the animal hides for their drums, there was a tinkling of glasses, a gentleman said something or other, one of the ladies started to laugh like a goose

"I can't believe it I can't believe it"

Carlos, who wouldn't stop blinking his eyes, knocked Rui's plate off the table on purpose, close to where Lady was, she was startled and ran off, Rui started bawling and it wasn't just one goose now there were hundreds of them laughing plus the glasses plus the clock ticking very quickly plus the gentleman who said something or other, indignant, as though shooing away birds with a stick

"I swear on my health that it's true"

my father in the kitchen

"Carlos"

Carlos running up the stairs

"Let go of me"

with no desire to be pushed on the tricycle or be held up to the branches of the golden rain tree or anything else, the geese went silent, the glasses went silent, the clock went silent, the gentleman who shooed away all the giggles with his voice

"On my health that it's true"

also going silent, my father looking at the stairs, I thought

"He's going to go up there"

he looked at Rui, looked at me, looked at the ceiling where Carlos's footsteps pounded from one side to the other, at first he gave me the impression that he was going to speak, and then the impression that he had become incredibly old, he fumbled around in the pantry until he found a bottle, uncorked it, and slowly headed back to the living room, Josélia and Maria da Boa Morte made comments to each other about him without words, the next day Carlos cut my pinafore with a pair of scissors and broke Rui's pull-string car, my mother raised her slipper at him with my grandmother nodding in approval, Carlos with his hand held out

"It doesn't hurt at all"

Fernando was tossing grains to the peacocks, the combine climbed a hill with a driver seated on a little chair that vibrated, and the machine sunk its blades into the earth, my father on the couch was nothing more than a pair of crossed legs and a newspaper, the shoe that wasn't on the rug, with mud on the tip of the toe, dancing all by itself, my grandmother set down her crochet, her nose and chin almost touching since she had no teeth

"I am not the grandmother of a mulatto"

the pages of the newspaper shrank, as if my father were withering away behind them, he crossed his legs the other way around, silly little man, you aren't going to stop until the little ones catch cold in this damp air are you, platters, gravy boats, tureens, pitchers of wine, cakes that we could only get a taste of the next day with hardened Chantilly cream covered in cracks and crumbling

I am not the grandmother of a mulatto

that tasted like sweetened plaster, my mother saying to my grandmother, dropping the slipper on the floor, with eyes that kept blinking, like Carlos

"I never imagined you could be so cruel"

who looked back and forth from one to the other, without understanding, hoping they would explain it to him, not feeling hatred for anyone

"What's a mulatto Mom?"

Carlos and Lena

you married him because you thought my brother was rich, that you'd free yourself from the slum, wear fancier clothes, live on the plantation, have servants, money, get to know the governor and the bishop, you accepted Carlos the way I accepted Luís Felipe

"I have to hang up dear you received my present didn't you merry Christmas merry Christmas"

because a job in a boutique or a hair salon or an art gallery with
a husband working an office job no thank you, get up at six in the
morning, arrive home without the energy to even raise a finger, look
like I'm fifty when I'm thirty, if it weren't for Africa and whiskey I
wouldn't live here

Carlos and Lena waiting for me in that rat's nest in Ajuda and me in front of the television eating popcorn, drinking Coca-Cola, and flipping channels, sports, cartoons, the Pope, a ventriloquist conversing with a duck, Italian Dutch Belgian Spanish Moroccan news channels, a bouquet of flowers with a greeting card and a check, a bracelet in a jewelry box, a box of chocolates, a dress, I'm going to stay in Estoril and watch the lights, which are out of focus because of the rain, the boats dripping down the windowpanes, my grandmother's voice aimed down the hallway

"My daughter who has no respect for me insulting me in my own home it's just as well that Eduardo is no longer with us so he doesn't have to suffer this humiliation any longer"

Carlos sitting on a stone beside the river, down below, past the lepers' bell, cotton on the opposite bank, better cared for than ours, it didn't belong to us, it belonged to Cotonang, where my father used to live when he was single, past the cemetery and past the dirt road that led to Salazar everything belonged to Cotonang, all of it belonged to the blond engineers, to the State, which didn't pay a red cent to the regional administrator for the transportation of Bailundos from Huambo, younger and stronger than ours, who could withstand six or seven harvests in a row, with their foremen forcing them to work twice as much and giving them half as much food as ours, I squatted down beside Carlos and Carlos

"Beat it"

motionless in the lepers' colony, paying no mind to the nightfall to Josélia to my mother on the back porch to the leopards to the wildcats until my father went to get him and carried him back, flailing his legs in rage

"Let go of me"

me sitting on a rock in Baixa de Cassanje

(my how everything is trembling right now, the house, the peacocks, the azaleas, my how everything around me is trembling right now)

just like I'm sitting here in Rui's chair waiting for the sleeping pill to kick in, me on the tips of my toes taking the glass globe down off the desk, in which snow swirled around the sleigh, the reindeer, the little bearded man, around me, gold-colored specks, around Luís Felipe's presents, around the couch, around the knick-knacks that I thought were pretty at first but which frighten me today, what do I care about a bar with nickel-plated hardware, the mirror on the ceiling at which the workers installing it couldn't stop laughing, they called me once or twice to ask me out, addressing me with the informal *tu*, those little porcelain dogs on top of the chest of drawers, ugly as hell, imitation Ming porcelain, which the owner of the antique store, after we showed them to him so he could appraise them, taking such care as I set them down on the counter, advised me to give to the doorkeeper lady for her birthday, Luís Felipe, pretending to be shocked, showing him some oriental characters on the pedestal

"You've got to be kidding me that can't be right"

me pointing at a stamp to the right of the oriental characters that you could tell someone had tried to scratch off

made in Singapore

Luís Felipe stammering out excuses

"They put that there on purpose so they don't have to pay import taxes"

coming by the next week to bring me extremely expensive gold earrings to make up for it and me hurling them out the open window, something that honest to God up to this day gave me the greatest pleasure in life

"I'm allergic to pinchbeck my dear it stings my ears"

and that night, what panacea, he called me every hour, locked in the bathroom, obvious from the sound of running water and his voice echoing off the tile, as soon as he started to speak

"Sweetheart"

I'd hang up the phone, a little while later the phone ringing twice

"Sweetheart"

hung up, a little while later the phone ringing twice

"Sweetheart"

hung up, a little while later the phone ringing twice

"Sweetheart"

and right after the

"Sweetheart"

his wife's voice echoing off the tile as well, but dampened by the distance

"What are you doing with the phone in the john, Luís Felipe?"

a woman with her hair dyed purple, with no waist, with cellulite-speckled thighs, whom I saw in a magazine about interior decorating, at the dentist's office, telling reporters about the treasures in her house, posing proudly in the first photo of the article between two porcelain dogs, identical to mine in their ugliness,

the stupid look on their faces, I bet even in the made-in-Singapore half scratched out and everything, I felt the urge to write
her a letter out of feminine solidarity recommending that she
foist those off on the doorkeeper lady as a birthday present and
that she at least demand real solid gold earrings that she could
toss out the window, a woman the same age as my mother and
lucky enough not to have to wander over hill and dale in Baixa
de Cassanje to escape from UNITA or the government soldiers,
lucky enough to have never had to search for friends among the
arms, legs, and crushed skulls piled up in a broken freezer at the
hospital in Malanje, we'd recognize them by a ring, a lock of hair,
a scar that was untouched by the bomb, half of someone's face
pressed against half of someone else's face and the stench and the
flies and the workers in the morgue ripping out metal-capped
incisors hoping to sell them when the war ended just like they
hoped to sell a pair of charred boots and a pair of charred sandals, friends or people we used to say hello to in high school or in
a café not just in morgues, hallways, hospital wards, the hospital
grounds, it's strange to take a step without thinking, stepping on
them like stepping on a leaf or a twig, hands, fingers, muscles
yielding underfoot

jellyfish on the beach jellyfish

and now Ming porcelain dogs, a bar with nickel-plated hardware, that stupid mirror on the ceiling that Luís Felipe adores

jellyfish on the beach

when the reporters from the magazine photographed her bedroom there was no mirror on the ceiling no sheer drapes hanging from the bedposts no paintings of nymphs anywhere, the

furniture was straight out of a sacristy and there was a gigantic crucifix with a furrowed-brow Jesus on it

jellyfish on the bea

to eliminate any romantic fantasies from the scene, I don't believe the plantation is even there anymore, or the golden rain tree or the peacocks, the troops roasted the peacocks when they destroyed the house, maybe they left behind some toucans or the setters, howling, devouring each other in the flower beds, if it weren't for Africa and whiskey my father wouldn't have died and I wouldn't live here, we'd open the little numbered windows

jellyfi

on the cardboard nativity scene, one two three four, uncovering angels and shepherds and sheep, the little baby behind number twenty-five, Our Lady conceived without sin and Saint Joseph with the gray-haired dignity of a grandfather, if it weren't for Africa and whiskey maybe my father would visit a young Angolan lady about my age on Tuesdays and Sundays, a young lady with an epileptic brother, in an apartment in Estoril furnished like mine with tacky valuables, he'd call her dear, sweetheart, tell stories about his colleagues, ask me to scrounge up some little girls

"Don't you know any sweet young things?"

to celebrate a business deal with the associates at his firm, we'd put on some romantic music, turn down the lights a little, light some Japanese candles, dance

jellyfish on the beach jellyfish on the beach jellyfish on the beach

we'll have lots of fun you'll see, but instead ashtrays overflowing, decrepit old men with their hearts in their throats, pinches, Carlos waiting for me in Ajuda, excited as streetcars approach, umbrellas make their way up the street, the lights of taxis appear, if it weren't for Africa and whiskey I'd keep the photo album from my honeymoon in my living room, a different living room, the opening page filled with one of the invitations, letters printed in gold so-and-so and so-and-so have the pleasure of inviting you, esteemed gentleman and your eminent wife to the wedding of our daughter Clarisse to the esteemed gentleman doctor so-and-so which will be held on such-and-such day of such-and-such month of such-and-such year at I-don't-know-what time in such-and-such church followed by a luncheon in such-and-such restaurant r.s.v.p. to such-and-such address, the menu on the second page with signatures of the guests and the rest of the pages filled with the newlyweds, the flower basket, the relatives, the priest's blessings, the ring bearers, the toasts, the cake cutting with one hand each on the knife, the car that I would like to be a tricycle, how old am I now that the sleeping pill has started to take effect and I feel like I'm dozing off, I mean I can still think and speak but from the waist down I'm no longer me, I've disappeared, I can't see myself, I can still flip channels, sports, cartoons, the Pope, Italian Dutch Belgian Spanish Moroc

excuse me

Moroccan news channels, a ventriloquist conversing with a duck, the same stare, the same struggle beneath his smile, the same open mouth, or is the duck conversing with me, or am I conversing with the duck and the audience is laughing, I can still see the lights in Estoril out of focus because of the rain, the boats dripping down the windowpanes, the cotton, the sunflowers, the corn, the halves of burned smashed faces in the morgue at the hospital, I no longer exist from the neck down, I've disappeared, I can't see myself but I can still see my father holding me up to the tree branches, I can get higher than you all

   jellyfish

watching them crawl around like ants below, insignificant, insignificant, the police chief from Malanje, the government troops, Luís Felipe, my mother, my brothers

   insignificant

waving good-bye to them because in no time flat it will be eleven in the morning, I'll wake up with the sun curled up on my knees like a cat and I'll have to take a shower to shake off the drowsiness and get dressed really fast because a person that I know is here at the door on the street waiting for me with a cane that will push me on my tricycle far away from Angola and Estoril and death pursued by a pack of porcelain dogs made in Singapore barking as they run behind us, falling further and further behind us, incensed with rage since they weren't able, aren't able, will never be able

   well done

   to catch us.

14 NOVEMBER 1994

Only after Maria da Boa Morte said
  "Behind you"
  and I turned around and saw the five vultures watching us from
the roof beam of the little hunting shelter and another two on the
hooks we used to clean antelopes, pecking at the bark on the tree
with their beaks, only then did I understand that we'd died and
we weren't sitting on the porch in Marimbanguengo, rather we
were bloated like the corpses of the victims of the war waiting
for the tall grass to grow over us after the birds finished and flew
off. My godfather used to say that the difference between Europe
and Africa was that Europe had forgotten about us, while Africa

didn't even remember itself and that he lived in Angola because he preferred to exist rather than existing in order to have existed one day, years and years in a tomb in the cemetery and in a portrait in a living room, where no one even knows who's in the portrait, the brother of a brother-in-law, an uncle, a grandfather, some anonymous cousin, the date erased and the signature illegible, while on the other hand Angola grew from the sepulchres outward, transforming them into fields and mango trees and jungles and what the photographer in Malanje really gave us was a smile floating on an island of silver iodide with the shadow of a tuxedo below, or what was assumed to be a tuxedo and could have been a topcoat, a tunic, a raincoat, a suit coat, Maria da Boa Morte

"Behind you"

the five vultures on the roof beam of the little hunting shelter and another two on the hooks we used to clean antelopes, pecking at the bark on the tree with their beaks and watching us, and since Luanda was the city of the dead, permeated from the coast to the slums with the stench and fumes of the dead which frightened off the living, even the Katangans who wore necklaces made of human ears and ate fat people, even the Cubans who swore they ate the placentas of pregnant women, even the beggars from the bay who ate themselves, their mouths doubling back on themselves, chewing away chewing away, since Luanda was the city of the dead

in the avenues, on the streets, in plazas, on the sidewalks, on the trails in Sambizanga, and in the palm trees, I even saw them at the top of the palm trees, which had maybe even grown taller with all the dead waving the palm fronds and their shirts in unison, keeping watch on the island maybe the dead protected us from vultures, wild dogs, and hyenas ambling diagonally like people with back problems, or maybe they outfitted a boat with cabin boys, machinists, and dead passengers, headed for Lisbon, which would run aground on a sandbank, falling to pieces on the sand surrounded by angry seagulls. My godfather used to say that the difference between Europe and Africa was that Europe had banished our bones from the continent to work as shop assistants or bricklayers in Brazil or France, while Africa built its skeleton out of them, all it takes is one glance at the baobab trees or the cassava roots drying in huts, convince me that they aren't bones, convince me, all it takes is one glance at the houses, all it takes is one glance, no need to go any farther, at us, at how everything dissolves, at how you aren't tripping over vestiges, ruins, remains, my godfather whose plantation disappeared along with him, the tobacco, the farm equipment, the mounted heads of lions and hippopotamuses, we went down to Dala Samba and we didn't find anything but weeds, shrubs that grew and got thicker until they transformed into acacia trees, at most a piece of a wall, a piston rod from a tractor, a gate hinge, and an old woman smoking a pipe sitting in a rocking chair in what we assumed had been, centuries before, the kitchen

the kitchen before us with its stone tabletop, cupboards, shelves filled with sugar and beans and rice and pasta and grains, a thousand flasks and bottles and jars in the pantry, the ice-cream maker with its little gasoline flame, the chickens, the she-goats, and the turkeys strolling around amid dishcloths, skillets, frying pans, and pots hanging from hooks, the sideboard cupboard with plates and glasses and faceted wine glasses from Porto which refracted the light from the electric lightbulbs, concentrating and bouncing off the surface like the way it did off the surface of the French woman's rings, an old woman with a pipe sitting in a rocking chair in what we assumed had been, centuries before, the kitchen stoking an imaginary woodstove with a makeshift fan made of twigs

"Armandina"

and her fanning the fire even faster

"Lamb will be ready in ten minutes sir"

and all this because going from Marimbanguengo to Luanda we had to pass through what used to be his home, amid the eucalyptus trees on the tobacco plantation, saw my parents and me alighting from the jeep and walking up the front steps, my father in his riding boots, my mother watching out for muddy puddles lifting a corner of her dress, proceeding underneath her open parasol, me in a pink bodice, a pink Panama hat with pink ribbons that ran down my back, my godfather's voice yelling from inside

"Armandina"

Armandina with her pipe sitting in a rocking chair stoking the woodstove with a makeshift fan made of twigs, not an old woman, a woman about thirty or forty years old and I say thirty or forty just as I could say twenty or thirty, or forty or fifty since I don't think there's a single person in the world who would dare presume to know or imagine they presume to know a black person's age, always much younger or much older than they look, with whites yes sir, animals and plants maybe maybe not, with blacks don't even think about it, except perhaps for when they smile

a woman about thirty or forty years old but in any case not an old woman

Armandina

"Lamb will be ready in ten minutes sir"

and in the living room with the windows opened out onto the sealike sound of the eucalyptus trees, the trunks and the fruit capsules making the sound of waves, the echo you can hear in a conch shell, the ebb and flow of little glass pebbles, in the living room, aside from us and my godfather, the traveling dentist

his van parked out by the ostrich pen, its doors covered in price lists in stenciled letters

Doctor Salema this much for tooth-pulling with no anesthetic this much with anesthetic this much for a filling this much for oral disinfectant this much for a cleaning this much for two crowns on molars one on each side this much for a complete set of crowns this much for haircuts even though this is not my specialty plus a surcharge meant to cover the cost of the shame of performing a lesser operation

and dozens of diplomas in Spanish and French with faux-silver seals stuck to the rusty van with pieces of tape, the dentist honking his horn from plantation to plantation with a chair that looked like a throne, which my godfather swore was bought off a shoeshine in Luanda, a wooden armchair in which we sat with a napkin tucked in at our necks, grinding our gums and the wooden slats of the chair out of dread, the drills, the little mirror for examining molars at the end of a metal rod, which he inserted down our gullets

"Say ah ah"

taking a step back to clean the mirror on his lab coat, delicately dusting off a speck of dust with his little finger

"Ah ah"

us afraid, rinsing out our mouths with a little cup

paper cups like they have at parties in elementary schools or better yet a lone paper cup that he reused, with holes in it, washing it in a fish tank

"Are there any problems doctor?"

the dentist rooting around in his bag, the jingle of metal tools knocking against each other

"Ah ah"

a sadistic pair of pliers that made him seem gigantic, a tiny man who suddenly became enormous, suddenly became God, demanding that we open our mouths, turning them into a vast space

"Ah ah"

the foreman inspecting a molar with an apprehensive finger, the dentist swirling around making gestures like a reaping machine

"Not a single root that can be used madam they've all gotta come out"

as we passed through what used to be a home among the eucalyptus trees on the way to Luanda, the eucalyptus trees turned dark before nighttime and lit up before dawn, just like the clock, which had a personal understanding of time the hours that bore no resemblance to the time and hours of the rest of the world, we saw my father in his riding boots, his collar fastened with a copper collar bar, and if we were to call out to him

"Dad"

he would look around without responding, my mother with her parasol open because of the sun, passing right by us without noticing us lifting up one of the folds of her dress with her gloved hand,

me in my pink bodice and pink Panama hat with pink ribbons running down my back, the Panama hat that I found some years ago in
the backyard stuck on top of a pole to frighten crows, but it was me it
really frightened, its arms outstretched in the shape of a cross and its
head made of rags with facial features hastily and carelessly scrawled
on it, it took me hours to put on my makeup, getting everything just
right, getting impatient with myself, doing it over, so ugly and defenseless against the birds that I had the urge to hug myself

"Isilda"

to take care of myself, to go get mascara and lipstick, to brush
the cornhusk hair with my hairbrush, fix the hat, put it back on
my head, to become an adolescent again, fill my room with dolls,
never marry anyone, walking behind my parents, back when I
could have said

"Wait for me"

but I was worried that I'd raise my eyebrows inquisitively, not
recognizing myself, or that I'd call out to my father and my father
would tell me to beat it

"Get out of here"

that even my own past will have forgotten me, the only person
who paid us any attention was that wretch with his van covered
in price lists and foreign diplomas, which was where he slept,
wrapped up in a blanket

"Ah ah"

disappearing into my mouth with the little mirror

"Ah ah"

me terrified

"Mom"

my mother not hearing me, only a meter away if that and she still didn't hear me, preoccupied with the muddy puddles, talking about seedtime and servants with my godfather helping her up the front steps, the roasted lamb, the smell of tobacco, the smell of the eucalyptus trees and the breeze that made them sound like the sea, I never saw any thunderstorms in Luando or in Lobito, just the patience of the waves as they tossed around conch shells, one time there was a big fish suffocating on the beach among the coconut palms, its gills giving up and bidding a gentle farewell, my mother and my godfather evaporated amid the mounted heads of lions and hippopotamuses, my father hesitated, as if he'd heard something, like a ferret scampering off, a mole rustling in the reeds, wiping the soles of his boots on the doormat and evaporating as well, and me passing in front of myself with the ribbons from my hat bobbing around my shoulders

"Isilda"

waving at me ever so slightly, an indifferent farewell

"You're so old"

Armandina twenty or thirty or forty years younger, which is about as close as you can get when you call a black person young before they smile, she served the lamb in the dining room, the disorderly household of a man without a woman in his life except for the black ones he had children with and who lived out in the workers' quarters, even after the harvest was over, washing his sheets and shirts in the river, mulatto children that we pretended not to notice so that we could come visit him without causing a scandal and to whom my godfather never paid any attention unless it was to ask them to drive the tractor or spray the plants with insecticide

Teófilo Plínio Marciano Nepomuceno Isaías

not living in straw huts but in brick shacks, all identical in the clearing, out behind the house, just as all the children were alike even though they had different mothers, silent, enormous, serious, each one cooking in his own clay oven like neighbors on bad terms with each other, Maria da Boa Morte and I peeking into the dining room wherein echoed the fruit pods, branches, and leaves of the eucalyptuses, the indecisiveness of the first drops of rain on the straw roof, my godfather at one head of the table, my father at the other one, the dentist to the right of my godfather

a doctor

trying to convince us to replace our real incisors with ceramic implants, which aside from never developing root abscesses could be cleaned with a little brush and obviated the need for toothpicks, Maria da Boa Morte and I sniffing the potatoes and the sauce for the lamb, unable to taste it, Armandina walked right in front of us as if we didn't even exist and in truth we didn't exist, barefoot, emaciated, batik cloths tied around our waists, with five vultures in the little hunting shelter keeping an eye on us plus another two on the hooks we used to clean antelopes, pecking at the bark on the tree with their beaks, Armandina called the dogs over to a pan full of scraps and we ran up right beside them, my mother froze with her fork halfway to her mouth while we ate, lifting her veil in a gesture of refined repulsion

"What's happened to you daughter?"

not in Dala Samba but in the bedroom at the plantation putting a jewel-encrusted brooch on her lapel, the bedroom that the government troops, the Cubans the Russians the UNITA soldiers burned and pillaged and which was buried by the grass, my mother picking her earrings out of a tortoise-shell jewelry box, thinking of the French woman's envy, placing the jewelry box in the drawer and hiding the key in a jar, not surprised, just displeased

"What's happened to you daughter?"

picking up the bottle of perfume with its satin-covered pear-shaped bulb that you had to squeeze to release the scent hoping that I wouldn't soil the scooping neckline of her dress with sand, seeds, hay, insects, my mother with no white hairs and no medicinal drops for blood pressure putting a beauty mark on her cheek with the dab of a pencil

"What's happened to you daughter?"

whom I helped Josélia shroud in her wedding dress when she died, my mother squeezing my father's knee in secret, hoping that nobody would notice me while he was busy selecting one of the cigars my godfather was offering him, passing one under his nose with eyes closed

"Eduardo"

Damião passed right through me on his way to the hallway carrying a bottle and a glass of anisette liquor on a tray, me playing with Maria da Boa Morte in the lepers' colony, my father straightening the knot of his necktie while the police chief from Malanje began to laugh

"You my dear?"

a chair against the doorknob in the study, pointing at my batik cloth, exacting revenge for me having treated him like a cashier in a shop, a Jinga

"I thought that you all took your clothes off the second you found yourself alone with a man aren't you going to take your clothes off?"

taking everything off the desk, the blotting paper, the inkwell, the picture of Amadeu at Cotonang with a group of engineers on their way back from a hunt, a little pot of azaleas that he always stepped on when he didn't knock over the planter with his jeep as he left or when the policemen didn't smash them beneath their espadrilles, the police chief ripping off the batik cloth that was tied around my waist

"I thought that you all took your clothes off the second you found yourself alone with a man aren't you going to take your clothes off?"

my breasts and my buttocks like an African's, stretch marks from the delivery of ten or fifteen children, skin scarred by ticks, by sewing needles, by cinders from the stove, by the fury of the thorn, I thought you all took your clothes off aren't you going to take your clothes off, the desk against the wall, the sound of Carlos breathing against the door, he wanted to knock, he knocked, tried the doorknob, knocked again, an owl outside on the windowsill, its feet wrinkled and rough the way my fingers are now, my mother

"What's happened to you daughter?"

asking Josélia to help her lie down in the coffin, putting a crucifix over her chest while explaining to me with her eyelids shut

"I can't do anything for you anymore daughter I can't"

four candles in the corners of the room and even more on the chest of drawers in candelabras, teacups, the tops of shoe-polish cans, plates, the flames changing from white to blue anytime someone came in or out, the smoke tarnishing the curtains, people from neighboring plantations, the bishop's secretary, the lieutenant-colonel, the governor's assistant, women with missals in hand, people in mourning clothes whispering, accepting tea cakes or waving them away, warning me

"We can't do anything for you Isilda we can't"

the clouds in Chiquita, a group of fifty or one hundred or two hundred mandrills jumping all over each other on the hillside, on the lookout, waiting for us, my father on the porch lining them up in the sights of his rifle, my godfather grabbing his arm

"No"

Maria da Boa Morte and I in Dala Samba on our way to Luanda to join the rest of the corpses that the government troops covered in gasoline and scraped into the bay with rakes and shovels, corpses mixed together with the beggars in the palm trees and the gnarled steel of white people's cars, the hoarfrost in Salazar and Dondo looked like cotton, water that the plants had secreted overnight, the damp grass impossible to burn, the dentist with no throat seated upon his throne of wooden slats, with a second mouth in his neck, wide open and boiling with flies, his lab coat spotted with brown stains the shape of peninsulas, the price lists and the foreign diplomas on the van, tipped over onto its side, the forceps, pliers, and pincers all on the ground, a bridge of ceramic molars falling out of his pocket

"I can't do anything for you madam unfortunately I can't"

the diplomas that he himself had written in an invented Spanish that he called Spanish, an invented French that he called French, an invented Latin that he didn't call anything and which he said had been personally presented to him by a cardinal from Rome in thanks for pulling that tooth right there, the second

look

the second one down from the top of the price list, the most expensive, unfortunately I can't do anything for you madam because they killed me on my way back from Baixa de Cassanje, no fillings no cleanings no partial dentures, a tree trunk down in the dirt road, the van's shocks absorbing the tree trunk, the tinny sound of beetles, the night sky above strata of branches, the headlights, the one on the right brighter, the one on the left dimmer, pointing at the roots of the jungle floor, fluctuating with the lurching of the motor, a fox frightened by the headlights or by what it thought at first, while the dentist was still trying to move the trunk out of the way, were headlights, up until the dentist saw the rocks that were holding the trunk in place and understood, without time to be afraid he thought of returning to the van, put it in reverse, get out of there, there's a place where I can turn the van around, if I can go a hundred yards back I'll turn it around at the crossroads and that's that, without noticing that he was speaking aloud, a place where I can turn it around a place where I can turn it around, now with time to be afraid, his gestures growing thick with fear, the steering wheel, the parking brake, the gearshift, the extremely complicated pedals that someone had switched around on him, making the van shake and squeal, refusing to move, the dentist not noticing that he was screaming because his voice had become an autonomous sound, at once noisy and silent, independent of him, a place where I can turn it around a place where I can turn it around, a fear that was still vague, out of focus, that became more and more precise, coming to life, impeding him from compelling the van to head out of the jungle or jumping out of the van and running, he thought he heard the rustling of animals, not squirrels, something bigger than a squirrel up in the treetops, a cheetah said the dentist, knowing that it wasn't a cheetah, it was impossible that it was a cheetah, a cheetah or a leopard or a gnu that had wandered away from the herd, trying to start the van while his fear

which now had the shape, smell, and density of fear, a shape, density, and smell that he'd known for a long time, fear of my older sister when she got serious, of illnesses, of the police, of geckos, of death, of falling asleep, night after night pinching my skin until it hurt, if I fall asleep I won't wake up and my sister will take this chance, look who's asleep, to bury me right away, fear, for example, of not being me, of being someone else, of going into my home and people telling me

"Beat it"

a hard, insistent, tepid, intense, heavy fear that ran down the length of my arms and legs, that extended its acidic tendrils down to my fingertips, that promised to dissolve, to evaporate, and instead of evaporating it again grew bigger and as such he wasn't scared by the uniformed Angolans who were walking toward him without haste, or the foreigner who wore a different uniform that made it seem like he was in charge of the Angolans, the dentist in the van with the price list and diplomas that concealed not only the need for a paint job but also holes, dents, craters, and other defects in the steel body, turning the steering wheel, pushing the gas pedal in vain, just as he wasn't scared when they put his dentist's chair in the middle of the dirt road and ordered him, in gestures not in words, in gestures, how strange, he thought, to sit down in it, the dentist suddenly completely unafraid and finding his lack of fear strange, he looked for it inside himself yet there was no fear, where's my fear he asked, watching the jungle grow dark as the headlights dimmed, grayish and red and then finally black, not as black as before but black, the shrubs and the grass blending into each other, little lights from butterflies, the rustling of rabbits in the distance, where is my fear he asked himself where is my fear, watching the foreigner grab a razor, pulling the blade open, pushing his chin up, a cloud of stars, sparkles burning in the void, minimal intermittent foci against a square piece of slate, rain clouds, lightning

where is my fear

on the banks of the Congo, I spent months looking for diamonds in that stupid river and found nothing but shards of rock, tiny pieces of coal, grains of sand that got caught in the sieve, I'd shake it a little and they'd disappear in the water, so when I found the dental instruments in a store in Catete I read up on tooth-pulling and cavities in an encyclopedia, I bought the van from a dry-goods salesman, fixed it up in my backyard, transformed it into a dentist's office, drew up the diplomas on pieces of poster board, and started the business, one of the headlights grew brighter, lit up the edge of a farm, a straw hut, a group of straw huts, and then went out, the other headlight wheezed in agony like the flame of a candle, illuminating the Angolans, the foreigner, what was left of the stone wall around a mission, a school, a well, I thought

"Where is my fear?"

feeling the wooden slats of the chair falling off one by one, abandoning me, the slats at my back, under my buttocks, under my elbows, hinges, pieces of wire, and nails that held the slats together, no fear of my older sister or of illnesses or of the police because I'm not a real doctor, because I'm a clerk at the treasury in Benguela, nine hours a day five days a week and forty-eight weeks a year for twelve years for an African's salary that barely covered the rented room until I was told about the diamonds, the Jews in Cassanje and a group of colonists who were heading north with chemical reagents and scales and tents, a cloud of stars, sparkles burning in the void, minimal intermittent foci against a square piece of slate, rain clouds, I thought

"Where is my fear?"

and that was the last thing I thought before I noticed that they were surrounding me, before I felt some sort of figure next to me and felt the razor blade open my throat, I want to say that it didn't hurt a bit, that I was thankful to them that it didn't hurt a bit

"It doesn't hurt a bit at last it doesn't hurt a bit"

talk with them, shake their hands, become friends, tell them that I didn't hold it against them, that I didn't care, that I didn't feel angry, the second headlight evaporated, the engine of the van evaporated, you could hear the Dondo River and the reeds of the Dondo, the crackling of the power plant that UNITA had destroyed, which is still in flames, I wasn't afraid and it didn't hurt a bit, mainly it didn't hurt a bit

"It doesn't hurt a bit at last it doesn't hurt a bit"

so as soon as the two old women, the white one and the black one, both of them barefoot and wearing batik cloths around their waists if you can call those faded dirty rags batik cloths, a couple of old women, like twins, sisters, perched on the back of the chair, eyeing me with their heads sunk down between their shoulders, looking just like vultures, as soon as they started to peck at the top of the chair with their beaks, fluttering their wings made of rags I understood that I had died and didn't care that I was dead, didn't care that one of them squawked to the other

"Behind you"

because when they pierced my skin and pulled out my entrails it didn't hurt a bit the same way it wasn't going to hurt a bit when the grass eventually closed shut over my corpse after the birds were gone.

24 December 1995

I don't know if I like my family. I don't know if I like anybody at all. I don't know if I like myself. Sometimes it's tough at night: I sit down on the couch, get up, sit back down, some indefinite thing is lacking in me, I want someone to call me, to pay attention to me, talk to me, I grab a magazine off the table, read the five-week-old horoscope on the penultimate page, health, take care of your liver, love, possibility of an unexpected reconnection, money, don't reject a business proposition from a friend, lucky number, twenty-six, color, violet, a second magazine with the spring-summer season fashions where they recommend warm colors, tight-fitting skirts, shorts that can make your sensuality explode, I turn on the television, a Bible movie, people in sandals who believe in God, I turn it off, those virtuous people in sandals reduced to a tiny point of light, I can't find any CD I like because I don't like any of them, I get back up, think about what would happen if I took all the sleeping pills in the mirror cabinet with three little doors in the bathroom, the little door in the middle never closed all the way, you don't hear a little snap when it closes like you do with the others, it opens by itself, I suddenly become aware of dozens of broken things in the apartment, for example the door to the pantry in the kitchen that I always push closed with my knee whenever I walk past it, that brown stain in the bidet caused by the faucet that won't turn off all the way, the handle for the vanity drawer which I have no idea where it went, or the frayed edge of the rug which I don't have the patience to sew, I become aware of the absurd importance of all the things in disrepair once it gets dark, shoes that need new leather uppers suddenly become impossible to ignore, the plastic bag with a suit in it that I left on top of the chest in the entryway so that I wouldn't forget to take it to the seamstress becomes the focal point of the entire world, I forgot to put laundry detergent on the shopping list for the maid and the fact that I forgot to put detergent on there tortures me, I write two boxes now, in capital letters, instead of just one, I don't include my usual thank you, as if it was her fault for forgetting, and at this point it is her fault, I take advantage of the moment to slam the door to the pantry, not with my knee but with the heel of my shoe, a nail in my heel leaves a mark in the paint, from the hallway the living room looks to me like a tomb with pictures hanging on its walls, the stupid entertainment center, the super-ugly plants, the curtains brown from cigarette smoke

not very brown I guess but just look at them

asking to be thrown in the washing machine, the bar irritates me with its flashy chrome finishing, the glimmering chrome almost laughing at me, I move from the couch to Luís Filipe's armchair, a striped monstrosity that cost him a fortune, the divot in the cushion from Luís's body bigger than my body and I disappear in the cushion, which bends in the middle like a pocketknife, my feet not even touching the ground, I take my address book out of the drawer, pricking myself on the scissors that some idiot

me?

left there, suck on my finger, worried about an infection, tetanus, someone used the last bandage and left me nothing, tricking me by leaving the empty box on the medicine shelf, I'll have to buy another, I flip through the names, Alcina (hairdresser) no, Lurdes (dressmaker) no, butcher shop no, pizza delivery no, plumber, what for, Amália's married, Graça will just hit me up for money, the letter *P* is missing, the fabric on the cover of the address book is turning to dust, there are some really elegant address books, I'll buy a leatherbound one that will last for ages, I hold myself up on the arms of the chair, my kidneys aching and my knee asleep, I put my nose up against the windowpane, you can see the streetlights in Estoril, trembling behind the raindrops on the glass, lights at front gates and in windows, headlights flashing between shrubs and trees ascending the hill, Luís Filipe's house with his kids' cars, his daughter's big jeep blocking traffic, his daughter, the same age as me, but taller and with blond hair, unlikable, flat-chested, with jingling bracelets on her wrist, with a new boyfriend every time I see her at the super-market, young guys, eighteen or nineteen years old, wearing vests with dozens of patches sewn on them, with ponytails, with earrings, God knows where she scrounges them up, shooting up in the arcade, trying to pick up foreign girls, sniffing around them like poodles with nauseating arrogance, you can see the palm trees, the bay, the sea, all of it very sad at nighttime during the winter, everything very sad today, no shops open, no bars, no restaurants, deserted galleries with a guard waiting around on a stool in the back, happy holidays in spray paint on the shop windows, pine trees with fifty-escudo notes pinned to the pine needles with a wooden clothespin, plaster mannequins that look like Luís Filipe's daughter, I don't know if I like my family, I don't know if I like anybody at all, I don't know if I like me, the television-guide magazine has this week's horoscope on the penultimate page, after the summaries of the soap operas, health, take care of your liver, love, possibility of an unexpected re-connection, money, don't reject a business proposal from a friend, lucky number, twenty-six, color, violet, it doesn't say anything about taking an entire bottle of sleeping pills, it doesn't say that there's something indefinite lacking in me, maybe it's a cardboard display with little doors and behind them angels and shepherds and white wise men standing in front of the black wise man, not the black wise man in front of the white wise men, the white wise men were in charge of the whites and the black wise man was in charge of the blacks, I asked my mother what a wise man was

"What's a wise man?"

my mother thought for a moment, opened her eyes wide, stuck out her lower lip then pulled it back in, so you could tell right away that she didn't know the answer, she freed herself of me with the phrase she usually used

"When I have time I'll tell you"

and so I hardly know anything at all because there was never time to explain what the wise men were or the reason why ice floats in water without sinking or the reason the refrigerator can get so cold if it runs on burning gasoline, my father would look it up in the dictionary but the dictionary would remain silent, he'd look in the encyclopedia and the encyclopedia would remain mute, if I take the whole bottle of sleeping pills the mysteries of the world won't intrigue me anymore, on Tuesday when I brought a glass of whiskey to Luís Filipe who as soon as he gets here takes his shoes off and loosens his belt, and it's obvious that he doesn't do the same with his wife, he shows some respect

I'm your whore aren't I you can admit it I won't get angry your lover out in the workers' quarters you don't have to humor me worry about me act loving toward me when I found that lump in my breast you vanished because all you have to do is pay up I'm your whore obliged to stay healthy who takes money in order to stay healthy not to be ungrateful and get sick you can admit it I won't get angry what's the point of getting angry

on Tuesday, as I brought a glass of whiskey to Luís Filipe, with two ice cubes, if I put one ice cube or three ice cubes in the glass it might as well be the end of the world, he sits there examining the glass, fidgeting, yelling at me the way you yell at a servant, two ice cubes damn it two ice cubes how many times do I have to say two ice cubes what on earth

I'm your whore aren't I

are you good for Clarisse, as I brought him a glass of whiskey and I laid down on his lap the way he likes, being careful not to touch his pacemaker which ticktocks like an alarm clock under his shirt

"Why does ice float in water but pebbles sink to the bottom?"

Luís Filipe does important business with the government, he was president of the city council and Secretary of State, his eyes widened, he stuck out his lower lip and then pulled it back in, so you could tell right away that he didn't know the answer, the pacemaker ticktock under his shirt, and me wondering what I'd do if the little gadget were to stop working, some battery which at any moment bye-bye, Luís Filipe not really a person, more like one of those dolls with a cord hanging down its back, me always expecting the expression on his face to freeze, for his movements to become more and more shaky and sluggish, for his legs to go numb and for him to fall over on his side, as rigid as a piece of wood

"When I have time I'll tell you"

in the same tone of voice as my mom, which the toy makers recorded onto a tape and installed inside her, the only phrase they ever installed, no matter what you said

"Good morning"

or

"Good afternoon"

or

"What time is it?"

and there'd be a hiccup, a little electric tremor, the ticktock going faster, eyes blinking, that jerking motion that machines make, which I don't understand and scares me, it makes you want to help them, to pat them on the back, ask them where it hurts, no one can convince me that inanimate objects don't suffer, and if so what to make of the furniture sighing in the dark, the houses vibrating in Baixa de Cassanje, I swear it's true, the walls moaned, that jerking motion that machines make right before they start rumbling, Luís Filipe's mouth, now shut, now open, his facial expressions not matching the movements of his mouth, repeating that phrase with the ecstasy of a parrot while his hand zigzagged back and forth searching for my skirt, or better yet not his hand, his poorly oiled fingers reaching out, joints creaking

"When I have time I'll tell you"

Luís Filipe looking to his left and right for people who might know him as he gets into his car, terrified of his wife, me at the window waving good-bye, it was an immense relief, it didn't happen this time, he didn't kick the bucket, he didn't die, and even though he was gone I could still hear the ticktock everywhere I went, I'd go into the bedroom and ticktock, the kitchen ticktock, the living room ticktock, out by the clothesline under the awning a ticktock coming from the laundry basket, there wasn't a chest of drawers or bookcase that didn't have an anxious little heart inside it, the clamor of tightly wound springs, a sickly little electric pulse, the whole building ticktock and me thinking if it stops it's all over, there would be dead dolls on every floor of the building, frozen in the middle of a gesture, in the middle of a conversation, in the middle of a bowl of soup, and nobody around to pull the string again, the maid shaking me and me motionless

"Young lady"

not like right now as I sit down on the couch, get up, sit back down in spite of the sleeping pill, the spring-summer fashions on a dozen pages, use warm colors, tight-fitting skirts, shorts that make your sensuality explode, when my parents would leave for the governor's palace they'd come up to our beds to give us a kiss and turn out the light

"Sweet dreams"

my mother's perfume, which I usually only smelled when I opened the bottle, lingered for who knows how long all around us, my mother with her ears stretched by slender filaments that looked like crystals from the chandelier, my father in coattails with his hair wet but it wasn't wet it was stiff, I'd reach my hand out toward his head, the sticky oil that smelled like almonds would linger on the palm of my hand, there was a second world inside the world we lived in that I didn't have access to, the way they breathed, the way they came near us without really coming close to us, the way they danced on certain Sunday afternoons as if a part of their bodies were made of vapor or liquid, at first I didn't pay attention to it and afterward I pretended not to pay attention to it, and then I started to turn to liquid as well, half of me fell into a strange state of torpor, consenting, Yes

I'm your whore aren't I you can admit it I won't get angry

half of me remained alert so I could spy on them, I'd hear the key in the lock, shoes falling to the floor, whispers

"The window the children are outside they'll hear us through the window"

the shutters pulled shut, my grandmother's crochet needles moving faster, warm colors, her noisy silence, her ruddy disapproving cheeks, I'd let Carlos and Rui water my part of the azaleas *tight-fitting skirts shorts that make your sensuality explode*

and crouch next to the creeping vine below the windowsill, consenting, Yes, without noticing that I was consenting and trying to listen in on what the swather engine wouldn't let me hear, noticing that I was liquid and that my bones were melting into a strange feeling of itchiness, not an itch, something like an anthill down around my ankles

a dozen pages of women in pink and blue head scarves

and around my wrists, Rui flooded my plants and splashed around in the mud, tried to splash Josélia and Lady

I wonder whatever happened to Lady

Carlos pushing him, taking the hose away from him

"Stupid"

Rui sitting on the ground, flailing his legs

"Grandma"

me on my tiptoes, hanging from the shutters, my grandmother not paying attention to Rui, not getting mad at Carlos, understanding what I didn't understand, what I came to understand later on with Renato but it wasn't exactly the same

"Clarisse"

it wasn't so

warm colors skin-tight skirts shorts that make your sensuality explode

nor did I feel like there was a separate, hidden world of perfumes and stiff hair that somehow coexisted with the golden rain tree, there was only this one world, get away from there Clarisse, it's a good thing that your grandfather passed away if he were still alive poor thing he'd die of sorrow seeing the miserable state of this family shameless sluts and mulattoes,

of his, my grandmother demanded an explanation from the sky over Baixa de Cassanje, which responded

"Eduardo"

his plantation that Cotonang was buying up little by little, the farmers complained about the government in Lisbon bleeding them dry with taxes, about the customs agents refusing their shipments of crops

they're no good

yet accepted much worse shipments from the state, shipments that weighed far less and contained far more impurities, but for which they paid double the price, the whites in Portugal who treated us like blacks, we're their blacks, the farmers would shut their mouths when the police chief came around, the police chief, in an indulgent tone of voice

"Conspiring, good sirs?"

from time to time one or another of them was summoned to the police station, he'd spend the whole morning there, then enter the pastry shop without saying a word, a single muscle twitching in his face, and take out a box of matches to light his cigarette, the matches would fall to the floor and the ones that didn't fall would snap in two against the striking surface

"Nothing happened"

a cripple selling lottery tickets going from table to table, the farmers taking their anger at the state out on him

"Get lost"

and the police chief was the only one who'd call him over, treat him like a friend, these bums get on your nerves sure but really they're just a bunch of poor bastards, leave him alone, and then he'd take a twenty-to-one ticket, mollifying him

"There there"

or a whole ream of tickets that he'd hand out to the farmers and which none of them would refuse, who knows maybe you'll win a small fortune, you haven't thanked me for all I do for you my good sirs, he'd try to cheer up the guy with the matches by giving him a little friendly pat on the back, cheer up man here take the one with the best odds buddy, the guy with the matches looking like his face was swelling up, a violet-colored spot on his cheek, the police chief, thoughtfully, you haven't hurt yourself there have you, asking one of the pastry-shop employees for warm water and a towel to ease the pain, putting the towel on the guy's face himself, don't squirm it's for your own good, hold still, when you get home you should ask your wife to rub some ointment on your face and you'll be fine, there are some things you shouldn't mess around with, things that are easier to prevent than to fix later isn't that true, the water running down his neck, the cigarette drenched and falling apart, and even without a cigarette the guy's fingers trembling trying to strike a match, the matches still snapping in two until the box was empty, the police chief extremely kind, handing the washbasin and the towel back to the employee, drying the farmer's mouth with his own handkerchief, some dried blood between two of his teeth, the police chief asking in a sulky, childlike tone of voice

"What do we say when somebody helps us out what do we say?"

the owner pouring a glass of rum, his arm frozen in the air, the beady eyes of the cook averted toward the pantry door decorated with *azulejo* tiles, a shoeshine guy bent over a shoe, pausing, the veterinarian's niece walking the dog outside by the palm trees, dry-season dust devils whirling in the garden out front, the last match, a labored murmur stifled by the dried blood, struggling with broken incisors to form the syllables

"Thank you sir"

the police chief sat back in his chair, happy, offering some last tender words

"Good boy"

the same way he addressed Carlos from the doorway to the study with his arm around my mother's waist after he'd taken the pellet gun away from him, and my mother silent, not submissive, merely inert

your lover out in the workers' quarters

"Good boy"

my grandmother hurried over to her altar with a rosary wrapped around her wrist, scandalized as she spoke to her little saints, complaining that she'd been abandoned by the clay figures she worshipped with offerings of hearts of palm, doilies, and little oil lamps, a multitude of martyrs in tunics and long hair, all of them out of work after she died, and whom I sometimes run into on the Cascais rail line, begging for change with a guitar strapped across their shoulders, that same compassionate look on their faces, those same virtuous thin bodies, that same faith in Eternity, those same bare feet, stretched out on the benches of the train station, playing a fife, with Uruguayan necklaces spread out in front of them on a mat or being harassed by those atheist national guardsmen, good thing that you died Grandma if you were still alive you'd die of sorrow, God's own intimate friends have fled from the mahogany altar in Baixa de Cassanje to beg for cigarette butts and sausage sandwiches, squatting on a street corner with no one offering them hearts of palm or doilies or little oil lamps, good thing that you died Grandma, maybe they pawned all your gifts and offerings, the little porcelain vase with a rosebud for Saint Stephanie, the little dried flowers for Nuno the Pious, the porcelain dove of the archangel Gabriel whose wings, instead of coming out of his shoulder blades, emerged from his flowing robes, hairy, this whole heavenly host of beggars forcing me to alter my route on the street and lock up my house tight, windows and doors, afraid that they wouldn't recognize that I'm the granddaughter of my grandmother, that they'd barge into my house and demand all my stuff, my watch, my jewelry, so they could trade it for smokable heroin, which is the incense of the seraphim, and then levitate, entranced, with their eyes closed, floating through the slums, helped along by the propulsion of the syringe, gathering a flock of followers from among the Cape Verdeans at the construction sites and the drunkards who live down by the columns of the aqueduct because they've taken a vow of poverty, mortifying their flesh for the sake of our sins, using newspapers as blankets, pieces of broken bottles, chicken bones, trash, locked up tight in Estoril, going from the couch to the balcony and from the balcony to the couch, angry about the presents from Luís Filipe, the flowers, the check, the dress, the bracelet, angry about the paper they were wrapped in, torn to pieces on the carpet, the little porcelain made-in-Singapore dogs in the niche in the wall, staring at me since the beginning of the night with the unfathomable stubbornness of corpses, the little dogs, the furniture, the paintings, the photographs staring at me as if I was an intruder, trying to make my cry, making the lights look sadder, daring me to take the whole bottle of sleeping pills, me making an colossal effort to hold back my tears

"I'm not going to take them"

me saying out loud

"I'm not going to take them"

I want people to pay attention to me, to take an interest in me, talk to me, love, possibility of an unexpected reconnection, lucky number, twenty-six, everything makes sense now, everything is coming together, how come I didn't think of this sooner, the solution's right in front of me, obvious, and me refusing to see it, I dial the number twenty-six on the telephone, well on my way to an unexpected reconnection, so many people say so on TV, educated people, lawyers, doctors, they say that astrology is a science, they don't take a single step without checking their horoscope and me here blind, there isn't a single interview with a movie star where they don't talk about their sign, we're happy because my husband is a Capricorn and I'm a Pisces, my life wouldn't have turned out right with any old Aquarius, health, take care of your liver, I have to take care of my liver, no more fried foods, fatty foods, eggs, the telephone ringing, of course, why shouldn't it be ringing, love, possibility of an unexpected reconnection, color, violet, maybe violet wouldn't look so bad on me if I didn't go overboard with it, there's no need to dress up in the purple robes of Our Lord of the Stations of the Cross, just some violet earrings, let say, a scarf tied around my neck, a necklace, perhaps, why not, there's a violet dress in the boutique downtown and I like the style of it, some things end up surprising you, shades of violet that are really quite different from one another, that don't make me look too serious, that don't make me look old, that don't turn me into Luís Filipe's wife, that don't put wrinkles on my face, the day before yesterday I found a white hair in my brush, I stared at it for ages, turned on some additional lights, searched around my temples, combed my hair for hours, terrified that I'd find another, but thank God no, an extremely long white hair, gigantic, the longest one I'd ever seen and it had to be mine, mine, soon enough I'll have back problems, anemia, my hormones out of whack, high blood pressure, doomed to go from hospital to hospital, sitting in hallways all morning long, the nurse

"You"

it hurts here, it hurts there, the sleeve of a white medical coat writing something down, handing me a piece of paper

"One tablespoon every eight hours"

an old folks' home, daytrips to the shrine of Our Lady of the Rosary in Fátima, a nonexistent waistline, a gut, open your mouth Dona Clarisse, an eighty-fifth birthday party for Dona Joana, a ninetieth birthday party for Dona Rita, candles on the cake that they can't blow out, blowing their own dentures out of their mouths, the nurses singing the birthday song, clapping their hands, clapping their hands, money, don't reject a business proposal from a friend, when someone picks up on the other end I'm going to wear warm colors, tight-fitting skirts, shorts that make my sensuality explode, a purple head scarf

color, violet, color, violet

and hide the next white hair I find, I'll send the little porcelain dogs back to Luís Filipe through the mail

"Best wishes"

no more of the absurd importance that I attach to all the things in disrepair once it gets dark outside, the little cabinet door of the mirror that doesn't snap when it closes, the pantry door that I push closed with my knee, the stain in the bidet caused by the faucet, the handle for the vanity drawer which I have no idea where it went, the frayed edge of the rug that I don't have the patience to sew

"Best wishes, all"

shoes that need new leather uppers, the plastic bag that I left in the entryway so that I wouldn't forget to take the suit to the seam-stress, the brown curtain begging to be thrown in the washing machine, the detergent I left off the list for the maid, eventually writing DETERGENT, the objects in the house finally affable, no longer daring me to take the whole bottle of sleeping pills, if the doorkeeper lady were to offer us a cat

"Isn't it just lovely?"

we'd accept it, and we'd start discussing, amid playful shoves pinches caresses kisses

after my father I don't think that any man

the name we'd give it, Cutie, no not Cutie, what a terrible name, Tigress, how tacky who's ever heard of such a name, can't use a person's name either because it's disrespectful, some funny word, a foreign word, but at the same time fun and childish, one of those names from the cartoons, Mickey Mouse's girlfriend, what's her name, Minnie, there Minnie it's settled, on top of that she even has Minnie's face, look how pleased she looks it seems she likes it, say Minnie Minnie Minnie, you look so cute when you say Minnie, whoever said that cats, so clean and clever, don't smile, come here Minnie, they can be as silly as they want, foolish without being ashamed, just play, health, take care of your liver, love, possibility of an unexpected reconnection, money, don't reject a business proposal from a friend, number, twenty-six, color, violet

Carlos never liked me, the same way I don't know if I like my family I don't know if I like anybody at all

sometimes it's difficult at night something indefinite lacking in me it makes me want

I hate to confess this

to cry

Rui busy torturing everybody, after my father I don't think that any man

he'd hold my hand if I sat down next to him

his knees trembling on the bed

he'd promise me that tomorrow we'd go for a stroll in Marimba a friend invited me to dinner and I forgot about it the light was still on in his bedroom he didn't get upset with me

"My daughter"

he'd smile at me happy to see me happy that we were together that I waved good-bye to him from the doorway

after my father I don't think that any man unless it were to happen right now

love, possibility of an unexpected reconnection, number, twenty-six, color, violet

father

warm colors tight-fitting skirts, shorts that make your sensuality explode, liquid like in Baixa de Cassanje, the perfume lingering around us, mixing with the smell of the golden rain tree, me hanging from the shutters, consenting, Yes, without even noticing that I was consenting, a strange itch, not really an itch, an anthill around my ankles and wrists, the engine of the swather chugging back and forth, back and forth, Carlos taking the hose from Rui, pushing him, Rui sitting on the ground, flailing his legs

"Grandma"

we'd go inside the house on the plantation

"Mom I would like to introduce you to"

my mother more relieved than happy for her daughter

let me knock on wood

so you don't end up working in a bar or a cabaret in Luanda

you can admit it I won't get angry I'm your whore

or spend my days hanging laundry on a clothesline with my girlfriends out on the island

no

not that way

my mother satisfied with him, beaming in his presence, at his appearance, his manners, standing to greet him

"Pleasure to meet you"

my grandmother grateful, lighting some additional votive candles and vowing to say some novenas in front of her altar, even Josélia and Maria da Boa Morte would be happy in the kitchen, make your sensuality explode, warm colors, but they wouldn't hug me

obviously

but still happy, smiling

"Young lady"

the apartment in Estoril all of a sudden habitable, the little Ming made in Singapore dogs finally almost tasteful, finally tasteful, if Luís Filipe's wife, who subscribes to magazines, frequents antique shops, and attends auctions has them in her house then they aren't something that should just be thrown out, that's for certain, the magazine, here it is, calls them collector's items, museum-quality treasures, the bar, the armchair, the niche, there isn't a respectable lady who doesn't have one, plates displayed vertically and illuminated by hidden lights, and then we'd end up living in Estoril, even on a dead-end street with buildings under construction, with the sheds and bricks and mounds of sand and workers hammering all day long, the phone ringing, color, violet, number, twenty-six, health, take care of your liver, love, possibility of an unexpected reconnection, a first connection in this case, but under my sign it says possibility of an unexpected reconnection, the other horoscopes say keep your relationship stable, don't confront a loved one with a difficult decision, remember that love is fragile, forgive, have hope but don't demand the impossible, mine on the other hand couldn't be clearer, there's no mistaking it, I'm pointing at it with my fingernail, possibility of an unexpected reconnection, another ring from the phone, the sound of his telephone in my ear, the presents from Luís Filipe that don't interest me in the least all on the floor, the bouquet of flowers, the check, the dress, the bracelet, the sound of the telephone connection, that little electrical sounding noise, click, the sluggish voice of a woman, a sleepy mumble

"Good evening this is Telecom"

me breathing into the little holes in the plastic mouthpiece in disbelief

"Good evening this is Telecom"

my mother, if she'd gotten up from her chair, sitting back down again, my grandmother going back to her crochet, the whores out on the island hanging their bras between the coconut palms, the peacocks running here and there, extremely annoying, idiotic birds,

Josélia going out to the patio with food for the setters, the swather going up and down the rows, the shutters open back up, if the little ones are outside they'll hear us through the window, I don't feel any strange itch, how silly, I'm not liquid, warm colors, tight-fitting skirts, the voice on the other end of the line getting furious

"Can't people show some respect these days geez"

I'll get my shoes repaired the day after tomorrow without fail, look for the handle for the vanity drawer, take the suit to the seamstress, sew the frayed edge of the rug, ask the doorkeeper lady's husband to come up here with his screwdriver and put an end to the torment of pushing the pantry door shut with my knee, deposit the check, put on the dress Luís Filipe gave me, the bracelet, put the flowers in a vase between the porcelain dogs, get some ice cubes from the freezer, not three, not one, two ice cubes Clarisse two ice cubes how many times do I have to tell you two ice cubes, the pacemaker

ticktock

turns him into a vulnerable man and I like vulnerable men who doesn't like them, maybe he'll get divorced someday or his wife will die and I'll have to open up a second niche in the wall, right next to the first one, illuminated by hidden lightbulbs, so I can put the dead lady's porcelain dogs in there.

27 September 1995

This can't be Luanda because I've never been here before, a city full of natives built by natives, ruins of buildings heaped up in piles, pieces of churches and timbers in the street, trash
    and when I say timbers I don't exactly mean timbers I mean detached shelves pieces of wooden chests wooden benches with no legs twisted pipes boards all of it descending toward the bay to die in the ocean or next to the coconut palms on the beach
    broken statues some birds
    a city mimicking another city the way the Africans mimic our gestures and our clothes, silhouettes of houses, silhouettes of gardens, ridiculous plazas, buildings that have been left unfinished,

stairs that lead to nowhere, a plaster gnome in a backyard that's not even there, a city they call Luanda

this can't be Luanda because I've never been here before

a copy of Luanda, right down to the island out in front, the government palace, the fortress that's not the São Paulo fortress it's a copy and when we look close we can tell that it's fake, a fortress just like the gnome in a backyard that's not even there, a fortress for fighting against the Dutch, who aren't there either, theater-prop cannons, battlements that are really stage flats, soldiers with fake machine guns pretending to be soldiers, if we were to push on the walls with our hands, you don't even need to push hard, all of it would fall over with a little hollow crashing sound and behind it there'd be wood, fabric, cables, there'd be a stool with a round lamp on top of it off in the wings

a dust-covered sun that you have to light with a burning piece of paper

actors masquerading as corpses, rags masquerading as children, pieces of Styrofoam masquerading as trees, dogs hastily dressing themselves up as dogs, taught to sniff pools of paint and cushion stuffing to make us think that they're sniffing at blood and guts, tearing out the fake intestines of the actors, biting one another, pretending to be starving, beggars with fake stumps in place of their real legs who are told

"Now stay here"

making their beds in what's left of the arcades, pastry shops, travel agencies, a city invented by the ministers of state in Lisbon in order to trick us and force us to leave, to make us think

"All right Africa belongs to the Jingas I'm out of here it's over" when Luanda clearly still exists, hidden, just a bit farther up or down the highway from all this, they've planted a jungle all around it, covered up the slums, camouflaged the highways, the real Luanda, the real palace, the real fortress, the real people, the authentic swallows, not fake ones strung up on a clothesline, real beggars with real sores the way it should be, the ministers of state in Lisbon want to take Angola from us, my cotton, my plantation, my house, so they can sell it all to the Americans or rent it to the Russians, getting rich off of us in one fell swoop, we're their blacks, my father used to explain, the same way that the blacks have their blacks and those blacks even have their blacks from one level to the next down to the depths of disease and misery, this can't be Luanda because I can't see, I don't know, I can't see Alvalade, all I see are ruins with no windows or doors, alleys littered with refuse, broken-down police jeeps, huts in place of the house where my cousins used to live, with a mime playing the part of a dead man hanging against the wall, if we clap our hands he'll get up and thank us, if we turn our backs he'll ask the stage manager, who's dressed up as soldier

"How was I?"

while he cleans the makeup and shoeblack off his face with a handkerchief, his colleagues will gather up the props, they've got the painting that my cousins used to have hanging in their living room and which I found on the ground, a child depicted next to a lake, his head now missing, what seem to be photographs, what seem to be letters, everything forged of course, everything done up to see if I'd fall for it, and my cousins close by waiting for me

"Isilda"

with the painting that hung on the wall, a child depicted holding a conch shell on his shoulder, pouring water into a pond, the photographs and letters all in order, Maria da Boa Morte no longer with me

naturally

back where she belongs, helping out in the kitchen with her own kind, this can't be Luanda because I don't see Samba Pequena, Samba Grande, Corimba, the boat that ferries over to Mussulo Island, all I see are the whites from Lisbon and the laborers who were brought here by foreigners when they bought Angola and drove me off the land that belonged to me, which they couldn't buy, trying to frighten me with carnival-prop corpses and ruins of buildings that were really cardboard, me to the dummies dressed up like soldiers and armed with toy machine guns as I shooed away some dogs

"I'm not going to leave"

me to Maria da Boa Morte thanking her for her applause and taking off my costume-batik cloth and my old-lady wrinkles

"How was I?"

to my husband, to my mother, to my father, with Damião in silhouette in the entryway to the living room with the tea tray

"How was I?"

me on the Corimba highway with no boat to ferry me to Mussulo, no native soldiers to protect me

(Maria da Boa Morte pushing aside the toy machine gun

"Ma'am")

no aide-de-camp from the governor's office, no regional administrator, nothing but the dummies dressed up as soldiers and that fool tugging on my arm, pleading

"Ma'am"
and pleading
"Ma'am"
and still pleading
"Ma'am"
amid the carnival-prop corpses, rags masquerading as children, pieces of Styrofoam masquerading as trees, the tumult of stage flats crashing down with a little hollow sound

"I'm not going to leave"

the toy machine gun blasting its cap-gun rounds, the dogs, who had memorized their part, running far away from us, the prop master tossing down tiles and boards from the rafters, Maria da Boa Morte pleading

"Ma'am"

as if she were truly scared and the plastic guns were really firing bullets, can you believe it, until the stage manager and the prompter ask her

"Well?"

Maria da Boa Morte, obedient, letting go of my arm, hurriedly putting a half-dozen splotches of paint on her belly, breasts, and face, trying to speak, falling silent, trying to speak again

"How was I?"

hoping that it would make me happy, how stupid, that I would be delighted with her, that I would get excited

"You were great"

Maria da Boa Morte now playing a corpse like the other actors lying facedown on the ground, their bodies being drained, stains stretching out on the ground that weren't blood, anything you like but not blood, no one can convince me that it was blood, extending down the length of her leg, me impatient

"Stop this right now it's not funny get up"

leaning over her, shaking her shoulder

"I said get up didn't I?"

a third of her nose still there, a third of her skull, a flap of flesh hanging over her only eye, if I were to scrape at it with a stick or my fingernails her real features would appear underneath, if I clapped my hands, if I applauded

"That's enough you were great"

Maria da Boa Morte would smile at me and that would be that, if I were to warn her that it's getting late, four hours of travel left at least and that's if the rain doesn't open potholes on the dirt road, the little ones are waiting for dinner in Baixa de Cassanje, Carlos who won't eat without her, Clarisse making all the tractor drivers uneasy, Rui making a mess all through the house smashing my mother's altar to pieces, tormenting Lady, plucking the feathers off the peacocks, if I can convince her that I need her, not that I'm her friend

let's be sensible here

that I need her, she'll say good-bye to the director, disobey the stage manager, and come along, the two of us down at the workers' quarters by the river with the doll with a missing arm perched up on a shelf as if it were a throne, if you squeezed her navel her expression stays the same but she says

"Mama"

that's the thing about the Bailundos that makes me furious, their expression never changes, the police chief would raise his

whip at them or hold his pistol up to their ear and there'd be silence, no complaints, they had no more awareness than inanimate
objects, a childlike innocence that had nothing to do with pride or
dignity or courage, I was going to say they had the temperament
of a chicken but chickens, good Lord, chickens at least kick their
feet, try to escape, you can see quite clearly that they're scared of
us, but the Bailundos at most

"Yes sir"

at most

"Yes boss"

never objecting, never revolting, apologizing for the inconve-
nience of making us punish them for no reason, just like us when
we go up to the whites in Lisbon, dragging around a sheaf of papers from office to office, apologizing for them robbing us, accepting their alms, meager meals, staying in prefab buildings next to
schools, in empty barracks, ancient palaces with wood-paneled
walls and no roofs in the middle of gardens overgrown with shrubs,
scattered weeds, fences with missing rails, dusty old gazebos, me
to Maria da Boa Morte in Baixa de Cassanje in the hut by the river,
in which, according to her grandmother, boa constrictors laughed
with the voices of children, me shaking her shoulder

"Get up"

the two of us watching, as we held hands, the arrival of my father's first automobile, a saucepan with wheels and a pair of round
eyes made of glass, my father bouncing in the seat on top of it and
my mother panicking on the porch

"The azaleas"

wearing a hat that would later be mine

"My how pretty you are Isilda"

and ended up faded, eaten by moths, in the chest in the attic, the wide brim, the veil, the little plastic fruits, the ribbons, my mother slowly grazing it with the tips of her fingers, my father putting the car in reverse, trying to swerve around the flower beds, driving the car onto the lawn, running into the front gate, then heading resolutely toward the flowers, trampling them before finally coming to a stop against the front steps, my mother on her knees among the plants straightening stems, gathering up petals, fixing smashed corollas, resurrecting what she'd created in order to conquer the French woman and her bracelets, her necklaces, her horses

"The azaleas"

me to Maria da Boa Morte on the Corimba highway

"Get up"

my father perplexed as he got out of the automobile, examining the engine with the owner's manual

a book that was bigger than a dictionary with a photograph of the saucepan-shaped car on the cover

open on the hood, drawings, arrows, paragraphs in English, my father tracing diagrams of wires and coils with his uncertain little finger

"I swear I don't understand what happened it drove beautifully in Luanda"

my mother going into the garage that night with an ax, turning on her flashlight, bashing the automobile, the doors, the roof, the windows, which were turned into tiny grains of glass, I could no longer hear the parakeets rustling in the golden rain tree, my father gesticulating in his nightshirt out of which emerged a faint plea

"My dear"

me to Maria da Boa Morte because it was getting late

"Enough of this it's not funny get up"

splotches of paint on her belly, her chest, her face, trying to speak, falling silent, a stain that wasn't blood, anything you like but not blood, stretching down the length of her leg, a third of her nose, a third of her skull, a flap of flesh hanging down over her only eye, if I were to scrape at it her real features would appear underneath, the soldiers with the plastic machine guns surprised by my applause

"You were great"

you were great but we're so old and it's getting late now, get up, so old, I won't go so far as to admit that I'm your friend

let's be sensible

I need you the same way that the white people in Lisbon need us so they can sell Angola, the coffee, the cotton, the corn, the tobacco, the scales and acids of the Jewish diamond merchants, and since they've already sold it we don't exist anymore, the theater director told everyone to put everything in its place, told my father

"Now don't forget to trample the azaleas with the antique car"

and turned out the lights, as if it were getting dark, spilled cans of motor oil and a handful of tools on the ground, directing the person playing my mother

"Now hit the body of the car, with feeling this time"

Maria da Boa Morte and I down at the workers' quarters by the river searching for hyena tracks in the fields, Fernando ringing the dinner bell, turning the person playing my mother into my actual mother

"Isilda"

the relatives in Moçâmedes enraptured

"My how she's grown"
a choir of old women with feathered fans that smelled like doves,
my mother pushing me towards a fluffy lap that smelled sour
"Twelve years old now Auntie"
the fans, which seemed very impressed by the passage of time,
flapped in unison in a frenzy of surprise
"My Lord"
from time to time a letter that had been sent months earlier,
its edges black with dirt, announced the burial of one of the old
women, and my mother, wiping away a corner of her sorrow with
the corner of a handkerchief, would add the woman's photograph
to the sepulchre, the top of a chest of drawers lined with photos
of the deceased, their frames on a linen tablecloth, which to judge
from its lack of decoration represented a shroud
"Poor thing"
the relatives in Moçâmedes offered me chocolates that had
melted during their trip, caramels glued together in sticky clus-
ters, packages of cookies reduced to musty grains of sand, my father's eyes would grow very wide, commanding me
"Don't eat it"
the aunties would take back the sweets wrapped in tinfoil, dirty-
ing their hands, sucking on their brown fingertips
"Did you lose your appetite little girl?"
my mother's eyes would grow very wide, staring down my
father's
"How insulting"
my father's eyes would get smaller and my mother's eyes would
grow wider as she looked at me
"Why don't you try just a little bite at first Isilda be patient"

my fingers dirty as well, my dress dirty, a drop of melted chocolate on the couch, my mother's eyes raised to the ceiling

"How terrible"

my father's eyes

"Didn't I tell you this would happen?"

my aunties' fingers, even though they'd been sucked clean, leaving fingerprints on the couch cushions, on the curtains, on the
upholstery, on my father's hand when they bid him farewell, my
father's eyes growing wider as he looked at his hand, as he wiped
his hand on his pants and stained his pants, growing wider as he
looked at my mother

"I'm going to kill you"

my mother's eyes distressed, apologizing

"What could I do?"

the aunties kissing my mother, leaving dark smudges on her
cheeks, trying to hold on to my father as they walked down the
front steps, my father trying to escape their grasp, recoiling from
them but trying to make it look like he wasn't recoiling from them,
examining his shirt, smiling at them, not a smile really, just rows
of teeth, whipping my mother with his pupils

"I'm going to kill them"

we'd step on caramels, which were a pain to scrape off the bottom of our shoes, even after scraping with a knife for hours our
shoes would still stick to the ground and would only come unglued from the floorboards with great difficulty, we'd lift our ankles and feel a strange pull, we'd be pulling the rug along behind
us and it was as if we were dragging the whole house along with
us, its foundations and everything, we'd sit down and bruise our

skin on cookie shards crushed beneath the weight of our bodies, crunch crunch, my father to my mother, livid, limping, the whole study stuck to his foot and dragging along behind him, the wooden floor, the ledgers, the furniture

"Get this entire business off of me when you get the chance"

for two weeks Fernando and Damião dusted, washed, and scrubbed, moving aside armchairs, tables, armoires, searching for any wily candy that might still be lying in wait in the shadows or hanging from the chandelier like a tick, ready to drop down on us in all its villainous stickiness, my father distrustfully inspecting the seats of all the chairs, taking half an hour to go from the bedroom to the hallway as he examined the hardwood floor, taking his revenge by knocking over the photographs of the deceased, kissing the letters that arrived to announce another death in triumphant joy, my father, who never kissed anybody

"Thank God one less"

maybe he kissed the French woman or the women in Luanda who my mother thought were of the same breed as the French woman, which is to say wearing low-cut blouses and smoking with a cigarette holder, my mother swore he kissed them, handing me the collars and cuffs of his shirt so I could smell them, showing me smudges of lipstick and eyeliner

"Look at this lack of respect this shamelessness"

but he never kissed me, he'd put his hands on my head and tousle my hair with the palm of his hand

"Little Isilda"

he never kissed my mother because he slept in a different room, he'd graze his lips across her forehead

"See you in the morning"

and go up the stairs with a newspaper, we could hear his key turn in the lock, the springs in the lock engaging, the sound of the generator breaking the silence, the lightbulbs now about to explode, now tiny anemic filaments, my mother to herself

"What did I ever do to him?"

weighing herself, examining herself in the mirror, going on a diet of grilled fish, grilled beef, greens, weighing herself again, showing me the slack in the waistband of her skirt, proud

"Two kilos"

buying new clothes, changing her hairstyle, putting on more makeup, wearing higher heels, buying rings, without saying anything to anybody, with her own money from her inheritance, from the jeweler in Malanje, to the point where all the savings that had been left to her evaporated into thin air, my mother taking her place in the living room an hour before my father arrived

"How do I look?"

my father not even noticing her

"Hi"

putting his hands on my head and tousling my hair with the palm of his hand

"Little Isilda"

not registering the new clothes, the new hairstyle, the makeup, the high heels, the rings, the pathetic sad face that tried to force a smile, the creams on her face washed away with tears, my father oblivious to it all, despite the rouged eyelids, the fluttering eyelashes, the breasts that her corset strained to contain, I woke up in the middle of the night with my mother tapping on his door

"Eduardo"

with her fingertips, waiting a moment, tapping again, trying the doorknob, then pounding on the door with an open palm

"Let me in Eduardo"

using the base of a bronze lamp to knock even louder, the lightbulb shattering, the lampshade about to fall off, me barefoot on the carpet runner in the hallway holding my doll to my chest, my mother throwing herself against the door

"You don't have the right to do this to me Eduardo"

the doll crying in anguish, not me, and so I sang to comfort her, not myself, as we walked through the house, it was for the doll's sake not my own that I yelled down to the first floor

"Come talk to me Mom"

but nothing, just metal handles that were transformed into threatening, scowling faces, the curtain puffed up by the wind, something that looked like a dead person gesturing at me, something that looked like a leopard about to pounce, things that looked like

they didn't look like, they were

spirits and skulls like they had in the Castle of Terrors that came to Malanje in February, you'd buy a ticket from a harmless little man who was always coughing, leaning against the doorway with a cigarette in his mouth, my father holding me by the hand, cautious, eyeing the witches near the entrance who shook their hips and rolled their eyes

"Do you think it'll scare the little girl?"

the little man who, up close, didn't seem very clean, and whom I admired for his unperturbed intimacy with spirits and bones, pulling his handkerchief out of his pocket, unfolding it, spitting into it, putting it back into his pocket, and cutting a corner off our tickets, doing all of this without the ash of his cigarette, which was extremely long, longer than the cigarette itself, so much as shaking

"It's a silly little puppet show it doesn't scare anybody"

as soon as we entered there were spiderwebs, coffins, howls, satanic laughter

I love the term satanic laughter if I could I'd say satanic laughter every five minutes

a greenish manikin pulling the lid off an urn with a frightful creaking sound

same goes for frightful, frightful frightful

my mother, lacking the courage to go in, waiting nervously outside, the little man consoling her, finished with his cigarette, a cylinder of ash that shook as he spoke, after he stopped coughing

"Don't worry ma'am only an idiot would be scared of this"

disdainfully cutting corners from the tickets of more trembling idiots, me extremely happy to be alive, how wonderful, my father, I'm not sure how he felt, with an ambiguous smile on his face, my mother backing away from the witches and their shaking hips with a girlish, anxious look on her face, absolutely amazed and timid

"Well?"

staring at us with a look of respect, as if we'd just returned from the depths of hell

"Are there dragons?"

dragons with smoke emerging from their throats, women with goat's hooves for feet, fur-covered dinosaurs, trapdoors, lizards, bodies hanging from nooses, my father, me, and a grown woman with tears in her eyes, about to swear to her that yes, it's true, but the spoilsport with the cigarette beating us to it in an explosion of cigarette ash

"Dragons what dragons ma'am it's just seven or eight poorly dressed scarecrows they're downright laughable"

my father, who could have strangled him for his impertinence, whispering into my mother's ear, confidentially, summing up the entire world for her

"This country's full of drunks don't pay him any mind"

and after the Castle of Terrors the Hungarian Giant in a tent, a melancholic creature seated on a little stool, protected by a transparent sheet, looking at us, and when there were enough people in the tent an elderly man who sold the tickets for the spectacle and who must have been the Hungarian's owner and maybe the brother of the little man with the cigarette zipped up the entrance to the tent, approached the transparent sheet, and ordered

"Stand up giant"

the melancholic creature abandoned his stool and stood next to a vertical ruler that read two meters and forty-three centimeters in capital letters, then sat back down, the elderly man unzipped the tent and we filed out, all of us thinking of suicide, infected by the sorrow of the sideshow, which slowly faded inside us, I was touched and I peeked through a hole in the canvas and there he was sitting still with his hands on his knees hoping that someone would take him back to Hungary where it never stops raining, the kind of rain that makes you catch cold, and where everyone is enormous and terribly sad, the people, the buildings, the villages, the streets, all of it in black and white, no colors, us on our way back to the plantation and me terrified that I'd suddenly become an orphan and be put on display in a tent

"Mom"

to make sure she was still there, that they were both still there, feeling reassured

"Never mind it's nothing"

and so I fell asleep and they carried me up to my bed, I remember them going up the stairs muttering under their breath with each step

"Our little girl is made of lead"

me dreaming that they were undressing me while they undressed me, their voices far off in the distance

"Bend your arm Isilda"

I remember my joints being someone else's, bearing no relation to my own elbows and knees, dreaming that they were turning off the light as they turned it off, thinking

"I'm going to be scared"

and even though I didn't know where my doll was, I wasn't scared, I listened to the clock, my parents' footsteps, the sunflowers shrouded in fog mingled with thoughts of witches and the little man with the cigarette, putting his handkerchief back in his pocket

"Don't worry ma'am only an idiot would be scared of this"

the little man with the cigarette who I looked for when I awoke and who wasn't in the bedroom, it was just my dress with the sleeves inside out, my socks turned inside out, one sandal on either side of the room, my doll on the floor, the native soldiers who worked for the civil servant in Luanda, who once a year came to collect taxes and set up a little table out on the patio, the workers in a single-file line that stretched from the patio to the workers' quarters, the chiefs, the wives of the chiefs, the lepers, the blind ones holding onto their children for support, the civil servant with his strongbox full of money called the names in his notebook, drew a cross next to the last names of those who paid and the native soldiers led the ones who didn't pay over to the government truck which took them to work on the railroad for a whole season, laying railroad ties at the edge of the jungle, shackled to a post at night so they couldn't run away and if they did run away they were hunted down like partridges, hiding in furrows in the fields, hopping around like terror-stricken animals as bullets flew at their feet, the same little animal feet weaving their way through the grass, the same wide-eyed gallop at first, the same gelatinous body after, the same gluttonous crows screeching and pushing each other aside, my father put his hand over my eyes

"Don't look Isilda"

the little man with the ashy cigarette coughed into his unfolded handkerchief, pointing at the birds

"Don't worry ma'am only an idiot would be scared of this don't pay it any mind"

Damião and Fernando silent, Josélia silent, Maria da Boa Morte silent lying facedown in Corimba, a pool of paint, not blood, growing larger beneath her

anything you like but not blood, you can't convince me that it was blood

"Enough of this it's not funny get up"

the sea down below wasn't the sea at all it was an illusion produced by oscillating pieces of paper and lights, the bay and the coconut palms and the governor's palace and the fortress were all stage settings, the city was made of wood, fabric, and plaster in order to mimic Luanda and if we were to reach out and push it, we wouldn't even need to push hard, it would fall over with a little hollow crashing sound, me to Maria da Boa Morte, shaking her shoulder

"I said get up didn't I?"

silhouettes of houses, silhouettes of gardens, ridiculous plazas, buildings that were left unfinished, stairs that lead to nowhere, a plaster gnome in a backyard that's not even there, a city they call Luanda but can't really be Luanda because I've never been here before, actors masquerading as corpses, rags masquerading as children, pieces of Styrofoam masquerading as trees, dogs masquerading as dogs so they can be more doggish than ever, taught to rip out the fake intestines of the actors, to attack one another, feigning hunger, beggars who were directed

"Now stay here"

making their beds in what's left of arcades, pastry shops, travel agencies, a city thought up by the ministers of state in Lisbon in order to trick us and force us to leave, to make us think

"All right Africa belongs to the Jingas it's no longer mine it's over"

then selling it to the Americans or renting it to the Russians, getting rich off of us in one fell swoop, we're their blacks, my father used to explain, the same way that the blacks have their blacks and those blacks even have their blacks from one level to the next down to the depths of disease and misery, me on the Corimba highway but it wasn't really Corimba the same way that Samba Pequena wasn't really Samba Pequena and Samba Grande wasn't Samba Grande and Mussulo wasn't Mussulo either

me on the Corimba highway at the place where my cousins used to live, ruins with no windows or doors, alleys littered with refuse, broken-down police jeeps, a mime playing the part of a dead man hanging against the wall, me surrounded by foreigners who bought Angola and carnival-prop detritus and ruins of buildings that were really cardboard, me to the dummies dressed up like soldiers who pointed their toy machine guns at me

"I'm not going to leave you can pretend to kill me but I'm not going to leave I'm not going to leave do you hear me you can do whatever you want but I'm not leaving here."

24 December 1995

Someone said my name, maybe it was Luís Filipe, maybe my mother was calling me, or maybe I just fell asleep without realizing it, and my own mouth screamed

"Clarisse"

and I woke up to the morning in Estoril on the couch in the living room, scared of my own name. Not yet morning: the lights outside were still on, the windows didn't display the palm trees or the sea, they reflected my seated body, my hands, which straightened out my blouse, fixed my hair, rubbed my eyes

a speck of mascara got in my eye and it burned

my hands crumpled up the check, found the bouquet of flowers, the dress, and the bracelet, which were slipping off the couch onto the carpet, Rui shook my father's knee right away

"Clarisse didn't like any of her presents she's throwing them out Dad"

my grandmother unwrapped her new martyr, turning it this way and that, distrustful

"Did you already give it to the bishop to bless it at least?"

because until they had been blessed it wasn't a saint it was a doll and try to get a miracle out of a doll, preposterous, they bought a Christmas tree in Malanje that they kept in the attic with all the decorations still on it and everything, nice and ready for the following December, we'd open the closet door up there and find the Christmas tree drying out, my father held his new shirt up to his chest to try it out

"Don't you like your new watch Clarisse?"

my first real watch after having toy watches with plastic faces and elastic wristbands, I'd twist the knob on them and the hands would spin around yet always maintain the same angle, quarter after twelve, one twenty, two twenty-five, three thirty, my first watch with independent hour and minute hands, and a second hand longer than the others, thinner, and scarlet, pointing at one little hash mark after another, moving to the side with a slight jolt, I'd put on my watch, walk on my tiptoes, and I'd seem at least five years older, I wouldn't pay the slightest attention to my brothers, two little kids, Carlos trying to trip me

"You snob"

me still on my tiptoes, jumping over his shoe, with my nose in the air since I didn't even hear him, the way my mother never heard the men in the pastry shop muttering under their breath

"Something or other something or other"

the two of us, my mom and I, deaf, superior to men, until we headed back toward the plantation in the jeep and the last of the slums evaporated behind us in a cloud of dust

"What did they want Mom?"

phrases that I didn't understand, gestures with their index fingers, difficult words, fenced-off pastures out the window of the jeep, shirtless children walking aimlessly amid a few scattered huts, mouths hidden behind hands repeating

"Something or other something or other"

if they let me smoke I'd have lit up a cigarette in the jeep

"What did they want Mom?"

a gaggle of wild geese something or other something or other in the sky, my mother who didn't seem angry the way I got angry at Carlos's stupid behavior

"You snob"

(the keychain for the jeep was a rabbit's foot and there was a second rabbit's foot hanging from the rearview mirror that was almost just a bone)

my mother, who should have offered me a cigarette since with my watch and on my tiptoes I was almost the same age as her, but she didn't offer me one, if I'd put a ring or two on my fingers and gone to the hairdresser with her they wouldn't be able to tell the slightest difference

"None at all"

the lights in Estoril motionless in the darkness except for a garland of lilac-colored lamplights that rocked to and fro

a ship?

if I could only embark on a cruise ship with nightly shows and a swimming pool, if only Luís Filipe would invite me on a cruise to Greece, I've got tons and tons of clothes that I haven't worn yet, it's a shame really, me looking at myself in the windowpanes, unable to find that little girl who was superior to the men

"Something or other something or other"

in the pastry shop, looking at the women I once longed to become and whom I now despise, taking off my shoes and walking around on my tiptoes wearing a toy watch with an elastic wristband, much better than a real one, women destined to become princesses asking me

"Do you have the time Dona Clarisse?"

me with a disdainful look on my face, not even glancing at them

"Ten to one"

them repeating, enchanted

"Ten to one imagine that"

all watches everywhere anxiously trying to hurry up and set their time by my watch, until I start wishing it was a quarter after three, because I hate lunch, winding the knob and bam, it's a quarter after three all of a sudden in the real world and the world is grateful, free of all those meatballs and soups and scoldings for putting your elbows on the table

"Elbows Clarisse elbows"

Josélia cutting Rui's meatballs and nobody getting upset about him having his elbows or even his chin on the table, my grandmother placing the sanctified martyr in the section reserved for martyrs murdered with rocks, arrows, crosses, flaming coals, rubble from collapsing temples, communists' bullets, lions, the martyrs in the middle who suffered the most those poor things

"And now sit up straight before you become a hunchback like cousin Deodata just think how pretty that would be"

me a little hunchback, in black mourning clothes, two wedding rings, one that belonged to me and one that belonged to the deceased, porcelain bears, Chinese boxes, maybe penniless, maybe starving, cousin Deodata as a young lady in a photograph without a trace of a hump on her back, my grandmother putting on her glasses to get a better look at it, her nose pressed against the glass of the frame, a young lady holding an umbrella

(it wasn't clear why she was holding an umbrella)

leaning against a high-backed armchair, the same one that was still fading in the corner of her living room

"You looked so different Deodata"

cousin Deodata with her forehead almost touching her belly, shuffling along, one slipper after another

"Thank you thank you"

if I'd wanted to all I'd have had to do is wind my watch with the elastic wristband backward and cousin Deodata would once again be leaning against the armchair, back to when my father didn't drink, back to the beginning of the evening and I'd go see Carlos in Ajuda, I'd buy some aftershave downtown, some perfume for Lena, any perfume at all would do as long as it has some sort of scent because Lena doesn't know anything about perfume, I'd hop on the trolley, hop on the bus, ring the doorbell

"Hi Carlos"

the hideousness of that ugly street, the mulberry trees, the buildings with their crumbling cement façades, back to when my father didn't drink, sometimes he'd distract me from the watch that had been bestowed upon me and I'd become a little girl again, my heels back on the ground, and we'd hop across the patio on one foot, the last one there was a rotten egg, Carlos upset

"No fair Dad let you win"

my mother winking at Carlos, telling him to be quiet, which I saw quite clearly

"No he didn't don't be silly"

my father hopping on one leg with me in his arms, the two of us against Carlos who still cheated by letting his other foot touch the ground even though my mother, who was the referee, didn't make him go back to the starting line, my father stopped all of a sudden, Carlos got to the flowerpot before we did and I wanted to punch him, not buy him any aftershave downtown, just hop on the trolley, hop on the bus, ring the doorbell in Ajuda, the hideousness of that ugly street, the mulberry trees, the buildings with their crumbling cement façades, and punch him

"Cheater" and run off through the cotton fields and live in Malanje all by myself, my father grabbed me around the waist as I ran down the trail and gently sat me down on the ground, or call him a

"Cheater"

or ask my father to pick me up again

"Pick me up again"

floating around and around, birds and trees spinning in reverse, me twirling around, a feeling of vertigo, gleeful panic

"I'm going to fall"

as if I was going to die but I didn't die my father caught me before I landed on the ground, I remember his smell, his hands, the damaged fingernail on his scarred thumb, which didn't leave a fingerprint, it felt funny when you ran your finger over the tip of it, my mother cheering for whomever was trailing behind

"Hurry hurry"

my grandmother sullen because nobody was talking to her, reprimanding the kitchen help

"Who filled the sideboard table with whiskey bottles?"

my father would go over to the sideboard table and sneak a drink, my mother would argue with customs agents from Cotonang in the study while my father stumbled around in his bedroom, uninterested in the Bailundos, either my grandmother or Carlos would be the one who counted them at night, my father's jarring voice resounded in the dark, singing, startling the owls, Lady would scurry around in distress, Carlos would get tripped up in his counting and have to start over, counting out loud, one two three four five six seven eight nine pointing at each one with a switch cut from a tree, speaking with the same authority my father had before he started in with the bottles, the ones sick with dysentery or malaria sat waiting on the ground wrapped in blankets and burlap sacks, the foreman taught them manners with the edge of his boot

"Hey you"

laborers who were starting to waste away after they'd barely arrived from Huambo, at first they were bigger than our blacks, more obedient, fatter, but now their ribs were sticking out, trying to stand up, then giving up

"Hey you"

and my father stopped singing for a moment to cough, whenever they turned on the generator the house would suddenly appear, the same size it was during the day but somehow different, the golden rain tree shining in the light, a house that was hidden behind another house, lying in wait, you could hear distant sounds that seemed to be right next to us, toads, frogs, a shivering fox, insects that weren't digging burrows in the ground, they were digging into my bones, someone said my name, not Luís Filipe, not my mother, not me, not cousin Deodata

cousin Deodata

"Clarisse"

and I woke up to the morning in Estoril on the couch in the living room with the bouquet of flowers scattered about, the dress and the bracelet on the carpet, as if some woman I don't know had taken them off and gone to lie down on my bed, there were times when I was so tired when I got home that I started to undress in the entryway, my jacket, my purse, my shoes, my contorted acrobat arms reaching around to pull the zipper at the nape of my neck, there was never a man here to help me unzip, that's what a marriage is, having a man to whom we can turn our backs and pull back our hair and he'll zip us up and fasten the clasp at the top and then step back and start thinking about something else

"All set"

I'd keep undressing as I came down the hall, without turning on the light, my bra on the back of a chair, my panties on the ground, my necklace in an ashtray, stubbing my toe on the flowerpot with the little rubber tree, writhing in pain, my earrings, which, who cares, I'll spend an eternity looking for the next day, down on my hands and knees, furious with myself, someone called my name, not my mother, not Luís Filipe, not my grandmother, not Rui, not the cartoons on TV, cars that belong to Luís Fillipe's kids swerving past people's lawns and gardens on their way to Alcabideche, to Cascais, to Sintra, except for me and the Air Force Major who lives on the ground floor nobody else lives in this building, the Major's wife doesn't respond to me when I say hello, she just shuts the door in my face as if she didn't see me, she shakes her head as she points me out to her husband with the tip of her nose, thinking I don't notice, same goes for the woman at the butcher shop, same goes for the tobacco shop where I buy my cigarettes, all these people involved in a conspiracy of whispers, the butcher-shop lady's stepson leaves notes in my mailbox next to bank statements and advertisements for plumbers all services performed, Wanna go to the movies with me sweetheart? on Sundays I'm startled by the rumble of his motorcycle going up and down the street, swerving around all the scaffolding and the mounds of sand, speeding off behind a billow of exhaust, disappearing the moment I pull back the curtain, if my father even dreamed of how they treat me he'd fold up his newspaper and set it aside, jump up off the couch, and invent some game to make me feel better, he'd hop across the patio on one foot with me, stopping before he got to the flowerpot, pretending to be tired so that I could win, he'd help me hunt for grasshoppers in the grass, we'd make boats out of paper and launch them in the little pond to the amusement of the fish, he'd promise me a bicycle with a headlight on it for my birthday, my mother would be arguing with my grandmother about the arrangement of stitches in one of their needlepoint magazines

"But that screws up the look of the flowerpots you can't tell what it's supposed to be"

just before he died he motioned for me to come to his bedside with his finger, I put my ear to his lips, a short breath, the tendons in his neck were flexed tight, his tongue tried to separate the words, line them up in a row, pronounce them in order, one syllable after another, putting together sentences like the pieces of a puzzle mixed up with lots of pieces from other puzzles, to tell me what he hadn't had time to tell my mother or his own mother many years before, those sentences that my mother or his mother didn't have time to tell him

snatches of songs, children's prayers, the tributaries on the left bank of the Douro River, the names of different kinds of marbles cat's-eye devil's-eye oxblood and aggie, hit it chase it hit it then chase it hit it, a shallow hole still open after a marble jumped it, playing soldiers, choosing partners by walking toward each other one foot in front of the other whoever steps on the other person's shoe has to go first, tell my daughter that as soon as I feel well, as soon as I feel better, the tributaries on the left bank of the Douro River, the hills of the Galaico-Duriense mountain range Peneda Soajo Gerês Larouco Falperra, I never knew what the Douro or the Galaico-Duriense mountain range were, me, for whom Portugal was nothing more than a pink-colored smudge on the map, full of kings and monasteries, and it wasn't clear how all of that fit in the tiny space next to the big green blotch that was Spain, I wanted to tell my daughter that as soon as I feel better, I can't find the rest of it in all these mixed-up sentences, who wants to see the beautiful boat today put out to sea, no that's not it, oh mary of mine mary my tender branch of rosemary, no that's not it either, when my grandfather fell ill he raised his head from the pillow, held up his hand to ask us to wait, all of us waiting for his final revelation, he swallowed, cleared his throat, held up his hand again, my uncle Joaquim to us

"Be quiet"

to my grandfather

"What is it Dad?"

all of us paying close attention to his final words of advice, my grandfather with his hand in the air, then setting it back down on the bed, his head collapsing onto the pillow

"I can't"

not desperate, just very distant, hearing something that no one else could hear, maybe it was Who wants to see the beautiful boat today put out to sea, maybe it was Oh mary of mine mary my tender branch of rosemary, maybe some ballad that's even older than those or maybe it wasn't even a ballad at all

"I can't"

just silence, his body all quiet and still inside, or maybe this little ditty, blood is flowing round and round then dances at the end of town, I could see him hesitate but he didn't panic because it's so simple, terrified of it our whole life, thinking about it our whole life, but it's really so simple

"As soon as I feel better we'll buy you that bicycle Clarisse"

when what I really wanted to tell my daughter is that it's so simple, I think I like you, I should like you but my affection for you has become so distant that I don't know, I should like you but I don't care if *you end up alone, I'm not worried about you, just as I'm not worried about me, Peneda Soajo Gerês Larouco Falperra, any one of those will do, faces that I recognize or don't recognize, and even if I once recognized them I no longer do, faces of people who are able to stand up on their own, able to move around freely, how odd, Who wants to see the beautiful boat today put out to sea, as soon as I feel better we'll buy you that bicycle Clarisse, but what bicycle, I don't want anyone to touch me, to talk to me, to take an interest in me, to ask me*

"Well?"

"Feel better?"

to whisper to me

"It's me Dad lie still don't move around don't overexert yourself"

I am still, I'm not moving around, I'm not overexerting myself, what exertions

"The firewood needs to be cut Amadeu"

lungs either breathe or they don't breathe, it has nothing to do with me, what really does have to do with me are my hollow arms, two weightless prosthetics, like leaves and branches carried off by the flowing water, a babbling brook that once had meaning for me but that I no longer understand

just before he died he motioned for me to come to his bedside with his finger, I put my ear to his lips, a short breath, the tendons in his neck were flexed tight, his tongue tried to separate the words, line them up in a row, pronounce them in order, one syllable after another

"Clarisse"

and I woke up to the morning in Estoril on the couch in the living room, scared of my own name, not yet morning because the lights outside were still on, the windows not showing the palm trees or the sea, they reflected my seated body, my hands, which straightened out my blouse, fixed my hair, rubbed my eyes, crumpled up the check, found the bouquet of flowers, the dress, and the bracelet, which were slipping off the couch onto the carpet, the indefatigable cat chasing around the annoying little chick with enormous eyelashes and a tiny, childish voice until I too felt the urge to strangle it, shut it up once and for all by clamping down on its little throat, not yet morning, still night, the seagulls in the eaves of the church or on boat-cabin roofs, sometimes you can tell that it's morning not by the sun but by the birds on the beach, dozens and dozens of birds walking along the sand, the generator rattling in Angola, I'd wake up to find Josélia snoring on the doormat in front of Rui's bedroom instead of keeping watch in case he had an attack, Josélia fell asleep Mom, my mom looking for a switch to whip her with

"Josélia"

Josélia not objecting, not saying

"But he won't fall asleep young lady he won't fall asleep ma'am"

finding the switch before my mother does, handing it to her, pulling her skirt up to her back, I remember those extremely dark marks on her back, the sound, my mother

"Are you trying to kill my son are you trying to kill us all, you all will never rest until you've finished us off"

Carlos slamming doors down the hall, furious with my mother, furious with me, muttering under his breath

"Something or other something or other"

like the men in the pastry shop in Malanje, all those things that men know how to say, all those things that men have always said to me, even Luís Filipe and all the ones before Luís Filipe, maybe even my father as well

"Something or other something or other"

in a hut near Cotonang muttering things to the cafeteria worker with whom he had Carlos, I don't know if I like my father, I don't know if I like anyone at all, I don't know if I like myself, my father, just a man

"Something or other something or other"

who at the end of the day is just the same as other men, just as coarse as they are, Carlos slamming doors down the hallway, my mother holding off with the switch

"Carlos"

pulling him by the arm, raising the switch to him without even waiting for him to pull up his nightshirt, again the extremely dark marks, the sound

"So you're defending your friends are you little nigger?"

the only time I ever heard her call him a nigger, the only time I truly understood that she hated him, that she treated him better than us precisely because she hated him so much, just as my grandmother hated him

"I should put you to work out in the cotton fields I should hand you over to the foreman he'll put you in your place"

the house suddenly felt strange, my mother going out on the balcony that looked down on the flower beds, my father to us

"It's nothing it's nothing"

my father to my mother

"Isilda"

Carlos and Josélia looking at us with the same expressionless expression on their faces, the same calm indifference, and what was there behind that calm indifference, I ask myself, there was nothing behind that calm indifference, I respond, not resignation, not panic, not respect, nothing, if you could only understand their motives for killing us, for running us through on pikes like animals, the sound of my father's boots on the balcony, my mother's voice

"Don't you ever think about touching me again for the rest of your life"

hovering over Carlos the next morning, ironing his shirts, insisting that he drink another glass of milk, serving him his food before the rest of us, leaving chocolates on his pillow, introducing him to a broker from Luanda

"My oldest son"

impulsively promising him a motorcycle for Easter and forgetting all about it a week later, yet still, I'd bet everything I own on it, my nearly genuine jewelry my nearly genuine French gowns my nearly antique made-in-Singapore porcelain dogs, yet still hating him, still hiding him from everyone, still tormenting him out of a mixture of rage and remorse, we never again raced across the patio hopping on one leg

"Faster faster"

we never again quarreled about it

"Cheater"

if I were to turn the hands of the toy watch back to the beginning of the night I would certainly find him waiting for me in the apartment in Ajuda surrounded by those horrific masks, those orange porcelain jars that Lena just adores, the codfish, the greens, the cruet set, two glass ducks that pour oil and vinegar from their open beaks, a Christmas tree decorated like a country bride, a tree that's, let's be honest, downright ugly, some stupid gift for me, some stupid gift for Rui, both of them bought on the cheap at a shop in Alcântara, Carlos keeping an eye out for us on the balcony, looking down at the avenue in that neighborhood full of mulberry trees and poor people, perfumed every night by the smell of broom shrubs wafting down from the Monsanto forest, if Luís Filipe knew I had a mulatto brother he'd faint the poor thing, his pacemaker ticktock, ticktock, slowly giving out beneath his undershirt, I'm not feeling very well sweetie, I swear I'm not feeling very well bring me some of those pills I put under my tongue they're in my jacket pocket, Luís Filipe's eyes rolling back in his head and me thinking that I'm done for, the door opening before I even ring the doorbell, Carlos in the doorway straightening his tie, nervous, unsure whether he should kiss me or stick out his hand, the type of hand that seems like it's always dirty and makes us want to wash our own hands after we touch it, not with soap but with a pumice stone and a stiff-bristled brush, Lena behind Carlos, sticking her head up over his shoulder to see, like a cuckoo bird popping out of a clock on an invisible spring, opening and shutting its painted wooden beak

"You haven't changed you haven't changed at all come in"

the cuckoo bird looking gaudy in her fripperies and necklaces, her fingernail polish chipped away at the edges, her hair dyed at some beauty school that even a Gypsy would scoff at, a pair of glasses hanging around her neck on a metal chain that made me realize that for them, but not for me, fifteen years had passed, they were like cousins who live in the country or elderly servants who had moved up in the world and no longer address you as young lady they address you by your name even though it sounds unnatural or uncouth when they say it and then they go back to addressing you as young lady, waiting for you to sit before they sit, getting out the fine china, shooing the cat off of the nicest armchair

"Sit here sit here"

hurriedly hiding a broom behind a window curtain, I realized that fifteen years had passed for them, they'd suffered illnesses, gained weight, had liver spots on their hands, I realized that even worn-out furniture can become more worn-out, that damp spots on the ceiling can get even darker, that dust can accumulate on top of dust until the first layer of dust disappears entirely, I realized that there can be old age on top of old age, wrinkles on top of wrinkles, webs of cracked plaster on top of other webs of cracked plaster, like on the frescoes you see in churches, Lena happy to see me, putting on her glasses

"You haven't changed young lady you haven't changed at all come in"

me uncomfortable on the uneven springs of the couch, its velvet fabric once blue now purple, spotted with tallow and grease stains, one of my butt cheeks higher than the other, something that felt like a metal thorn digging into my leg bone, a wooden crossbar bruising my back, Carlos bringing me a glass of water on a tray with fingerprint smudges on it and decorated with an embroidered cloth

(a chapel, peasants dancing, a stork perched on a chimney)

pushing aside a miniature lighthouse figurine on the end table, setting the tray down next to me

"Are you thirsty young lady?"

solicitous, anxious, emotional, grateful that I came, that I deigned to converse with them, as I left they'd dry their eyes on their sleeves, write to their children to tell them all about it, explain who I was to the neighbors, rifle through drawers to find a picture of me when I was little, one of its corners bent, and putting it up in place of the miniature lighthouse, still emotional as I drink the water, they'd bring out a package of cookies on a second tray with a second embroidered cloth, blowing some tiny crumbs off of it

"Would you like another glass of water young lady some cookies?"

Lena's ankles swollen, breathing heavily like a fat person, pausing for a moment to catch her breath when speaking, her hand on her chest, fingers splayed and touching her necklaces, just like Maria da Boa Morte or Damião, just like Luís Filipe on the afternoons he was able to get the job done

"Sweetie"

the afternoons when he didn't apologize to me afterward, it's all the work at the office sweetie, all the pressure in this business, it was such a hassle trying to persuade those Frenchmen, if a few things come together we'll spend a weekend in Madrid or the Canary Islands, lying out under the sun at a nice hotel with no cell phone, no worries, no problems, spending the whole time together just the two of us, spending the whole time snuggling and kissing, I'm a much better lover than I seem right now, you'll see, I'll be like a twenty-year-old kid, twenty, forget that, fifteen or even twelve years old so I can be your little baby, your little son, who knows maybe this will be the last Christmas we have to spend apart, the last one where I leave you all alone, without me, turn off the cartoons, grab the dress and bracelet I gave you, put the bouquet in a vase, put the check in your purse before you lose it, sit on my lap and don't cry, most importantly don't cry, it's not worth crying because I'm all yours for two hours every Tuesday and Saturday, I'm here to take care of you, to talk to you, to keep you company, what more could a woman, frankly, dry those tears for me, what more could a woman want out of life.

And so I decided that we'd celebrate Christmas at home this year.
I told the servants to use whatever was left of the generator to
light up whatever was left of the garden, there's got to be a gas can
somewhere around there, forgotten in some corner of the storehouse or underneath a pile of ashes in the basement and maybe
if a couple of the generator parts were fixed it would start up
again, I want everyone to be able to see the big azalea blossoms
and the golden rain tree properly, the neat flower beds, the cut
grass, the metal bars on the front gate without a spot of rust, the
patio covered with big blue canopies, and me making my grand
entrance the way I did on my father's arm as we walked around

the churchyard, my father and I in front, smiling, and my husband behind us fidgeting with the wedding ring on his finger, fidgeting in his rented, misbuttoned double-breasted suit coat, which you could immediately tell was used because the elbows and knees were shiny from overuse and the stitches on the breast pocket were coming undone, even the carnation in his lapel, which he certainly rented along with the suit itself, looked withered to me, a carnation that wasn't quite red, faded, with petals that had wilted over the years, worn-out after dozens of weddings, weddings of foremen and managers, poor things, weddings of poor people

my dear lady, Mr. Eduardo, Dona Isilda, bowing solemnly and repeatedly, guests looking out the window of the car as they drove off and there they were, still waving good-bye

dozens of weddings and probably a number of baptisms at least, the wives of my father's friends pointing at Amadeu whispering into their gloves their fans the veils of their hats

pregnant pregnant I'd bet my niece's dowry that she's pregnant and me glaring at them furiously without ever ceasing to smile which they clearly took note of

"I'm a virgin"

the bishop with his secretary, the governor with his aide-de-camp, the police chief, not that one, the one that they'd sent to Baixa de Cassanje before we complained in Luanda, the one who never arrested anyone, not even a measly adolescent, the Jingas just did whatever they wanted without regard for anyone else, buying their dried fish and tobacco at the general stores in the villages and giving the excuse that it was cheaper than our company store, and we were either obligated to let them go at the end of the harvest because they didn't owe us anything or pay them a salary that was almost as much as a white person would get, tables covered with gladiolas and roses, Dutch porcelain and silver-plated utensils that we used for the first time after we bought them at the estate auction of a Belgian man who'd passed away, and which had come all the way from Bié in straw-filled crates, my mother to Josélia as she held up the plates, blowing the dust off them one by one

"Be careful"

my father running his thumb along the edges looking for cracks, flaws, silverware, porcelain, crystal glasses that didn't match, you'd tap one with a knife and it would make this interminable sound, as if it contained all the sadness of an ailing dog, the simple fact of their existence seemed to make them suffer, perhaps, or else it was the sound of the Belgian man bemoaning the loss of some of his cattle via the crystal that once belonged to him

pregnant pregnant I'd bet my niece's dowry that she's pregnant

the Belgian man who instead of getting on a ship bound for Europe hanged himself from a roof beam in his barn with his ticket in the pocket of his vest, he piled up all his suitcases balanced on top of them took a step forward and good-bye

doesn't it disturb you to use a dead man's things Eduardo there are times when I look at these things and I feel a sort of chill

"Don't be silly dear"

honestly some sort of chill it makes me think that that foreigner is going to barge in here any minute and reclaim his things stare at me silently furious with me, demanding that I return all of it to him I felt his presence in the hallway I could hear the damn keys turning

*in the locks of the door I'm certain I heard his footsteps following me
for the love of God before something terrible happens*

"Don't be silly dear you always told me that you wanted a decent
set of china"

get these dishes and silverware away from me so I can sleep in peace

the china, the silverware, and the crystal glasses that didn't
match, which the government troops didn't touch, the Belgian
man appeared before them hanging from the roof beam in the
barn and they ran off, terrified, the crates surely still intact in the
pantry, Damião and Fernando cleaning them all afternoon, setting the tables out on the patio, placing the china on the same
tablecloths we used my wedding day, gladiolas, roses, little printed
place cards set in front of each place at the table, Carlos, Lena,
Clarisse, Rui, Amadeu, my mother, the Christmas tree in the
middle, not in just any old pot, in the Sèvres vase from the living
room, its branches covered with candles and silver-colored balls,
not in a million years that old tree we bought in Malanje when
my children were little, which wasn't really a pine tree, I swore to
them it was a pine tree but it wasn't, it was just a branch from an
acacia or a cedar, this time it will be a real pine tree with real pine
needles from Norway or Sweden, with clumps of snow still stuck
to its branches, a tree that's seen tiny men, old ones, with chubby
cheeks, big bellies, red tunics, and white beards in sleighs pulled
by reindeer, popping in and out of chimney tops with a clamor of
jingling bells, the first real Christmas that I've ever given them, I'll
get my dress out of the attic, my hat

*fingers caressing the silk, idly, melancholically lingering on it, bid-
ding me farewell*

you're not going to die Mom I won't let you
"You look so pretty Isilda"

I'll starch all the pleats in them, cover up the spots eaten away by moths with a little stitch here and there, a scarf, a kerchief worn around my waist as if it was a belt, I won't move around too much so I don't rip the seams and no one will know the difference, it will be harder with the hat which has been nothing more than a snack for the moths for so many years, I'll rearrange the little plastic fruits on it, trim the veil a little bit, even if it isn't completely perfect no one will notice at night when even the mirrors themselves don't show it, the mirror in my bedroom for instance, with a little help from my makeup, almost reflects a young lady, shoulders firmer, the wrinkles on my neck masked by my smile and my necklaces

me never ceasing to smile glaring at them so they soon fell quiet swallowing the scandal
"Where did Isilda dig up this idiot?"
"I'm a virgin"

my children proud of me, Carlos and Rui in their Sunday suits, Lena in one of those gaudy Sevillian outfits that slum-dwellers adore, if I didn't say anything about her and accepted her it was because I could never really want very much for my son, it was impossible that people wouldn't notice something in his nostrils and hair, even if he only had a great-great-grandfather with black blood in him the nostrils and hair never lie not to mention a certain nimbleness in his movements, Clarisse just a little too immodest in the way she walks but this year I won't make a single comment, just a question, feigning disinterest, about when she's going to find a man and get married, like she should, this year together in

Baixa de Cassanje, so many years later, my husband not drinking, the cotton and sunflowers shining, my mother who never experienced this war, we buried her before there were corpses chopped to pieces with machetes and sickles out in the fields

I don't want to talk about it right now

my mother almost happy in spite of her son-in-law and her grandchildren

a drunk, a mulatto, an invalid, and a slut who'll end up in a hut out on the island hanging clothes on the line with the other whores while they wait for a client to arrive, it's a good thing that illness saved you from seeing this, Eduardo

sitting to my right squeezing drops of her blood-pressure medicine into her glass in such a way that it's impossible not to count along with her, the whole universe focused on the number of drops, after she took her medicine my mother would disappear with her crochet basket into a corner of the living room, superfluous, like a candlestick that's missing its mate, my mother, with whom we never talked, in whom we never took any interest, about whom we constantly forgot, muttering behind her knitting needles about the dead French woman, suddenly falling silent with her hand cupped to her ear

"Wait"

so she could hear the sea in Moçâmedes, the voices of cousins buried centuries ago which became interwoven with the sound of the corn and helped raise her spirits

"Wait"

the walls in the living room, the trinkets, the paintings, all echoing the rhythmic sound of the trees and the cadence of the waves, like the sound of the cotton during dinner when Fernando brings out the chicken soup, the turkey, the fruitcake, the jelly-filled *sonho* pastries, the French toast, the champagne, my husband lighting the candles on the Christmas tree, Damião stacking up the presents against the vase

"Only after midnight only after midnight"

the house painted, weeds pulled, broken tiles replaced with marble ones

the government troops and the foreigners in UNITA were never here, the Bailundos never ran off into the jungle, I never left my children on the docks to embark for Lisbon, there wasn't a single corpse in the streets of Luanda, and my husband, what a silly story, never hid a single bottle in a drawer, I didn't get married because I was pregnant and my father didn't scrounge up a fiancée for me and pay him to cover up the shameful mess, I'm a virgin

the tractors in front of the storehouse, the flickering lamplight from the workers' quarters mixing with the reflection of the rippling water of the river and the edges of the stones where the women washed their clothes in the morning, me telling Fernando to serve the chicken soup and turkey and at the same time I'm not told to get in the pickup truck with the other convicts and they aren't taking us to the end of the Corimba highway, out past the baobab trees, where they'd dug big ditches, which you could spot from far away because of the birds circling above them, they'd shoot at the dogs to shoo them away but they always came back, snouts low to the ground, whining, limping, the smell of bodies upon bodies covered in flies almost reached Luanda when the wind changed directions, a barefoot soldier with a shotgun across his lap keeping an eye on us, us squatting on the ground, not feeling the mosquitoes biting, cleaning the encrusted dust from our mouths and noses with our batik cloths, if Fernando hurries up I'll have time, since the machine guns haven't started firing yet and after the machine guns a few scattered shots here and there and after the scattered shots the quicklime and after the quicklime a layer of dirt, time to have dinner with my children, hand out the presents, ask Carlos to uncork the champagne, tell them not to worry about me, gather up all the china and silver-plated utensils, watch them all leave, help turn off the lights out in the garden, bound up the steps to the attic, stumbling on the runner, feeling the rest of my way up the stairs, taking off the dress and the hat, closing the chest, taking off my scarf, tying these rags around my waist and squatting down on the ground with the other prisoners, breathing the odor of their sweat, their feces, I thought about telling Clarisse and Carlos to take care of Rui but I was scared of being overly sentimental, of getting emotional, that my children would think that these people are going to stand me up in front of a ditch and shoot and after that the quicklime and after that a layer of dirt, scared of ruining their Christmas after spending eighteen years apart, my children who traveled for who knows how many days from Lisbon to Baixa de Cassanje just to have dinner with me

Carlos Clarisse Rui

there are times when I think I should have, could have, that it would have been easy to have had a different life, even here in Africa where we came

my father used to explain

not in search of money or power but black people with no money or power at all who could give us the illusion of having money and power which in fact we wouldn't have even if we did have it since the people in Lisbon only tolerated us, nothing more, they looked down on us the same way we looked down on the people who worked for us and thus in a way we were their blacks, just like the blacks have their own blacks, and those blacks have their blacks and so on going down from one level to the next to the absolute depths of disease and misery, cripples, lepers, the slaves of slaves, dogs, there are times when I think that my children hate me, just as my husband hated me, because the sound of the desk knocking against the wall was louder than the peacocks, the clock, the generator, Carlos hiding up in the golden rain tree throwing rocks at the jeep, the police chief running toward him, the smell of azaleas overpowering the smell of the sunflowers, the corn, the freshly washed sheets, the lavender, the starch

"Piece of shit mulatto piece of shit mulatto"

what we came in search of in Africa wasn't money or power, the machine guns on the Corimba highway, the first burst of shots, a pause, the second burst of shots, a pause, the third burst of shots, a pause, and now a few scattered shots from a pistol, the backhoes working to dump in a layer of dirt, the police chief shaking Carlos by the neck at the base of the golden rain tree, his mouth insulting me, forming the words with his lips then shutting his mouth, but not just with his mouth, with his eyes as well, my blouse low-cut like Clarisse's blouses, my skirt even tighter than hers, the window to my husband's bedroom open

"Say it I dare you say that you aren't scared say it"

my son silent, it was the peacocks who said it not my son, the police chief grabbed him so he could shake him some more, Carlos's legs slack and dangling, his head, his buttocks, something different about his eyebrows, a bruise, a red splotch on his face, and yet his mouth was still closed, his mouth didn't tremble the way his eyes did, the pickup trucks empty on their way back except for a lone sandal, a crutch, and a ring, but the people driving us weren't white, they were Angolan, when we finish eating dinner and Damião brings out the champagne I'm going to ask Clarisse and Carlos to take care of Rui, to never leave him alone, to never put him in a home, Lena who was raised in the slums and learned to share her misery evenly, one bucket of water for everyone, one chicken for everyone, Lena understands, poor people understand this better

"Keep your money"

since they're used to splitting their nothing evenly, they're able to make nothing into something you can eat, something that can protect you from illness, from the cold

"Keep your money I said keep your money I don't need your money to be able to take care of Rui"

this African money that in Lisbon is worth less than conch shells or seashells or rusty cans of preserves or ripped up pieces of newspaper, the illusion of money and power, my father used to explain, which we wouldn't really have even if we did have it, we'd only have blacks who have their own blacks and those blacks have their blacks and so on going down from one level to the next to the absolute depths of disease and misery, cripples, lepers, the slaves of slaves, dogs, those same humble beasts who despite being shot at always come back, the snouts low to the ground, whining, limping, back to the ditches of Corimba, the azaleas lit up, the patio lit up, great big blue canopies, orchids and roses on the table, the bishop, the governor, the police chief, not that one, the one the government appointed before this one and who never even arrested one measly adolescent, lying in his hammock every afternoon in front of the police station swatting away insects with his hand, the smell of the spikenard plants inside the church, the sound of the organ breathing in between the notes

"Why Isilda?"

the sacristan annoyed with my fiancée who couldn't stop fidgeting out of shyness, howling into his ear

"Face the front and stand still sir"

the wives of my father's friends pointing at Amadeu whispering into their gloves their fans the veils of their hats, like birds on the river staring at me with their cruel little pupils, swallowing their syllables whole, like fish

"Pregnant I'd bet my niece's dowry that she's pregnant"

me glaring at them, never ceasing to smile, capable of knocking them into the ditches in Corimba

baobab trees, they've even cut down the baobab trees

watching them topple over in a whirlwind of skirts, fox-fur stoles, purses, little pillboxes filled with their bladder-medicine pills, capable of covering them with a layer of quicklime, a layer of dirt, and even after that you'd still be able to hear their shrill voices, persistent but getting weaker and weaker, fortunately getting weaker still, now just a hiss

"Pregnant I'd bet my niece's dowry that she's pregnant"

dozens and dozens of cars in front of the house, my father told the foremen to open the company store, dried fish, beer, flour, tobacco, which of course they noted down so they could take it out of their salary, with an additional surcharge since it was after six o'clock, there are times when I start to wonder if, as the communists in Luanda claim, or the UNITA leaders, those hideous monkeys from the south, pillaging our lands in Cacuaco, those thieves, thieves, I start to wonder if we really treated them unjustly

and thus, in a certain way, my father used to explain, we were other peoples' blacks just as the blacks had their blacks and those blacks had their own blacks as well and so on going down from one level to the next down to the absolute depths

and when I think about justice and injustice I remember that when I was a child as soon as I got a stain on my clothes I'd immediately wash it with so much water and so much soap that I could no longer tell whether it was the original stain or my attempt at washing it off that was discoloring the fabric, and when the stain and the soapy water dried it looked like they were both still there, one on top of the other, two discolored aureoles that infuriated my mother, who would grab a hairbrush to hit me with the handle

"Hold out your hand Isilda"

I don't know if she was mad about the little stain or the big one, me fighting back tears with my hand held out, me waiting in the overgrown grass with the other prisoners, I wasn't afraid that they'd hit me, I was afraid of the face they'd make as they hit me, that they'd leave, that they'd leave me alone on the plantation, the garden lit up, the porch lit up, the azaleas and the golden rain tree lit up, the great big blue canopies, the Belgian man's china and silverware, the Christmas tree, the Christmas Eve dinner, chairs

and more chairs, me left all alone, except for the owls and the noc-
turnal insects, at the table decorated with orchids and roses, me
wearing the dress and hat from the attic surrounded by admiring
hordes of the dead, surrounded by the prisoners who waited with
me, the soldiers' pickup trucks, the mutts with their snouts low to
the ground, whining, limping

I'm not afraid that they'll kill me I'm afraid of the face they'll
make as they kill me, afraid that they won't like me, of the expres-
sion on my son Rui's face as he raises the pellet gun and lines me
up in the sights, his face disappearing behind the rifle, firing, and
it wasn't a feeling of loneliness, it wasn't that I was far away from
them, it wasn't pain, it was that my son didn't like me, if I tugged at
my mother's bedsheets in the middle of the night

"Do you like me?"

she never hugged me, never told me

"Come here"

never laid me down next to her

not money, not power, but blacks with no money or power to
speak of

she'd sit up, startled, and turn on a lamp to see what time it was,
her hair as I'd never seen it before, a curl falling in front of her face,
the smell of sleep, tiny eyes open just a crack, surrounded by her
eyelids, no, not her eyelids, a web of tiny swollen veins, my father
just a lump facing the wall, his back to us, with no facial features,
no limbs, a bracelet on the ground, an upside-down shoe, lungs that
deflated and seemed like they'd never fill up again, thank God they
filled back up with air, with a rattling noise that sounded like some-
one shaking a piggy bank, my mother would turn off the lamp in a
vague gesture of protest, the bracelet and the shoe would disappear,

the window would reappear, the ashen halo of the plantation, the tiny fires down in the workers' quarters, the house a cave in which the drapes slowly flapped their enormous wings

"Do you like me?"

not a house, just a space in which the furniture and fixtures could go to ruin, wobbly towel racks, doors loose in their frames, shaky shelves, cracked hinges, the little corn stalks walking across the carpet, the troops, Mom, they're going to rob me, they're going to take me with them, lock me up in a hut, hang me from a mango tree, the flagstones and overgrown grass of the cemetery in the hallway, crucifixes, a fragment of a stone angel

"Isilda"

me tugging at my mother's bedsheets in the middle of the night, grown-ups are so big

"Do you like me?"

if I put on one of their shirts I can't even see my fingers, I have to run three steps for every step they take, they can pick me up as if I weighed nothing, I don't weigh anything, the slightest breeze would

"Do you like me?"

I'm not tall enough to see myself in the mirror on the wall, my mother with the lamp turned off, abandoning me

"What kind of question is that?"

the golden rain tree won't stop moaning, it won't stop, I'm not afraid that they'll kill me

I'm afraid of the pickup trucks that finally came to a stop here on the Corimba highway, exactly like the ones in which the laborers arrived from Huambo, the foremen refused to take one or two of them because they were too old or they were pregnant or throwing up, my father would check them out, pressing his palm

to their kidneys, tell them to walk up and back, sign invoices, pay
the driver, the pickups bouncing down the road toward Malanje,
four hundred kilometers from Malanje to Luanda, six hundred
kilometers from Luanda to Nova Lisboa, I'm cold
   when my daughter Clarisse asked
   "Do you like me?"
   I got annoyed, pushing her hand away
   "What kind of question is that?"
   afraid as well, afraid
   "What kind of question is that?"
the pickup trucks in Corimba, the government troops opening
the tailgates of the pickup trucks, some of them wore colored ties,
mirror-lens sunglasses with a metal frame, as if they were made
of silver
   speaking of mirrors how long has it been since I had a good look
   at myself, since I've gauged how old I look, how much hair I've lost,
   my wrink
   one of them in patent-leather ankle boots, like a groom
   pregnant I'd bet on it pregnant
always hanging behind the others, polishing the cracked patent
leather with the cuff of his shirt, not threatening us in the least,
he'd talk to us, press his palm against our kidneys, tell us to walk
up and back, if they pressed their palms against my kidneys and
asked me to walk up and back they'd refuse to take me, I wouldn't
last more than an hour with a grain sack, I can't walk through all
those thorns, the cotton bolls prick my fingers, you try to grab it
and it pricks you, the pickup trucks on the Corimba highway to
take us to Baixa de Cassanje
   what we came in search of in Africa

a climate different from my climate, the earth a different color, the river

what we came in search of in Africa wasn't money or power it was the foremen dividing us up shoving us toward deserted huts

"You you"

which need some work, some adobe to patch them up, grass for the lawn, pots and pans rented from the company store, beer, fish, and tobacco ten times more expensive then anywhere else, don't put Rui in a home, Lena who was raised in the slums, one bucket of water for everyone, one chicken for everyone, she understands, dressing up the way poor people dress up, cheap, gaudy stuff, keep your money, I said keep your money, don't put Rui in a home

hospitals where they treat people like

pointing toward the pickup trucks

"You you"

the one with patent-leather ankle boots helped me up, slapping my backside

Josélia

and then paused to polish his boots with a corner of his handkerchief

why do they treat Africans like humans when they aren't human at all I've never seen an African grieve at the death of a child

he hit a Bailunda who's around my age, and another one, and a third, and they, those deformed creatures, those ducks, geese

not humans

as their kerchiefs slipped off their heads, exposing the web of cracked, wrinkled skin on the napes of their necks, their white, kinky hair, they didn't complain at all not humans

not a single lament, not a single protest, not a single word, the soldiers riding on the fenders, the hoods, the running boards of the pickups, sunglasses with metal frames like silver, the Corimba highway gliding across their mirrored lenses, tree trunk after tree trunk, remains of thatched huts, a torn piece of fabric, the innards of combat vehicles, felled cannons, a lone schoolhouse wall, suddenly I realized that there weren't any birds, it wasn't that there weren't any people around, except for the corpses being torn to pieces by the dogs

I'm not afraid that they'll kill me I'm not afraid of

it was that there weren't any birds, vultures, that species of long-legged seagull in Mussulo that flies behind the trawlers or sits on the beach between the coconut palms

the face they'll make as they kill me wobbly towel racks, doors loose in their frames, shaky shelves, cracked hinges my mother with the lamp turned off abandoning me

"What kind of question is that?"

I wanted to explain to my children and to the government soldiers that even on my tiptoes I can't see myself in the mirror on the wall, behind which my parents hid my birthday present for months

my children spoke to each other without hearing me, the government soldiers didn't doff their berets in my presence

what we came in search of in Africa

Carlos Clarisse Rui bidding me farewell on the Corimba highway smiling as they wave good-bye, Rui bigger than his brother and sister, the doctor in Malanje showing me the test results, epilepsy, I was the one who cleaned up his urine, held his arms down during his fits, his face bright red, his knees twisted, a look of manliness in his naked body that terrified me, a mulatto, an invalid, and a whore who'll end up with the other whores out on the island waiting for their clients to show up, the garden lit up, the back porch lit up, great big blue canopies, orchids, roses, my husband in a rented double-breasted suit, misbuttoned, you could tell that it wasn't new from the stitches that were coming undone on the breast pocket, even the carnation in his lapel looked withered to me, petals that had wilted over the years, worn-out after dozens of weddings of foremen and managers, poor things, weddings of poor people

my dear lady, Mr. Eduardo, Dona Isilda, bowing solemnly and repeatedly, guests looking out the window of the car as they drove off and there they were, still waving good-bye

the pickup trucks parked next to the ditches, the dogs always returning with snouts low to the ground, whining, limping, the smell reached all the way to Luanda when the wind changed directions, the government troops wearing colored ties, mirror-lensed sunglasses with metal frames as if they were silver

speaking of mirrors how long has it been

flower-print suspenders holding up their military pants, the soldiers inviting me to get out of the pickup

"Ma'am"

the flight of birds overhead, their wings made of felt, screeching, the sea below, Mussulo, the coconut palms, we walked down to the beach, my parents and I, my father in a cream-colored suit and cream-colored Panama hat, my mother in the shade of her pink parasol, me in my straw hat that tied under my chin, we brought lunch in a basket covered with a cloth which we spread out on the sand with the containers of food on top of it, a bottle of juice for my mother and me, a bottle of wine for my father, my mother never took off her gloves or her shoes, sitting on a little stool cooling herself with her fan, my father fanning himself with his newspaper, the birds overhead weren't the same as the ones circling above the ditches in Corimba, with their dusty woolen wings, but I wasn't afraid because it was daytime, the soldiers, even the one in the patent-leather ankle boots, weren't going to rob me or take me with them or do me any harm, there wasn't a single darkened room in the house in Malanje, they raised their machine guns, lined me up in their sights, disappeared behind their guns, the way their muscles hardened, the way they all shut their mouths, and me running in the sand toward my parents, my straw hat sliding down to the nape of my neck, happy, without needing to ask them if they liked me.

FINIS LAUS DEO

ANTÓNIO LOBO ANTUNES is the internationally acclaimed author of *Knowledge of Hell*, among others. Born in Lisbon in 1942, Antunes was trained as a psychiatrist and served in the Portuguese Army during the Angolan War of Independence. He lives in Portugal where he continues to write.

RHETT MCNEIL has translated work by Machado de Assis, Gonçalo M. Tavares, and A. G. Porta.

PETROS ABATZOGLOU, *What Does Mrs. Freeman Want?*
MICHAL AJVAZ, *The Golden Age.*
The Other City.
PIERRE ALBERT-BIROT, *Grabinoulor.*
YUZ ALESHKOVSKY, *Kangaroo.*
FELIPE ALFAU, *Chromos.*
Locos.
JOÃO ALMINO, *The Book of Emotions.*
IVAN ÂNGELO, *The Celebration.*
The Tower of Glass.
DAVID ANTIN, *Talking.*
ANTÓNIO LOBO ANTUNES, *Knowledge of Hell.*
The Splendor of Portugal.
ALAIN ARIAS-MISSON, *Theatre of Incest.*
IFTIKHAR ARIF AND WAQAS KHWAJA, EDS., *Modern Poetry of Pakistan.*
JOHN ASHBERY AND JAMES SCHUYLER, *A Nest of Ninnies.*
ROBERT ASHLEY, *Perfect Lives.*
GABRIELA AVIGUR-ROTEM, *Heatwave and Crazy Birds.*
HEIMRAD BÄCKER, *transcript.*
DJUNA BARNES, *Ladies Almanack.*
Ryder.
JOHN BARTH, *LETTERS.*
Sabbatical.
DONALD BARTHELME, *The King.*
Paradise.
SVETISLAV BASARA, *Chinese Letter.*
RENÉ BELLETTO, *Dying.*
MARK BINELLI, *Sacco and Vanzetti Must Die!*
ANDREI BITOV, *Pushkin House.*
ANDREJ BLATNIK, *You Do Understand.*
LOUIS PAUL BOON, *Chapel Road.*
My Little War.
Summer in Termuren.
ROGER BOYLAN, *Killoyle.*
IGNÁCIO DE LOYOLA BRANDÃO, *Anonymous Celebrity.*
The Good-Bye Angel.
Teeth under the Sun.
Zero.
BONNIE BREMSER, *Troia: Mexican Memoirs.*
CHRISTINE BROOKE-ROSE, *Amalgamemnon.*
BRIGID BROPHY, *In Transit.*
MEREDITH BROSNAN, *Mr. Dynamite.*
GERALD L. BRUNS, *Modern Poetry and the Idea of Language.*
EVGENY BUNIMOVICH AND J. KATES, EDS., *Contemporary Russian Poetry: An Anthology.*
GABRIELLE BURTON, *Heartbreak Hotel.*
MICHEL BUTOR, *Degrees.*
Mobile.
Portrait of the Artist as a Young Ape.
G. CABRERA INFANTE, *Infante's Inferno.*
Three Trapped Tigers.
JULIETA CAMPOS, *The Fear of Losing Eurydice.*
ANNE CARSON, *Eros the Bittersweet.*
ORLY CASTEL-BLOOM, *Dolly City.*
CAMILO JOSÉ CELA, *Christ versus Arizona.*
The Family of Pascual Duarte.
The Hive.
LOUIS-FERDINAND CÉLINE, *Castle to Castle.*
Conversations with Professor Y.
London Bridge.

Normance.
North.
Rigadoon.
HUGO CHARTERIS, *The Tide Is Right.*
JEROME CHARYN, *The Tar Baby.*
ERIC CHEVILLARD, *Demolishing Nisard.*
MARC CHOLODENKO, *Mordechai Schamz.*
JOSHUA COHEN, *Witz.*
EMILY HOLMES COLEMAN, *The Shutter of Snow.*
ROBERT COOVER, *A Night at the Movies.*
STANLEY CRAWFORD, *Log of the S.S. The Mrs Unguentine.*
Some Instructions to My Wife.
ROBERT CREELEY, *Collected Prose.*
RENÉ CREVEL, *Putting My Foot in It.*
RALPH CUSACK, *Cadenza.*
SUSAN DAITCH, *L.C.*
Storytown.
NICHOLAS DELBANCO, *The Count of Concord.*
Sherbrookes.
NIGEL DENNIS, *Cards of Identity.*
PETER DIMOCK, *A Short Rhetoric for Leaving the Family.*
ARIEL DORFMAN, *Konfidenz.*
COLEMAN DOWELL, *The Houses of Children.*
Island People.
Too Much Flesh and Jabez.
ARKADII DRAGOMOSHCHENKO, *Dust.*
RIKKI DUCORNET, *The Complete Butcher's Tales.*
The Fountains of Neptune.
The Jade Cabinet.
The One Marvelous Thing.
Phosphor in Dreamland
The Stain.
The Word "Desire."
WILLIAM EASTLAKE, *The Bamboo Bed.*
Castle Keep.
Lyric of the Circle Heart.
JEAN ECHENOZ, *Chopin's Move.*
STANLEY ELKIN, *A Bad Man.*
Boswell: A Modern Comedy.
Criers and Kibitzers, Kibitzers and Criers.
The Dick Gibson Show.
The Franchiser.
George Mills.
The Living End.
The MacGuffin.
The Magic Kingdom.
Mrs. Ted Bliss.
The Rabbi of Lud.
Van Gogh's Room at Arles.
FRANÇOIS EMMANUEL, *Invitation to a Voyage.*
ANNIE ERNAUX, *Cleaned Out.*
LAUREN FAIRBANKS, *Muzzle Thyself.*
Sister Carrie.
LESLIE A. FIEDLER, *Love and Death in the American Novel.*
JUAN FILLOY, *Op Oloop.*
GUSTAVE FLAUBERT, *Bouvard and Pécuchet.*
KASS FLEISHER, *Talking out of School.*
FORD MADOX FORD, *The March of Literature.*
JON FOSSE, *Aliss at the Fire.*
Melancholy.
MAX FRISCH, *I'm Not Stiller.*

Man in the Holocene.
CARLOS FUENTES, Christopher Unborn.
  Distant Relations.
  Terra Nostra.
  Where the Air Is Clear.
WILLIAM GADDIS, J R.
  The Recognitions.
JANICE GALLOWAY, Foreign Parts.
  The Trick Is to Keep Breathing.
WILLIAM H. GASS, Cartesian Sonata
  and Other Novellas.
  Finding a Form.
  A Temple of Texts.
  The Tunnel.
  Willie Masters' Lonesome Wife.
GÉRARD GAVARRY, Hoppla! 1 2 3.
  Making a Novel.
ETIENNE GILSON,
  The Arts of the Beautiful.
  Forms and Substances in the Arts.
C. S. GISCOMBE, Giscome Road.
  Here.
  Prairie Style.
DOUGLAS GLOVER, Bad News of the Heart.
  The Enamoured Knight.
WITOLD GOMBROWICZ,
  A Kind of Testament.
KAREN ELIZABETH GORDON,
  The Red Shoes.
GEORGI GOSPODINOV, Natural Novel.
JUAN GOYTISOLO, Count Julian.
  Exiled from Almost Everywhere.
  Juan the Landless.
  Makbara.
  Marks of Identity.
PATRICK GRAINVILLE, The Cave of Heaven.
HENRY GREEN, Back.
  Blindness.
  Concluding.
  Doting.
  Nothing.
JACK GREEN, Fire the Bastards!
JIŘÍ GRUŠA, The Questionnaire.
GABRIEL GUDDING,
  Rhode Island Notebook.
MELA HARTWIG, Am I a Redundant
  Human Being?
JOHN HAWKES, The Passion Artist.
  Whistlejacket.
ALEKSANDAR HEMON, ED.,
  Best European Fiction.
AIDAN HIGGINS, A Bestiary.
  Balcony of Europe.
  Bornholm Night-Ferry.
  Darkling Plain: Texts for the Air.
  Flotsam and Jetsam.
  Langrishe, Go Down.
  Scenes from a Receding Past.
  Windy Arbours.
KEIZO HINO, Isle of Dreams.
KAZUSHI HOSAKA, Plainsong.
ALDOUS HUXLEY, Antic Hay.
  Crome Yellow.
  Point Counter Point.
  Those Barren Leaves.
  Time Must Have a Stop.
NAOYUKI II, The Shadow of a Blue Cat.
MIKHAIL IOSSEL AND JEFF PARKER, EDS.,
  Amerika: Russian Writers View the
  United States.
DRAGO JANČAR, The Galley Slave.
GERT JONKE, The Distant Sound.

Geometric Regional Novel.
  Homage to Czerny.
  The System of Vienna.
JACQUES JOUET, Mountain R.
  Savage.
  Upstaged.
CHARLES JULIET, Conversations with
  Samuel Beckett and Bram van
  Velde.
MIEKO KANAI, The Word Book.
YORAM KANIUK, Life on Sandpaper.
HUGH KENNER, The Counterfeiters.
  Flaubert, Joyce and Beckett:
  The Stoic Comedians.
  Joyce's Voices.
DANILO KIŠ, Garden, Ashes.
  A Tomb for Boris Davidovich.
ANITA KONKKA, A Fool's Paradise.
GEORGE KONRÁD, The City Builder.
TADEUSZ KONWICKI, A Minor Apocalypse.
  The Polish Complex.
MENIS KOUMANDAREAS, Koula.
ELAINE KRAF, The Princess of 72nd Street.
JIM KRUSOE, Iceland.
EWA KURYLUK, Century 21.
EMILIO LASCANO TEGUI, On Elegance
  While Sleeping.
ERIC LAURRENT, Do Not Touch.
HERVÉ LE TELLIER, The Sextine Chapel.
  A Thousand Pearls (for a Thousand
  Pennies)
VIOLETTE LEDUC, La Bâtarde.
EDOUARD LEVÉ, Autoportrait.
  Suicide.
SUZANNE JILL LEVINE, The Subversive
  Scribe: Translating Latin
  American Fiction.
DEBORAH LEVY, Billy and Girl.
  Pillow Talk in Europe and Other
  Places.
JOSÉ LEZAMA LIMA, Paradiso.
ROSA LIKSOM, Dark Paradise.
OSMAN LINS, Avalovara.
  The Queen of the Prisons of Greece.
ALF MAC LOCHLAINN,
  The Corpus in the Library.
  Out of Focus.
RON LOEWINSOHN, Magnetic Field(s).
MINA LOY, Stories and Essays of Mina Loy.
BRIAN LYNCH, The Winner of Sorrow.
D. KEITH MANO, Take Five.
MICHELINE AHARONIAN MARCOM,
  The Mirror in the Well.
BEN MARCUS,
  The Age of Wire and String.
WALLACE MARKFIELD,
  Teitlebaum's Window.
  To an Early Grave.
DAVID MARKSON, Reader's Block.
  Springer's Progress.
  Wittgenstein's Mistress.
CAROLE MASO, AVA.
LADISLAV MATEJKA AND KRYSTYNA
  POMORSKA, EDS.,
  Readings in Russian Poetics:
  Formalist and Structuralist Views.
HARRY MATHEWS,
  The Case of the Persevering Maltese:
  Collected Essays.
  Cigarettes.
  The Conversions.
  The Human Country: New and

SELECTED DALKEY ARCHIVE PAPERBACKS

Collected Stories.
The Journalist.
My Life in CIA.
Singular Pleasures.
The Sinking of the Odradek
  Stadium.
Tlooth.
20 Lines a Day.
JOSEPH McELROY,
  Night Soul and Other Stories.
THOMAS McGONIGLE,
  Going to Patchogue.
ROBERT L. McLAUGHLIN, ED., Innovations:
  An Anthology of
  Modern & Contemporary Fiction.
ABDELWAHAB MEDDEB, Talismano.
GERHARD MEIER, Isle of the Dead.
HERMAN MELVILLE, The Confidence-Man.
AMANDA MICHALOPOULOU, I'd Like.
STEVEN MILLHAUSER,
  The Barnum Museum.
  In the Penny Arcade.
RALPH J. MILLS, JR.,
  Essays on Poetry.
MOMUS, The Book of Jokes.
CHRISTINE MONTALBETTI, Western.
OLIVE MOORE, Spleen.
NICHOLAS MOSLEY, Accident.
  Assassins.
  Catastrophe Practice.
  Children of Darkness and Light.
  Experience and Religion.
  God's Hazard.
  The Hesperides Tree.
  Hopeful Monsters.
  Imago Bird.
  Impossible Object.
  Inventing God.
  Judith.
  Look at the Dark.
  Natalie Natalia.
  Paradoxes of Peace.
  Serpent.
  Time at War
  The Uses of Slime Mould:
  Essays of Four Decades.
WARREN MOTTE,
  Fables of the Novel: French Fiction
  since 1990.
  Fiction Now: The French Novel in
  the 21st Century.
  Oulipo: A Primer of Potential
  Literature.
GERALD MURNANE, Barley Patch.
YVES NAVARRE, Our Share of Time.
  Sweet Tooth.
DOROTHY NELSON, In Night's City.
  Tar and Feathers.
ESHKOL NEVO, Homesick.
WILFRIDO D. NOLLEDO, But for the Lovers.
FLANN O'BRIEN,
  At Swim-Two-Birds.
  At War.
  The Best of Myles.
  The Dalkey Archive.
  Further Cuttings.
  The Hard Life.
  The Poor Mouth.
  The Third Policeman.
CLAUDE OLLIER, The Mise-en-Scène.
  Wert and the Life Without End.
PATRIK OUŘEDNÍK, Europeana.

The Opportune Moment, 1855.
BORIS PAHOR, Necropolis.
FERNANDO DEL PASO,
  News from the Empire.
  Palinuro of Mexico.
ROBERT PINGET, The Inquisitory.
  Mahu or The Material.
  Trio.
A. G. PORTA, The No World Concerto.
MANUEL PUIG,
  Betrayed by Rita Hayworth.
  The Buenos Aires Affair.
  Heartbreak Tango.
RAYMOND QUENEAU, The Last Days.
  Odile.
  Pierrot Mon Ami.
  Saint Glinglin.
ANN QUIN, Berg.
  Passages.
  Three.
  Tripticks.
ISHMAEL REED,
  The Free-Lance Pallbearers.
  The Last Days of Louisiana Red.
  Ishmael Reed: The Plays.
  Juice!
  Reckless Eyeballing.
  The Terrible Threes.
  The Terrible Twos.
  Yellow Back Radio Broke-Down.
JOÃO UBALDO RIBEIRO, House of the
  Fortunate Buddhas.
JEAN RICARDOU, Place Names.
RAINER MARIA RILKE, The Notebooks of
  Malte Laurids Brigge.
JULIÁN RÍOS, The House of Ulysses.
  Larva: A Midsummer Night's Babel.
  Poundemonium
  Procession of Shadows.
AUGUSTO ROA BASTOS, I the Supreme.
DANIËL ROBBERECHTS,
  Arriving in Avignon.
JEAN ROLIN, The Explosion of the
  Radiator Hose.
OLIVIER ROLIN, Hotel Crystal.
ALIX CLEO ROUBAUD, Alix's Journal.
JACQUES ROUBAUD, The Form of a
  City Changes Faster, Alas, Than
  the Human Heart.
  The Great Fire of London.
  Hortense in Exile.
  Hortense Is Abducted.
  The Loop.
  Mathématique.
  The Plurality of Worlds of Lewis.
  The Princess Hoppy.
  Some Thing Black.
LEON S. ROUDIEZ, French Fiction Revisited.
RAYMOND ROUSSEL, Impressions of Africa.
VEDRANA RUDAN, Night.
STIG SÆTERBAKKEN, Siamese.
LYDIE SALVAYRE, The Company of Ghosts.
  Everyday Life.
  The Lecture.
  Portrait of the Writer as a
  Domesticated Animal.
  The Power of Flies.
LUIS RAFAEL SÁNCHEZ,
  Macho Camacho's Beat.
SEVERO SARDUY, Cobra & Maitreya.
NATHALIE SARRAUTE,
  Do You Hear Them?

FOR A FULL LIST OF PUBLICATIONS, VISIT:
www.dalkeyarchive.com

Martereau.
The Planetarium.
ARNO SCHMIDT, *Collected Novellas.*
Collected Stories.
Nobodaddy's Children.
Two Novels.
ASAF SCHURR, *Motti.*
CHRISTINE SCHUTT, *Nightwork.*
GAIL SCOTT, *My Paris.*
DAMION SEARLS, *What We Were Doing
and Where We Were Going.*
JUNE AKERS SEESE,
Is This What Other Women Feel Too?
What Waiting Really Means.
BERNARD SHARE, *Inish.*
Transit.
AURELIE SHEEHAN,
Jack Kerouac Is Pregnant.
VIKTOR SHKLOVSKY, *Bowstring.*
Knight's Move.
*A Sentimental Journey:
Memoirs 1917–1922.*
Energy of Delusion: A Book on Plot.
Literature and Cinematography.
Theory of Prose.
Third Factory.
Zoo, or Letters Not about Love.
CLAUDE SIMON, *The Invitation.*
PIERRE SINIAC, *The Collaborators.*
KJERSTI A. SKOMSVOLD, *The Faster I Walk,
the Smaller I Am.*
JOSEF ŠKVORECKÝ, *The Engineer of
Human Souls.*
GILBERT SORRENTINO,
Aberration of Starlight.
Blue Pastoral.
Crystal Vision.
*Imaginative Qualities of Actual
Things.*
Mulligan Stew.
Pack of Lies.
Red the Fiend.
The Sky Changes.
Something Said.
Splendide-Hôtel.
Steelwork.
Under the Shadow.
W. M. SPACKMAN,
The Complete Fiction.
ANDRZEJ STASIUK, *Dukla.*
Fado.
GERTRUDE STEIN,
Lucy Church Amiably.
The Making of Americans.
A Novel of Thank You.
LARS SVENDSEN, *A Philosophy of Evil.*
PIOTR SZEWC, *Annihilation.*
GONÇALO M. TAVARES, *Jerusalem.*
Joseph Walser's Machine.
*Learning to Pray in the Age of
Technique.*
LUCIAN DAN TEODOROVICI,
Our Circus Presents . . .
NIKANOR TERATOLOGEN, *Assisted Living.*
STEFAN THEMERSON, *Hobson's Island.*
The Mystery of the Sardine.
Tom Harris.
JOHN TOOMEY, *Sleepwalker.*
JEAN-PHILIPPE TOUSSAINT,
The Bathroom.
Camera.
Monsieur.

Running Away.
Self-Portrait Abroad.
Television.
The Truth about Marie.
DUMITRU TSEPENEAG,
Hotel Europa.
The Necessary Marriage.
Pigeon Post.
Vain Art of the Fugue.
ESTHER TUSQUETS, *Stranded.*
DUBRAVKA UGRESIC,
Lend Me Your Character.
Thank You for Not Reading.
MATI UNT, *Brecht at Night.*
Diary of a Blood Donor.
Things in the Night.
ÁLVARO URIBE AND OLIVIA SEARS, EDS.,
*Best of Contemporary Mexican
Fiction.*
ELOY URROZ, *Friction.*
The Obstacles.
LUISA VALENZUELA, *Dark Desires and
the Others.*
He Who Searches.
MARJA-LIISA VARTIO,
The Parson's Widow.
PAUL VERHAEGHEN, *Omega Minor.*
AGLAJA VETERANYI, *Why the Child Is
Cooking in the Polenta.*
BORIS VIAN, *Heartsnatcher.*
LLORENÇ VILLALONGA, *The Dolls' Room.*
ORNELA VORPSI, *The Country Where No
One Ever Dies.*
AUSTRYN WAINHOUSE, *Hedyphagetica.*
PAUL WEST,
Words for a Deaf Daughter & Gala.
CURTIS WHITE,
America's Magic Mountain.
The Idea of Home.
Memories of My Father Watching TV.
*Monstrous Possibility: An Invitation
to Literary Politics.*
Requiem.
DIANE WILLIAMS, *Excitability:
Selected Stories.*
Romancer Erector.
DOUGLAS WOOLF, *Wall to Wall.*
Ya! & John-Juan.
JAY WRIGHT, *Polynomials and Pollen.*
*The Presentable Art of Reading
Absence.*
PHILIP WYLIE, *Generation of Vipers.*
MARGUERITE YOUNG, *Angel in the Forest.*
Miss MacIntosh, My Darling.
REYOUNG, *Unbabbling.*
VLADO ŽABOT, *The Succubus.*
ZORAN ŽIVKOVIĆ, *Hidden Camera.*
LOUIS ZUKOFSKY, *Collected Fiction.*
VITOMIL ZUPAN, *Minuet for Guitar.*
SCOTT ZWIREN, *God Head.*